"A SUPERBLY PLOTTED AND CRAFTED NOVEL . . ."

—*Washington Post Book World*

Conroy wrenched open the door, and crawled out of the crazily canting car. He was firing at the Mercedes, which was now backing slowly closer, like some deadly killing machine. Conroy cast a desperate look around. Karen was lying behind the rear of the Volvo, calmly aiming at the cab of the Mercedes. The window shattered, but the driver could not have been hit. After a moment's hesitation, the menacing vehicle resumed its inexorable backward progress. A few more feet and Conroy and Karen would be exposed and shot to pieces like clay pigeons.

"Get away from it!" Conroy yelled. "Away!"

She grasped his intentions at once. While Conroy fired continuously, hoping to force the gunmen to keep their heads down, she ran, doubled up, towards him. Conroy put his last bullet into the petrol tank of the Volvo.

THE BRINK

N.J. CRISP

PUBLISHED BY POCKET BOOKS NEW YORK

 POCKET BOOKS, a Simon & Schuster division of
GULF & WESTERN CORPORATION
1230 Avenue of the Americas, New York, N.Y. 10020

ISBN: 0-671-45605-9

First Pocket Books printing April, 1983

10 9 8 7 6 5 4 3 2 1

AUTHOR'S NOTE

I am grateful for the help and advice of my son, Robert Crisp B.A. Robert is a computer consultant. He has gone to great pains to ensure that the alarming developments described are feasible. Any errors which remain are mine.

N. J. Crisp
London, 1981

ONE

The darkness was dissolving into a dim form of daylight, slowly and reluctantly. Somewhere above those low, threatening clouds, the sun was easing above the horizon, bathing high-flying jets in its golden rays, but the expected front was creeping eastwards, as predicted. Here on the ground, visibility would remain limited all day, and night would fall early. Not that Goss was much interested in the rest of the day. Only the next thirty minutes.

It was chilly in the camouflaged observation post. Goss turned up the collar of the trenchcoat he habitually wore, and thought about breakfast.

He raised his powerful binoculars, and studied the landscape before him again, carefully refocusing as he examined each feature. Every detail was already imprinted on his mind, as it was, as it had been, and as it would be, either if events took their planned course, or if they did not. He wondered if, over on the other side, there was someone like him, minutely checking for any hint of a false note, the slightest indication of something unexpected which might betray an impending double-cross. Goss hoped there was someone, some senior officer of the KGB, whose existence might be recorded under some arbitrarily allotted code-name in the secret computerized Intelligence records, access to which was limited to the handful authorized to receive the 'key' code, itself changed twice daily. A man whose real name Goss might never know and, God willing, would never meet. If there were some KGB general over there, anxiously swallowing, like Goss, on an empty stomach, it would mean that, having examined the bait during the prolonged and secret negotiations, they had decided the balance of advantage lay with them, and were prepared to take it.

They bloody well ought to take it, Goss thought bitterly. It was not so much a bait, as a damned great fish, one of the biggest ever landed. In their position, Goss would have taken it, he knew that. He pushed aside the uncomfortable question *that* posed. This was a poker game for two, and the essence was that both players must believe they were going to win. Goss wished he were more confident that the discard he was prepared to make was the right move.

The sluggish river which formed the frontier at this point, bisected no-man's-land. On the other side, set back three or four hundred yards, was a high, electrified wire fence. Behind that were the ominous watch-towers, wooden structures spaced at rifle-shot intervals along the border. Should any would-be escaper evade the alert guards, and fail to kill himself on the lethal fence, the remaining innocent-looking grassland running up to the river was mined and booby-trapped.

Goss focused on the nearest watchtower. The guard's

automatic rifle was visible, and he too was peering through binoculars, although not at Goss. He was studying the British Army vehicle which was crawling at walking pace along the narrow, rutted, unrepaired road on Goss's left, towards the timber bridge which spanned the river.

This first sign of movement was on time to the second. Goss panned his binoculars, searching for the answering movement on the other side, and found it. A troop carrier, fur-hatted soldiers sitting stiffly to attention, the red star prominent on the armoured side, its engine no more than a distant rumble from here in the observation post, as it bumped and jolted slowly onwards, through the gates in the electrified fence as they were opened, coming to a stop just short of the bridge.

The fur-hatted soldiers jumped down, rifles slung, stretched their legs, and stared with casual interest at their counterparts across the river on the Western side.

Goss lowered his binoculars, and put his horn-rimmed spectacles back on. His eyes were watering, and he felt as though he had been screwing them up and staring through those bloody binoculars all night.

'So far, it looks OK,' Goss said to the young captain beside him, who wore the badge of the Coldstream Guards in his beret. 'I don't anticipate trouble, but if there is any, there's to be no bloodshed—at least, not *their* blood—but our man's to land up on this side, alive and well. Clear?'

'That's understood,' the young captain said. He had no idea why the man called Goss, with the lined face, baggy eyes, and large ears, who somewhat resembled a weary old hound, should wield so much power and authority. Nor did he much care at this moment. He was more concerned with the problems which would present themselves, should he be obliged to snatch a man from the other side, in the face of what he strongly

3

suspected were crack troops—not to mention the mines and the armed guards in the watchtowers—while the man himself remained unharmed. All that, without starting World War III.

'You've rehearsed the necessary action enough times,' Goss said unconvincingly. 'Anyway, it probably won't come to that.'

I bloody well hope it doesn't come to that, Goss thought, as he left the observation post and walked towards the staff car, which was parked out of sight, behind a clump of trees. There was no reason why it should. So far, every detail of the timetable, so painstakingly drawn up during those prolonged, frigidly courteous negotiations, had been rigidly adhered to. Why should they initiate a charade, unless they intended to go through with it? But Goss knew the answer to that one. Because some bugger in the Kremlin might put the boot in at the last minute. Just as some bugger in Downing Street had nearly put the boot in at the last minute.

Otherwise, leaving aside the possibility of some Kremlin high-up with nervous ulcers, or one who could read his mind, Goss was reasonably satisfied. This place met all the necessary requirements, or at any rate, *his* requirements. On the other side, they were not burdened with a press which would regard this transaction, should it ever come to light, as a 'good story', front-page news. Goss despised the Western press for its venality, its mixture of servility, corruption and malice; but he deeply respected its ability to make trouble for people like himself. They would love this one, if they ever got to hear about it. Goss was taking considerable pains to ensure that they never did.

Before the country was divided, when the Western Allies, having fought a world war supposedly for democracy and self-determination, settled for what

4

they could get, which was arguably less than they had started out with, the timber bridge had linked two small villages, one each side of the river, both about ten miles away. Now, the road led only to the death trap of the frontier, and the decaying bridge would not support the weight of a vehicle.

Seven miles to the west, that road had been sealed off two days earlier, because of 'military manoeuvres', an event so common this close to the border that the scattered local populace, bored, accepted it without question. There were no dwellings within sight. The crossing was no longer used, and the road normally carried no traffic. Like the young captain, the soldiers now staring impassively at their opposite numbers across the bridge all wore the insignia of the Coldstream Guards. In fact, they were SAS men, and the SAS were trained, and could be trusted not to talk.

No. The arrangement would never become public knowledge, a possibility which had much exercised a small Cabinet sub-committee, meeting in secret, with no minutes being taken.

There were two men in the camouflaged staff car. The driver, sitting erect, eyes front, temporarily an RASC corporal, was a taciturn Welshman, whose name was Jenkins. Jenkins had one role in life, apart from acting as Goss's chauffeur, and that was to keep Goss alive and, if necessary, to die in his place in the process. Various types of practice ambushes and assassination attempts were sprung upon Jenkins, at random intervals, as a form of training, and to ensure that his reflexes were up to the mark. So far, no one had seriously attempted to eliminate Goss for real, a state of affairs Goss was perfectly content with, and hoped would continue unchanged throughout the few years remaining until his retirement. Goss cherished few private ambitions, but they included surviving to spend his gratuity on a peaceful, unhurried round-the-world cruise, first-class, and thereafter living on his handsome pension in quiet obscurity.

However, Goss was well aware that, like the KGB colonels and generals his department had managed to identify to a greater or lesser degree, he, for his part, figured in their records under a code-name. He even knew what it was. Nikita. Although not, unfortunately, where the Soviet secret master computer was located, much less how to gain access to it. The possibility of acquiring that particular piece of information belonged to the area of wild fantasy, and Goss did not waste his valuable time on it; merely allowing himself to day-dream occasionally in his bath, with the wistful yearning of one longing for the impossible.

Goss was not sure whether they had picked on Nikita because his Christian name, which few people ever used, happened to be Nicholas, or whether, with grim humour, the Russians thought that he bore some slight facial resemblance to the late, and not much lamented in the USSR, Nikita Khrushchev.

Either way, according to the Soviet defector whose debriefing had lasted six months, and who had formerly combined his KGB activities with those required of a sociable, well-liked station manager for Aeroflot, they knew of Goss's existence and had photographs of him. Thankfully, however, their information was otherwise sketchy, and they did not regard him as a senior or important figure.

The Aeroflot official had chosen to defect after becoming wildly enamoured of a British girl, whom Goss had thoughtfully arranged for him to meet on the off-chance of indiscretions in bed. This bewhiskered ploy had succeeded beyond anyone's most optimistic expectations. The Russian developed a doggily devoted passion for the girl and declared that he could not live without her, and would embrace the West as well as her, in return for guarantees of his safety, a house, and an income.

It was the most astounding piece of luck, except possibly for the girl who never did much like the breezy, hard-drinking Russian in the first place. The dedicated lady still submitted monthly reports concerning any titbits her Russian let slip in or out of bed, which had not figured in his debriefing. The reports were growing slimmer as the months went by and, once satisfied that the Russian was truly milked dry, Goss would authorize the end to the affair, which was the lady's keen ambition, and which she so richly deserved. Meanwhile, money from a secret fund over which Goss presided was accumulating in her bank account. Goss chose to call it a hard-lying allowance, but like so many of his private jests, the audience principally concerned failed to find it very amusing. The rather lovely young lady had lost a perfectly good English lover, who could not be told the reasons for her infidelity, and would not have understood them anyway. Which was sad, but one of those things in the subterranean world which Goss and his kind inhabited. Goss's own marriage had collapsed in hopeless ruins many years before.

Nikita was, Goss knew from the defector, shown as 'Divorced' by the KGB, and his ex-wife's second marriage was faithfully recorded among the other, mostly unimportant, pieces of information about him which they possessed. The defector had spent his six months' debriefing singing about far more important matters than Nikita, of course, but Goss was only human, in his own estimation at least, and he found the subject of considerable personal interest.

He had been much heartened to find that they knew so little about him, after so many years on active service, even if his last decade as department head had been spent largely in the background.

They would soon know a lot more about Nikita

though, Goss thought, glancing at the man who was sitting, indifferently, in the back of the car. He had considered that unpleasant fact, although without attaching much weight to it, before making his decision. Compared with the enormous risk he had advised his government to take, in making this discard, his own personal safety mattered little.

Just the same, as they fleshed out their knowledge of Nikita, and became able to deduce more, Goss could well come to figure high in the league table of desirable targets. Should they further deduce more than Goss hoped and as much as he feared, and if the KGB computer kept on spewing out his name for submission to their Action Committee, events would take a disagreeable turn. A patient, anonymous hit man would be assigned to Nikita, ready to live and wait under cover for months, or even years, until he could manipulate the right opportunity.

Goss sighed and dismissed the thought from his mind. Should that unpleasant moment ever arrive, he had every confidence that Jenkins would obey the unthinking instincts so rigorously implanted in him, and do his utmost to interpose his body between Goss and the bullet, or the poisoned dart, or the knife intended for him, and die in place of Goss as he was trained to do.

Goss glanced at his watch, opened the rear passenger door of the staff car, climbed in, and sat beside the man already there.

'Won't be long now,' Goss said.

Garnett nodded, but said nothing. Garnett was good at saying nothing. The Spy of the Century, as the tabloids had christened him, almost lovingly, when his trial was splashed across the front pages day after day, had spent a year in custody before appearing in any dock. During that period, teams of skilled interrogators had used every known technique, and some which Goss had invented as they went along. The upshot, although lengthy, and a damning indictment, was substantially no more than Goss already knew before Garnett was arrested.

Everyone except Goss believed that the interrogation had been completely successful, that the evidence obtained—not all of it presented at the trial, even when the court went into secret session—comprised all there was to know about Garnett's activities. Goss did not share this comforting belief. Goss thought that he had suffered a personal defeat at Garnett's hands. Unfortunately, he would not prove it, even to himself. Even more infuriating, he did not know what to do about it.

There was a sickly smell of peppermint inside the staff car. Garnett sucked mints continuously, his prim lips twitching as he did so.

'Got enough mints?' Goss asked.

Garnett took his hand from his pocket and showed a full packet.

'Good,' Goss said. 'Should last you. You'll probably be driven straight to the airport.'

Garnett offered the packet to Goss and lifted his eyebrows enquiringly.

'No thanks,' Goss said. 'Can't stand them myself.'

Garnett had been a heavy smoker until he was arrested, three packs a day of untipped cigarettes. Early on, Goss deprived him of cigarettes, along with a good many other things. Like the other deprivations, cutting off his cigarettes had no discernible effect. Christ, Goss had thought, I wish my people were as well trained in counter-interrogation techniques as this bastard. Later, when his trial started, and Garnett became entitled to certain privileges, such as not being exposed to Goss and his interrogation teams any more, he became addicted to mints.

9

'The corporal's got some cigarettes, if you'd like to try one,' Goss offered. Jenkins obediently opened the glove pocket and held up a packet of Players.

'I don't think so, thank you,' Garnett said, speaking for the first time that day. 'Now I know I can do without them, I may as well stick to mints.'

'Probably a good idea,' Goss agreed.

'One of the several things I have to thank you for,' Garnett said. He gave Goss a small, ironic smile. Now, as so often before, the effect of that intimate, little mocking smile was to instil instant rage into Goss's whole being. He fought back the familiar desire to smash the face which mirrored that smile into a bleeding pulp.

'You're very welcome,' Goss said. 'My pleasure, I assure you.'

Garnett was a small, mild, studious-looking man. With his half-moon spectacles and the neatly greying hair of early middle age, he looked exactly like what he had been—a senior scientific civil servant. A clever boffin, an academic bureaucrat, whose masters, it had transpired much too late, had their offices in Moscow, not Whitehall.

His round, guileless face was unnaturally pale, but after a year of Goss and his teams, when he had never so much as glimpsed daylight, and a further spell in the maximum security wing of Parkhurst Prison, that was hardly surprising. The maximum security precautions had been a waste of time. Garnett made no attempt to escape. Nor did he need to. He was content to wait. Neither was there the slightest sign of the complex operation necessary to spirit him out of a cell under twenty-four-hour guard, with the further problems of getting him off the Isle of Wight, for which the prison authorities watched so anxiously. That, too, was unnecessary. From the day he was sentenced, Garnett's real masters were at work, using contacts from Hanoi to the

United Nations to Delhi, in the delicate, protracted series of feelers, and finally the negotiations which would never be acknowledged, and of which no record existed.

'Well, you always said they'd get you out before long,' Goss said. There was a deliberate note of resentment in his voice. It was unlikely that Garnett had the slightest notion that Goss might have had a hand in the arrangement, and vital that the possibility did not cross his mind.

'I thought it reasonably likely, all factors being taken into account,' Garnett said. He bestowed that small, limpid smile on Goss again. Goss did not have to mimic any expression of tight, helpless fury. He simply allowed nature to do its work and achieve the desired effect.

Goss had been in the public gallery on the day Garnett was sentenced. For the first time, the judge allowed his feelings to show.

'You are a man who has cold-bloodedly betrayed the country of your birth, to which you owe your natural allegiance,' he told Garnett. 'You are a traitor whom all decent, right-thinking men will despise. As such, you deserve no shred of mercy, but more important, over and above the question of the severe punishment which is your due, the ordinary citizens of this nation must and shall be protected from the slightest risk that you may resume your treacherous activities. You will be sentenced to thirty years imprisonment, and in my belief you should serve every minute of that sentence. However, in case the memory of your most heinous crimes should grow dim as the years pass, this court will recommend with all the power at its command, that under no circumstances should you be considered for parole until at least twenty-five years have elapsed. You will then be an old man, and no further danger to your countrymen. And if anyone should consider these measures harsh, to them I would say, reserve your pity for those whose freedom and security you have deliberately set out to endanger. A traitor such as you is not worthy of a moment's compassion. He is worthy only of lasting contempt.'

'You silly old fool,' Garnett said from the dock, quietly yet clearly.

'Silence,' the judge ordered.

'I shall be released before your funeral,' Garnett said. 'And from the look of you, I doubt if that happy event is very far off.'

'Take him down,' the judge said.

The warders each side of Garnett hustled him below to the cells, and the judge turned to the more pleasant task, as he put it, of congratulating those responsible for bringing Garnett to justice.

The Special Branch chief superintendent and chief inspector thus singled out listened with a modesty which was well justified. Neither of them had so much as known of Garnett's existence until they were provided with *prima facie* evidence, and requested to arrest him. But it was they who had been the arresting officers, they who had spent days in the witness box, and they who collected the glory.

Goss did not begrudge Special Branch the praise, or the limelight, in the slightest. It was a useful fiction, this pretence that Special Branch were the ones who hunted down spies. That way, attention was diverted away from those whose business in life it really was. Goss and his department coveted publicity about as much as the plague.

Goss sat in his seat while the judge rambled on about a perilous chapter in British history being closed, and wished he could share the old boy's satisfaction. Goss did not believe that it was closed, or even half-written yet. The evidence against Garnett, which in the end

12

amounted to vanloads of files, documents and papers, conclusively proved his guilt. The trouble with half-written chapters, if Goss was right about that, was that the reader might think he knew how they were going to end, but he did not. He could guess. Or he could wait and see. Goss thought it might be dangerous, and conceivably catastrophic, to wait and see. And he did not like indulging in guesswork.

Enough had come to light to prove Garnett's guilt, but too little else had been discovered for Goss's liking. The whole world now knew 'what' Garnett had done. What was still unknown was 'how'. Had Garnett chosen to make that lack of certainty the mainstay of his defence, the brilliant QC who had done his best on Garnett's behalf would have been able to make hay. He could certainly have induced doubts in the jury's collective mind. The prosecution case would have been made to look incomplete. Garnett might even have been acquitted.

But Garnett had not chosen to take this sensible course which was open to him. Instead, he had chosen to make certain admissions during his interrogation. Those admissions could neither be proved nor disproved but, if true, they did outline a possible 'how'. However, even supposing that those admissions were inadvertent, Garnett had had plenty of time to think again before the case came to court. Yet his defending counsel had never once set out to challenge this one, wobbly part of the prosecution case.

Such oversights did happen, of course. In the kind of forensic duel which had occupied the Old Bailey for weeks, one side was always liable to slip up, and no one worried about it except Goss. Goss worried intensely. Goss thought that Garnett regarded being caught as a personal insult and had no wish to go to prison. He thought that Garnett was far more than the merely clever man he appeared to be. If agents were discussed in the same terms as artists, he thought that Garnett would have justified a 'genius' rating. Yet despite what seemed at the time to be his emptily defiant words to the judge, Garnett had, or so Goss's guts told him, in effect chosen to go to prison. Goss thought that Garnett had fed a harmless 'how' to his interrogators, and then allowed the prosecution to wing it on the one thing they could not definitely establish. If that was indeed so, the 'how' was still a mystery. That was why Goss was worried. That and the possibility that the 'how' had some bearing on the way the chapter was intended to come to an end. Which was, to put it mildly, unlikely to be to the advantage of Great Britain, NATO, or the West in general.

Goss sat on his hard seat while the court proceedings wound down into anti-climax. Goss had arrogance in plenty, which he deemed well justified. He also knew his limitations. The trouble was that, in this case, he could not delegate his problem to some team of experts with a request for a recommendation, as he normally would. The sour feeling that he was beaten sprung from a gut reaction. It was not a product of his mind. And it was hard to delegate a gut reaction.

Goss had pulled one of his large ears reflectively, as the court began to clear, and he left his seat. He was a realist. He knew what was needed. And that was, a better man than him. Not better all round—Goss did not believe that any such individual existed. Better equipped to run this particular course. Not one who would regard it as an intellectual problem. The approach of such men was too leisurely. They were prone to make a career out of arriving at a solution. No. One who could be prodded and goaded, used and harassed. If necessary, to the point of exhaustion. If necessary, to the point of death.

'Seven days from now, you will die,' Goss remarked.

'I rather thought I might,' Garnett said. 'How?'

'A massive coronary,' Goss said. 'You will be cremated at Parkhurst Prison.'

'No religious ceremony I trust,' Garnett said. 'I'm an agnostic.'

'If I had my way,' Goss said, 'you'd be burned alive.'

Garnett smiled and chewed a fresh mint. The two-way radio in the car crackled, and the voice of the young captain said, 'Sparks to control, opposing staff car moving into position.'

'Acknowledged,' Jenkins said into his microphone.

Goss opened the door of the staff car, and climbed out. He looked at Garnett.

'I shall be at your funeral,' he said.

'I might have the pleasure of attending yours, too,' Garnett said. 'You never know.'

Goss slammed the car door, and tapped on the roof. The staff car moved from behind the clump of trees, on to the rough road, and came to a stop.

Goss made his way through the trees until he had a clear view of the distant bridge. He took off his glasses, raised his high-powered binoculars, and focused them.

The limousine with the stars on the side had stopped half a mile short of the river. A man was getting out of the back. He shut the car door and stood, waiting.

Goss heard the sound of the British Army staff car's door closing, to his left, and knew that Garnett would be standing beside it, facing the watchtowers.

Goss adjusted his binoculars a fraction. A full minute was decreed for identification, and Goss allowed sixty seconds to elapse—but he was positive after five.

He had known the man he was looking at for twelve years. For two years Goss had been his field commander. Since Goss's elevation to head of department, contact had been less frequent. Frequent enough though. It was him all right. Just under six feet tall, thirty-eight years old, square, pleasant face, dark brown hair, cut short. Not especially good-looking, but neither did he have any irregular features which might be readily remembered. The sort of man who might be middle management, or a sales representative, or a skilled technician. The sort of man you might stand next to in a lift without noticing him; the sort of man who walked through the green Customs channel without being challenged; the sort of man who sat in hotel dining rooms and restaurants without anyone recalling his name. The sort of man able to pass anywhere without attracting attention, or being noticed. That was his trade.

That had been his trade.

Goss knew certain other things about him which were not apparent. How sinewy and powerful the body was, deceptively concealed under the deliberately slightly loose-fitting clothes. The aggressive independence, uncommon in men who followed his profession, but which Goss thought he knew how to use and exploit. The quickness of mind, not in a reasoned way, but using instinctive leaps from one premise to the next to a conclusion, which could leave a merely intelligent, clever man feeling flat-footed and envious.

Goss was probably the only person still alive who knew him that well. The fact that he knew so much did not induce any feelings of admiration or liking. In so far as Goss had any personal feelings about him he disliked the man keenly, but that was irrelevant. He also knew him well enough to know that there was much about him which he did not know, but could only guess at or suspect. But there was one thing about which there was no doubt at all. It was him.

The chance that they would try and pass off a substitute had always been in the order of 1,000 to 1 against, but Goss took all chances into account. Now, he was satisfied. They were going to go through with it. Goss took a small, low-powered walkie-talkie from his pocket, and held it to his mouth.

'Marks to Sparks,' he said. 'Positive identification. Clear to proceed.'

Goss had chosen the code-names to be used on this occasion. He had recalled the motto of the great retailing company, known affectionately as Marks and Sparks, in which they claimed to exchange any article without question. No one else thought that was especially funny.

Nor did Goss, not now, as he stood and shivered and waited in the rising wind.

The driver, standing beside the car with the stars on the side, received a signal, marched briskly round, and opened the door.

Conroy got back inside, where it was blessedly warm. They had returned his own clothes to him, and someone had gone to some pains to clean and press the suit and launder the white shirt, which was a nice, if belated, touch of consideration. However, that meant he was dressed for dining in a Berlin restaurant, not for standing about on a lonely frontier, and he was relieved to be back in the car.

It seemed to be a carbon copy of an old Cadillac. Not that Conroy drew any conclusions from that. There were times when the mindless rantings of the obediently conservative British press made him laugh out loud.

On the one hand, they scoffed at the lack of consumer goods in the USSR, which proved, so they assured their readers, that communism did not work, that it was a grossly inefficient way to organize production, and that therefore capitalism was an infinitely superior method, under which all its lucky readers were much better off even if, increasingly, they were unable to afford the glossily advertised goodies.Q.E.D.

On the other hand, sometimes on the next page or even in adjoining columns, awful warnings appeared about Russian superiority in missiles, tanks, guns, planes and submarines. This, however, was not used to illustrate the superiority of communism as a system capable of outstripping capitalism in complex high technology, but as proof of Soviet aggressive intentions.

Leaving aside the motive of the Soviet Union in its choice of priorities, Conroy found it mysterious how two such mutually contradictory points of view could be offered simultaneously. It was true that Russian hardware was technologically superior to that produced by the Western powers, and that they had more of it. Had the Soviets, however, chosen to pour the same effort into dishwashers, colour television sets, and refrigerators, it seemed highly likely, given the quality of their scientists, research capabilities, and technicians, that the resulting consumer goods would also have been technologically superior to those of the West, even if the power to operate them was in conspicuously short supply on both sides.

Russian superiority in arms, and inferiority in churning out consumer trash, might tell you something about who was better equipped for war, and who intended to win it if it happened, but Conroy failed to see how it proved anything about the merits of two rival political systems.

He wondered how those leader writers, peddling the party line as assiduously as any *Pravda* hack, thought they could get away with it. He supposed that they contemptuously regarded all their readers as dummies.

Conroy possessed the profoundest possible respect

for Russian technology, and their ability to manufacture exactly what they wanted, in the quantities they wanted.

The car moved slowly forward and came to a stop just before the electrified fence. A Red Army captain got in and sat beside Conroy. The car crawled on again. On the other side of the river, Conroy could see the British Army staff car, matching his own progress, yard for yard.

The carbon-copy Cadillac rolled gently onwards, its driver watching the British staff car as intently as a pilot keeping close formation. The two cars halted simultaneously. Both engines were switched off. The Red Army captain got out and held the door open for Conroy. Conroy did not acknowledge the courtesy in any way. What had happened to him might be one of the hazards of his trade, but the experience had been extremely unpleasant, and a few formal courtesies at this late stage did nothing to redress the balance.

The Red Army captain marched on to the bridge, his boots echoing on the creaking timbers. From the other side, the young captain wearing the insignia of the Coldstream Guards approached, keeping step, so that only one set of footfalls could be heard. They met in the middle of the bridge, halted in unison, and exchanged courtesy salutes.

Conroy remained where he was. For the first time, he realized who was waiting to cross over into the East when he was given the signal to return to the West. Astonishment jolted him as though a high-voltage current had passed through his body. Garnett!

Bile rose into the back of Conroy's throat, and he swallowed it back. Garnett, whom it had taken two long, patient years to track down. Garnett, who should be serving thirty years in prison. Garnett, who for a time had succeeded in rendering Britain's independent nuclear capability utterly useless, as alarming to any potential aggressor as a handful of snowballs.

Conroy would have been marginally less surprised to see his monarch standing there. All that time and effort wasted. What the hell did they think they were doing. Letting that treacherous little shit go?

The signal came, and Conroy began to walk, as did Garnett. Once on the bridge, he could feel it moving slightly under his feet. He stopped beside the Red Army captain, and stared at Garnett, while the two soldiers exchanged salutes again. Trust the military to make a meal of it. All it needed now was for brass bands to give a solemn rendering of the two national anthems, but instead there was silence, apart from the creaking of the bridge and the thin hiss of the chill wind.

Then the two captains smartly stepped back two paces. Conroy and Garnett walked forward. They passed within arm's length of each other. Garnett's eyes were alight with amusement. His lips twitched in a brief smile of recognition.

The young captain about-turned and followed Conroy to the staff car. Conroy saw that the corporal driver was no corporal, but Jenkins. So bloody Goss was here too.

Jenkins opened the door, expressionless. Conroy got in. The young captain sat beside him. He relaxed, and gave Conroy a cheerful grin.

'I expect you'd rather be on this side than over there, sir,' he said.

'You're right,' Conroy said. 'I would.' He would too, but he did not think he was worth his Sovereign, or Garnett. He wondered what the hell was going on.

Jenkins made a neat three-point turn, and drove towards a clump of trees half a mile away. Once there, shielded from the watchtowers, he stopped. The young captain got out, exchanged a few words with the waiting Goss, and saluted. Goss climbed in. The car accelerated and drove away fast.

'Welcome back,' Goss said. 'How did you enjoy your spell in foreign climes?'

'Not a great deal,' Conroy said. He did not like Goss. No one in the department liked Goss. Even in a profession ruthless and pitiless by its very nature, Goss was regarded as an unpleasant brute, and quite possibly a sadist. Those men and women under his control who had been around long enough were prone to reminisce nostalgically about the days when the urbane, civilized Lionel (now Sir Lionel) had been head of department. There lay a significant difference. Everyone had always thought of Lionel as Lionel, and addressed him as such, in an affectionate manner which was reciprocated. No one ever called Goss anything but Goss, and there was no affection given or received. True, the department had changed radically in the ten years since Goss had taken charge. It was no longer a relatively small offshoot of Intelligence, serving as the PM's private link between, and private check on, the military and civilian branches, an ancillary arm of the more clearly defined Intelligence Services. The scandals which had surfaced and rumbled damagingly on had eroded such confidence as remained in the main operational branches. A new look was needed, and DI3 by chance or otherwise had remained relatively 'clean'.

Nowadays, under its deceptive title of Defence Information, which made it sound like a cross between a reference library and a public relations office, DI3 had absorbed many of the functions of MI5, MI6, and the SIS. In theory its stance was still a defensive one, but under Goss it had become an aggressive organization, initiating rather than reacting, in pursuit of the old maxim that attack was the best form of defence. So it might be, but you tended to get more casualties that way.

Whether some government had deliberated and willed this, or whether Goss had brought it about through a sheer monomaniacal lust for power, no one knew for certain. Most put it down to the latter. Empire building. Conroy was not so sure about that. Goss did not seem to him to resemble an empire builder, so much as the captain of a Roman war galley, lashing the rowing slaves into exhaustion and collapse in his urgent, manic drive for speed and yet more speed towards some unknown destination.

Somehow, despite DI3's steady, unrelenting expansion, Goss had managed to retain its private links with successive prime ministers, although how he had contrived that with the present occupant of that high office, God alone knew. It was hard to imagine how two creatures who appeared to be not so much chalk and cheese as members of entirely different species could communicate in any way, but apparently they did.

This exchange must have been cleared with the PM personally, for one thing. They were taking a hell of a chance in letting Garnett go. His trial was still too fresh in the public mind. His release would be regarded as a scandal. Governments had fallen because of scandals before now.

'All right,' Conroy said. 'What makes me worth as much as friend Garnett?'

'You're not,' Goss said disdainfully. 'It was a package deal. Garnett fetched a good price. We've retrieved six other assorted bodies besides you.' He glanced at his watch. 'Who will now be enjoying their freedom after being handed back in places like Helsinki, Aden, and Ho Chi Minh City.'

'I'm the one selected for the personal greeting from the Big White Chief, though,' Conroy said.

'You're one of mine,' Goss said. 'You vanished. One minute you're in West Berlin, the next you're in Moscow. I want to know why.'

'It took longer than minutes,' Conroy said, with feeling. 'Jesus Christ, my cover's blown for good. They took casts of my teeth, they took my fingerprints, they even did a myelogram.'

'Why? Were you poorly?' Goss enquired. 'Some trouble with your spinal cord, is there?'

'A lumbar puncture, done slowly, during interrogation, is no joke,' Conroy said. 'And the stuff they use, it just stays there in your body and shows up on X-rays for years.'

'I wish I'd thought of that,' Goss said, annoyed. 'That's good. So simple, too. No point in trying to change your appearance. A simple scanner at sensitive places, a glance at the X-ray screen as the crowd passes by, bingo, that fellow's worth questioning, and they've got you again. I like it.'

'You would,' Conroy said.

'Well, your operational days are definitely over,' Goss said. 'You'd be about as much use in the field now as a spare prick at a wedding. End of promising career. Have to find you some sort of desk job, I suppose. There is one vacancy coming up. SADHCC. How would you fancy that?'

'The crummier the job, the more initials, in my experience,' Conroy said.

'Special Assistant to the Deputy Head of Communications Control,' Goss interpreted. 'It means you get a cubbyhole office, and all the shit no one else wants to deal with.'

'Thanks very much,' Conroy said.

'What did you expect?' Goss queried contemptuously. 'A medal? The red carpet and promotion? You're blown because *you* blew it. A perfectly simple assignment. Necessary, but routine. Run of the mill. And what happens? You get yourself lifted, and your contact's found dead. Jesus, what a shambles.'

'I'm surprised you didn't leave me where I was, to rot,' Conroy said. 'So Hans is dead.' He thought about that.

'Men don't rot peacefully, like dead leaves,' Goss said. 'They get desperate. Some get to the point where they'll do anything. That's when they can be turned round. I've seen it happen. I've done it myself. Men working for them—just as good as you.'

Conroy laughed. The sound was a harsh bark. 'I can just imagine it,' he said. 'Coming back, and trying to take you in.'

'So can I,' Goss said stonily.

'They could have turned me years back, for all you know,' Conroy pointed out.

'Yes, they could,' Goss said. 'That's one reason why you're out. To establish that very thing.'

'When you were a boy,' Conroy said, 'you're the sort who'd save up his pocket money and hire private detectives to check back and find out if his mother had been screwing around nine months before he was born.'

'Not quite,' Goss said.

'A pity you didn't,' Conroy told him. He turned his head and stared at Goss. 'On the evidence I'm looking at, your birth certificate should have read "father unknown".'

'I do the only job I've got the only way I know how,' Goss said. 'I don't know of another way that works. In my considered opinion, an alternative doesn't exist. I suppose you're thinking that Lionel would have patted your hand, sympathized, and made you feel good. Well, Lionel's gone, long since. It's time you got used to that.'

'Lionel was a human being,' Conroy said. 'Unlike you.'

The car had gained a main road. Jenkins signalled a right turn into a narrow, winding lane. The trafficators clicked in the silence. Jenkins showed as much interest in their conversation as though they had been snapping at each other in Japanese. If Jenkins heard what was going on around him, he gave no indication to that effect, and never, ever, reproduced so much as a word of it. Even Goss, Conroy supposed, needed one living being whom he trusted implicitly. The dour, taciturn Jenkins was it.

At that moment, Conroy devoutly wished that he was in the kind of business—any kind but this would do—where he could not only tell his boss what he thought of him, but also what he could do with his lousy job.

No one, however, was permitted to resign from the department, any more than a soldier in the middle of a battle was allowed to change his mind and opt for a quiet life at home with his Mum and Dad, or his wife and kids. The parallel was exact.

Department personnel who reached retiring age, although there were not too many of those, were put out to grass. Rather more became disabled in one way or another, usually spinal or brain injuries incurred in the field. For these, a rehabilitation centre was thoughtfully provided where hope of recovery usually died, and they began to learn to come to terms with their disabilities; after which a residential nursing home run by the department was at their disposal. Some disappeared without trace, or were killed in one corner of the globe or another. But resignation was an option which was not open to anyone. It did not exist. Not since Goss had taken over. That had been one of Goss's first rulings. He called it 'tightening things up a bit'.

Conroy sighed tiredly. He *was* tired. Sleep was not a commodity he had enjoyed too much of during the last few months. He felt depressed, as well as weary. In his own detached assessment, he was the best field operator the department possessed. And although he was still alive and more or less in one piece, his active career was over. His cover was blown to ribbons. He would eventually moulder in some office, shuffling memos and reports and attending meaningless meetings. Meantime, he still had Goss on his back. From Goss, there was no escape.

'At first, I didn't believe it when they told me,' Conroy said reflectively. 'I thought it was straight out of the book. Raise my hopes, get me going . . . and then, "no, not yet. Not until we know this or that". Then it began to seem as if they really meant to go through with it. And I felt good. I couldn't help it. The thought of getting out . . . away from them. Feeling good didn't last long. That began to go brown round the edges when I saw Garnett. Realized you were springing him. That he was going to get away with it. Garnett was someone I felt personally about.'

'We all did,' Goss said, watching him carefully.

'When we crossed on the bridge, not much more than a yard apart,' Conroy said, 'I thought: I could take this bastard into the river with me, and hold his head under. I near as dammit did.'

'You'd have got wet for nothing,' Goss said. 'We had a team of frogmen standing by, against any such little accidents, and I expect they did too.'

'Now you,' Conroy said. 'With a welcome like a load of wet fish.'

'It's the only welcome you're entitled to,' Goss said. 'When an experienced man gets snatched like a novice, I need to know why. Whatever the reason, I'm not going to like it. Something smells, and it's not wet fish.

You're going to help me find out where that smell's coming from.'

'You don't have to look very far,' Conroy said.

'You think you know?' Goss enquired.

'They knew,' Conroy said bleakly. 'That's the point. The identity of my contact, the meeting place, everything.'

'How can you be so sure?'

'I was there first, as arranged,' Conroy said. 'When Hans arrived, he didn't join me. He asked a waiter where he could park his car, and went out again. That was the prearranged signal. Something wrong.'

'What did you do?'

'Ordered a meal and a bottle of wine,' Conroy said. 'Ate the first course. Asked where the men's was. Went there. Everything seemed OK. Went out the back way. They were waiting. I'd been set up from the word go.'

'How did they get you across to the East? Do you know?'

'Not for certain,' Conroy said. 'One of them was bragging a bit, later. Showing off. Or pretending to. He said I'd crossed Checkpoint Charlie in the boot of a diplomat's car. Might be true, might not. I don't know. I wasn't conscious at the time.'

'That part doesn't matter much anyway,' Goss said.

'Until just now, I thought it was Hans who'd shopped me,' Conroy said. 'I didn't know the poor bastard was dead.'

'Found in a sewer,' Goss said. 'Throat slit open like a calf's.'

'Only three people knew all the arrangements,' Conroy said. 'Hans, me . . . and Karen.'

Goss nodded. 'Karen Dewar,' he said thoughtfully.

'Karen,' Conroy said vindictively. 'The bitch. I hope she fries in hell.'

The car had entered an Army post. They passed a

row of huts and headed for a helicopter pad, on which a chopper was sitting like a dreamy dragonfly.

'He'll ferry us to the airport,' Goss said. 'We'll have time for breakfast before the next flight to London.'

'If Karen knows I've been swapped,' Conroy said, 'she'll have gone as soon as your back was turned. She'll be in Warsaw or Prague by now.'

'I doubt that,' Goss said with irritating self-satisfaction. 'When I left, she was at the Home.'

There was only one reason why Karen should be at that place.

'So you already knew it was her,' Conroy said.

'I felt she might benefit from a period of refresher training,' Goss said obliquely. 'Unarmed combat, techniques of resisting interrogation, that sort of thing.'

'Serves the cow right,' Conroy said pitilessly. The Home, as it was known in the department, was set on a hillside between two small Devon villages. It was a large, gracious-looking, rambling building, in the middle of twenty acres of private land. The sign on the locked gates beside the porter's lodge said PURBRIDGE CONVALESCENT HOME. Ambulances sometimes drove in and out. The staff lived in. The Home had been open for eight years now—it was one of Goss's bright ideas—and the few local inhabitants had lost interest. There was no outward sign that the ambulances were as secure as prison vans, that the staff were armed, that the extensive cellars had been modified, now contained some unusual features, and were sound-proofed. Nor that the innocent-looking grounds, and the perimeter, were patrolled night and day.

The Home was an interrogation centre which compared well in sheer callousness, Conroy thought from his recent experiences, with anything on the other side. Garnett had spent six months there. The Home was also used for advanced training. 'Refresher Training' was something which was viewed with apprehension, and avoided if at all possible. Sometimes it was just that, but it could be something else altogether. It depended if you were under suspicion or not. The trouble was you never knew. Even when you got there.

At any other time, Conroy would have felt sorry for Karen. Refresher Training at the Home was not something he would normally wish upon his worst enemy. But not only had Karen betrayed him, she was also responsible for what had happened afterwards, at the very recollection of which his mind and body winced in vicarious agony. Whatever was happening to her at the Home, she deserved it. He hoped she held out for at least as long as he had been obliged to do. Let her find out what it was like, as minutes dragged out into endless days, and endless days into interminable weeks.

'Come on,' Goss said. 'He's waiting for us.'

As they climbed out, the engine of the helicopter began to whine, as if winding itself up, and the rotor blades slowly started to revolve.

Jenkins fell in discreetly behind. They walked towards the helicopter pad.

'It'll be quite a reunion,' Goss remarked. 'You and Karen together again.'

'What are you talking about?' Conroy demanded. But he knew. He knew at once, and there was lead in his stomach.

'Well, naturally, you'll be going to the Home too,' Goss said conversationally. 'For debriefing.'

The rotor blades lifted. The engine roared. The pilot glanced towards the three men and signalled 'ready'. Conroy had stopped dead, facing Goss.

'I've just spent six weeks in the bloody Lubianka,' he shouted, above the snarl of the engine. 'Hasn't anyone ever told you what that means?'

'Of course,' Goss shouted back. 'That's why you'll be sent to the Home. To find out what you told *them*.' The downdraft from the rotor blades sent cold air down

29

Conroy's back. 'Get a move on,' Goss shouted. 'I'm hungry.'

Conroy turned and climbed into the helicopter. Goss and Jenkins followed. A crewman pulled in the steps and closed the door.

The chopper took off. Its nose dipped, it swung on its axis, and headed West.

TWO

At Heathrow, Goss, Conroy and Jenkins remained on board while the other passengers disembarked. The aircraft taxied to its refuelling point, where a car was waiting. They transferred to that and were driven round the airport perimeter to the cargo area.

Most of the passengers would travel into London by bus or the rail link. Cars still swirled around the airport, but in markedly fewer numbers than in years gone by. The last temporary reimposition of petrol rationing had proved to be about as temporary as income tax.

Ration coupons, even if it was often hard to find a filling station which would honour them, were now a permanent fact of life. So were the queues of cars which formed like magic when rumours of a bulk delivery to some filling station spread. Those disappointed fell back on bribing attendants for a precious few gallons, or the black market in priority petrol. Both were offences punishable by heavy fines, but desperate non-priority motorists risked that in their efforts to keep their cars on the road. Not so many risked the airport with coloured priority petrol from the state-run filling stations in their tanks. There were frequent and well-publicised spot checks at the airport.

Goss indicated the parked ambulance and the two uniformed attendants.

'A laddie we've finished with is being transferred to Brixton Prison this afternoon,' he said. 'So you may as well travel to the Home with them. Save the country a bit of fuel and money. Keep the public-sector borrowing requirement down a fraction. Every little helps, they tell me.'

Conroy supposed that was one way of saying: 'You're a prisoner. You don't get the chance to make any phone calls, or contact anyone.' He climbed in the back. The rear doors were slammed, and bolted and locked from the outside. At least he was to be left alone. Neither of the ambulance crew joined him.

Being left alone, he soon realized, only meant that he was as secure as an animal in a cage. He had never travelled in one of these vehicles before, and he examined the interior curiously.

He had no idea which route they were taking. The windows were opaque. Not only were the doors of hard steel, so were the floor and the roof. There were no bolted or riveted joins. It was, in effect, a welded box. The windows were of reinforced plate glass, sealed into their frames. An oxyacetylene cutter would have been needed to get out of this thing, and the likelihood of occupants travelling with such equipment was remote.

Not all travellers, it appeared, however, were allowed the privilege of his unsupervised freedom of movement. There was a rack on the left-hand side of the doors, at present empty, into which Conroy thought sub-machine-guns might fit comfortably. Thick nylon straps, hooked back now, could only have one purpose —to lash a man tightly to a stretcher. Three straitjackets were folded neatly in a locker.

A gorilla in the prime of life could have been safely left unsecured in this thing, without any risk of its escaping. Conroy supposed that it was occasionally used to transport men and women who were mad with pain, or bent on self-destruction.

There was also an Elsan closet in one corner. Conroy used it with relief. He was urinating more frequently than usual, and he noted that he was still passing blood.

Checking into the Home was rather like arriving at a quiet, discreetly comfortable hotel. Conroy signed an index card, which already carried his name and service number, and initialled, as requested, the date and time of his arrival. He was allocated a room and given his key.

His room was on the first floor. It was larger and more agreeable than most hotel rooms Conroy had inhabited, and possessed its own private bathroom. There was full air-conditioning, keeping the atmosphere fresh but warm, although there seemed to be no way of opening the double-glazed windows.

On the inside of the door—just like a hotel—was a notice, which was headed in large red letters: IN CASE OF FIRE . . .

Conroy read it, and learned that, if trapped in his room, he was to keep his door closed and wait until the windows were opened from the outside.

Provided, he thought, someone remembered where the keys were kept which fitted the exterior lock to the window frame. Otherwise, he and a number of others, no doubt, would slowly roast.

Propped up on the dressing table was a card, with PROGRAMME printed on it, and his name and service number written underneath. Inside, his activities for the next seven days were listed, broken down into morning, afternoon and evening sessions. Day One, simply said 'Arrival' written in the round backward-sloping hand of some female clerk. Day Two was wholly devoted to 'Medical Examination'. After that, it got monotonous. Every session had the same thing written in. 'Debriefing'.

The English language, with its rich store of wonderfully vague synonyms, had a lot to answer for, Conroy thought.

On the bed was a suitcase. The last time Conroy had seen it was when he closed the door of his hotel room in Berlin, and set out for the restaurant. He opened it.

Inside were the toilet articles, which had also been retrieved from his Berlin hotel, together with a quantity of clean clothes, neatly packed. Two suits, back from the cleaners, still on wire hangers, shirts, underwear, socks, shoes, slacks, sweaters, and a track suit.

Either, Conroy supposed, whoever had invaded his London flat and removed this lot from his bedroom expected him to change twice as often as any woman, or he was destined to remain in this place for rather more than the one week his "Programme" indicated. There was enough here for a month. He began to transfer it all in to the fitted wardrobe. He wondered how long it would be before he was able to put his possessions back where they belonged.

Conroy's flat was in a large block, close to Ravenscourt Park. Field personnel like himself were free to live wherever they chose, provided the department approved of their choice. Small, cosy mews were out. So were conversions, where old houses had been turned into a dozen flats; the mail came through the front door in one bundle for the residents to sort out, and everybody knew everybody. Neighbourly relations were to be avoided. Neighbours, even subconsciously, were liable to clock erratic comings and goings, to remember nocturnal arrivals and departures.

Sprawling estates in Ilford were OK. Half the taxi drivers in London seemed to live in Ilford. Since, their ration of diesel fuel being insufficient to keep their cabs on the road continuously, they worked to no set pattern of hours or days off, individuals who behaved similarly became part of the norm. Tower blocks of council flats were even better. Most of the wretched tenants were dying to get out of those planners' aberrations, and meantime kept their doors locked and spent no time at all hanging about, for fear of thugs and vandals.

Conroy liked neither option, but his choice of residence had passed muster. The block of flats was vast. From the outside, it resembled a grim Victorian prison, but inside the flats were pleasantly spacious, and Conroy could see the park from his living room window.

For more than a decade, the harassed owners had been trying to get the tenants out and sell the flats instead of renting them. The resulting turnover was steady. Buyers tended to take their profits and move upmarket, so neighbours changed frequently and were no problem. Conroy was pretty well the oldest inhabitant now. The giant block, built in an L fronting two different roads, had five separate entrances. A man as careful as Conroy need never worry about being noticed coming or going.

In truth, Conroy's flat really needed modernizing, a fact he was well aware of, but had never quite got around to doing anything about. On a practical level, he was rarely in London for long enough to organize all the details of such an operation. Besides which, he rather liked it the way it was. Impersonal formica was no improvement on a solid, if worn, pine kitchen table, in his opinion. The flat was the nearest thing to a home which Conroy had known for a very long time.

There had been a period when he had contemplated selling it. With its three bedrooms, it was much too large for him, as things had turned out. He still thought about moving out from time to time. But the spasms grew less frequent and could be lived with. Besides, he did not want to have his base in Ilford or a tower block, or somewhere similar.

Conroy closed the wardrobe and put his suitcase away. There was a telephone extension beside the bed, but it remained silent. Perhaps he was to be left alone all day. He savoured that idea, and liked it.

He picked up the 'Programme' again, and turned it over. Printed on the back were mealtimes. Breakfast, lunch, tea, and dinner. The bar would be open, he noticed, at lunchtime and during the evening.

Conroy looked at his watch. He decided to skip tea ('served in the lounge') and settle for the luxury of a long, hot, relaxing bath, instead.

Conroy slept for ten hours that night and woke up feeling better. A few days of blissfully doing nothing like this, and he would be his normal self again. Whether 'Debriefing' as Goss interpreted that word, would not sharply reverse the process, and be intended to do so, was another matter. He would find out in due course. Today, at least, should be all right. Conroy was cautiously optimistic, although not absolutely positive, that the 'Medical Examination' might be merely intended to ascertain what, if any, damage he had suffered— and therefore considerably less painful than those he had experienced in the Lubianka.

The night before, he had had a couple of drinks in the comfortable, discreetly lighted bar, with its padded stools and leather armchairs, before strolling into the dining room.

There, he had been shown to a corner table. Places were laid for two, but no one joined him. He studied the menu and ordered smoked salmon, rump steak, sauté potatoes, and half a bottle of claret. The food was excellent. So was the wine. He ate and drank slowly, and with enjoyment.

The remaining diners were, he assessed, mostly attached to the staff. He knew one or two of them, and gave and received friendly nods; but did not recognize the others, which did not surprise him. The department's work was organized so that as few people as possible ever got to know each other. It was safer that way.

The tablecloths and napkins were spotless, freshly laundered, the glasses were of crystal, the cutlery silver-plated, the servants helpful and courteous, if uncommunicative. But with the heavy velvet curtains drawn, and the shaded, individual lamps on the tables, there was a relaxed atmosphere, and a good deal of cheerful laughter from the other tables. It reminded Conroy of an officers' mess, when the CO was dining elsewhere.

After dinner, he looked into the bar again, but decided against a brandy and small talk, and in favour of an early night.

There was no sign of Karen, which was a relief. Accustomed as he was to being someone else, dissembling, standing truth on its head, and lying about himself, his actions, and his motives, with utter conviction, Conroy would have found it hard to say anything to Karen which was not obscenely abusive.

There was no sign of Goss either, which was another relief. Conroy could do without Goss any time at all.

Now, back in the dining room, Conroy relished the well-cooked eggs and bacon, and the splendidly hot buttered toast. This place had its merits. With such inviting food and swift, efficient service, a man could easily become fat and lazy. Or off his guard.

At nine o'clock, Conroy presented himself at the surgery. There was no need to ask where it was. Signs clearly indicated the way to the various sections although, Conroy noted, only to what might be called the public rooms.

Every six months, Conroy was obliged to undergo a rigorous physical checkup, and he had got to know the doctors attached to the department, but this one was a stranger.

He was dark-haired, in his thirties, affable, shook hands warmly, but did not introduce himself.

'Well, now,' he said, 'strip off, and let's have a look at you.'

It was a rerun of the examination Conroy had some months before. Blood pressure, lungs, ECG, testing reflexes, peering into each orifice in turn, the lot.

'On the face of it, you seem to be in surprisingly good shape, considering what you must have been through,' the doctor said. 'Apart from aches and pains, have you noticed any ill effects yourself?'

'I pee a lot, and there's blood in it,' Conroy said.

'Roll over,' the doctor said. His fingers explored gently, and then pushed harder. 'Does that hurt?'

'Yes,' Conroy said. 'A bit.'

'There's no sign of external bruising,' the doctor said, peering at Conroy's flesh closely.

'There wouldn't be,' Conroy said. 'They were artists.'

It was not necessary, if skilled men wished to inflict pain upon another human being, to leave him bruised or gashed or cut. It was usually desirable that no outward sign should be visible, should the victim later appear in an open court—or become a possible candidate for an exchange.

'We'd better do an IVP,' the doctor said. 'An intravenous pyelogram.' He studied his diary. 'I can book you into X-ray for two o'clock this afternoon. Will that be all right?'

'Fine,' Conroy said. 'I just appear where I'm told, when I'm told.'

It was eleven-thirty. The bar would be open. Conroy rejected the idea. He would confine himself to a light lunch too. He did not wish to become fat and lazy. Or off his guard.

Conroy lay on his bed, comfortably, and settled down to finish reading the morning newspaper. He was about to put it down, when a small, obscure item, tucked away at the bottom of the page, caught his eye. He read it carefully, and with concern. It referred to earlier reports, but Conroy knew nothing about those. Where he had been, British newspapers did not appear at breakfast time. Nor did breakfast, come to that, except the day before his release.

A Foreign Office official named Ernest Harrington had, it seemed, vanished in Rome some weeks before, as he was changing planes, en route to Pakistan. Mr Harrington had not been seen since. The Italian police discounted claims that he was being held captive by the People's Union Free Liberation Army (PUFLA). They still believed that Mr Harrington was the victim of a kidnapping, and were awaiting ransom demands.

Conroy dropped the newspaper on to the floor, and lay on his back, staring at the ceiling. He had a fair knowledge of most of the subversive organizations operating in the West, and he had never heard of PUFLA. However, new ones were always being invented. They sprang up, served a specific purpose, and disappeared again.

What bothered Conroy considerably more was the possibility that Mr Harrington was not a Foreign Office official, nor was his name Harrington; although the part about being on his way to Pakistan might be correct, even if not for recognized diplomatic reasons. If so, the Italian press must have got hold of what seemed a perfectly ordinary news story, and everyone was desperately trying to do a cover-up job.

Conroy could not be certain that his unease was justified. He had been snatched himself before the start date of the operation. It was not one of 'his', but while visiting Karachi he had developed good personal relations with the man who later became one of the most effective Afghan 'rebels', and he had thus been peripherally involved in the planning.

The whole thing typified the department's 'positive posture', as Goss liked to call it, which revealed either a taste for weasel words, or a private, sardonic sense of humour. The British involvement was to be that of honest—or dishonest—broker.

No one really believed that the Russians could be forcibly dislodged from Afghanistan, which, in any case, despite all the hullabaloo, had never been much of an oriental haven of liberty, freedom, and democracy. On the world stage, beloved by statesmen with a taste for the theatre of the absurd, a 'solution' had been fudged up, mostly by the simple device of not talking about it any more after a vague conference had concluded a vague agreement concerning Afghan immunity from outside intervention, which left the Third World more or less satisfied for the time being, the Russians firmly in control, and the West muttering darkly about a Vietnam-type situation.

The Viet Cong, however, had been exceedingly well armed, and it was no secret where their weapons came from. Times had changed since those increasingly far-off days. It might be safe to nip the Bear so that he scratched himself, but anything which might provoke him to use his teeth was to be avoided. Russian power, in conventional and nuclear hardware, was now too great, the likely cost of any misjudgement too alarming. The Cuban Crisis was no more than a nostalgic memory in the minds of a few ageing hawks, yearning for simpler days. That kind of calculated gamble belonged to the past, when the chances were that the bluff would not be called. Today, the chances were that it would, and it would be the West which would be obliged to climb down.

Back in the early eighties there had been a comforting, if brief period when many, especially those prone to believe that problems which were too daunting would somehow go away of their own accord, felt that the Russian empire was somehow on the point of crumbling away, under the strain of its Afghan commitment, and events in Poland. This optimistic delusion had long since receded into the realms of myth, only comparable with the so-called 'oil surplus' of the same period. Both myths were arguably connected.

Viewed as an oil tank, the earth was steadily being drained. Consumption might be slowed during recession, but 'recovery' meant increasing it again. In any case, the level continued to drop and would eventually reach 'empty'. A free-market economy depended upon surplus, freely available. Communism did not. It might visualize some distant utopia, but the means comprised rigid control and allocation, about which its subjects complained, but largely as a fact of life, comparable to the weather. The West was racked by unfulfilled expectations. The Russian empire contained expectations more easily and, in the Kremlin's judgement, it was the West which was crumbling.

The USA having, in its view, 'fallen behind', to achieve first parity with Russian might, and then superiority. 'Superiority' proved elusive. There was always some new weapon which must be developed, some extra contingency which needed guarding against. The cost was awesome. The means of destruction were ever more advanced, more complex. Technology ruled rather than men. Incredibly expensive systems rather than armies would fight opposing armies. And the race for improved hardware was continuous as, after a few years, sophisticated weaponry approached obsolescence and needed replacing with even more advanced devices.

Even America could not sustain such a burden alone and maintain large armed forces overseas at the same time. Her allies, supplied with the necessary hardware, must take more of the strain. Europe must be capable of defending itself, without relying on American manpower.

The end result was hardly what President Reagan and his planners had originally intended. In effect, if not by design, American forces, short of a world conflagration, were on the retreat. And Russia knew it. Her attitude became harder, her responses in disputed areas more daring, and often close to the bellicose.

A very fine line had to be drawn. Just the same, the idea of Afghanistan as a constant running sore in the Russian backside was an appealing one, and might be just possible with the narrow, remaining limits of manoeuvre. The same kind of 'rebels' who had once stubbornly mauled the British and turned the Khyber Pass into a death-trap were eager to continue with their natural, warrior trade. Weapons were the problem. A very large problem.

The 'rebels' could not be supplied with brand-new British or American or German arms. 'Rebels' suffered as well as inflicted casualties, and even in their mountain retreats, got hunted down and killed. The Russians had made it clear that any Western arms found lying around would be regarded as 'provocation'. They did not elaborate. They did not need to. The world was too full of trouble spots, no longer neatly divided into East and West, but a simmering cauldron, which only a little extra heat would bring to the boil.

There was only one practicable solution. The Afghan

'rebels' must be supplied with a steady stream of Russian weapons, from which the serial numbers had been obliterated. They could then claim that they were using guns captured from the Soviet Occupying Forces, or 'advisers' as they were labelled after the vague conference, and even if the Russians knew that was bullshit, they would be unable to make such propaganda or diplomatic mileage out of it.

Plenty of nations had plenty of Russian weapons, but most of them would not look with sympathy upon such an idea. The Chinese might not. They had, in any event, been doing it from the start, allowing a dribble of small arms through to the 'rebels' via Pakistan.

The object was to increase that dribble to a steady, constant flow, with some additional features which men like Goss thought might prove interesting. A few SAM missiles, even if obsolete, which could shoot down the occasional Soviet troop transport or helicopter gunship, would do wonders for the rebels' morale, and very little for the Russians'.

The Chinese, however, not renowned for hasty decision making at the best of times, were cautious. They had an uncomfortably long border with the Soviet Union, defended by an army still mostly equipped with Russian weapons. If they were to surrender significant quantities of those weapons, they wanted them replaced, in a ratio of two to one. In addition, the replacements must be of an advanced, up-to-date nature. And without China becoming dependent on Western factories. The Chinese, reasonably enough, trusted nobody.

It was a long drawn-out process, in which the department was involved from the British end because it was good at secrecy and could be disowned if necessary. It had got to the stage where agreement was close. Replacement weapons bearing a striking resemblance to those used by NATO, would be manufactured in

China, in factories equipped with imported machine tools operated with the aid of technical advisers from the manufacturers, the whole thing funded by a trade credit which would never be repaid. This it was hoped, would meet the various Chinese objections.

The documentation verifying and detailing the much-amended plan was to be carried by a department courier to Pakistan, where what was hoped would be a final meeting would take place in the north. This location had been chosen so that the main Afghan leaders could more easily attend.

The travel arrangements called for the courier to take off from London, and change planes in Rome.

Conroy lay on his bed for an hour, staring at the ceiling, before he roused himself, glanced at his watch, and went down to a late and hurried lunch.

There was no mention in the press report of any missing documents, but even if they had fallen into the wrong hands, they were unlikely to be damaging in themselves. They were highly technical and could be passed off as the kind attached to any trade deal. Without the other half of the equation—the Chinese *quid pro quo* in channelling their Russian-made weapons to the Afghans—which was known to very few people, and only to Conroy though his acquaintance with the Afghan 'rebel' leader, they would mean little or nothing.

But Conroy knew that the courier was to have been not some Ernest Harrington, but Karen Dewar. She would have travelled to Karachi, and thence to the north, as an official belonging to a relief organization. Karen was the original chameleon. If she chose, she could be the embodiment of sexiness, stopping all conversation dead when she walked into a room, obliging every man present to turn his head and look at her. If she chose differently, she could wait beside a warship in Portsmouth Dockyard, as it returned after three months at sea, and not one randy sailor would give her a second glance.

In this latter manifestation, she was the ideal courier. Invisible. With practical shoes and sensible clothes, hair pinned back, lips pursed, eyes downcast, hands bare of rings hugging a well-worn briefcase, Karen would have attracted no attention at all, even in a remote town close to the Afghan border, where the men tended to be on the chauvinist side. There was also a good deal of deprivation and disease, and they were accustomed to efficient, self-sufficient ladies working for charities. Karen could pass for one of those beautifully. One of her most frequently used covers was that of a charity worker.

Had Karen been to Pakistan, completed her mission and returned, before she was confined to the Home?

Or had she been replaced by someone else, using the name of Ernest Harrington, who had then—coincidentally—vanished?

If so, Goss had not mentioned it. And Goss would most certainly know. Some uncomfortable questions were arising in Conroy's mind. It was inevitable that he should be 'debriefed', although the fact that this process was to be carried out at the Home meant that he was under suspicion in some way, for some reason. He was beginning to think that the implications might be rather wider than he had first imagined.

He drank his coffee in the agreeable, comfortable dining room, and wondered when the kid-glove treatment would stop.

The nurse injected what seemed like a gallon of liquid into his left arm.

'Let me know if you feel faint, or anything like that,' the pretty nurse said, smiling at him. She slid the camera along into its gantry above him, and lined it up. 'Just a general snapshot first, to make sure everything's working OK,' she said, disappearing into another room and closing the door.

It was the doctor who emerged a couple of minutes later.

'I see you've had a myelogram recently,' he said.

'Yes,' Conroy said. Just as effective as being branded, and not a damn thing he could do about it.

The nurse came back. Conroy did as he was told and let her get on with it. There was a burning sensation in his arm, which felt swollen, although it was not, and he experienced a creeping nausea. The minor discomfort was negligible, but his body protested with a vehemence which was out of all proportion. The traditional last straw, perhaps. Or he was more exhausted than he had thought.

He turned his mind back to Karen. The cold anger he felt towards that woman was guaranteed to make him forget everything else.

He wondered when she had been turned. The time when it was feared she had been taken in Helsinki, but had turned up unscathed in Stockholm? During the prolonged Garnett investigation, when she had been infiltrated into his office, playing her self-effacing secretary role, and worked closely with him? Possibly. But perhaps she had never been turned at all. Perhaps she had been recruited when she was at university, studying Russian. If so, they had waited for ten years before activating her; but the Russians, a patient people, were always ready to let their sleepers lie until the right time. Besides, the longer a sleeper was allowed to become part of the scenery, completely accepted, the more he or she was likely to achieve.

Not that Karen seemed to have achieved very much. Conroy snatched, and possibly Harrington. Still, it would be her role to pass information, not to assess its importance. Judging by the treatment Conroy had received in the Lubianka and elsewhere, the KGB regarded him as a prize catch, worthy of a great deal of time and trouble. But in the process, Karen had blown herself. Was it worth that, just to render one field operator useless? Or possibly two, if you included Harrington? But of course, there might be more, for all Conroy knew. He knew practically nothing, and no one was telling him anything. There was another alternative. Karen did not have to be one of 'them'. She could have betrayed him from personal motives of her own. He wriggled with irritable frustration.

'Do keep still, please,' the nurse said. She sighed. 'We'll have to do that one again.'

When it was all over, Conroy dressed, went for tea, as instructed, and returned to the surgery at 16:45. The doctor was studying X-ray plates.

'You'll be glad to know,' he said, 'that you appear not to have suffered any kidney damage, as far as we can tell.' Medicos always hedged their bets. He handed over some tablets. 'Take these, and things should clear up reasonably soon.' Conroy pocketed the capsules. 'Ideally,' the doctor went on, studying Conroy's notes, 'I'd like you to have a period of rest while we keep an eye on you, and then go on leave.'

'Sounds like a good idea to me,' Conroy said. 'Any reason why not?'

'Well, that's it, as far as I'm concerned,' the doctor said cheerfully, which did not exactly answer the question. 'I know you only drink in moderation, but it might be a good thing to cut out alcohol entirely, for a while. Plenty of liquid though, as much water as you can manage. Give the kidneys a holiday at least. All right?'

Perhaps that was an answer.

At 09:30 the following morning, Conroy tapped on the door of Room B3 and walked in.

The previous evening, in the bar, he had fallen into conversation with someone called George, whom he had got to know by sight, which was not difficult. George stuck out. George always wore a track suit. He ate a hearty breakfast, chewing each mouthful carefully, was not seen for the rest of the day, and reappeared at dinner time, when he ordered a large steak and a green salad.

Underneath his track suit, George possessed a muscular, powerful body, as formidable and subtle as a pile-driver. Conroy found his conversation equally subtle, but he seemed a neutrally safe companion in this strange place.

George revealed that he was a former Commando, and in charge of physical training at the Home. He gave the impression that it was his task to restore field personnel to the peak of physical fitness, although Conroy doubted if it was quite like that. He thought that George was not as dumb as he looked.

In all probability, like Conroy, George was being deliberately neutral, and chose to talk about the various bees which buzzed in his bonnet, all of which concerned the human body. This, he regarded as an engine, which the vast majority of people, even those who should know better such as department personnel, fail to service or fuel properly. Alcohol, George maintained, was a poison, and he approved of Conroy's abstinence, but urged him to drink carrot juice, instead of the tonic water which Conroy was sipping.

George was deep in his exposition of the merits of carrot juice, when a hand touched Conroy's elbow.

'Sorry to interrupt,' the square-faced, red-haired man said. 'You're Richard Conroy, aren't you? Glad to meet you.'

'How do you do,' Conroy said. They shook hands.

'I'm your debriefing officer,' the man said. 'Call me Derek. If it's all right with you, we'll make a start at nine-thirty in the morning. Room B3.'

'I've nothing else to do,' Conroy said.

'Fine. I'll see you then,' Derek said. 'Full of carrot juice, if George has his way.'

'It's no joke, sir,' George said. 'A glass night and morning wouldn't do you any harm.'

So 'Derek' rated a 'sir' from George, Conroy noted.

'Have a carrot juice now,' George suggested.

Conroy accepted politely, but noticed that George was not calling *him* 'sir'. Which could indicate that the staff knew rather more about what was due to happen to him while at the Home than he did, and assessed his standing accordingly.

If so, nothing too disagreeable was going to take place yet, apparently. Room B3 was on the top floor. It was light and airy, and the large windows commanded a fine view of the gentle Devon countryside.

So far, Conroy's presence had not been required in the underground section, in what had once been the cellars, nor had he found any means of access. There were two lifts in the Home, one each side of the reception area, but neither went any lower than the ground floor. Nor had Conroy seen any stairs which led down below ground level. Not that he had gone out of his way to search. It was Conroy's ambition to depart from the Home without, if humanly possible, spending any time in the cellars at all.

'Morning, Richard,' Derek said. 'Sit down and make yourself comfortable.'

He indicated the deep, inviting armchair, which was set at an angle in front of his desk. Behind the desk, Derek lolled casually, in a revolving executive-type chair.

'As you know, we've allowed five days for debriefing,' Derek said, 'but that's a moveable feast. We may get it wrapped up much quicker, but if we find we need more time, then it's available. We'll see how it goes. To begin with, perhaps you'd give me a general outline of events, and we'll fill in the details later.'

Conroy began to speak, repeating what he had already told Goss. There was no tape recorder visible, and Derek, apparently in something approaching a daydream, was not taking notes.

Conroy looked for, and eventually found, the camera lens. It was concealed inside a box file, one of dozens which stood in rows on some shelves in the corner he was facing. The lens glinted briefly in the sunlight streaming in from outside when he moved his head slightly. The interview was being videotaped. Small, directional microphones would also be aimed at him.

Conroy continued his account without a pause, giving no indication that he knew it was being recorded. He spared a brief thought for those who would later spend their time watching hours and hours of tape, alert for any inconsistencies. Good luck to them. The trouble with videotape, of course, was that it could easily be edited to provide practically any inconsistency required; but if that was Goss's game, there was nothing he could do about it.

Derek asked a few questions as he went along, but not many. Most of the time, Derek was either listening with his eyes closed, or quietly dozing.

Conroy was trained to remember detail and, knowing from the first that this moment would come, had spent several days organizing what he would say in his head. He was careful to differentiate between facts he was certain of, logical deduction, and speculation. There were not too many of the former. Conroy had travelled by car, in a sealed van, and by air. Sometimes he was conscious, sometimes not. What his captors had called 'preliminary questioning' had lasted approximately two weeks and had taken place in a desolate, hutted camp.

'Where do you think that was?' Derek murmured.

'Somewhere near the border,' Conroy said. 'That's all I know.'

'Inside the Soviet Union then,' Derek said dreamily. 'Go on.'

Coffee and biscuits arrived at 11:00. They paused for fifteen minutes and casually discussed world affairs, mostly the West German election campaign, which was coming to its vituperative climax. Both agreed that the stability enjoyed under the one-time chancellor, Helmut Schmidt, was beginning to look like a golden age, and on the dangers of the polarization between far Right and far Left, which had since taken place. Proportional representation, while theoretically fair, could lead to horrors of its own, with a ramshackle government unduly dependent upon pressure groups composed of fanatics. The idea of a Greater Germany, comprising both East and West in one form or another, was being played for all its emotional worth; but Conroy thought that, provided the election passed off peacefully, serious trouble could be avoided. Derek nodded, looked at his watch, and they resumed.

Conroy had never been in any doubt about being in the Lubianka. The Russians had made a point of telling him where he was the moment he recovered consciousness after his arrival.

'The name does have a certain ring to it,' Derek said. 'Calculated to generate shivers in the spine.'

'Justifiably,' Conroy said drily.

'Any visual confirmation though?' Derek asked.

'When I left,' Conroy said, 'I was driven to the airport in an ordinary car.'

Conroy got to the point where he had walked past Garnett on the wooden bridge.

'I think we may as well break for lunch now,' Derek said.

They walked down to the dining room together, but Derek did not offer to join him. As before, Conroy sat alone at the table for two in the corner. With the exception of the egregious George, Conroy was receiving about as much social attention as the Invisible Man.

After lunch, Derek became more businesslike, and turned it into a question-and-answer session.

'Was any one person in charge of your interrogation?' he enquired.

'Yes,' Conroy said. 'Both at the camp and at the Lubianka. About sixty years old, heavily built, spoke good English. Thick grey hair, prominent nose, grey eyes, heavy eyebrows.'

'Any idea of his rank?'

'He always wore civilian clothes,' Conroy said. 'But from the deferential way he was treated, I'd place him as a general in the KGB.'

'Was he at the frontier when you were exchanged?'

'He didn't travel with me,' Conroy said, 'but I caught sight of him while I was standing beside the car. I'd say he was in charge of the operation. Their version of our beloved Goss.'

'Anyone you recognize from our picture gallery?' Derek asked, letting that one go without comment.

'No,' Conroy said. The department possessed photographs of those persons who, while fulfilling diplomatic or commercial functions, might or might not be KGB men. 'I very much doubt if he's ever operated in the West. But if he turns up as the leader of their trade-union movement, I'll know the bastard again.'

'Later on, we'll construct a profile and a photofit picture of him,' Derek said. 'Meantime, let's give him a code-name.' He paused, waiting.

'Andrei,' Conroy said.

'Any special reason for suggesting that?'

'I don't know,' Conroy said. 'It came into my mind for some reason.' He wondered why. There was one possible reason, which he had had no call to mention yet.

'I see,' Derek said. 'Now, you were interrogated first at the camp, and then at the Lubianka, for eight weeks in all.'

'As near as I can judge,' Conroy said. 'I had no watch, I never knew if it was night or day. I tried to keep track. That's my best estimate.'

'It's a long time,' Derek said reflectively. 'How much do you think you told them?'

'Nothing,' Conroy said. 'I stuck to my cover story. I was a self-employed computer consultant, hoping to drum up business in Berlin.'

'Obviously, they tried to break your story down.'

'They didn't have to try,' Conroy said. 'They knew from the start that it was all rubbish. They even had my real name.'

'They had it? You didn't tell them?'

'No, I didn't tell them,' Conroy said sharply.

'Did they know why you were really meeting Hans?'

'No,' Conroy said. 'And I didn't tell them that either.'

'There's no need to be aggressive, Richard,' Derek said gently.

'I feel aggressive,' Conroy said. 'So would you, if you'd been shopped.'

'Yes, I expect so,' Derek said. 'Did they try and test your claims in any way? Show you a computer and tell you to write a programme or anything?'

'They did that,' Conroy said. 'With some computer experts of theirs firing questions.'

'Do you think that's when you might have given yourself away?'

'I did not give myself away at any point,' Conroy said stubbornly. 'I've used that cover off and on for years. I know enough to pass. In any case, a lot of real computer consultants don't write their own programmes. They prefer to steal other people's.'

'Would they know that? The concept of a self-employed expert living off his wits could be fairly foreign in the USSR.'

'Don't make the mistake of patronizing them,' Conroy said. 'They're probably better informed about us than we are about them. And as a by the way, the computer they made me operate was a damned good one. I've learned enough to know that, technically, it was highly advanced.'

'I wasn't so much patronizing them, as testing the validity of your reply,' Derek said. 'So you believe that they failed to shake your story, but they knew it was false from other information in their possession?'

'Test it any way you want,' Conroy said. 'That's how it was.'

'Let's come to the means they employed to try and force you to admit that you were lying.'

'The combination you'd expect,' Conroy said. 'Psychological and physical. Weakening resistance in all the usual ways. Extremes of heat and cold. Deprivation of food, water, sleep, and lavatory facilities of any kind. Not even a bucket.'

'An attempt to make you feel no better than an animal.'

'After a while, that's exactly how you do feel,' Conroy said. 'The beatings are designed not only to inflict pain, but to leave you with about as much dignity as a cringing dog.'

'You found this loss of dignity the hardest thing to tolerate, I gather.'

'I think they overdid it,' Conroy said. 'Admittedly, it reduced me to my lowest point very quickly, but then I began to get angry. Angry with them. To that extent, it was counterproductive. That anger saw me through. When they switched, and the general played the soft, reasonable man who only wanted to help me, I could feed off that anger. I just sat there, thinking "you bastard".'

'The application of such techniques are extremely difficult to judge. One sometimes gets it wrong,' Derek said. One professional scrutinizing the work of another, like a painter commenting upon the brush strokes of a fellow practitioner. 'Let's discuss pain,' Derek said. 'If that's not too painful.' He smiled pleasantly, with mild approval of his own minor play on words. 'Beatings, you've mentioned. I have a note from Goss about an ingenious quasi-medical variant which, apart from being highly unpleasant at the time, also served to mark you indelibly for several years to come. They must have decided to let you go from the beginning, it seems.'

'Not necessarily,' Conroy said. 'They did that fairly late on. Goss's negotiations must have been pretty protracted.'

'But they took care not to inflict any external injuries right from the outset.'

'At one point, they were talking about putting me on trial,' Conroy said. 'If they were considering an open show trial, it wouldn't have had such propaganda value if I'd clearly been tortured.'

'Why do you suppose they did not put you on trial? Especially if, as you say, they knew exactly who you were, and that you worked for the department?'

'They did know,' Conroy said. 'But they couldn't prove it, even in their terms, unless they could extract some damaging admissions as well.'

'If they failed to do so, that reflects great credit on you,' Derek said. The 'if' was not emphasized, but it was there.

'All the training, the conditioning, the imposed reflexes, the brainwashing, which is what it amounts to, they come into play when it finally happens,' Conroy said. 'The cover story's imprinted on the mind, the truth would be a lie. So you just keep on repeating the cover story.'

'That would probably be true of most men and women in the department,' Derek said. 'But you have been continually assessed as someone who does not readily accept imposed ideas. You question. You have a streak in you which might be called rebellious. You're something of an odd man out. That's all splendid in some ways. It makes you a highly resourceful individual in the field. Outstanding, in fact. But under interrogation, that's another matter. Interrogators like a man with a mind of his own. If he's prepared to question old ideas and look at new ones, he's vulnerable. They can use that trait to nudge him towards doubt. Doubt about himself. Doubts about what he's doing.'

Conroy rubbed his face reflectively. He remembered the camera, which he had forgotten about for the moment, and wondered what they would make of that automatic gesture. That of someone gaining a little time to work out a good evasion, probably.

'Well, you know your own trade,' he said. 'Looking back now, perhaps there were moments when they nearly got the kind of lever you're talking about locked into place. But they overplayed their hand.' He leaned his head back. The sun had evaporated an hour ago. Dark, bulbous clouds were gathering outside. It would rain soon. 'I don't think I can give you a direct answer,' Conroy said eventually. 'Certainly not a general one. Only how it seemed to me. There's nothing noble about pain and degradation. If the last couple of months had been from agonizing illness, I'd have resented it, to put it mildly, even had it been from natural causes. Because it was deliberately imposed, the resentment, in the end, was all the greater. Not because we're always right, and they're always wrong. I don't believe either is true. I wouldn't put it any higher than a choice of evils. But if that was the lever they were looking for, they didn't find it. They were putting me through it, trying to manipulate me, to get what they wanted, but without

. . . I don't know . . . passion, if you like. It was all detached, as impersonal as a scientist carrying out vivisection to prove some theory he'd dreamed up in the bath. And I thought "Sod it, no. You're not going to use me like that". No grand ideals, or anything. Sheer bloody-mindedness, really. It's that simple. Or that complicated. I don't know which.'

'Nor do I,' Derek said. He smiled, faintly. 'It's a point worth bearing in mind, though. The virtues of being bloody-minded. Apart from the myelogram, did they try anything else which you would not have expected?'

'Only one,' Conroy said. 'I spent a week on heroin.'

'Heroin? Were they trying to turn you into an addict?'

'I doubt it,' Conroy said. 'Supposedly, it was to relieve the pain. Which it certainly did. They were using medical doses. If some people get addicted after that, I'm not one of them. It was an experience all right, but I hated it.'

'Then what do you suppose the purpose was?'

'I think someone had had a bright idea, and they were trying it out as an experiment,' Conroy said. 'A different way of achieving disorientation.'

'While they continued to interrogate you, presumably?'

'The bits I remember,' Conroy said. 'Most of that week is pretty much of a blank.'

'So you can't be certain that you didn't tell them something during that period?'

'I'm certain I did,' Conroy said. 'A lot of jumbled garbage. I didn't make sense to myself, let alone them. I had brief rational periods, and I could tell they were getting frustrated and fed up.'

'Do you know why they stopped the heroin treatment after seven days?'

'I wasn't eating,' Conroy said. 'My physical condition

was deteriorating. Perhaps if they'd kept it up, I'd have gone right round the twist, and a gibbering lunatic wouldn't have been any use to them. I'd guess that time was running out, it wasn't working, they weren't getting anywhere, and they abandoned the idea.'

'How can you be so sure that it wasn't working? You spoke of rational periods, which implies that otherwise, you were irrational. In other words, disorientated, as they wished.'

'When I wasn't rational,' Conroy said, 'I was hallucinating like crazy. They couldn't get through to me.'

'Do you remember what form these hallucinations took?'

'Some,' Conroy said. 'Once, they faked a phone call for me. Told me it was Garnett on the line.'

'Did you believe them?'

'Completely,' Conroy said. 'But I had a Latin master at school. He was also our football coach. His name was Garnett. To my knowledge, he's never crossed my mind since the day I left, but I thought it was him. Rambled on about Virgil, and Caesar's Gallic Wars, and whether I shouldn't play deeper, and try and overlap in the next first eleven match. The poor sod the other end got very confused.'

'He would do,' Derek remarked.

'Another time, I was in my room with two of them. It wasn't a cell. More like a hospital ward. I was convinced we were in the Members' Pavilion at Lords. We were watching a test match, England against Australia. I was explaining the game to them. That was when I realized that they were getting pissed off with the whole thing. One of them, I remember, threw me on the bed, and shouted: "Stop it. Stop pretending. Talk properly."'

'But you weren't pretending?'

'I was there. At Lords,' Conroy said. 'I could see

every detail. England were 243 for 7. Australia had just taken the new ball. I was telling the two goons why it would probably swing in the air a lot, and that was when I got thrown on the bed. They weren't much interested in the finer points of cricket.'

Derek smiled. 'I can imagine,' he said. 'Tell me about your other hallucinations.'

'I don't remember any more,' Conroy said. He preferred to keep the most vivid one of all to himself. The one which was straight out of Kafka.

He was in a small room, facing a raised dais. Three men took their places, with solemn dignity, behind the dais. They began to question him. It was a tribunal. He was on trial. No charges were preferred, but they accused him just the same. Conroy defended himself. The three men became more menacing, accusing him in turn. Even though they did not say what offence had brought him before the tribunal, they knew that he was guilty. Conroy answered them back defiantly. But they were relentless. Implacable. They ordered him to make restitution. Conroy pleaded that he did not know how to do so. He repeated, that it was not his fault. It was not his doing. It was not his wish. The three judges nodded their understanding, but the verdict remained unchanged. Conroy refused to accept the authority for the court. He would appeal. The judges rose and filed out. The verdict was final. He was guilty.

'You said that you spent most of that week halluci- nating like crazy,' Derek said.

'I also said that most of it was a blank,' Conroy said.

'This could be more important than you imagine,' Derek said seriously. 'Your subconscious conjured up a Latin master you thought you'd forgotten. It may also have brought back other, and rather more important things, which they might have been able to use against you.'

Conroy said, 'I know I can't prove it, but I'm positive that I told them nothing, whether under the influence of heroin or not.'

'Perhaps I should have mentioned that, by training, I am a psychiatrist,' Derek said. 'Your subconscious was bobbing about, in your own words, "like crazy". That is, out of control. All human beings lock away things they would rather not dwell upon. You're no exception —despite your training. You may have revealed, not information—I'm not saying that—but doubts, or fears, or guilts, which normally you don't even know you possess. They could use that. It would be a good lever. They would use it.'

'Possibly,' Conroy said. 'But it didn't happen.'

'You may not be aware of the significance of some seemingly bizarre hallucination,' Derek said. There was a trace of worry in his eyes. 'You must recall fragments, at least. I think we should try and build them up. Complete them. And then analyze them together. See if there's any meaning there which you may have overlooked. Some chink in your protective armour, into which they may have been able to insert their lever.'

'I'll go over it again tonight, and let you know,' Conroy promised. Fuck that, he thought.

'You're not in the Lubianka now,' Derek said. 'Here, it's your duty to tell the absolute truth, and answer every question I put to you without evasion, and without holding anything back. I think you're concealing something. Whether deliberately or not, I don't know. But it's my job to find out. I'm not satisfied, Conroy, and you may as well know it.'

'How fragile was the chumminess, the 'glad to meet yous', the use of Christian names. The cellars, Conroy thought, had come noticeably nearer, in sixty seconds flat.

'Whether you're satisfied or not is your bad luck,'

Conroy said. 'I really don't care. I don't need any reminders about duty from someone who's never been out in the field, and I doubt if you have. If I remember anything else, I'll tell you.'

He would have to invent a couple more hallucinations for the fellow, and give him something to analyze. That should keep him happy. Meanwhile, he stared at Derek, with the rancorous gaze of the honest man, resentful of the unfair allegation that he was holding something back.

'Very well,' Derek said, after a long pause. 'Reflect overnight, and we'll come back to it tomorrow.'

Conroy believed that if he could beat the bastards in the Lubianka, he could beat the bastards here too.

Some things were private. Nothing to do with the department. Nothing to do with this merchant, with his psychiatric training. Nothing to do with Goss.

Least of all to do with Goss.

THREE

At 18:45 on the evening of the fourth day, the cheerful buzz of conversation over drinks abruptly halved in volume, and became a muted murmur.

Goss had walked in.

He crossed to the bar where, as though he were Moses parting the Red Sea, a space magically opened up for him at once.

Those nearby muttered polite greetings. Goss grunted with all the charm of a teety grizzly bear. Conroy turned his back on him, finished his drink, and walked into the dining room.

The tables filled up rapidly. Everyone else seemed to have much the same idea. If only it were feasible, Conroy thought, to nominate Goss for *Private Eye's* 'Shit of the Year' contest, it would be a walkover.

He was halfway through his main course, when Goss arrived, sat at the vacant place beside him, and ordered the roast.

'Settled in all right?' Goss enquired. 'Looking after you, are they?'

'No complaints,' Conroy said. 'Quite the rest cure. Up until now.'

'We'll have to do something about that,' Goss said loudly. 'You're not here to idle your time away. The staff must have got slack. Come to regard it as a soft number. Need a good kick up the backside.' His head rotated as he stared malevolently at the offending members of staff. Those within earshot pretended they had heard nothing and were unaware of his presence.

'You'll enjoy that,' Conroy said.

'You think so?' Goss enquired. 'Well, we'll see how much you enjoy it, perhaps.'

All the malevolence was now focused on Conroy, who gave Goss the equable smile which would certainly be interpreted as insolence. What the hell did that matter? Goss had made up his mind already, like those three judges in his hallucination. Conroy wondered why his mind had not cast Goss as one of them. But for some reason, it had not. They were all strangers.

'Men perform more efficiently when they're led, rather than driven,' Conroy said. 'Respect is a better spur than fifty lashes, right, left and centre. The Navy found that out a long time ago.'

'Don't give me that crap,' Goss said. 'This isn't the Navy. A nice guy running this department would be a menace. You think Lionel was a nice guy? He was ruthless, he was heartless. Only he had the sort of good manners the upper class acquire at Eton and Balliol, and he liked to be liked, even when he was sticking the knife in. Me, I don't give a damn, and that's the only difference between us. Jesus,' Goss breathed, 'you think I care about being respected? Keeping the department one step ahead in the dirtiest game on God's earth, that's all I care about.'

'I haven't seen Karen around,' Conroy said, changing the subject. He was slightly surprised by Goss's vehemence.

'You wouldn't,' Goss said. 'No alcohol allowed during refresher training.' He took a swig from the glass of iced whisky, which he had brought in with him. 'I'm glad to see you're off it.'

'Doctor's advice,' Conroy said. 'Is Ernest Harrington a Foreign Office official?'

'You read about that,' Goss said, eyeing him.

'Wasn't I supposed to?'

'Karen's replacement,' Goss said. 'Still no word of him. Don't know what it's all about, except he's the second of ours they've lifted recently, counting you. Perhaps they're trying to shake morale. Make us feel no one's safe. Doesn't make sense otherwise.'

'Karen's second bullseye,' Conroy said. 'First me, then Harrington.'

'Well, she won't be be scoring any more,' Goss said. 'If she was the source.'

Conroy stopped toying with his glass of water. 'What do you mean "if"? She's the only possible.'

'Not necessarily,' Goss said. 'There's another one. Put yourself in my place, and think about it.'

'In that case,' Conroy said, 'I come up with you.'

'Not if you're in my seat, you don't,' Goss said. He speared a large piece of lamb, chewed on it, and spoke with his mouth full. 'Derek seems to think you're concealing something. Believes we should take some pains to find out what it is.'

'He's a jingoist,' Conroy said, 'if he thinks our techniques for taking pains are superior to theirs. I've run a consumer test. In my considered opinion, they're not.'

'Ah, but whether you really sampled the goodies they had on offer remains in the realm of speculation,'

Goss said. 'You could have viewed the samples and decided on discretion instead of valour.'

'My debriefing isn't going too well, I gather,' Conroy said.

'You're not going anywhere else yet, if that's what you mean,' Goss said. He started on the roast potatoes.

'I hate to quibble,' Conroy said, 'but how does your quack think I managed to pass blood? Are they supposed to have taught me how to do it? That'd be quite a trick.'

'There's no discernible kidney damage,' Goss pointed out.

'I should have warned them you'd be hard to fool,' Conroy said. 'They'd have shoved more lead inside the rubber.'

'Anyway . . .' Goss began. He shovelled brussels sprouts into his mouth as well. '. . . Derek isn't suggesting the thumbscrew, or attaching electrodes to your balls. Others might, but that's not his style. His idea is to put you back on heroin for seven days and encourage you to cough up these hallucinations you're not telling us about.'

A chill of apprehension rose from the bottom of Conroy's spine. He had every faith in his conscious resistance; much less in the ramblings of his subconscious.

'Please yourself,' he said casually. 'I don't suppose I'm entitled to refuse, anyway.'

'Not while I'm in charge you're not,' Goss said. He attacked his carrots. 'The trouble with trick cyclists,' he grumbled, as his fork left his mouth, 'is that they always imagine there's all the time in the world. They get carried away. I'll tell you his assessment. He thinks you're a man they'd be unlikely to break by conventional means. But if they found out something which you couldn't bear anyone else to know, "secret guilts" to use his jargon, then maybe, just maybe, they'd have the key they wanted. They could wear you down that way. Especially if you resisted it, this thing you're supposed to be ashamed of. And he argues that there must be something, or you wouldn't have minded telling him . . . whatever it was. What's your opinion?'

'If you argue from a hypothetical premise, you can prove anything you like,' Conroy said.

'I see what he means,' Goss remarked. 'You *are* being evasive. Just suppose he's right for the minute, for Christ's sake. Do you reckon they could crack you open that way?'

'I think he's vastly overrating his own trade,' Conroy said.

'Could be,' Goss said reflectively. 'But I remember that short story of H G Wells' about the fellow who didn't believe in God, and when he died he found himself, much to his surprise, standing on the palm of God's hand. And God told him his fortune, about things he'd done on earth which he'd never seen that way, because he thought he'd been a pretty good bloke, really. And God reduced him to a snivelling wreck.'

'Yes, well, I expect God's a bit brighter than Derek is,' Conroy said, annoyed. 'Or you are. Or they are, for that matter.'

'Trick cyclists want to play God anyway,' Goss said. 'That's the only reason they become trick cyclists.' He pushed his plate away with a sigh of pleasure. It looked as though a dog had licked it clean. 'I haven't decided, as yet,' he said. 'It seems to me Derek's got you taped.'

'Only by way of your supposedly concealed video camera,' Conroy said.

'I told you they'd got slack here,' Goss said grumpily. 'They're supposed to know we're not dealing with innocents. All right. You've scored. Tell me.'

'It's not set deep enough,' Conroy said. 'The lens reflects the light from certain angles.'

66

'I'll have it fixed,' Goss said. 'Plus the merchant responsible,' he added. He brooded for a while, his chin sunk into his collar, which enlarged his jowls considerably. 'The trouble is, time could be short,' he said at last. 'I'm not sure if we can spare seven days listening to you gibbering like a lunatic. Fascinating though the insight into the filthy recesses of your mind would no doubt be.' He peered at Conroy from under his shaggy eyebrows. His eyes were bloodshot in the corners. 'I'm tempted though,' Goss said. 'So don't think I'm not. Depends whether we can afford a week to send you on another trip. Or whether we need that time more urgently. For something else.'

'Up to you,' Conroy said. 'Let me know.' He pushed his chair back pointedly. 'Anything else? If not, I'm going to bed.'

'Meet me at 07:30 in Reception,' Goss said. 'If you want an early breakfast, you have to order it tonight.'

'OK,' Conroy said. 'Good night.' He stood up.

'One more thing,' Goss said. 'Pack your suitcase. Someone'll collect it during the day. You're being moved to different quarters.'

Conroy did not sleep well that night. Goss was a high-class professional, and even though Conroy recognized every move in his game, that did nothing to detract from the effect. In slightly over one hour, Goss had generated more unease and apprehension than had Derek in days. True, Goss had more going for him in that respect. There was a chilling menace about Goss, born of the ultimate power which he wielded. In the undercover world which Goss ruled, habeas corpus and the Judge's Rules did not exist. Goss was required to account to no one except the PM, and then only in general terms.

When things went wrong, and the secret war was being waged against a resolute and tough opponent, it was sometimes necessary to account for the untimely death, in some parts of the globe, of whoever it was who had given himself or herself away by a moment's lapse, or been betrayed by others. Properly certified death certificates were neatly filed, giving the cause of death as cancer, or coronary thrombosis, or multiple injuries in a road accident, depending on the victim's cover in use at the time. Funerals always ended in cremation. Surviving relatives, sometimes close enough to be grief-stricken, used the imaginative death certificates to acquire death benefits and the proceeds of insurance policies. Wills were proven, and homes and bank accounts changed hands.

It did not require too much of a suspicious nature to suppose that Goss might well authorize the same treatment for the very occasional traitor or double agent unearthed in the ranks of the department. Department personnel could hardly be tried and convicted in the ordinary way. Goss could easily 'lose' such an individual, in his next report to the PM, merely remarking with regret that a loyal servant of the Crown had unfortunately drowned while unwisely bathing off Beach Head, or fallen from the balcony of a tenth-storey flat in some tower block. And the PM would nod, and not ask awkward questions.

'It's your own fault,' Conroy told himself. 'You should have stayed in Army Intelligence. Instead, you allowed Lionel to flatter you with his glowing admiration of your successful undercover work in Northern Ireland, and his honest, oh so honest, belief that you were just the man for the most testing, the most daunting, the most rewarding . . . in short, he bullshitted you into the department. Yes, you knew it was bullshit even then, but Lionel could charm virgin novices out of a nunnery, and into a brothel. Here was a man, you thought, it would be a privilege to work for.

And you went on thinking so. You only forgot one thing, didn't you. Lionel would retire at sixty. And his successor might be a very different man indeed. His successor might be a Goss.'

Had Lionel really been as heartless and ruthless as Goss maintained? Conroy, older now, and centuries wiser, thought about it.

At just after one o'clock in the morning, during those most vulnerable few moments for any man or woman, when sleep had almost embraced him but not quite, the raised dais and the three implacable judges entered his mind again. Conroy swore, switched the bedside light on, stared at the tasteful, full-length, heavy brown curtains, and banished the scene from his mind.

What sneaky, underhand tricks the human brain played, even one as largely conditioned as his must be by now. That relatively brief episode in his life had been closed for years. He could not remember the last time he had given it a thought. Yet under heroin, it had been reincarnated, twisted and distorted out of all recognition, as though it were still important, and as though anything else had been possible. It was no longer important, damn it, even if it ever had been. And in any case, the decision had not been his, it had been hers. Not only had he not been informed or consulted, he had not even known anything about it until it was all over. He could not be considered responsible in any way. What was it all about, for Christ's sake? Nothing. Such things happened all the time. At worst, a misunderstanding. A combination of unfortunate circumstances. When he thought about what he was occasionally obliged to do in the course of his job . . . things for which he would have been tried at the Old Bailey if his work was like other men's . . . crimes in the view of society . . . violent crimes

. . . sins in the eyes of most religions . . . but the hallucinatory tribunal had not summoned him to answer for those, but for—that!

For even though the tribunal had accused him without saying of what he was accused, and condemned him without mentioning his supposed offence, Conroy knew what it was all about.

It was the effect of the heroin of course, shredding his brain, depriving him of reason, leaving him with the mental capacity of a retarded idiot, the random imaginings of a maniac. By the lights of any normal man, it was laughable. A joke.

For a start, there was his family-sized flat, with its three bedrooms. Buying that demonstrated in practical terms how deeply he had been involved, how genuine his emotions were. Not that they needed demonstrating. Even though it was like looking back upon another man, he could still remember. Even now.

Eventually, they would get married, that was understood almost from the beginning. The department could raise no conceivable objection. In the meantime, there was no hurry. They were as settled as any married couple. As always, he was away a good deal. He had recently assembled the necessary, if fairly superficial, expertise to pass as a computer consultant, and was enjoying the flexibility of his new cover, which had served him well ever since, until it was blown in Berlin.

Her work confined her mostly to London, at that time. She kept her own flat on, but she had the key to his. Towards the end, when he came back unexpectedly early, he found her busy decorating his flat. The woodwork shone brilliant white. The walls glowed in soft pastels. At the time, he did not perceive the significance, but simply took her out to dinner as a gesture of thanks. Now the decorations bore much the same resemblance to her handiwork as an old oil painting badly in need of restoring does to the original. The pastels no longer glowed, the woodwork was off-white rather than brilliant. Conroy had got used to it as it was now. It took an effort of memory to recollect the effect, when he had walked in and taken her by surprise that day.

Shortly afterwards, Conroy was ordered by the department to cancel his leave and fly out the following morning via Paris. It was hoped, overoptimistically as it transpired, to enlist the support of the French.

'Where are you going?'

'After Paris, the Middle East,' Conroy said.

'How long for?'

'Two, three weeks, something like that. Perhaps a bit more.'

'It seems to me that you're breaking a promise, and I don't like that.'

'There's nothing I can do,' Conroy said. He had tried to get out of it and failed. 'This is important. The client's making trouble. It only means postponing for a while. I'll be able to call you now and then. We can talk on the phone.'

It was three and a half months later before Conroy returned.

'Well, at least you didn't cock it up,' Goss said. 'Even though you did take your bloody time about it.'

'Thanks very much,' Conroy said. He knew a compliment from Goss when he heard one. 'I take it I can go on leave now.' That was before he knew. 'But I want a personal interview concerning my status, as soon as possible.'

'Oh, gawd,' Goss groaned. 'Not another one. When are you young fellows going to learn to appreciate the virtues of public libraries? You don't have to buy the bloody book, you know. All right. Monday morning, first thing.'

Later, Conroy cancelled the appointment. Goss did not ask why, nor did he ever so much as refer to the matter again. He was not interested.

Conroy had been engaged in securing the release of a party of British diplomats taken hostage by a disowned offshoot of the PLO. The affair never achieved anything like the column inches given to the American hostages in Teheran, for a very good reason. Goss had been obliged to inform the PM that, as bad luck would have it, two members of the party had rather more to do with the department than with diplomacy. Should that come out, there would be shrieks of 'Spies!' throughout the entire troubled region. The less publicity the better, and no busybodies from the UN with high ideals at any price. The whole thing should be played down and dealt with discreetly.

It was because of the need for discretion that it took Conroy so long. Working with two operatives stationed in the area, he stitched together one compromise after another, only to see them fall apart. Absurd demands were made and gravely considered. One deadline after another came and went. Local informers were recruited and came up with useless information, mostly invented.

Eventually, the disowned offshoot of the PLO probably became bored or frustrated, or both. One of the intermediaries said too much to one of the informers, who for once had something accurate to sell. The remote hideout where the hostages were being held.

Even then, the negotiations with the Emir ran into weeks. The potentate was a nervous man, not nearly as rich as his more fortunate brothers, who was deeply alarmed to find that his territory was being used in this way, for causes in which he had not the slightest interest. He could only foresee trouble, and his first, instinctive reaction was to refuse to believe it. Patiently, he was persuaded that the problem would not go away of its own accord. He then communed anxiously with the official PLO, and only when assured that they would raise no objection, did he sanction a rescue operation. On two conditions.

The first was that his own troops must carry out the rescue. The second had to do with a deposit to be made in a Swiss numbered bank account. The Emir had no great faith in his own long-term future as a ruler. The two conditions were referred to London. The first presented no problem, and a detachment of the SAS was placed on standby. The second, since it involved money, took longer to resolve. Conroy sweated and fumed, but at last the authorization came through. After that it was plain sailing.

The SAS struck at dawn, disarmed the kidnappers, injuring only one of them slightly, and withdrew out of sight. Then the Emir's troops went in and were filmed triumphantly leading the captives to safety. The SAS detachment changed back into the civilian clothes in which they had arrived and returned to the UK. Their part was never mentioned but, like the department, they preferred it that way.

Conroy had managed to make a few private phone calls, but not many. He could not use the consular facilities which were available to him for official coded messages, and he sometimes thought not only that there seemed to be more Rolls-Royces than telephones in the Emirate, but that they also worked a damn sight better, too.

She either sounded more and more distant as the weeks dragged by, or the decrepit system was on the verge of giving up the ghost entirely. For the last month and a half, he was unable to get through to her at all. He supposed that she must be working away from home, but sent a cable giving the date and time of his return on the off-chance.

She was not at the airport. He reported to Goss and went home. She was not there either, nor was the scribbled note he had more than half expected. The flat was airless and dusty. There was no sign that she had been there.

He phoned her, but there was no answer. It was nearly ten o'clock at night. Feeling flat, let down, and hungry, he went to a restaurant which they often used. She was just leaving, hugging the arm of some man he had never seen before. She gave him a brilliant smile and his front-door key, and stepped into a waiting taxi.

It came out later, in a coldly angry row in which she gave as good as she got. She was always his equal, at least, which was perhaps why she was the only one he had ever really cared about.

Conroy's fury withered into disbelief when she told him, head held high, that while he was away she had had an abortion.

'Why didn't you tell me you were pregnant, for God's sake?'

'I didn't know until after you'd gone.'

'On the phone . . .'

'The day it was confirmed, you announced you were staying on, and you didn't know when you'd be back. I decided it was my problem.'

'It wasn't your problem, it was ours. And it wasn't a problem, either, damn it. What the hell made you do a thing like that?'

'Because I took a good look at myself. And you. I've been behaving like a stupid schoolgirl, mooning over her first crush. It was never going to come to anything. Your work's all you give a damn about. I didn't want to bring a child into the world with an absentee father who's always dashing off somewhere at a moment's notice.'

'I doubt if you'd have made an ideal mother either, since your first thought was to get rid of it!'

'Fine. Then I did the right thing, didn't I? Let's just forget it, shall we? We were neither of us being ourselves. It was useless from the beginning. We never had a hope in hell.'

In a world which had become steadily more deadly and uncertain, where the so-called balance of terror no longer decisively favoured the USA, a world which had teetered uncertainly on the brink of nuclear war for longer than the general public realized, the life of one unborn child could be of no consequence whatever. It had never existed. Nor was it in any way exceptional. Millions of women had had abortions since the Act making it legal. And the chances were that the numbers were marginally, if at all, smaller before the Act. Nowadays, they were officially recorded. That was the only difference. Finally, it had not been his decision anyway.

Logically, the tribunal's accusations were nonsense.

They were even more ridiculous when they went on to hold him responsible for her. She had changed, certainly—or appeared to have changed. Since then, she had used men, formed no lasting attachments, briefly satisfied herself, and then moved on. Well, why not? Her body was her own, to do with as she liked, as the Women's Lib movement might have maintained, in the distant days when their case still needed arguing.

True, there was a sharp contrast between her way of life since, and the girl she had seemed to be when they were together. The girl who lovingly and carefully decorated the flat with its extra rooms, implicitly ready to receive a family. But he was not responsible for that, either. People did not really change. She was older now, and that was all. She was the woman whom that girl would have become anyway. All that demonstrated, was that the whole thing would have ended in disaster at some point. That point happened to arrive a few years earlier than it otherwise might have done. Regret for a relationship which was always doomed was permissible. Relief that it had ended before too much harm was done was sensible. The dotty tribunal's assumption of some kind of guilt, was not.

There was no basis in logic, or any kind of morality. That tribunal was an idiotic mutation, born of his youthful reading of Kafka, and could only flourish in a demented mind, crazed by drugs.

Conroy could find no flaw in his reasoning, even in the dismal small hours of the morning. Satisfied, he turned out the bedside light. The absurd ramblings of the tribunal would trouble him no more.

At 06:45, Conroy was the only one in the dining room. The newspapers arrived at 07:00. He glanced through them, but there was no mention of Ernest Harrington. At 07:30 exactly, Conroy joined Goss in Reception.

They stepped into one of the lifts. Goss palmed a plastic code card and slid it into a slot, which was underneath the metal casing enclosing the buttons. He pressed the one marked 2 and removed the code card.

The lift began to descend steadily.

'Do I get one of those?' Conroy asked.

'We're entering a Security Area,' Goss said. 'Authorized personnel only.'

'One of these days, you'll answer a simple question,' Conroy said.

'I answer questions when I know the answers,' Goss said.

They stepped out into a whitewashed corridor. Fluorescent lights forbade all shadows. As soon as the automatic doors closed, Conroy heard the lift whine upwards.

Goss led the way. He turned right, then left, then

right again. It was like a maze. He stopped outside a
door marked CONTROL, opened it, and they went in.

Inside resembled a small version of a television
gallery. A desk carrying rows of buttons and switches
faced a bank of blank monitor screens.

Goss sat down behind the control panel and gestured
at the chair beside him.

'If you're going to play back my debriefing, I'm going
to sleep,' Conroy said. 'It bored me rigid first time
round.'

'You look tired,' Goss said sympathetically. 'Have a
doze, if you want to.'

He caressed a switch, punched up one of the moni-
tors, and sat back, lounging comfortably in his chair.

The room which came up on the screen was devoid of
windows or furnishings. It seemed to be about twelve
feet square. The walls and floor were thickly padded.

'You treat nut cases, do you?' Conroy said. 'People
who need padded cells?'

'For safety reasons,' Goss explained. 'We don't want
anyone getting hurt.'

'Or people who might want to hurt themselves
perhaps?'

'Occasionally,' Goss agreed. 'Depends who we're
dealing with. Not today. Department personnel are
never suicidal. Too carefully screened, in the first place.
You should know that.'

Somewhere below the camera, out of its range of
vision, there was the sound of a door opening. A figure
came into view. The door closed with a metallic clang.

'I think we'll do without the sound,' Goss remarked.
'I find it distracting.' He switched the sound off. There
was silence, except for a slight, regular whistle, as Goss
breathed in and out. He blew his nose vigorously, and
the whistle stopped.

Conroy's eyes were fixed on Karen. Her long black

hair was pinned up, with a scarf tied round it. She wore a leotard, and her feet were bare.

She backed up against the wall facing the unseen door. For a moment she seemed to be staring straight at Conroy, as her eyes flicked towards the camera. She had probably located it during previous visits to this room with its padded walls and floor. Then she remained still, gazing at the door. Waiting.

Her face seemed to be thinner. Her high cheekbones were prominent, as was her collarbone.

'What's she on?' Conroy asked. 'Six hundred calories a day?'

'People pay out fortunes to go to health farms and be starved,' Goss said.

'They get plenty of fluid,' Conroy said.

'She's not dehydrated,' Goss said curtly.

Conroy leaned forward, peering at her intently.

'You want a closeup?' Goss asked. Obligingly, he moved a lever. The zoom lens answered. Karen's face filled the screen. There seemed to be a slight tremor round her lips.

'What's the temperature in there?' Conroy enquired.

'Not terribly high,' Goss admitted. 'But she'll soon get warm.' He moved the lever back again, and the lens returned to its normal wide angle.

Conroy saw Karen deliberately relax, as if taking hold of herself. Then she began to do warmup exercises. She was wonderfully supple still, but her lips parted, and she was breathing hard sooner than he would have expected.

'She looks in pretty poor shape to me,' he said.

'There are thresholds which are disagreeable to cross,' Goss said. 'The vast majority of mankind never come anywhere near them. Our people must be able to. It's essential.'

'When did you last go hungry?' Conroy asked sarcastically.

'There are other kinds of threshold more difficult to handle,' Goss said cryptically.

Karen stopped doing her warmup. The door must have opened and closed, out of sight. George came into vision, wearing his inevitable track suit. His round, genial face broke into a broad smile, and he said something to Karen. She did not reply, but tensed herself, staring at him fixedly.

Then it began.

George moved in and, with startling speed for such a big man, aimed to put an arm-lock on her. Karen slithered away from his grasp with the speed and grace of a fish, and unleashed a kick at his momentarily exposed chin. Had her heel connected, George would have been in trouble. But he swayed sideways, clamped his hands on her leg, twisted it violently, and threw her. She crashed into the angle of the wall, rolled immediately sideways, but too late. George had flung his full weight upon her, and his knee was in her back, his forearm under her chin in the lock which would break her neck, if he so chose.

'She's slowed down a lot in the last few days,' Goss mused.

George released her and stood up, with a laughing remark. Karen's breasts rose and fell under her leotard. Her mouth was open as she gasped for breath. But some of that distress must have been feigned. Unexpectedly, she launched herself at him with the speed of a cheetah. George was taken by surprise. She got a scissors lock on him, but could not hold it.

'George is getting slack, too,' Goss complained. 'Too bloody complacent by half. She'd have had him then, if she'd been in peak condition.'

It went on. And on. And on. George was not taken by surprise again. There was never a moment when his iron, yet flexible, body was not in command. Eventual-

THE BRINK

ly, as her exhaustion grew, he began to play with her, his cheery grin teasing her.

'Now you see why her unarmed combat needs brushing up,' Goss said. 'If it ever happens for real, you still have to be able to inflict damage, no matter how tired you are.'

'If she weren't half starved, she'd damage him all right,' Conroy said.

'It could happen when you're on the run,' Goss said. 'When you've forgotten what three square meals a day are like.'

Whatever his feeling about Karen, as the minutes dragged slowly by, Conroy found it a pathetic sight. Normally, Karen could see off any ordinary man without taking a deep breath. Conroy would not have bet too heavily on his own chances, if she had the slightest advantage of surprise. If he were in charge, instead of Goss, George would be dispatched elsewhere, to deal with recruits. George had been in 'refresher training' too long. He was immensely skilful, but it was all theory. That vital edge, needed in the field, had gone. Karen knew this too, that was apparent. She could see the openings, but weakened as she was, she could not exploit them.

George was doing as he pleased now, twisting her limbs and throwing her about like a woman-sized doll. The thick padding on floor and walls protected her from 'getting hurt' in the way which Goss had presumably been referring to, the kind which caused bleeding or extensive bruising, but there was another kind which did not show, and Conroy knew about that kind. He knew how her tormented muscles were screaming in agony every time she was twisted and thrown. He could see it in her face. Goss must have been able to see it too, but he was merely gazing at the monitor screen with bland interest. That bastard was probably enjoying it as much as George was.

80

And George *was*, there was no doubt about that. George was finding the whole thing highly exciting. When he turned, and his track suit was pulled tight, the bulge was clearly visible. George's iron body had developed an iron-hard erection, and he seemed to be panting slightly, although not from his exertions.

George could afford to be careless now, and he developed a taste for a bear hug, pressing his urgent projection into her small buttocks, while his hands clamped her breasts and crotch, reluctantly throwing her eventually, and then moving in again.

Karen's humiliated, helpless fury was obvious. Her lips moved as she spat what looked like four-letter abuse at him. George laughed and said something back. Karen kicked at his genitals.

'Perhaps we should have had the sound up after all,' Goss remarked.

George had seized Karen's ankle before her instep could reach its target. Gently, almost in slow motion, he turned her leg until she lost her balance. He fell on her, his paws clamping her thighs to his shoulders, his face a few inches from the smudge of black pubic hair peeping from under her leotard, his eyes fixed and intent.

'For Christ's sake,' Conroy snapped violently. 'This is obscene.'

Goss's shaggy eyebrows rose.

'Really? Do you find it so?' He shook his head. 'Degrading, yes. Definitely degrading. But then degradation is one of the objects of the exercise, as your own experiences will have shown you. The form it takes varies, that's all.' He returned his attention to the screen. 'George won't rape her. The state he's in, there's nothing he'd like more, but he daren't. The poor sod's suffering now, nearly as much as she is.' He waved one hand. 'Coffee in the machine behind you, if you feel like one.'

'No, thanks,' Conroy said bleakly. There was an unpleasant taste in his mouth, and he swallowed.

Goss moved the lever again, the focus changed, and Karen's body grew bigger on the screen.

'I'll bet she'd be a damn good screw though,' Goss said thoughtfully. 'Look at those legs.'

FOUR

The canteen in this section of the Home was small, only four bare, wooden tables.

'Those on a strict regime eat in their quarters,' Goss said.

Plates arrived on a dumbwaiter. The metal covers were supposed to keep the food hot, but after its lethargic journey from the kitchens above, it was little more than lukewarm.

Conroy toyed with his tepid chop, new potatoes and cabbage. Facing, as seemed likely, the 'strict regime', it would be sensible to eat as much as he could while he had the chance, but his stomach refused to cooperate.

Goss ate with apparent enjoyment, polishing his plate clean. He said nothing and seemed oblivious to the uneasy silence between them. Conroy watched him until Goss sat back with a sigh of pleasure.

'It might save a lot of time if you told me what kind of game we're supposed to be playing,' Conroy said.

'We're not,' Goss said. 'You may be. That's possible. But not me. One thing this definitely is not, and that's a game. I'm going to have some pudding. How about you?'

'I'm not hungry,' Conroy said.

At first sight, it was not clear what the 'Assessment Room' was intended to assess. It was quite large, with a few wooden chairs against the walls. Conroy sat on the one near the door, which Goss indicated.

In one corner was an enclosed booth, the top half of which was plate glass. Inside, there was just about enough space for a hard-backed chair. Angled to face the booth was an ordinary table, on which sat a microphone.

Behind the table were two chairs. Beside one of them was a trolley, which housed some sort of control unit. Goss padded about in a leisurely fashion, inspecting everything as if he had never seen any of it before.

Karen came in, escorted by George. She had changed into a lightweight cotton sweater and slacks. Few women's clothes were of man-made fibres derived from hydrocarbons any more. Cotton was abundantly available from the Third World countries. If she saw Conroy, she gave no indication that she had done so.

'Ah, Karen,' Goss said benignly. 'Good to see you again. How's the refresher course going?'

'That's what you're supposed to tell me, isn't it?' Karen asked. Her normal speaking voice was pleasant and musical. When she chose, it could be something else.

'Wouldn't be fair to comment yet,' Goss said. 'To be frank, if your life depended on it, up to now you'd be for the chop. Still, bags of time left to make up lost ground. Perhaps today's session'll tell us something. Here he is, bang on time.' Derek had walked in, with an armful of thick folders. 'Right then,' Goss said, smiling at Karen. 'Into the box with you, and let's see if you can win the jackpot.'

George opened the door politely. Karen sidled into the booth and sat down. George closed the door. A metal clamp secured it tightly.

Derek sat down behind the microphone and assembled his folders. Goss eased himself into the chair beside the trolley. Karen lifted the earphones which were hanging up inside the booth and put them on.

'Can you hear me?' Derek said into the microphone.

'I hear you,' Karen replied. Her voice was disembodied and spectral, coming as it did from a loudspeaker close to Conroy's right ear.

Goss chuckled to himself. There was no need for him to share his grisly joke. By accident or design, it was all a grim parody of a giveaway television show. Karen was going for the big prize. Or Goss was, in this instance, more likely.

'All right, Karen,' Derek said pleasantly. 'This is a further exercise in the course designed to refresh you in resisting interrogation. One of the problems we face, of course, is to simulate the techniques and pressures which would be applied were this genuinely a matter of life and death, but we have done our very best in that respect. What we shall ask you to do now is to cooperate in a dummy interrogation. To assist us in checking your performance, you will be interrogated concerning operations in which you were, in fact, recently involved. Is that quite clear?'

'Perfectly clear,' Karen's disembodied voice said.

'Right, we'll begin,' Derek said. 'Did you betray Richard Conroy?'

'I did not.'

'Did you later betray Ernest Harrington?'

'I did not.'

'We believe you did. We have ample proof to hand

which clearly indicates your guilt. However, the normal rules of justice do not apply in this case. The proof we have assembled would convince any court, but a trial might not be politically desirable. Your friends have disowned you. You are entirely in our hands. They will not lift a finger to save you from summary execution. You are required to prove your innocence. Your life depends upon it. I hope you believe that.'

'I believe it.'

'However, you cannot prove your innocence, because you are guilty. We know you are guilty. You have only one hope of saving your life. That is, to confess, here and now. To tell us who else was involved. To give us the names of all your contacts.'

'There's nothing to confess,' Karen said. 'I was involved with no one. I had no contacts. There are no names I can give you.'

Derek said, 'There's plenty of time for you to change your mind. Remember, unless you tell us the truth, you are dead. The only way you can save your life is to make a full admission. Let's go back to the beginning. Who told you that you were to be infiltrated into Garnett's department?'

'Mr Goss,' Karen said.

'With whom else did you discuss the operation?'

'Richard Conroy,' Karen said.

'Why? That was a breach of security, wasn't it? What were you trying to find out?'

'The exact nature of my task,' Karen said. 'Conroy briefed me, and I discussed it with him, that's all.'

'What was your task?'

'Garnett was under suspicion, but no connection could be proved. Conroy suggested that I form a relationship with Garnett.'

'What did you take that to mean?'

'Go to bed with him,' Karen said. 'That's what Conroy meant when he used the word relationship.'

'Did you do so?'

'No,' Karen said. 'Garnett was a homosexual. I'd have thought someone might have taken the trouble to find that out first.'

'Garnett's homosexuality was already known,' Derek said, glancing at the open file before him. 'So why do you suppose Conroy made such a suggestion?'

'You'd better ask him,' Karen said shortly.

'I'm asking you,' Derek said. 'Do you believe he intended to mislead you?'

'I don't know,' Karen said.

'Hoping perhaps that some clumsy action from you might make Garnett suspicious?'

'Conroy had already been working on the Garnett case for over a year, before I came into it,' Karen said.

'But was it not you who provided the final proof?'

'The proof which was used in court, yes,' Karen said.

'So Conroy could have been dragging his feet?'

'Your guess is as good as mine,' Karen said. 'I'm not making any accusations.'

Aren't you? Conroy thought. Well, you're doing a sweet job. And what was Derek up to? He seemed to be spreading his innuendoes widely for a man who, for the purposes of this 'exercise', was supposed to be convinced of Karen's guilt. He glanced quickly at Goss, but Goss was absorbed in the control unit on the trolley.

'Well, we'll leave that for the moment,' Derek said. 'When you decided that Garnett was a homosexual, what did you do?'

'Garnett was careful,' Karen said. 'He dared not risk having a steady mate, and he avoided boyfriends. They tend to be too promiscuous and unreliable. He was a very solitary man, but he didn't dislike women. Like many homosexuals, he enjoyed their friendship. I became his friend.'

'You became close to him. He trusted you.'

'He wasn't suspicious of me,' Karen said. 'I'd go no further than that. Garnett didn't trust anyone. But he relaxed. Just enough. He made a mistake.' She seemed to be in distress for some reason, shaking her head slightly, as if to clear it.

'Through his meeting with a Russian journalist, when he was kept under surveillance, seen to hand over certain documents, and arrested. How was that achieved?'

'Conroy gave me the documents. I concealed them in the desk of a newly arrived senior assistant. I pretended to be worried. Told Garnett I thought security were checking on us. That I'd seen the new man behaving strangely. That I was afraid the telephones were tapped, which they were, of course.'

'That seems a strange thing to do,' Derek remarked. 'It sounds to me as if you were trying to warn Garnett, not trap him.'

'Nothing of the kind,' Karen said sharply. 'And it worked. Garnett stayed late in the office one evening. When he left, he used a public telephone. He was arrested the same night.'

'With the evidence you'd arranged for him to find,' Derek said. 'Or to put it bluntly, planted.'

'Those were my orders,' Karen said.

'Do you always obey your orders?'

'I've no choice, any more than you have,' Karen said. She passed her hand across her forehead.

'Who ordered you to betray Richard Conroy?'

'No one,' Karen said tiredly.

'When you started work in Garnett's department, did you know of what he was suspected?'

'Mr Goss told me,' Karen said. 'I think he wanted me to realize how important it was.'

'What did he tell you?'

'That exact information was being passed about the

patrol routes of our nuclear missile submarines, and where they were to sit on the sea bed, waiting to fire.'

'Were you impressed?'

'I could hardly believe it,' Karen said. 'It meant that their hunter killer submarines could wipe out our nuclear deterrent any time they liked. In the worst scenario you can imagine, where Europe was threatened and the Americans were hesitating, we'd have had no alternative but to surrender. If he hadn't been discovered, Garnett would have pulled off the biggest espionage coup ever.'

'You sound as if you admire him,' Derek accused.

'If someone from the department could come up with the patrol routes of the Russian missile submarines, we'd think he was a genius,' Karen said. She cleared her throat. She was growing hoarse. 'I didn't like Garnett, but what he nearly pulled off was unparalleled.'

'Just as well he didn't,' Derek said. 'Do you know how it was discovered that the nuclear submarine patrol routes were being passed to the Russians?'

Karen said, 'During a Navy exercise, I believe our own submarines were shadowing some Russian hunter killer subs. Someone realized that the Russians, in turn, were keeping just out of range of the detection devices of our nuclear missile submarines. That they knew where they were.'

'I wonder why you believe that,' Derek said softly. He referred to another file. 'The version given in court was entirely different. That piece of information is restricted. You were certainly never informed.' He looked up toward the booth. 'Did Conroy tell you?'

Karen hesitated.

'It's a simple question,' Derek snapped. 'You don't need any time to invent an answer.'

'I suppose Conroy did in a way,' Karen said. Great,

Conroy thought. Goss had turned his head, and was gazing at him thoughtfully. 'The bait which Garnett was supposed to swallow . . . which he did swallow . . . consisted of what I took to be genuine Navy orders . . . orders to shadow Russian hunter killer subs which had been detected . . . detected near our nuclear subs . . . it seemed to follow . . . I assumed . . .' She broke off into a fit of coughing.

George had been sitting, watching the proceedings with mild interest. Now, he glanced at his elaborate wristwatch, stood up, tiptoed quietly toward the door, and paused beside Conroy.

'I'll leave you to it,' he whispered. 'You'll find your gear in number seven—your new quarters. We're due to have a preliminary workout in Exercise Room Number Two at 18:00, so I'll see you there with your track suit on, OK?'

Conroy nodded, and George crept out. The cause of Karen's distress had become apparent. Perspiration was pouring down her face as though she were under a shower. Goss fiddled with the controls again. The booth she was sitting in was a sweatbox.

'. . . but the one thing you haven't mentioned,' Derek was saying, 'is how Garnett obtained this information about the nuclear submarine patrol routes.'

'I don't know how,' Karen said huskily.

'Does Conroy know?'

'If so, he didn't tell me,' Karen said.

'Garnett must have had a contact high up in Defence or the Navy. Very few people had access to the patrol routes, even fewer to the sea bottom positions. Who might Garnett have talked to, to your knowledge?'

'To my knowledge, no one. My job was inside the office, and occasional social meetings with Garnett. Conroy was working outside.'

Goss evidently decided on a change of gear and took over. He shouted, he hectored, he threatened. He fitted the role of bullyboy like a glove and visibly enjoyed every second of it.

He succeeded in confusing Karen in a way Derek had not. Her replies became fainter, weaker, disjointed, as she practically fried in the glass-fronted booth. She began to wander, she rambled, she repeated herself.

Goss took instant advantage, showing all the mercy of a thug on the rampage. It was a distasteful perform- ance, but Conroy was obliged to recognize the man's skill. Behind the shouting and the bullying was an ice-cold brain, functioning like a machine. A chess player's mind, not taking random advantage, but plan- ning how to secure it long in advance. In its own unpleasant way, it was an exhibition of great forensic ability. The brute should have been a barrister. Except that no judge would have allowed him to carry on like that for two minutes.

The end came when Karen's eyes glazed and went blank. She fell forward and toppled on to the floor.

'God, I've been hoping she'd faint for the last half an hour,' Goss said conversationally. 'I'm worn out.'

Room seven was a cubicle containing a narrow bed against the wall, a wash basin, a hanging wardrobe, and a deal chest of drawers. No curtains were required. There were no windows. Anyone swinging the tradi- tional cat would have fractured its skull.

The door could be locked and bolted, but only from the outside. Conroy turned the taps on experimentally. Water gushed out freely. As yet, then, he was not on a 'strict regime'. He changed into his track suit and pulled a pair of plimsolls on. The floors of the corridors were bare concrete.

As in the more civilized section of the Home up above, everything was neatly signposted. He met George outside Exercise Room Two.

'Plimsolls off, if you please,' George said. He pointed to a sign on the door. It said, KINDLY REMOVE FOOTWEAR BEFORE ENTERING. As though they were about to visit a mosque. Conroy kicked his plimsolls off.

'Hygiene more than anything,' George explained genially, as they walked in. 'Don't want bits of grit all over the padding.' He closed the door, which was padded on the inside.

Exercise Room Two was either the same one which Conroy had seen earlier on the screen in the control room, or its twin. He recognized what Karen had briefly glanced at immediately. There was only one place where a camera could be concealed, and that was behind a ventilation grille, recessed high up on one wall.

George was in no hurry to begin.

'I've looked at your notes, Mr Conroy,' he said. 'I see that your fitness is assessed very highly for a man who's nearly forty. On the other hand, I believe you've had quite a bad time these last two or three months. I expect that's dragged you down a bit.'

'I didn't get too much of the protein and sound sleep you so warmly recommend,' Conroy said. 'And definitely no carrot juice.'

George laughed. 'Well, we'll just take it nice and easy this time,' he said. 'Work up a bit of a sweat, but not overdo it. That OK with you?'

'Great,' Conroy said. 'Suits me fine.' George, he thought, would not deceive a trusting boy scout.

Perhaps George had little faith in his powers of deception either. The feint for a head-lock was fast, the unexpected chop which would have numbed Conroy's right arm delivered with rapier speed.

Conroy swayed, dropped his shoulder, seized George's momentarily available wrist, spun round, and sent him thudding spreadeagled against the wall.

George began to straighten his powerful legs for his tiger-spring response. His face fell apart as Conroy's instep landed in his genitals. He began to double up. Conroy grasped his shoulders, rolled backwards and, using his knee as a pivot, threw George over his head. The centre of the pivot happened to be George's nose.

Conroy stood up. George was curled up, moaning, and bleeding profusely over the padding.

'What happens now?' Conroy enquired, addressing the grille set high up in one wall.

'You come up to the control room,' Goss's voice said. There was a click as he spoke to someone else. 'George needs some first-aid. I think he's got a broken nose and two rapidly swelling balls.'

Conroy put his plimsolls back on and followed the signs back to the control room. The monitor screens were blank. Goss was extracting two cups of coffee from the machine. He handed one to Conroy.

'Thank you,' Conroy said.

'I don't think much of that for a workout,' Goss complained. 'It was supposed to have gone on for an hour.'

'I didn't fancy an hour,' Conroy said. 'I'm not up to that yet. I'd have run out of steam.' He sipped his coffee. 'This is foul.'

'Tastes all right to me,' Goss said. He perched himself on the desk. 'George is only doing his job, you know.'

Conroy said, 'He's become a Mr Body Beautiful. Thinks about his own muscles too much. Otherwise, he wouldn't have got caught. He's far too overconfident. I'm surprised you didn't see that before.'

'All right, all right,' Goss growled. 'You've made your point. It's time he was moved out. But I think you were giving him one for Karen.' He glared at Conroy. 'Come on. That's what it was really all about, wasn't it?'

'You say he was doing his job,' Conroy said. 'Perhaps

he was. But I didn't much like the way he was enjoying it.'

'No one asked you to,' Goss said. 'Nothing's done which doesn't serve a purpose.'

'If you care to tell me what that purpose is,' Conroy said, 'perhaps I'll believe you. Perhaps.'

'Follow your nose, and you might find out,' Goss said. 'You told me Karen was the only one who could have passed the information which led to you being snatched. So why are you feeling sorry for her?'

'It's like seeing men in prison,' Conroy said. 'They may be murderers or rapists. They deserve to be there. But the stinking conditions they're kept in, I've felt sorry for them. That doesn't mean to say I think they should be let out. It's the same thing.'

Goss finished his coffee, and threw the plastic cup into a waste bin.

'Karen's been through it,' he said. 'The bits you've seen . . . nothing. No more than a taste. We haven't broken her. That lady's got guts, I'll give her that. But she's bending, by God. She's dreading the dawn of every new day. What she needs now is a bit of sympathy. Some loving kindness. Someone on her side. Take the pressure off. That's when people like her finally break. When the pressure's off, not on.' He gazed at Conroy seriously, and rubbed his face. 'I get pissed off with having to shave twice a day,' he said.

'I see. Someone to play the soft guy. Catch her when she's down. At her most vulnerable.' Conroy leaned forward and examined Goss's face. 'You should use an electric razor.'

'Tried it. Don't get a clean shave,' Goss said. 'Anyway, you might enjoy it. She'll be so grateful for a few kind words, you could be on to a good thing. I'll bet you didn't get anything like that in the Lubianka.'

Conroy shook his head. 'I don't think I'm qualified,' he said.

'You're the only one who is. You feel sorry for her. Christ knows why, but you do. You're halfway there. You're the obvious candidate. You've just elected yourself.'

'Why the hell go to all this trouble?' Conroy enquired peevishly. 'She's the one. She's got to be. Why are you so keen on getting an admission? It wouldn't be difficult to fake enough evidence for Special Branch, if you want her arrested and tried.'

'After the Garnett business, another trial would be deeply embarrassing,' Goss said. 'Make us look like a lot of dummies. Certainly, I could deal with her by administrative action, but that's not the point. I'm not convinced that it's just Karen. I think there's more to it.'

'What do you mean? Others in the department involved?'

'That's what I'm hoping to find out,' Goss said. 'By a happy chance, her quarters are next to yours. Number six. Her door will be left open from now on, in case you get the chance of any midnight pranks in the girls' dorm.'

'She won't buy it,' Conroy said. He wondered why he was putting up obstacles. 'I don't need telling that those quarters are under surveillance night and day. Nor will she. She'll smell a king-sized rat if I wander in and start being nice to her.'

Goss said, 'It's up to you to find a way round that. One step at a time. Christ, the wise remarks I come out with.' He looked at his watch. 'I need a drink. Can't invite you to join me, I'm afraid.'

'You're stopping over again? How long for?'

'I don't know,' Goss said. 'A few days. Hard to tell.'

'With the department to run? You should learn to delegate,' Conroy told him.

'I can look after things from here,' Goss said. 'One bit of this place that's still up to scratch is the communications section. What's more, you cheeky bastard, I do delegate. I'm very good at it. There's more than one way to do it, that's all. But there are some bucks I can't pass. If it matters enough, then I have to see it through. There's no one else. That's what the head of this department's paid for. If you were in my shoes, you'd damn soon appreciate that.'

'Being snatched was important to me,' Conroy said slowly. 'But it's not a big deal for the department. It doesn't justify your personal attention for days on end. Karen's finished. She can't do it again. Even if she was involved with other people, the link's broken. It'll take time to mend. There's no hurry. You're either talking in riddles, or bullshitting.'

'I don't know how you ever got into the department,' Goss said. 'Whoever ran your personality test was incompetent. You should have been rejected. Still, there it is. We're stuck with you. At least, for the time being. You'll miss your grub if you don't hurry up. The canteen closes early down here.'

'I think you enjoy playing peeping tom,' Conroy said.

'There may be some truth in that,' Goss admitted. He opened the door, and they walked along the corridor. 'Riddles or bullshit,' Goss mused. 'A bit of both perhaps. But I'll tell you this. If I knew the answer to the riddle, I wouldn't be wasting my time here, free peepshows or not.'

'Tell me the riddle,' Conroy said. 'Perhaps I know.'

'You don't,' Goss assured him. 'Anyway, perhaps it's more like a skeleton crossword than a riddle. I don't even know where one down starts, let alone what it is. Given a very large chunk of luck which we need rather badly just now, you might accidentally fill in a couple of blank spaces. That'd help. Anything'd help.'

Goss disappeared into the lift.

* * *

96

Conroy took his plate from the dumbwaiter, sat down, and removed the cover. It was a casserole, which had probably been excellent when piping hot. He ate it anyway. A security man appeared with a key in his hand, and looked at his watch significantly. Conroy nodded, returned his plate to the dumbwaiter, and left. The security man locked the canteen door behind him.

The door to room six was slightly ajar. Conroy opened it and looked in. Karen was lying on the narrow bed. She opened her eyes and looked at him.

'What do you want?' she asked. The tone was neutral.

'I wondered how you were feeling.'

'I wonder why,' Karen said.

Conroy stepped inside, and tried the cold water tap. Clear water flowed freely.

'It came on a few minutes ago,' Karen said. 'And a real meal arrived too. Tomorrow I can use the canteen. Wonderful. I gather you've been playing with George.'

'A brief session,' Conroy said. He was still wearing his track suit. He leaned his behind against the chest of drawers, identical to the one next door. There was nowhere to sit, and Karen did not offer to make room for him on the bed. 'He retired hurt. Groping women isn't something that'll interest him much for a few days.'

'How many performances have you seen?'

'Only this morning's,' Conroy said. 'That was enough.'

'So you avenged my honour at the first possible opportunity.' Her voice was not her pleasant, musical one.

'The chance came to hand,' Conroy said. 'Or foot in crotch, to be more exact.'

Karen laughed. 'I'm glad to hear it,' she said. 'Now you can fuck off.'

'You're supposed to be grateful,' Conroy told her. 'Then we have a heart to heart. Tomorrow, I win you over by giving you some of my pudding. You're then in the right mood to cry on my shoulder, metaphorically at least, and whisper sweet confessions in my ear. I'm your local, friendly stool pigeon.'

'I don't think you've got a very bright future in front of you,' Karen said.

'I told Goss you might find it a bit sudden. Fresh water on tap, a square meal, your door unlocked, and me behaving as if I liked you.'

'I'm sure he had some suggestions,' Karen said.

'Yes. He told me to get round it somehow.'

'Is this your idea of getting round it?'

'I couldn't think of anything subtle,' Conroy said.

'He'll adore this when he plays it back.'

'I sincerely hope that he has an apoplectic fit, and perishes on the spot,' Conroy said. Karen neither agreed nor disagreed. 'Where's the camera?' Conroy asked. 'I haven't had time to take a good look round my cubbyhole yet.'

'I don't think there is one,' Karen said. 'If there is, I haven't been able to find it. Probably only microphones embedded in the walls.'

'I don't mind what I've got to say being taped. How about you?'

Karen pulled herself up into a sitting position and leaned her back against the wall, cross-legged.

'I don't know,' she said. 'It depends. Sit down if you want to. You don't look very comfortable.'

'Thanks.' Conroy moved about two paces, and sat on the end of the bed. 'Goss got it wrong for once. He confused a fleeting moment of pity with sympathy as sticky as treacle. Through you, I've been through what we all know is on the cards, and we try not to think about. I'll tell you something as a newly qualified expert. All the preparation we get in counter-interrogation techniques bears about as much resemblance to the real thing, as a soldier's battle training does to the time when he goes into action, and the enemy are trying to kill him with real bullets and real high-explosives. When they're really trying, it's different, believe me.'

'But you survived it all with flying colours,' Karen said mockingly. 'You took it until you could be exchanged, and left them none the wiser. What a shame no one ever gets any medals in this outfit. You deserve the VC. I hope you were suitably modest during your hero's welcome.'

'So far, the welcome home's left something to be desired,' Conroy said.

'I don't think I can be bothered with this performance after all,' Karen said. 'Go away. I'm getting bored.'

'Listen,' Conroy said steadily. 'It's very simple. They knew who I was. They knew where to lift me. They knew who my contact was. Whoever passed them the information had to know all of that. There weren't many, to put it mildly. To begin with, I thought it was Hans. Now I know it couldn't have been.'

'I never did think it was Hans,' Karen said.

'I spent several weeks hating his guts,' Conroy said. 'OK. Apologies to Hans. That leaves you. There's no one else.'

'I happen to be in the best possible position to know that it wasn't me,' Karen said.

'I'm told there's a form of mathematics in which two plus two don't necessarily add up to four,' Conroy said. 'I've never grasped that conception. To my observation, they always do. Without exception.'

'I'd have expected better from you,' Karen said. 'This isn't a case of simple addition. It's the three-card trick. Find the lady. And as always the game's crooked.'

'Not even three cards,' Conroy said. 'Only two. We've discarded Hans.'

'Right. And since I know it wasn't the lady,' Karen said, 'that leaves you.'

'I arranged a holiday for myself in the Lubianka?' Conroy stared at her coldly. 'As a resort hotel, it's not to be recommended. Would you like a detailed account of the kind of activities and fun they lay on for inmates like me?'

'For all I know, you could have spent your time drinking vodka with the comrades,' Karen said. 'With girls laid on to keep you warm at nights. You've lost a bit of weight since I last saw you, but you don't look like a man who's been through any terrible ordeal.'

'How long have you been here? You're supposed to have been put through the wringer, but right now, it doesn't show. I could say you look like a sexy woman who's taken off a few pounds to wear the latest fashions. What does that prove?'

'Everyone knows where I've been,' Karen said flatly. 'The same can't be said of you. Your version isn't corroborated. You disappeared. I know that wasn't through me. It certainly wasn't Hans. There's only one remaining possibility. You set up Hans. The snatch was a put-up job. You crossed over for fresh orders, or to spend a few weeks telling them everything you knew about the department, all the detail you've acquired over the years which can only be handed on face to face. Probably both. You believed you were above suspicion. That Goss would swallow it, and finger me. All you had to do was sit in Moscow and wait for your exchange to be arranged. And it's all worked out, hasn't it? As a last twist, you're on hand to make sure Karen Dewar's dealt with. Once that's done, you're safe. You've pulled it off.'

'Now I know why you didn't mind this conversation

being taped,' Conroy said sourly. 'It's a good try, sweetheart. Better than you realize.'

'I don't know why Goss has waited,' Karen said. 'He's not going to risk any trial, he's made that perfectly clear. I suppose he's like a cat. He likes to spin out the game with his prey. Before I was ordered into this place, I thought I knew what fear was. I didn't. I could face dying, I think, if I knew that was it, the decision taken, condemned. But Goss keeps hope alive. Little tantalizing glimpses of possible freedom. Then that escape route's blocked off. That glimmer of hope dies, and you die a little with it. And just when I've thought: "Face it. Come to terms with it. Goss is a pig. He uses women, but they're always lesser beings in his eyes. Given that the only evidence he's got is circumstantial, he'll believe Richard Conroy, because Conroy's a man. For no other reason." Just when I've really got that worked out, accepted that hope itself can be used as a form of torture . . .' Karen waved her hand. '. . . the door's left open, the water's running, and I realize how little it takes to make me go on fighting back, even though I know it won't be any use, not in the end.'

'You may be underrating your chances,' Conroy said. 'I get the feeling that Goss is a step ahead of you. And two steps ahead of me.'

If Goss already believed that Conroy's disappearance could have been faked, that he was dealing with two suspects, not one, it would almost make sense of his peculiar behaviour. Not entirely. There was a remaining niggle somewhere in Conroy's mind, which he could not quite identify. Conroy had something of a chess player's brain too, and he could perceive the various options which Goss's play was designed to open up, but not where some of them were supposed to lead. Probably they were mere bluffs on Goss's part. Distracting feints. It was always hard to know what Goss was really aiming at, but the most likely alternatives did not appear to imply a particularly agreeable or healthy future.

Karen's green eyes were fixed on him unwaveringly. There were other distractions for Conroy, very near to hand. The curve of her breasts. The shape of her mouth.

'There's only one thing we know for certain,' Conroy said. He wished that he did not find the woman so damned attractive. 'One of us is lying.'

'Right,' Karen said. 'And it's not me.'

'I don't know where the hell we go from here,' Conroy said.

'Where did you dig up that "we" from all of a sudden?' Karen said. She gave him an ironic smile, which revealed perfect white teeth, and no affection whatever. 'As I read it, it's you or me.'

'Not necessarily,' Conroy said. 'Goss has two versions on record, neither of which can be proved. One thing he can do is to discard both of us. He'd be certain to get it right that way.'

Conroy came awake as soon as the light was switched on. Derek was standing in the doorway.

'All right,' Conroy said. He sat up, and groped for his trousers. It was just before 06:00. Derek was shaved and fully dressed. He would be the more alert of the two during the dawn interrogation session, which was what Conroy supposed it was.

'Mr Goss wants to see you at once,' Derek said. There was a curious tinge of strain in his voice.

Derek used his plastic key card to summon the lift, and took Conroy up to Reception.

'He's in his private office,' Derek said, pointing. The door adjoined the communications section.

Conroy tapped on the door, and opened it. Goss was

speaking into a red scrambler telephone. He waved
Conroy in.

'. . . say I'm leaving at once,' Goss finished, and
hung up. He stuffed documents into a briefcase hurriedly. 'I liked the way you got round it with Karen last
night,' he said. 'Very neat.'

'I was sleeping the sleep of the innocent,' Conroy
said. 'So I hope that's not all you wanted to tell me.'

Goss snorted. 'Hardly,' he said. 'The shit has really
hit the fan in bucketfuls.' There were a number of
foreign newspapers on his desk. His finger stabbed at
them. 'Our own press checked with the Ministry of
Defence. There was no point in telling them not to
print it. There's no way we can keep this quiet. It'll be
in the British papers tomorrow.'

Conroy's German was marginally better than his
Italian. He took in the exclamatory headlines with
foreboding, and began to scan the text quickly.

Ernest Harrington, the missing British diplomat,
had been found wandering in Siena, dazed but
unharmed . . .

'Read them later,' Goss said curtly. 'Karen'll tell you
what *Pravda* had to say about it.' He laughed shortly.
'Although I don't suppose their reaction'll take you by
surprise all that much. It's predictable. You could have
written it yourself.'

Conroy wondered what, precisely, that was supposed
to mean.

'Why the devil was Harrington carrying documents
like that?' he asked.

'He wasn't,' Goss said. 'The whole thing's a fix. The
biggest piece of disinformation either side's ever
pulled. And damned neatly done. Harrington was
grabbed to provide a convenient British agent, which
he was. We can deny that until we're blue in the face.
We can deny that he was carrying any such material.
No one's going to believe it. Too many ordinary,

perfectly decent people are going to be frightened out of their wits to worry about such niceties. They'll follow the ones who know what to do, with ready-made organized plans. And there'll be plenty of those crawling out of the woodwork.'

Conroy thought about that for a while.

'Whether that matters much depends on whether the so-called documents are genuine,' he said at last.

'In themselves, no,' Goss said. 'They're not copies of any extant documents. What his alleged Liberation Army has released to the world press amounts to a summary of information, clearly souped up and popularized by another hand. To that extent we could deny their authenticity with a straight face. The trouble is that the first protest marches, which I've no doubt are assembling even now, will soon find that the damn things are exactly where the bloody newspapers say they are, and be forcibly kept out, probably at the cost of bloodshed, and quite likely a few lives. That'll serve their purpose just as well.'

'So ignoring the purple prose, what's there is accurate,' Conroy said, nodding at the pile of newspapers.

'Right on the button,' Goss said. 'Down to the targets in East Germany and the USSR at which each individual missile is aimed.'

In brief, the newspaper reports told their readers the exact sites where Cruise missiles were concealed, ready to fire, and which city or tank assembly area on the other side of the Iron Curtain they were intended to destroy. Restrictions on the range of Cruise had long since been removed, and the missiles were under shared NATO rather than solely American control.

'To the people of Western Europe! In the name of Peace and Freedom!' Conroy said, translating the sub-headline on the top newspaper.

'Yes. In the name of peace and freedom,' Gross said. His teeth bared in a bleak smile. 'I expect they enjoy their little jokes. Well, they've got something to smirk about now, the bastards.'

'Who could possibly have leaked anything like this?' Conroy wondered.

'Only a handful of top NATO military brass had access to so much detail,' Goss said. 'Even the senior politicians who agreed to the policy decision wouldn't know as much as any bugger across Europe, who can read, can now find lying on his breakfast table. I'd have said it was unthinkable. Out of the question. Which only proves how wrong you can be. Talk about treachery in high places. God almighty, it doesn't even end there. No one man could have been responsible for this. It would take a small army. Have the KGB penetrated the whole of our defence and intelligence establishments from top to bottom? The implications are enough to make your hair fall out overnight.' He looked at his watch. 'I must get going. My presence is required at Downing Street, for obvious reasons. Any ambitious sod with his eye on my job could well be in luck.' He took his trenchcoat from its hanger and shrugged it on.

'I'm no better informed than the man in the street about Cruise missiles,' Conroy began.

'Are you trying to make my job easy for me?' Goss enquired. '*Qui s'excuse, s'accuse,* I was always taught.'

Conroy ignored that.

'Laymen like me were told that Cruise missiles were simply stored at places like Greenham Common,' he said. 'That, being mobile missiles, there was no need to deploy them until the international situation deteriorated to the point where war appeared to be imminent.'

'The thinking changed,' Goss said. 'And not before time. The conception of a neat fourteen days' warning of approaching hostilities during which such decisions could be taken was always the dotty invention of some wild-eyed optimist, diligently bending facts to suit inadequate plans. Cruise is on site, and ready to fire. The locations were supposed to be secret. Sure, they can be moved. But if my guess is right, there won't be time. Not before the protesters start trying to storm the perimeters.'

There was only one reason why mobile missiles should be deployed, targeted, and ready to fire instantaneously.

'So it's true,' Conroy said. 'We've moved over to a new policy. Launch on Warning.'

'Don't be disingenuous,' Goss said. 'It was bound to happen. Missiles that can be taken out by a pre-emptive strike are no use to anyone.'

'I knew it was in the wind,' Conroy said. 'But unlike you, I'm not privy to top policy decisions.'

'Well, you are now, along with everyone else,' Goss said wearily. 'If the public can't work it out for themselves, any half-witted defence correspondent will be able to explain it to them. And there's nothing we can do about it. The one major defence reappraisal of recent years which it was hoped would never, under any circumstances, become public knowledge.'

'It's not exactly designed to make people sleep easy at nights,' Conroy said. 'The idea that we're geared to launch when the first enemy missiles appear on our radar screens. Suppose there's a mistake, and that "missile" coming from the East turns out to be something else? God knows, there have been enough spurious warnings in the past.'

Goss shook his head. 'Our warning system's much improved nowadays,' he said. 'It's most unlikely. And even if it did happen, there's a fail-safe device which is foolproof, and far ahead of anything the Russians have been working on. But it's impossible to reveal what that device is. First of all, the man in the street wouldn't be reassured because he wouldn't understand it. Second, it would tell the Russians about it. Thank God they haven't got hold of that, at least.'

'If it's a fail-safe device designed to prevent accidental war, why should they bother? The last thing they'd want to do is prevent that working.'

'The policy of Launch on Warning isn't credible without it,' Goss said. 'Also there is another factor built into the device, which we'd rather the Soviets didn't know about. Luckily, they haven't the capability in that area, and it's far too complex for any one man to hand over, or even a group of men. It would need an industrial complex of traitors, and if the Russians had that kind of leverage, they could take over the bloody country anyway, from the inside.' Goss turned up the collar of his trenchcoat and seemed to grow smaller in the process. 'The present problem's quite big enough, thank you very much. All over Europe, peaceful citizens will have discovered they're living a few miles from targeted Cruise missiles, ready to launch. Already, the Russians will have fed new aiming points into their SS20 missiles in retaliation. Those good citizens, living in peaceful country towns, will be on the receiving end of the first nuclear exchange. What do you think the probable reaction will be?'

'I don't suppose they'll like it very much,' Conroy said drily.

'Thank you for that brilliant analysis,' Goss said impatiently. 'You're supposed to know a bit about Europe. The likely effect on the anti-nuclear lobby was more what I had in mind.'

'They'll gain a lot of recruits,' Conroy said, stating the obvious. 'It won't be a lobby any more, it'll be a mass of popular movement. There'll be trouble in every country where Cruise missiles are deployed. But I'd say it'll be most serious in West Germany. That's where the violence will be orchestrated, and the ex-

tremists on both sides will be only too ready to join in
The election could turn into something more like a civi
war. They'll be lucky to come out of it with a govern
ment which is able to govern. NATO could fall apart.

'We do live under the American nuclear umbrella, o
course,' Goss observed. He gazed at Conroy enquir
ingly.

'If that ever was a reality, it ceased to be one the da
the Russians developed ICBM's,' Conroy said. 'The
might swap New York for Moscow, Los Angeles fo
Leningrad in an all-out war between the superpowers
but not to defend Europe. To them, Europe's a usefu
advanced launching pad and a potential battleground
nice long way away from home for a conventional o
limited nuclear war. But come the crunch, the
wouldn't press any buttons for us.'

'You're a pessimist,' Goss said. His own face was no
that of one readily associated with optimism.

Conroy said, 'The American Dream has gone sou
on them. They went on believing in the myth o
eternally increasing affluence even longer than we did
Now the chickens are roosting. The three-car family'
become the one-car family and before very long, th
no-car family. Great industries are sliding into collapse
They're no different to us. It can't be their fault. It mus
be someone else's. Like us, they look for someone t
blame. We got rid of our empire when we could n
longer afford to defend it. To a nation like the USA
trying to adjust to declining living standards, Europe'
beginning to look more and more like an outpost whicl
served its purpose in better days. In the last resort, the
won't opt for oblivion for our sakes.'

'Very interesting,' Goss said. 'That sounds ver
much like the more sophisticated party line to me
Perhaps they brainwashed you in the Lubianka. O
perhaps they didn't need to. Bring those newspaper
with you.'

He picked up his briefcase, went into the corridor, waited for Conroy to join him, and locked his office door. They walked into Reception. Conroy supposed that he should have kept his mouth shut, although why Goss should bother to elicit opinions which could be used against him at a time like this was beyond him.

'I'll be in touch,' Goss said absent-mindedly. 'Don't know when.'

'Just a minute,' Conroy said. 'I can't get back to the dungeons without a piece of plastic.' There was no one else in sight.

'Oh.' Goss waved vaguely. 'You're being moved. Just hang about a bit. Someone'll see to it.'

He went through the first door. Conroy heard the respectful greeting from the armed guard on the outer door. Then both closed, and he was alone.

FIVE

Conroy was back in his old room, with its bath en suite. His suitcase was on the bed. This, he thought, as he transferred his clothes to the wardrobe again, was worse than a cultural coach tour for frequent packing and unpacking. A television set had mysteriously appeared in his absence and was parked in the convenient place for viewing in bed.

He was not unduly surprised when Karen walked in, her lips compressed.

'I expect you want this,' he said, holding out the copy of *Pravda*. She took it. 'Where are you?' he asked.

'The room opposite.'

'Bathroom? All mod cons?'

She nodded.

'Cosy isn't it,' Conroy said.

'Very.' She eyed him warily. 'All mod bugs too, I suppose.'

'Probably,' Conroy said. 'I've given up looking. Who cares?'

'As Goss's poodle,' Karen said, 'I don't suppose you do.' She folded the copy of *Pravda* and tucked it under her arm.

Conroy sighed.

'Evidently we're supposed to converse with each other,' he said. 'Since the only subject we have in common is who did what to whom, I assume that's the intended topic. Otherwise, I haven't the faintest idea what's going on.'

'The first part I believe,' Karen said. 'The last sentence, I don't.'

'Oh, go and do your homework,' Conroy said impatiently, 'and let me do mine.'

He ran a hot bath, undressed, and lay in it for a long time. Goss had shown him the newspapers and briefly discussed some of the implications. He had not been obliged to. Conroy could have been confined to his pocket cubicle in the cellars and told nothing.

Perhaps he intended to question Conroy later about the affair, believing that he would betray himself. But that implied that Goss thought there was some connection between Conroy being snatched in Berlin and a momentous, dangerous international cock-up about Cruise missiles. Any such connection could only exist in Goss's convoluted mind, and that was a mystifying maze which it was pointless to try and enter. The man was the worst of all combinations, a brutal, unpredictable enigma, with the power of life and death. Conroy turned his mind to the news story which would have to break in the UK, at the latest, on the early evening television bulletin.

The whole thing, of course, had been deliberately engineered by the Russians, but there were a number of facets which Conroy found puzzling and, in the end, baffling.

They had scored an enormous propaganda victory and no doubt precipitated all kinds of trouble of the variety which Goss had predicted—but why? Was that the only purpose? If so, to achieve it, they had played an important Intelligence card which Conroy would have thought there were compelling reasons to keep quiet about—the fact that they *knew* where the Cruise missiles were deployed, ready to fire.

For, of course, there was no way of telling how long ago they had acquired this crucial piece of information. Certainly many weeks—the kidnapping of Harrington was not done on the spur of the moment. More probably, months. Conceivably, ever since the NATO decision was taken. If so, why use the information now? And why use it in that particular way?

Try looking at it from their point of view, Conroy thought. It was a mistake to divide humanity into black and white, good and bad. Implacable opponents and likely enemies 'they' might be, but whatever collective evil might result from a nation's actions, that nation was composed of human beings who, individually, mostly believed that on the whole what they were doing was right, or at least expedient. And it was very easy to see the Russian point of view in this instance.

They would have learned from whatever their source was, and with an unpleasant shock, that the West had decided to change the rules of the nuclear game and move to a policy of Launch on Warning.

The Russian reaction would have been immediate. Whenever they received that information, however many weeks or months ago, once satisfied that it was accurate, they would themselves have moved at once to a Launch on Warning state.

In that case, the world had lurched much nearer to imminent oblivion. Launch on Warning required a foolproof fail-safe device, and Goss had been adamant —whatever the device might be—that the Russians did not possess the necessary technology. Mistakes could occur on Russian radar screens, too.

But it seemed to Conroy that the Russians were taking terrifying risks, in a way which was unlike them. Unless they took out the Cruise sites tomorrow, the mobile missiles would be transferred to different locations or, if necessary, kept on the move continuously, which would be inconvenient, but possible. And even if Cruise could be neutralized, that still left the nuclear missile submarines, now safe from detection once more. The Russians might calculate that, in the last resort, the Americans would refrain from launching their ICBM's unless the heartland of the USA itself was threatened; but even if that proved to be correct—which Conroy happened to believe was fairly likely—the Launch on Warning policy meant that Russia itself would receive appalling devastation from a doomed Europe in the few minutes before that continent turned into a lifeless radioactive wasteland.

It did not make sense. There could be no profit for the Soviet Union in such an exchange, and despite their addiction to the Marxist analysis, they had always shown a keen regard for profit and loss in international affairs.

Conroy had grown up in the days when the West had hallucinated as crazily as had Conroy himself during his heroin trip, about automatically increasing prosperity for all, about economic miracles, based on eternally expanding growth—a geometrical progression which was always fatuously impossible, but which had fuelled expectations, not only in the rich West, but throughout the world.

Even then, a few, dismissed scornfully as cranks, had argued that the industrialized West was only comparatively rich because it had successfully looted the remainder of the globe. Human nature being what it was, the people of the wealthy countries preferred to believe that affluence was acquired by merit, by superior intelligence, ability, and capacity for hard work, and that backward peoples were deprived because they lacked these admirable qualities. It was a modern version of the feudal system, where God allotted each man to his rightful station in life for evermore.

The successive 'oil crises' which began in the seventies should have exploded the myth. From then on, the standard of living in the West was inexorably on a declining curve, but governments either preferred not to say so, or clung, Micawber-like, to the hope that something would turn up.

Inflation conceded what was really happening. More and more paper bought fewer and fewer goods, but 'incomes' rose, as measured in paper money, which usefully postponed facing reality. No politician in Great Britain or anywhere else cared to state that the people of the West were destined to become poorer, no matter what.

Bouts of manic optimism punctuated those years of decline. One such was generated by microprocessors, the so-called 'miracle chip', which was to solve everything and be the salvation of everyone.

But the 'chip' was no more than a multi-functional switch. Highly complex and a miracle of technological achievement, perhaps, but still just a switching device. True, it could replace men on a production line by governing 'robot' devices, but those men had used muscle power fuelled by replaceable grain and protein. The 'chip' required significantly more energy to perform the same functions, and by and large that meant fossil fuels which were due to run out in the foreseeable future.

Microprocessors, alas, did not resolve the problems of the Western world after all. Nothing had turned up to replace oil. The scientists, as ever, were optimistic, and annually renewed their promises to come up with a solution but, like those guaranteed by politicians dependent on the ballot box, those promises were only redeemable next year or perhaps the year after. Next year and the year after duly came. The solutions did not. In the meantime, the practical men were finally obliged to acknowledge what the dotty prophets of doom had been saying for years. Oil, once burned, had gone for ever. The electric car was a mirage, and nuclear power might light cities and drive public transport, but it could not fuel motor cars. Within only a few years, it was now clear, oil would be too precious to burn. The last reserves would have to be painfully eked out to provide protein, drugs, fertilizers, and the many other life-saving commodities which could be derived from hydrocarbons—rather more useful, ultimately, than the ability to convey individuals from A to B. 'Then' really meant 'now', but as ever, the ghost of Micawber stalked the West.

Millions of years and countless living creatures had gone into the formation of those oil deposits. The industrial world had succeeded in using up nearly all of them in slightly less than a century. Future historians would regard the people of the twentieth century as insane—on the assumption that their insanity allowed for any future for historians to inhabit.

The West staggered from crisis to crisis, society became more divided, more bitter, more violent, the cracks were showing, the seams were creaking.

Perhaps is was no paradox that the Soviet Union became relatively stronger as the West became more fragmented, more insular, ever more inclined to study its own navel. Communism was better equipped to organize shortage than societies which still paid lip service to a free market economy, which required a vanishing abundance in order to work properly. Unlike the major industrial nations of the West, the Russian economy was not heavily dependent on the production of motor cars which required oil, a factor which had belatedly turned out to be a blessing in disguise for the Soviets, for they were short of oil too.

More miles per gallon did not constitute a long-term answer. When there was no gallon available, a car's mpg was still zero. Increasingly, such was the case. Sky-high prices, ration coupons, half-mile queues to buy petrol and closed service stations combined to keep an increasing proportion of cars immobile. Conroy, of course, had priority, a special card which entitled him to fill up with as much as he liked at any of the state filling stations. Or he would have priority, if ever he got out of this place.

He dried himself lethargically, dressed, and lifted the telephone.

'Switchboard,' a girl's voice said.

'I want to place a call to London,' Conroy said. His own flat would do as well as any. 'Seven four one . . .'

'Sorry,' the girl interrupted. 'No outside calls.' That answered that one.

'How about Miss Dewar?' Conroy enquired. 'Am I allowed to speak to her?'

'One moment, please.'

'Hullo,' Karen's voice said cautiously.

'I've been given a television set,' Conroy said. 'Unless you've got one too, how about joining me to watch the news?'

There was a pause, as if she was prodding the suggestion to see where the catch lay.

'All right,' she said eventually.

They sat watching the newscaster.

Karen was wearing a blouse and skirt, with a pair of sandals which did not match. Conroy guessed that, when ordered to the Home, she had only been given sufficient time to throw a few clothes into a bag at random.

The Prime Minister had faced a worried and angry House of Commons. Great Britain was a loyal member of NATO . . . NATO policy was framed in the light of an ever-changing situation . . . the policy of Launch on Warning was one of many options kept under continuous review . . . it would not be helpful, except to a potential enemy, to go any further than that at this stage . . . yes, Honourable Members could be assured that every precaution was taken against the possibility of an accidental outbreak of war . . .

There were filmed reports of ugly scuffles between marchers and police at some of the named Cruise launch sites in Essex, Norfolk, and Yorkshire, but the crowds, finding nothing, were dispersing.

Britain had had a few hours' grace, and no doubt the Cruise missiles were being shuffled around the country in a madly harassed game of hide and seek. From the continent, the pictures were more bloody.

Bombs had exploded outside government offices in Italy. At the Hague, riot police were struggling to contain a massive demonstration. But it was in Germany where the fuse was well and truly alight.

Spontaneous demonstrations, led by men who appeared to be remarkably well briefed, and swollen by the nervous, fearful people who lived nearby, had assembled at all the named sites. The West German riot police, with a lot of practice in the application of their ruthless tactics behind them, had temporarily contained most of the demonstrations, but at a place near Minden it had gone badly wrong.

There, anti-nuclear demonstrators had invaded a site and discovered menacing missiles spread out, ringed by groups of armed soldiers.

It was then that a neo-Nazi counter-demonstration

arrived, intent upon dealing with the 'traitors, communists, and Jews'.

Who fired the first shot was not clear. Official reports claimed that an officer was callously shot dead. The Left asserted that the riot police and the neo-Nazis had acted in concert. The neo-Nazis accused the Left. All declared that they had only acted in self-defence.

Only the casualty figures were reasonably precise. Eight riot police, four soldiers, and seventy-eight demonstrators were dead. Three hundred and twelve police, soldiers, and demonstrators were being treated in hospital.

Right and Left counted their martyrs and swore revenge. It was already known as the Minden Massacre.

Conroy switched the television set off.

'Let's go and eat,' he said.

In the dining room, they were shown to the table for two in the corner.

'I think we're being flung together, as they say,' Conroy remarked. 'What do you think Goss is hoping to achieve?'

'One of us is supposed to trap the other,' Karen said.

'That's what I think,' Conroy said. 'Though considering what he's got to contend with just now, I wouldn't have thought that was top priority any more, to put it mildly.'

'Goss has a tidy mind,' Karen said. 'When the roof falls in, before he patches it up, he clears up the pieces. The one who set up Harrington triggered off the whole mess. That makes him a pretty important piece.'

'I'd have said "her",' Conroy remarked. 'Apart from that, I expect you're right. Suppose we order a bottle of wine?' He saw very little point in coddling his kidneys any more.

'None for me,' Karen said.

'For me, in that case,' Conroy said. 'I need it, if you're going to tell me what was in *Pravda*.'

He sipped his wine and ate silently while Karen told him. Goss was right. It was entirely predictable. Shock, outrage, the villainy of the Capitalist Imperialist warmongers threatening the peace-loving peoples of the Soviet Union—all the things the Western press would have said, had the position been reversed. As Karen finished and bent over her meal, he noticed that she was not wearing a brassiere. Not that she needed one anyway. She had plenty of uplift of her own. When she was using her dowdy secretary or charity worker cover, the brassieres she wore then were designed to compress and conceal.

'Goss wants us to talk,' Conroy said. 'And I think we should, although not necessarily in the way he has in mind. But first, I suggest we do something else.'

'Oh?' Karen placed her knife and fork neatly on her plate and pushed it away. 'I think I shall have fresh fruit salad now. Do what?'

'Go to bed,' Conroy said. 'Together,' he added.

Karen stared at him. 'Is that another of Goss's ideas?'

'I do have a few of my own,' Conroy said. 'I thought you might have it in mind, too.'

Karen laughed.

'Vanity, vanity,' she said. 'Thy name is not woman, it's man.'

'There's nothing under that blouse except you,' Conroy said. 'I'm sure you're well aware of the effect.' He looked around at the other tables. 'Which one of this crowd were you trying to impress if not me?'

Karen glanced down at herself, as if surprised.

'I forgot,' she said.

'Oh, well, that explains it,' Conroy said. He gestured

119

to the waiter. 'We'll both have fresh fruit salad and coffee, please,' he said.

Karen's fingernails clawed into the skin of his back. Her body moved under his.

'This doesn't mean a thing,' she breathed.

'Not a thing,' Conroy agreed.

They were in his room. The bedside lamp was on. He raised himself a little and looked down at her long black hair spread across his pillow, at her wide eyes, her serious expression. She turned her head aside, and closed her eyes. Her stomach muscles contracted, her lips parted slightly. Conroy waited for her, allowed her to pass him, caught her up, and they finished together, in a frantic variation on the oldest melody in the world, which left them breathless, clasped limpet-like together.

They lay side by side, while pounding hearts slowed and breathing returned to normal. Conroy turned his head, and looked at her finely sculptured body, her velvet-smooth skin, the rise of her breasts.

'God, what a beautiful woman you are,' he said.

Karen smiled faintly.

'You're supposed to have got all that out of your system,' she said.

Conroy said, 'What I should have said is that you're an arrogant bitch, with a good deal to be arrogant about.'

'If I have to do something, I prefer to do it well,' Karen said. 'Even if I don't like doing it.'

'In that case, it was a very good performance,' Conroy said, annoyed with himself for feeling mildly annoyed.

'Thank you,' Karen said. 'It's still stalemate, isn't it?'

'I don't know,' Conroy said. 'That depends on whether you agree to a different game. Don't go to sleep now, for Christ's sake.'

'I can listen with my eyes closed,' Karen said.

'All right,' Conroy said. 'I was lifted in Berlin and given the works. I say someone betrayed me, and that someone could only be you. You *claim* that it was all a fix, and I set myself up.'

'I don't claim anything,' Karen said, her eyes still closed. 'I *know*. Because it certainly wasn't me.'

'Just listen, and stop talking for the benefit of the bloody microphones, wherever they are,' Conroy said irritably. 'Then there's Harrington, and all this mess about Cruise missiles. Now I didn't know it was going to be Harrington. You were supposed to be the courier, and I was in the Lubianka when the switch was made, so that one couldn't possibly be down to me.'

'Nor me,' Karen said dreamily. 'I'd been brought here.'

'You knew the travel arrangements,' Conroy said impatiently. 'Which hotel in Rome, which room number. That would have been quite sufficient to identify him.'

'You knew that, too,' Karen pointed out.

'Look at it from Goss's standpoint for a minute, if that doesn't make you ill,' Conroy said. 'Both Berlin and Rome, it has to be one of us, from where he sits. The way the department's organized, as few people as possible ever know the details of any operation, to minimize the risks. We're the only ones who qualify in both cases, and that's the point. We both deny it. Neither of us can prove it. Saying yah-boo every two minutes isn't going to achieve anything.' Karen opened her eyes then and stared at him coldly. Conroy said, 'There's only one alternative that I can see. Suppose we call a truce? An armistice, if you like?'

'And what is that supposed to achieve?' Karen enquired.

'Well, we're not getting any bloody place this way,' Conroy said tartly. 'Let's pretend that we're both right, and neither of us was involved.' Karen opened her mouth, about to say something. Conroy hurried on. 'Don't bother repeating yourself until I've finished, and not even then if you can possibly help it. I know where you stand. You're virgin, pure and innocent. Well, innocent, anyway. Pretend I believe that. Pretend you believe me.'

'I find that extremely difficult,' Karen said.

'Just try,' Conroy urged.

'And pointless,' Karen said.

'Not if it were true,' Conroy said. 'Because in that case, there must be some other explanation for them knowing about me and Harrington. God alone knows what it could be . . .'

'I doubt if He's available,' Karen said.

'No, but we are,' Conroy said. 'And with sweet nothing else to do. I modestly believe that I was probably the best man working in the field until my cover was blown. I know you were the best woman. Between us, we either ought to be able to come up with it, or . . . well, there's no "or" is there? If we don't, one or both of us becomes Goss's ritual sacrifice.'

Karen appeared to be interested. She sat up in the bed, and leaned her head back reflectively. This brought her glorious breasts into full view. Conroy tried not to look at them.

'OK,' he said. 'Berlin and Rome—is there any connection?'

'None that I'm aware of,' Karen said.

Conroy said. 'The big blockbuster, of course, is how the hell they got the information about the Cruise missile sites, but that's Goss's problem, not ours.'

'Goss is the only man in the department who would have known where they were deployed,' Karen said. 'Goss also knew about your meeting with Hans.' She seemed to be paying more attention to the game now, as though she were beginning to enjoy it. 'And about Harrington as well.'

'I've considered that,' Conroy said. 'Goss as traitor and Master Spy. On a personal level, I must say that I find the idea deeply appealing. But it's so unlikely . . .'

'It's possible,' Karen argued. 'The obvious answer is one of us. Any other explanation is bound to be so unlikely that no one would ever think of it. And Goss fits the bill.'

'Against all my better instincts, I wonder,' Conroy said dubiously. 'The department's done the other side a lot of damage since Goss took over. More than in Lionel's day, to be honest.'

'That's his cover,' Karen said. 'The best front there is.'

'Garnett had rendered this country pretty well defenceless,' Conroy said. 'How about him?'

'No one knows how he got hold of the nuclear submarine patrol routes and sea bottom positions,' Karen said. 'He could have got them through Goss.'

'Would even Goss know that?'

'He'd know how to go about it,' Karen said.

'Yes, but dammit, you know what Goss was like during that investigation,' Conroy said. 'He was the driving force behind the whole thing. He never let up. He was like a man possessed. He went after Garnett like a hound after a fox. And bloody near tore him to pieces at the end, too.'

'He also arranged for Garnett to be exchanged,' Karen pointed out. 'That must have taken some doing.'

'Yes, that's true,' Conroy said slowly. 'But Garnett was safe until Goss went after him in the first place. Why should Goss nail him and then exchange him? It doesn't make sense.'

'We're not going to piece together everything, sitting here in bed,' Karen said impatiently. 'Perhaps Garnett was needed in Moscow for some reason. Anyway, you're forgetting that it was the Navy which discovered by pure chance that the Russians knew where the nuclear subs were. Goss had to do something then. Perhaps Garnett was no use here after that. The big plan hadn't come off, but that wasn't through Goss. That was through some bright commander in the Admiralty, who put two and two together.'

'That's right!' Conroy said. He felt that old, familiar tingle of excitement which always coursed through him when some distant quarry began to come into focus. 'It could all be a gigantic double-bluff. I'm not saying it is, not yet, but it bloody well could be.' Absently, he leaned forward and straightened the counterpane. 'Goss could have arranged for me to be lifted in Berlin. Nothing easier. But in that case, why was I part of the exchange? Why bring me back again?'

'He must want to use you in some way,' Karen said. 'A particular role which only you could play.'

She watched Conroy covertly as he leaned back, his face serious, his eyelids half-closed in thought. She too felt that thrill which she knew so well, and which was always associated with danger. Conroy was a formidable man, and in playing his game, she was taking risks. It was certainly possible that Goss was engaged in some double-bluff, but while she was far from certain about that, she was dead certain about Conroy. If her far-fetched invention about Goss was true, she had no doubt whatever that Goss would be using Conroy, and that he was performing his designated role here and now.

Conroy was thinking that Karen could be right in one respect at least. In his mind, he was going over Goss's behaviour since the exchange had taken place: it appeared contradictory, almost random, but must be neither. For some reason which was inexplicable to Conroy, Goss was nudging him towards some course of action, which he was unable to perceive or define.

'It's a nice hypothesis,' Conroy said at last. 'Goss could well play the kind of mastermind that any espionage service would give its eye teeth for, much less the KGB. He could have done everything we've said. He could have set up Harrington. But where Cruise missiles were deployed is another matter. The British, yes, he could have known about those. But not on the continent. That's NATO headquarters stuff. Goss wouldn't have access to that. It would mean he's working with high-ranking allied military people. The kind of spy ring which is unimaginable.'

'That kind of sensitive material might not cross Goss's desk,' Karen agreed. 'And the days of photographing secret files in Whitehall are over. Information isn't stored in files any more. But even given all the security precautions under the sun, there must still be ways of retrieving it. Perhaps Goss had found out how to do it.' She yawned delicately. 'Oh . . . I'm getting tired.'

'That's a pity,' Conroy said. 'My mind's beginning to wander off the subject again.' He stroked her flanks gently.

'Your mind seems to wander fairly frequently,' Karen said. 'I shall close my eyes and think of England.'

Conroy snapped awake, and sat up when the light went on.

'When the cat's away, eh,' Goss said. His head craned forward from the turned-up collar of his trenchcoat like that of a lascivious tortoise. 'Still, I'm glad you've found an agreeable way to pass the time. I told you she'd be a good screw, didn't I?'

Goss leered at the exposed portion of Karen's naked body and walked out.

'I don't know whether to laugh or be sick,' Karen said. 'So he told you I'd be a good screw, did he?'

She got out of bed and gathered up her clothes.

SIX

Karen did not appear for breakfast. Nor did Goss. Conroy thought it quite possible that they were together in some other part of the Home, talking privately. There was a lot of playacting going on which he could not fathom. His own part rather resembled that of a man pushed on to a stage and told to improvise, while knowing nothing about the plot, what the other characters were doing, or even who they really were.

Last night's instinct that he was on the verge of glimpsing something had weakened in the light of a new day. The gut reaction was still there, but he could find nothing to support it, and several queries which diminished it. Probably, it had been little more than wishful thinking.

He had set out to persuade Karen to talk, to say *something* at least, to edge her away from her repeated flat denials, which got no one anywhere. To some extent he had succeeded, but at the cost of being carried along by participation in his own invented game of make-believe. That brief moment of seeming semi-perception had been sparked off, on closer examination, entirely by suggestions made by Karen Dewar. She could have had her own motives among which, quite likely, would be a desire to mislead. Conroy did not entirely abandon the possibility that the distant quarry he had almost glimpsed might be Goss himself, but it bothered him that it had been Karen who pointed him in that direction. Karen might have been the more skilful player in last night's game. Conroy had few illusions about Karen. Desirable when she chose, feminine when she chose, the epitome of womanly elegance when she chose, she was also an experienced and skilful field operator and brilliant at lulling even the most suspicious and careful men into a false sense of security —as Garnett had discovered to his cost.

Conroy paused over that thought for a moment. The very finest lies were always half truths. If Goss had been working in collusion with Garnett, then Karen could well be part of the ring too. Perhaps she had not deceived and ultimately trapped Garnett. Perhaps, knowing that he would be exchanged in due course, Garnett had walked into that trap of his own free will.

Conroy sighed. There were so many endless permutations when speculation ruled, that it would take a computer to analyze them, compare them, and reject those which did not match the few known facts. The human brain had the capability, but not the time, at its disposal. The brain could guess and make imaginative leaps, which the computer could not. But the computer, once programmed, could unerringly select from a million alternatives in micro-seconds, a process which it would take a team of men decades to accomplish. He paused, examining the reason why *that* comparison had come into his mind. Karen again. She had not mentioned the word 'computer', but her use of the word retrieve' implied it. He thought about that carefully, and for a long time. An inspired instinctive guess? Or, again, pointing him in the direction which might suit her? Which was it?

Conroy began to read the morning newspapers. Between the lines it was clear that West Germany was in serious trouble. That section of the Left which had always seen Ostpolitik leading to an accommodation, neutralism, and eventual withdrawal from NATO was receiving large-scale support from ordinary people with little interest in politics; like the citizens of Minden, who did not relish the discovery that they had become, in effect, personal targets for Russian missiles.

The patriotic constitutional Right had acquired its own strange allies in the form of the neo-Nazis, who had emerged into the open not only in greater numbers than the democratic optimists had ever thought possible, but well organized, with a lot of support, financial and otherwise, from certain quarters, and with all the aggression and violence shown by their predecessors.

The members of staff in the dining room ignored Conroy, ate their breakfasts, and went about their business. No one told him to present himself anywhere. None of them so much as wished him good morning. He had, apparently, been consigned to a kind of limbo.

He ordered more coffee. It was supposed to be a diuretic, but he was now urinating normally and had stopped passing blood. The doctor's pills must be doing the job. Although possibly nature would have seen to it anyway. Outside the sealed, double-glazed windows, nature seemed to be in a cheerful mood. It was a fine, sunny day, with only a few fair-weather, fluffy cumulus clouds dappling the blue sky.

Conroy drank his fresh coffee slowly, since he had no reason to do anything else. He was, he realized, feeling a lot better. The regular meals and rest he had received in the Home were restoring him, physically at least, after the debilitating effects of his sojourn in the Lubianka.

At first, he had supposed that his betrayal had no particular significance, that it was one of the risks a man took in his line of work, and he had seen it in much the same light as a professional footballer might view a broken leg. Now he was beginning to wonder if he had not been deliberately selected, picked out, if it had not been him, Richard Conroy, they wanted, and no one else.

The KGB must have pinned a lot on Garnett. The nuclear submarine patrol routes represented a great espionage coup, but they would not have sat back, pleased with themselves. Such was not their nature. They would have had other plans, possibly even more ambitious, if that were possible. Garnett's arrest would have negated those plans, whatever they might be. That would be a deadly serious matter for the Soviets. The inquest on what had gone wrong could well concern the ruling committee in the Kremlin itself.

Perhaps that was why Conroy had been lifted. They wanted to find out how Garnett had been discovered. They not only knew that Conroy worked for British Intelligence, and in what capacity, they also knew that he had been involved in the Garnett affair.

If such was the case, they had failed to get what they wanted. Conroy, despite everything, had stuck to his cover story. He had told them nothing.

And perhaps, Conroy thought, groping his way through a mental fog, they had agreed to release him, once they had negotiated Garnett's exchange, because they no longer needed him. Garnett would be able to tell them what had gone amiss in person.

All that seemed to make sense, but if it were so, it threw doubt on the idea of Goss being in the service of the KGB. Any traitor must have means of communication. Goss would have told them because Goss had organized it all anyway.

Conroy chewed that one over thoughtfully until his coffee was finished and tables were being pointedly laid for lunch all around him. He still fancied the concept of Goss as the joker in the pack and was reluctant to let it go. Well, he could keep it. He was not certain that he had been specially picked out. It was more likely that his betrayal was merely part of information which some double agent—Goss himself—had been feeding to the other side.

But of one thing Conroy was absolutely certain. Goss, whether loyal or a traitor, did nothing without a reason, some end in view. He would have had a reason for telling them about Conroy's appointment with Hans. That brought Conroy back to Karen's theory, and he did not trust that lady, not one fraction of a millimetre.

Conroy left the dining room and wandered aimlessly around the Home, inviting someone to stop him and order him to go somewhere else, but the staff ignored him as though he no longer existed. The door to Goss's private office was closed and locked, he noted.

Conroy ceased to be the invisible man when he opened the door in Reception and passed through into the lobby where the armed guard sat at a desk beside the outer door.

'This is a restricted area except for staff,' the armed guard said.

'I feel like going out for a walk,' Conroy said.

'Do you have a pass?'

'No,' Conroy admitted. 'But I'm not trying to leave. I'd simply like to take a stroll in the grounds.'

'Not without an authorized pass,' the armed guard said.

'OK. Where do I get one?'

'You don't get one,' the armed guard said. 'It's either issued or it's not.'

Conroy supposed that that defined his status pretty clearly. He went upstairs. Karen's room was empty. There was not so much as a Gideon bible to read, although perhaps there would have been something almost blasphemous in having a book like that in a place like this.

Conroy switched the television set on in desperation, found himself watching the Open University, and learned something about ergonomics, until the telephone rang.

'The rest cure's over,' Goss said. 'Downstairs.'

Karen was waiting with Goss in Reception. She wore a cashmere sweater and the same skirt and sandals.

'Neither of you two hungry this morning?' Conroy enquired ironically.

'Didn't you go down to breakfast?' Goss asked Karen, surprised. He patted her fondly. 'Can't have that. You're supposed to be getting your strength back.'

'She wasn't in her room either,' Conroy said. 'Just vanished. Isn't that strange?'

'I don't see why,' Karen said coldly. 'I've been having a medical.'

'I hope the doc gave you a cervical smear,' Goss said solicitously. 'Most important for ladies who lead an active sex life, I understand. Come on. I'll show you the grounds.'

'Have you got a pass?' Conroy enquired.

Goss grinned. 'Only arseholes like you need passes,' he said.

Outside, Jenkins was waiting, like some immobile statue. He came to life and followed at a distance as Goss led the way, tramping across the grass.

Jenkins remained well out of earshot, but not out of

pistol shot. Jenkins was a top marksman with all kinds of small-arms, and he was always armed, day and night.

In the days when the Home had been a manor house, the surrounding acres had been a park. There were clumps of trees dotted about, and the flower beds were still well kept, although the grass was longer than it had once been in grander days.

Goss came to an abrupt stop.

'All right,' he said to Conroy, 'you take over.' He waved his arm. 'Anywhere you like. The place you'd choose for quiet conversation.'

Conroy glanced at the pleasantly organized rural scene. He walked away from the nearby clump of beech trees, skirted an ornamental pond, and headed for a grassy rise. At the top, there were no trees for a hundred yards.

'This'll do,' Conroy said.

'Fair enough,' Goss said. 'Trees might be bugged, but not every blade of grass. Satisfied?'

'No,' Conroy said.

Goss took off his jacket, shook it, showed Conroy the lining, and hurled it on the ground.

'You are a suspicious sod,' he said. 'You want me to take my shirt off too, in case there's a mike concealed under my bloody armpit?'

Conroy shook his head and glanced over his shoulder.

'Jenkins, bugger off!' Goss bellowed. 'He thinks you're eavesdropping with a directional microphone.'

Jenkins retreated uncertainly, like an uneasy sheep-dog which had received an unfamiliar order.

'Now you've got him worried,' Goss chuckled. 'Look at him. He doesn't know what to do. He can't be both sides at once, and if you rushed me and bundled me downhill, you'd be out of his line of fire.'

'We'd never get past the perimeter,' Conroy said. 'I can see the patrol from here.'

'He doesn't give a fuck about you making a run for it,' Goss said. 'Stopping you killing me, that's his job in life. Not you specifically, of course. Anyone.'

'Now you've pointed out the possibility,' Conroy said, 'I'm tempted.'

'Well, try and control yourself,' Goss said. 'Confine your animal passions to the delectable Miss Dewar here.'

'What's the matter with you, Goss?' Conroy demanded, just about controlling a surge of fury. 'Are you one of those who can't do it, but likes looking at it and talking about it? Or are you trying to make me go for you so that Jenkins can demonstrate his marksmanship? Is that it?'

'I wouldn't risk that,' Goss said mildly. 'You're sharp. You'd break my neck before he could kill you. But I have to point out that your satisfaction would be short-lived, because he would shoot you a second later. So unless you're bent on suicide, calm down and listen.'

Conroy shoved his hands into his pockets.

'All right,' he said flatly. 'I'm listening.'

'I must say, with some admiration, that you two weren't in the least inhibited by the knowledge that everything you said was being recorded,' Goss said. 'I've listened to it all, including the heavy breathing. Goss as the Master Spy, eh? Goss as the villain of the piece behind it all. You've got a bloody nerve, I'll say that for you.'

'It got you here,' Conroy pointed out.

Goss gazed at him malevolently.

'I don't like people who imagine they can manipulate me, Conroy,' he said.

'I've been debriefed,' Conroy said. 'She's been through her so-called refresher training. Either return us to duty, or if you're going to take administrative action, let's find out if you can get away with it now, without a few awkward questions being asked.'

'Pure self-preservation,' Goss said. 'And to achieve that, you'd even try and finger me.'

'The sound engineer should have checked the tapes for quality before you listened to them,' Karen said dreamily. 'He might remember that sequence if one or both of us happened to disappear.'

Conroy said nothing. Such a thought had certainly been in his own mind, but as for Karen's, he preferred to take a rain check. All the time, he was conscious that he could be dealing with a double act.

'You'll have to do better than try and smear me,' Goss said affably. 'Won't wash, my girl. For one thing, no sound engineer checked it. I'm the only one who's heard that tape, which, incidentally, won't be processed in the normal way, since it contains nothing of any interest.'

'Surprise, surprise,' Conroy said.

'Bloody hell, I wasn't born yesterday,' Goss said. 'People'll do the most incredible things when their own lives are at stake.' He eyed them both in turn. 'Take you two. What a marvellous pair you make. Neither of you believe a word the other's saying. Both of you would cheerfully shop the other to get off the hook. You don't give a damn how you do it. You'll clutch at any straw. If you thought it would come off, you're quite prepared to join forces in the hope of using each other, even to the extent of trying to pin the blame on some innocent third party. Someone like me,' he said, aggrieved. 'Someone entirely above suspicion.'

'All the really good traitors *are* entirely above suspicion,' Conroy said. 'That's why they're successful. You'll be running the rule over every high-ranking NATO planner in sight, men without a single blemish on their characters. Or you would be, if you weren't wasting your time here.'

'I never waste a second,' Goss said. 'We're standing here like three idiots, and I'm shivering in my shirt-sleeves, because what's said now is off the record. I want you to be sure of that. There's no tape which may or may not be used or get lost. This conversation never took place. I'm not responsible for what you do from now on. I may back you, I may not. That depends on whether I'm satisfied. Or not.'

'Do you know that he's on about?' Conroy asked Karen. She shook her head.

'I'm going to grant your own wish,' Goss said magnanimously. 'You both claim you're innocent, whiter than the driven snow. Secretly, you both believe the other's as guilty as hell. All right, prove it. Richard Conroy, Karen Dewar, or Mr X. Give him or her to me, and you're off the hook. I might even consider a spot of promotion for whichever of you is the survivor. Or both of you, should you produce a Mr X. But daft accusations won't do. It's got to be proof. Cast-iron—in my terms, if not the law of the land's. Now, I couldn't be fairer than that, could I?'

'Thanks for nothing,' Conroy said tartly. 'What are we supposed to do in this dump? Beat the hell out of each other?'

'You can piss off,' Goss said. 'You're released. Go and ferret wherever you like. I don't give a shit which one of you gives themselves away, or if you come up with someone we've never thought of, provided I get an answer that'll stand up. You can talk to whoever you like. I'll open any door for you. But be clear on one thing. You clear everything with me as you go along. If you don't, the deal's off, and you're back in the Home.'

'And you call that a fair offer?' Conroy demanded.

'More than fair,' Goss said. 'Generous. Warmhearted, even. So much so, that I think I must be going soft in the head in my declining years.'

'Jesus,' Conroy breathed, exasperated. 'Look, Goss, on or off the record, I don't know if you're a KGB agent, but the things that have happened, there are some around, and at top level. You could be one of them. You fit. If we were released, that's the first lead I'd want to follow up.'

'Fine,' Goss said equably. 'You think I qualify, chase that by all means, and see where it takes you. You're entirely free to prove that I deserve to be shoved into the top security wing at Parkhurst until the day I die. If you can,' he added.

'Exactly,' Conroy snapped. 'If we can. While you're breathing down our necks all the time. That could be a very good way of checking if your cover'll stand up to close investigation.'

'That's what I like,' Goss said cheerfully. 'That's what I need. A man who believes nobody and suspects everybody.'

'And if we should happen to be on the right lines,' Conroy said, 'we could meet with a fatal accident of the kind you're good at arranging, after which the flaw in your cover would be repaired.'

'That's a chance you'll have to take,' Goss sighed. He looked at his watch, picked up his jacket, and put it on. 'It is entirely up to you,' he said in a friendly fashion. 'If you prefer, you can stay here at the Home. Back in the cellars though. And for deep interrogation this time. See how we compare with the Lubianka. The choice is completely yours. I wouldn't wish to influence you in any way.'

They were in Goss's private office. Goss pitched some keys on to his desk.

'Your car's been brought here,' he said. 'It's been serviced. You'll find it in the garage. I think that's it . . .'

'Personal weapons,' Conroy reminded him.

'Not necessary,' Goss said. 'Since you'll have no call to use them.'

'I see,' Conroy said. 'Passports?'

'Your passports will remain lodged,' Goss said.

'We may need to go abroad,' Conroy said.

'If so, you clear it with me, and I arrange it,' Goss said. 'And don't waste your time trying to obtain substitutes. That would be regarded as a breach of good faith.'

'That would never do,' Conroy said.

'I am a much misunderstood man,' Goss said sadly. 'When I have such trust in you, as my actions prove, I really can't understand why.' He scribbled on a note-pad. 'Since you regard me as a prime suspect, I expect you'll want to see my personal file. See if you can track down any left-wing affiliations . . .' He handed Conroy the slip of paper. 'You present this at the Cabinet Office at 10 Downing Street. My personal documents aren't kept in the department, for obvious reasons. Wouldn't do for my inferiors to know all about my Achilles' heels.' He chuckled blandly. 'Right. I promised to open any doors. Name them.'

Karen said innocently, 'It's going to waste an awful lot of time if we have to keep continually referring back to you. Why don't we just go and talk to people? Make our own contacts, the way we usually do.'

Goss grinned, which made him look even more like Khrushchev genially promising to bury the West.

'Because you're on a kind of parole,' he said. 'You don't have quite the same standing as usual. Everyone will know that. Result—no one will talk to you without my personal approval. You're on a very short lead, my darling.'

'A casino that rigged the play like this wouldn't attract a single customer,' Conroy said.

'House rules or forget it,' Goss said. 'You don't have to play.'

Conroy looked at his car keys, lying on the desk. Freedom would be illusory, they would be under surveillance all the time, but it was tempting, as compared with the cellars of the Home. Merely to drive along an open road would be something, no matter where it might lead. He saw no alternative. Without Goss's say-so, they could go nowhere.

'I want to know how to rob a computer,' he said.

'What made you think of that?' Goss enquired sharply. His gaze shifted to Karen. 'Her small-hour inventions?'

'You didn't stipulate explanations when you laid down the rules,' Conroy said. 'The dice are well and truly loaded in your favour as it is. What more do you want?'

Goss thought about it, drumming his fingers on the desk top, staring at Conroy hard.

'All right,' he said eventually. 'The door's open.'

Conroy drove towards London, allowing his car to drift along at the legal speed limit. Karen glanced behind again, as she had done several times before.

'No one's tailing us,' Conroy said. He indicated a police car ahead, parked on the hard shoulder. 'No need to yet. They'll be logging the car number and reporting in as we go along.'

'We could dump your car and hire one,' Karen said.

'The first appointment we don't keep,' Conroy said, 'and every copper in the country'll be briefed to arrest us. That's a quick route back to the Home. Anyway, what do you have in mind?'

'I don't know,' Karen said. 'Except that I don't like the feeling of being a puppet on a piece of string.'

'Get used to it,' Conroy advised. 'Enjoy the drive.'

'This is senseless,' Karen complained. 'What on earth do you think you're going to do?'

'I know what I'm going to do,' Conroy said. 'I'm going to see if my flat's fit to sleep in. My cleaner's got a key, but she hasn't been paid for three months. The old biddy's probably given up. Thinks I've dropped dead.'

The note on the coffee table was carefully written, a legacy of the days when schools believed that handwriting should be legible.

"Dear Mr Conroy,

Sorry to hear you have been taken ill, even if not serious. Your friend told me, and paid me up to date, so we are all square. Hope you will soon be back from the nursing home, and fully recovered. Ring me at my daughter-in-law's when you want me to come again, as usual.

Yrs., faithfully,
E. Bond (Mrs)

P.S. Have emptied the fridge. It was all going off."

'Goss thinks of everything,' Conroy remarked.

He took off his jacket, left the living room, walked along the corridor, opened the door of the cupboard next to the bathroom, rolled up his sleeves, set up a pair of steps, climbed up, and felt around inside the cold water tank.

'But everything,' Conroy said, resigned. There should have been a deceptively small, but highly efficient, automatic wrapped in waterproof material, resting on the bottom of the tank, in case of emergencies.

He climbed down, put the steps away, went into the bathroom, and dried his arms. Karen did not need telling what he had been groping for.

'Like all nest eggs,' she said drily. 'Never there when the rainy day arrives.'

'Have you got one?'

Karen shook her head.

'They found mine when I was invited to the Home,' she said. 'That was regarded as highly suspicious.

Possession of an unauthorized weapon, and concealed to boot.' She watched him as he hung the towel back on the rail. 'Just who are you expecting to shoot?'

'No one,' Conroy said. 'With any luck. I'd just feel more comfortable, that's all. Still, that's not insoluble. The gentry who can supply the odd shooter on the side aren't the kind who'd have been briefed by Goss. Let's have a drink.' They walked back to the dusty living room. 'Unless E. Bond (Mrs) has knocked off all the gin,' Conroy said. He held up a bottle. 'No, bless her, she's left some.'

Mrs Bond had thriftily turned the refrigerator off when she emptied it, so there was no ice. Conroy poured two gin and tonics without, and handed one to Karen.

'I shall go home and change after this,' Karen said. 'I'm fed up with wearing the same things.'

'OK. I'll drive you,' Conroy said.

'Goss didn't stipulate that we had to stay together,' Karen said.

'I expect he assumes we will, though,' Conroy said. 'For some very good reasons.'

'Respect, affection, consideration, tenderness. Things like that?' Karen supposed ironically.

'That's right,' Conroy said. 'Plus all those other sweet emotions like suspicion, dislike, disbelief, which give two people an urgent desire to keep an eye on each other.'

'What did I say that made you come up with that stuff about computers?'

'You spoke of retrieving information,' Conroy said.

'I was inventing as I went along,' Karen said. 'I'd almost forgotten that I said it.'

'Unless you're in some great hurry,' Conroy said, 'I could take you over to your place in the morning.'

'If you're not going to leave me alone for a second,'

Karen said, 'there's no hurry.' She studied Conroy thoughtfully. 'Does it give you some kind of kick? Screwing someone you think might have betrayed you?'

'I could ask you the same question,' Conroy said.

The various functions of the Ministry of Defence were carried on in a number of buildings, mainly in Holborn and Whitehall, including the old Admiralty and War Office Buildings, with outposts in Southwark and Woolwich. DI3 was in Victoria, not all that far from the Royal College of Defence Studies.

The Office of Defence Information was, as it were, the shop window, where callers were welcome. This occupied a relatively small area which backed on to what appeared to be a block of flats fronting on to a parallel street. The block of flats was nothing of the kind, and here, casual callers were not welcome.

Conroy and Karen presented themselves to the 'hall porter' at the front entrance of the block of flats. That vigilant individual knew them both by sight, was expecting them, logged their arrival, and directed them to the basement. To both, this was strange territory. They were more familiar with the fourth and fifth floors.

They were met by the chief security officer, a greyhaired man called Mellish, who shook hands briskly and came straight to the point.

'I'm told that you want to know if unauthorized personnel could extract secure information from our computer system,' Mellish said. 'The answer is, no. It's completely impossible.'

'Why is it?' Conroy asked.

'Even commercial systems,' Mellish said patiently, 'are designed to avoid any security exposure. No IBM customer, for instance, who could simply be buying time on a computer, would fancy the idea of a competitor being able to extract confidential information. There are password protection procedures for all data-sets. In our case, where we're storing information which can be not only confidential, but the kind of top secret stuff that only a handful of people are entitled to see, those security procedures are absolutely foolproof. It's quite out of the question for anyone to retrieve information which he isn't entitled to see.'

'Look, don't get too defensive,' Conroy said cordially. A flush of mild annoyance flitted across Mellish's face. 'Perhaps your security procedures are as perfect as you say they are. But someone with authorizations as long as your arm could presumably see what he likes.'

'No, no, no,' Mellish said, horrified. 'Strict safe-guards are universally enforced. How can I put it?' He pondered how to explain his complex mysteries to two simpletons.

They were in an air-conditioned, quiet room, divided into glass walled sections. In each section was a computer terminal, at which was seated an operator. Mellish led them to a terminal which was not in use. He pointed at it.

'In simple terms,' he said, 'imagine that information is stored in a series of boxes, diminishing in size, each one inside another one.'

'Like Chinese boxes,' Karen offered helpfully.

'Exactly,' Mellish said. 'But carried almost to infinity. Each box requires a key, but each key will only open one box. The more boxes you need to open, the more keys are required, and the fewer people have access to those keys. Have I made myself clear?'

'Keys can be copied,' Conroy said.

'It's an extremely crude analogy,' Mellish said loftily, ruffled again. 'For key, read code-word. And the code-words are changed at frequent intervals. They are selected on a random basis so that they cannot be predicted, and they are issued in strict relation to the security classification of the person wishing to retrieve information.'

'Sticking to your own crude analogy for the moment,' Conroy said, 'can a skeleton master key be constructed by means of collusion between those who issue the code-words and those who receive them?'

'No,' Mellish said definitely. 'Because there is no direct relationship between the two. The whole thing resembles a pyramid. At the top, those with access to the most information, but each enquiry is controlled and logged. Even, if you like, the chief of the defence staff, shall we say, will receive his "key" on the random basis I spoke of. That is, from some unpredicted layer or segment at the bottom of the pyramid. I promise you, Mr Conroy, this system was evolved by the finest brains in this field. It genuinely is foolproof.'

'All right,' Conroy said doggedly. 'Let's take a practical example and follow it through. A while ago, I was involved in a particular operation in Germany . . .'

'What was the nature of this operation?' Mellish interrupted.

'You know I can't tell you that,' Conroy said sharply. It had been a combined effort between DI3 and the German Secret Service. Both had been worried about the infiltration of legitimate German political parties by people who made democratic noises, but whose first loyalties, it was suspected, lay on the wrong side of the Iron Curtain. The division of Germany made for ambivalent loyalties at the best of times. Conroy only knew about the segment of the operation in which he had been personally involved. General policy would have been guided by Goss, but not the day-to-day details. Conroy had acted as his own field sub-commander, in this instance, reporting to a field commander in Brussels.

'Yes, I know perfectly well that you can't tell me,' Mellish said, with a trace of smugness. 'A question like that, and all your training comes into force, an immediate conditioned reflex. The point I want to make is that all computer personnel are subject to the same kind of training. What's more, they are as carefully vetted as those who work in the field, and their security classification is as frequently reviewed. Just in case you had any red herrings in mind about computer operators extracting unauthorized information on their own account with, shall we say, dubious purposes in mind. That can't be done either.'

Mellish was like all experts, Conroy thought. Full of what could not be done, so much in love with his own subject as to be incapable of imagining how the object of his affections could possibly be less than perfect in any way.

'I don't think we should entirely rule out the possibility of a bent operator,' Conroy remarked.

'I can assure you that we must,' Mellish said, 'as I'm sure you will find yourself obliged to agree in due course. However, what aspect of this operation would you like to see retrieved?'

'A meeting in a Berlin restaurant with a man called Hans Braun,' Conroy said. 'At least, that's not his real name, but that's how he should appear.'

'Assuming this meeting was logged beforehand or reported afterwards,' Mellish said, with the air of one who had the upper hand and knew it. 'Not even a computer as advanced as ours possesses the functions of a crystal ball, you know.'

'It was logged beforehand,' Conroy said patiently, although it took something of an effort. Mellish's confidence was beginning to irritate him, mostly because the chance, odds-on in truth after all, that it might be well-founded, was worrying him. 'I didn't

145

really have much of an opportunity to report it afterwards. I was in the Lubianka at the time.'

Mellish blinked rapidly. In this safe haven, personal
experience of such nasty outside occurrences rarely
intruded.

'Oh, I'm sorry,' he said. 'I beg your pardon. I didn't
know.'

'Forget it,' Conroy said, regretting his own words,
which seemed as needlessly cruel as showing a safely
domesticated animal the savage wilderness in which it
would not survive. 'No reason why you should.'

'How did you log this meeting?' Mellish asked.

'By telephone to Field Control in Brussels in the
usual way,' Conroy said. 'Coded, naturally, since I was
using an open line.'

'Was the control assistant someone you'd spoken to
before?'

Conroy thought about that, recalling the sound of the
girl's neutral voice.

'Yes,' he said at last. 'Once two weeks beforehand,
and several times at intervals over the previous two
years.'

'But with a considerable gap each time,' Mellish said
happily, his self-confidence restored. 'Our precautions
start there. Informational calls from field operatives are
rotated so that their contact with each control assistant
is as infrequent as practicable. You yourself know as
little as possible about each operation to which you are
assigned. Any individual control assistant will only
receive fragments of the fragments you know, and
furthermore will be unable to decode your message.
The computer then stores it in coded form. Security,
Mr Conroy, begins at square one.'

'That's very comforting,' Conroy said. 'I still got
shopped.'

'Not through any fault or leak in our system,' Mellish
said. 'I can promise you that. Now, this meeting. If you

can give me the date and the password of the day with which you preceded your message . . . ?'

'The password was Saracen,' Conroy said. He gave Mellish the date.

'That's convenient,' Mellish said. 'The word Saracen indicates that the information is only available to those with a security classification of 1A or above. I happen to be 1A, so I can retrieve it for you. But first, I must speak to the duty officer and obtain an additional password to add to my own. We reach him on the green telephone here.' He picked up the instrument.

'I don't want you to do it,' Conroy said. 'I want to know how Goss could do it.'

Mellish seemed both startled and apprehensive.

'Why Mr Goss?' he enquired. He replaced the green receiver.

'Because I say so,' Conroy said. 'Because I fancy exploring that particular avenue.' There was, he noticed, an amused expression on Karen's face. She had changed into a two-piece which, on anyone else, would have qualified for the neat and serviceable label; but her high heels and her long legs turned it into something else again.

'I thought I'd explained the system reasonably clearly,' Mellish said petulantly, 'so that even a layman could understand it. I cannot retrieve highly sensitive information on behalf of Mr Goss. No one can. Mr Goss would have to do that himself.'

'I don't see your problem,' Conroy said. 'Fetch him.'

'I am authorized to tell you anything you want to know about our computer system and its built-in security precautions,' Mellish snapped. 'I am not authorized to go any further than that. I can demonstrate anything you like. There's no need to disturb Mr Goss.'

'For Christ's sake,' Conroy said sourly, 'I've told you

what I want, and you've just told me you can't demonstrate it. Only Goss can do that, it seems. He won't have you beheaded if you phone and ask him. He can only refuse.' That in itself would be quite interesting from Conroy's point of view.

Mellish, his lips tight, moved away and spoke into another phone, evidently a direct line to Goss.

Karen gave Conroy a sympathetic smile.

'If, as you claim, this was my bright idea in the first place,' she said, 'I'm beginning to think it was a lousy one.' She glanced round at the glass-walled cubicles which surrounded them. 'Apart from the myriad precautions which are making my head swim, every operator's under visual supervision all the time.'

'Maybe we'll draw a blank in the end,' Conroy said, 'but we haven't bloody started yet. All we've had so far is the PR guff.'

Mellish put the phone down and came back, his lips compressed more tightly than ever.

'In half an hour,' he said. 'But he's not pleased.'

'I really don't care if he's frothing at the mouth,' Conroy said pleasantly. 'All right if I play with your toy for half an hour?'

Mellish sighed and nodded. Conroy sat down at the terminal keyboard. Karen, interested, stood behind him, watching.

Conroy, although he lacked the lightning speed of a skilled operator, knew the drill. Experimentally, he typed in 'Traveller' and 'Saracen' and a request for information. The reply came up on the screen before him immediately.

'DATA NOT AVAILABLE. INSERT CODE-WORDS.'

Conroy made up some, scribbling notes as he went along. The same message reappeared on the screen. Conroy tried a few variations and received repeated brief messages of rejection. Karen began to giggle.

'I don't think much of this machine,' Conroy complained. 'It only knows how to say one thing.'

'I did tell you,' Mellish said wearily.

Goss arrived in a curt, bellicose mood.

'We'll get this stupid, time-wasting crap out of the way as quickly as possible,' he said to no one in particular, and lifted the green telephone.

'A special password is required to retrieve 1A material,' Mellish explained to Conroy, like some parrot repeating itself, 'which Mr Goss is now obtaining from the duty officer, who will log his request.'

'How does the duty officer identify Goss?' Conroy asked. 'By means of a voice print?'

'That's right,' Mellish nodded. 'Automatically checked, and as accurate as fingerprints. If anyone else tried to impersonate him, another circuit would be triggered. Security would be placed on full alert, and the building sealed off.' Goss hung up, and glared at Mellish impatiently. 'Mr Goss now has two elements of the necessary "key",' Mellish said nervously. 'His own personal coding, which is changed weekly, and the special password issued by the duty officer for secret information. Even now, that is not enough. The operator must add the section prefix which each shift receives when it comes on duty. I shall act as the operator for the purposes of this demonstration.' He sat down at the keyboard.

'I hope you don't have to go through this palaver every time you want to use the thing,' Conroy said.

'Not for routine work, of course not,' Mellish said. 'This kind of retrieval is relatively uncommon.'

'Zero zebra one two. Meridian,' Goss said, with ominous impatience.

Mellish's fingers flickered across the keys so fast that Conroy, although watching closely, lost him halfway.

'A Thor 5,' it began, 'OZ12 Meridian Traveller recall Saracen . . .'

The answer flashed up on the screen at once:
OPERATION TRAVELLER/00147298 it was headed.

There followed full details of Conroy's planned meeting with Hans, the date, the time, the name and address of the restaurant.

Mellish's fingers hovered over another key.

'Do you want a printout?' he asked.

'No,' Conroy said. 'Now I want to know how many times that information has been requested before, and who by.'

'God almighty,' Goss breathed. Mellish glanced at him apprehensively. 'All right, all right,' Goss said. He blew his nose noisily.

'How many code-words have to be issued for that?' Conroy enquired grouchily. Reason was telling him to abandon the whole thing.

'None,' Mellish said stiffly. 'It falls into the category of a routine security check.'

His fingers flickered. The screen answered. The information had been requested previously . . . a list followed.

Conroy's eyes fastened on the first two words.
RECIPIENT:HOD. Head of Department (HOD) was, of course, Goss.

'Now that raises an interesting . . .' he began, but stopped as he took in the rest. It was timed 08:10, and dated the day after his meeting with Hans had gone wrong.

'The only interesting thing about it is why I should bloody worry about you,' Goss said. 'You'd failed to report in. I wanted to know what your planned movements had been. Later that day, Hans was found dead.'

'Are you quite sure there was no request *before* the meeting?' Conroy asked Mellish.

With exaggerated tedium, Mellish punched in the

same enquiry and received the same answer. Conroy studied every item on the screen carefully. First, was Goss's retrieval the day after Conroy had been snatched. There followed, dated today, the laconic report RIGHT ENQUIRIES TERMINAL DI3/9. INCORRECT CODE GIVEN. INFORMATION NOT PROVIDED.

'This, of course, is DI3 terminal number nine,' Mellish said.

'Very impressive,' Karen said. She smiled at Conroy. 'You've been caught in the act.'

Conroy grunted. He picked up his crumpled note, glanced at them, and slipped the piece of paper in his pocket.

Finally, the screen recorded Goss's demonstration enquiry.

'Satisfied now?' Goss enquired sardonically.

'No,' Conroy said. He had detected what he thought could be a flaw, which he was disposed to keep to himself for the time being.

'We'll borrow your office,' Goss told Mellish. He gripped Conroy's arm and marched beside him to the room in the far corner. Once inside, Goss slammed the door, leaned his back against it, and folded his arms.

'Mellish has shown you that the computer can't be tampered with,' he said. 'You're nothing but a bloody amateur in this area, and Mellish is an expert.'

'He's still the monkey,' Conroy said. 'Now I want to talk to the organ grinder.'

'Not without giving me some good reason,' Goss said. 'You've had your free run, and a wild idea only justifies one, no more. You've got nothing to go on. You've just been playing a hunch, haven't you?'

Conroy hesitated, considering how much to say.

'Come on!' Goss ordered brusquely. 'Talk sense, or you come off the short leash and go back on the choke chain.'

'It's a bit more than a hunch,' Conroy said carefully.

'Call it instinct. Making connections. I can't chart those connections for you, but they're there.'

'On what premise?' Goss demanded. 'You must have some damn thing.'

'You should know that no premise exists,' Conroy said. 'Only a supposition. That is, suppose that both Karen and I are both telling the truth.'

'That supposition always needed more than a grain of salt,' Goss remarked. 'The way things are going, it must run into bloody tons by now.'

'You set up this game!' Conroy flared. 'What's wrong? Are you afraid I'm getting closer than you'd like?'

'No,' Goss said grimly. 'I'm afraid you're getting nowhere.'

'If Karen isn't lying,' Conroy said, 'and I'm the first to agree that it's a very big "if", then I was set up in Berlin by someone else, and in some other way . . .'

'You've just seen that idea comprehensively disproved with your own eyes,' Goss said.

'All I've seen,' Conroy said, 'is that if it can be done that way, I still don't know how.'

'You've got a huge great "if" in there,' Goss pointed out. 'You mentioned connections. What connections?'

Conroy thought that perhaps the time had come. He watched Goss's face carefully. The man's reaction might conceivably tell him something.

'The submarine patrol routes,' he said. 'Berlin. Ernest Harrington. Cruise missile deployments.'

Goss stared at him. His face might have been carved from stone. His eyes were as lifeless, and the combination told Conroy nothing.

'Why take on the impossible?' Goss asked eventually, in a quiet voice. 'You've had it proved to you that neither I nor anyone else extracted any information about your meeting with Hans before it took place.' Conroy listened, expressionless. If the flaw he imagined he had detected was indeed there, no such proof existed, but he chose not to say so at this point. 'You've also had it proved to you,' Goss went on relentlessly, 'that there's no way the computer could have been robbed of that information by anyone else. You've seen the precautions that are taken, how impossible it is . . .'

'I'm right about one thing though, aren't I?' Conroy said. 'Submarine patrol routes and Cruise missile deployment sites are stored in the computer.'

'Compared with getting access to things like that,' Goss said, 'finding out about your meeting in Berlin was like listening to the town crier. It's incredible. It doesn't stand up. And you can't show me a way.'

'It's far-fetched in the extreme,' Conroy agreed. 'But at least it's a method by which one man, or a small group could, theoretically anyway, acquire such information.'

'Theoretically bullshit,' Goss snapped. 'I could come up with theories just as good as that. How about little green men from outer space with extra sensory perception?'

'Fine. If they were little green communists,' Conroy said. 'Look, what's your alternative? Not one traitor in one government or military organization, but a whole team of them, working in collaboration throughout NATO. All people who've spent their lives achieving high rank, or sitting in Cabinets. Is that more credible? You may think so, but there's not much in it, and any such set-up is historically unheard of. It defies imagination.'

'Not your imagination,' Goss said. 'Not the way you're carrying on. Haven't you learned how incredibly complicated it would be to rob a computer of that sort of stuff we're talking about?'

'That's why I want to talk to the organ grinder,' Conroy said. 'That's the next door I want opened.'

Goss squinted down at his watch, unfolded his arms, and rubbed his face reflectively.

'I'll consider it,' he said at last. 'You'll be busy this afternoon on your biographical studies, so we'll make it my office, 18:00. And don't be late. You've already put me behind. I can see that I shall be here until midnight anyway, thanks to your stubborn determination to waste my time.'

SEVEN

Conroy was admitted to Number 10 Downing Street, for the first time in his life, by way of the Whitehall entrance. He was shown into a small office, where a principal secretary, with a look of youthful age about him, indicated a desk with only a bulky file lying on it. Conroy sat behind the desk. The principal secretary pulled up a chair and sat opposite. Conroy glanced at him enquiringly.

'The chief secretary instructed me to remain with you,' the principal secretary said distantly. He seemed none too enamoured of the idea. He was probably thinking, with resentment, about all the work he would have to take home, because of Conroy's unwelcome intrusion.

Conroy nodded and opened the file, which bore on the cover a reference number, and the legend SECRET. RESTRICTED TO CABINET OFFICE ONLY. He began to read.

By the time he left, Conroy had learned much about

Goss which he did not know and refreshed his memory about some things which he had half forgotten, such as Goss's Christian name, Nicholas, and the fact that he was divorced. It was hard to imagine Goss ever having been in sufficiently tender a mood to get married in the first place.

It was all there, including Sir Lionel's annual confidential reports on Goss in those far-off, better days when Lionel had been head of department, reports which, unaccountably to Conroy, were soberly glowing in unexpected ways. Lionel had evidently never seen through Goss.

Some of it was predictable, given Goss's behaviour. The humble background, born in Battersea, the only son of a labourer, a mediocre school record, enlistment into the RAF as a boy apprentice. Some of it was less predictable. That somehow, Goss had contrived to acquire a degree in law while still in the RAF, after which, his period of service over, he had joined Customs and Excise, been called to the Bar, and rapidly transferred to the C and E's small, elite Investigation Branch, where he had been responsible for busting arms and drugs smuggling rings, cases which were notorious enough for Conroy to remember reading about them when he was a boy.

At that point, Lionel, head-hunting as usual, had recruited Goss into the department. Conroy skimmed rapidly through Goss's field service record, which was distinguished, as would befit a future head of department.

He paused over the revelation that Goss appeared in the KGB files, code-named 'Nikita'. That could be no more than the sketchy information which any Intelligence organization sometimes acquired about individuals on the other side. Or it might, conceivably, be something else. A cryptic record of one of 'theirs' cross-referenced to another, more explicit file, to which the defector who had passed on the information had not had access.

Yet for the latter possibility to have the slightest shred of credibility, there had to be some history of contact somewhere with the ideas which could have shaped him in that direction. Not the kind of establishment treason acquired, in the first instance, intellectually, at agreeable universities, as in the case of people like Burgess, Maclean, and Philby. Goss had never been near a university. His law degree was an external one. Moreover, one of Lionel's few mildly disapproving comments on Goss was to the effect that he appeared to possess an impatience with the establishment bordering upon contempt.

Nor would it be about money. Goss was not an extravagant man, but in any event, high-class traitors rarely acted from monetary motives. Those who did it for cash were small fry, and the one Conroy was searching for was big. So big that he had already rocked nations, and shaken the very foundations of NATO. Nor did Conroy imagine that it was due to end there.

He hunted through Goss's field service again, looking for that missing element. Mostly Goss had used the cover of an engineer, a role which would have fitted him like a glove.

Only once, soon after joining the department, had he put his legal training to use. Conroy read that brief precis several times.

Goss had been infiltrated into a Community Law Advice Centre, which was regarded as a front organization. It was situated in a borough where the hard-line Far Left had taken over the Labour Party constituency organization. Goss had played his part, undetected—it said—for six months. The section ended, 'Possible links established with several other suspected front organizations believed to be in contact with Czech and Russian embassies, and various individuals identified. (See operational reports).' The detailed reports would not, of course, form part of Goss's personal file.

Typed underneath was one further sentence: 'Operation suspended on PM's orders. No further action.'

Translated into plain English, Conroy thought, that meant the prime minister of the time had developed cold feet. But would the department, even in Lionel's more traditional day, have informed the PM that such an investigation was taking place? Conroy thought it somewhat unlikely. In that case, someone had become suspicious for some reason and privately complained to the PM that Intelligence were taking an interest in people who were doing nothing illegal, engaged in perfectly legitimate work on behalf of a legitimate political party. Intelligence did just that all the time, of course, but politicians were sensitive about their own if they were obliged to take notice of what was going on.

Conroy recognized that it could mean nothing. The Far Left were highly paranoid—with some reason— about the activities of the Intelligence services at the best of times. But someone could have leaked it. Someone could have told them.

It was desperately thin. But at least in that poor, industrial, multi-racial borough, there had been the opportunity for Goss to come into contact with the ideas and the people—to develop the doubts which were necessary if a man was to turn against his own country. Goss had been there for six months. Six months could be a long time. What would Goss have been like at thirty? Might he have been capable of being appalled by squalor, poverty, injustice, racial persecution? Might he have been receptive, in that state of mind, to the slick and easy cure for all these ills?

Conroy found it hard to imagine. It did not seem like Goss at all. But that could be Goss's best protection. He must constantly bear that in mind.

Conroy went back to the beginning of the file again, looking for he knew not what. The man had no affiliations which, by the wildest stretch of imagination, could be regarded as suspicious. Goss was not much of a 'joiner', it seemed. The only organization to which he belonged was the Chelsea Supporters' Club. Chelsea? Conroy had moved on several pages before it struck him.

Garnett had been a faithful supporter of Chelsea Football Club.

So were about twenty-five thousand other people of course. But still . . .

Conroy, in the days when he was shadowing Garnett, had spent several Saturday afternoons in the stand, watching Garnett and seeing nothing of the game. A football ground, with its milling crowds, was an ideal place to make contact if, like Garnett, you had good reason for extreme discretion. Conroy had not witnessed him make contact with anyone, much less Goss. But still . . .

The electric clock on the wall told Conroy that it was time to go. He closed the file. A look of relief appeared on the principal secretary's face.

'Tell me something,' Conroy began.

'I am not authorized to answer any questions,' the principal secretary said hurriedly.

'Go on,' Conroy urged. 'Just try it for size. When everything else is computerized, why do you keep bulky great files like this here?'

The principal secretary warily examined the query for possible booby traps.

'I believe it may be possible, although I cannot be certain,' he said at last, 'that the contents of such a file might also appear in the computer records.'

'Why the duplication?' Conroy asked. He hoped that the principal secretary had run out of qualifying words and phrases.

'It could possibly be the result of some kind of traditional hangover,' the principal secretary suggested carefully. 'The PM has always had instant access to the personal file of the head of the department. That dates back to the time before the computer records existed. I assume . . .'

'Nobody's ever got around to changing the system,' Conroy supposed. 'That figures.'

Karen was waiting in the reception area outside Goss's office on the fifth floor. She looked bored. She had spent the afternoon with Mellish's assistant, a young man who had responded enthusiastically to his brief, which was to give her a crash course. She listened to a lot of jargon; repeated explanations of the security system which, she realized, was scarcely dependent on the human element, but programmed into the computer itself; reached the conclusion that Conroy was trying to crack something which was clearly impregnable, which could only mean that he was deliberately laying a false trail for some reason; and finally, deeply disappointed the young assistant, who had formed heady visions of a delectable near future, by declining his eager invitation to a candlelit dinner.

'I hope your afternoon's been more interesting than mine,' Karen said.

'I doubt it,' Conroy said offhandedly.

'No dirt? Not so much as an innuendo? Nothing at all?'

'Not a thing,' Conroy said. He intended to keep the connection between Goss and Garnett via the Chelsea Football Club strictly to himself.

They were shown into Goss's office at 18:02. He waved them into chairs. The room looked like a clone of any office anywhere in the world, and could have belonged to a banker, a businessman, or a lawyer, except for the presence of two red scrambler telephones side by side on the desk.

Goss lowered one heavy eyelid in a conspiratorial wink at Conroy. 'How about the Chelsea connection then?' he enquired slyly.

'Slender,' Conroy said. 'But positive.' He managed to refrain from grinding his teeth. Goss appeared to possess an infinite capacity for both taking him aback and annoying him intensely.

'My Dad used to take me when I was a boy,' Goss reminisced. 'Walked all the way there, and all the way back. Stood on the terraces, rain, sleet, snow, or shine. When I joined the Customs and started making a few bob, I bought him a season ticket for the stand as a birthday present, but he never used it. He'd rather perish on the terraces, silly old fool.'

Karen was looking thoroughly bewildered.

'Fascinating,' Conroy said.

'I still support them, when I can spare the time,' Goss said. 'Don't really know why. They're still a bunch of cripples.' He gave Conroy a large grin, revealing teeth like tombstones. 'Of course, I made a point of not going when you were tailing Garnett. I thought it might have confused you.'

'It might have done,' Conroy agreed.

'Even spies like to relax now and then,' Goss remarked. 'I suppose Garnett'll be cheering on Moscow Dynamo these days.'

'Have you had any reports on him from our people there?' Conroy asked curiously.

'Nothing very definite,' Goss said. 'Officially, he's dead, of course, buried on the Isle of Wight. So he's not going to reemerge as head of the KGB's English section. Not under his own name, anyway.'

'I assume that was part of the deal you made with them,' Conroy said. 'I'm surprised they agreed. They could have made a propaganda ball out him appearing at functions in Moscow wearing the Order of Lenin, or whatever, when he should be serving thirty years in a British prison.'

'They wanted him back too badly to worry about candyfloss like that,' Goss said. He appeared to be on the verge of picking his nose reflectively, but changed his mind in favour of thoughtfully caressing that prominent object. 'Anyway,' he went on, 'someone resembling our man has been sighted in Moscow, riding in a Zis limousine. He could have been Garnett with a newly grown beard, but it wasn't a positive identification.' He decided on a change of posture and linked his spadelike hands behind his head. 'I suppose you thought it was a bit of a coincidence, me and Garnett, both spending Saturday afternoons at Stamford Bridge.'

'You don't live nearby,' Conroy said neutrally. 'Nor did Garnett.'

'When bilious, pretentious critics want to have a go at Dickens, they usually knock his use of coincidence,' Goss said thoughtfully, as if he were a man with time to kill. 'Me, I think Charlie Dickens got it right. There's a hell of a lot of outlandish coincidences happen in real life. Too many books are too tidied up with a neat explanation for everything. Real life isn't like that.'

'True,' Conroy said. 'But the argument could be that he sometimes used coincidence to get himself out of a spot.'

Goss smiled a small, mocking smile.

'Chase it, my lad, if you must,' he said. 'But if you will follow will-of-the-wisps, be careful they don't lead you into dangerous swamps.'

'I'm always careful,' Conroy said. 'Like you.'

Goss eyed him in silence, while the seconds ticked past. The mockery had left his face.

'Yes,' he said, at last. He unlinked his fingers and

leaned forward on his desk, getting down to business. 'Right,' Goss said. 'Let's get down to business. I've just received an informed forecast of the German election result. There's only been one real issue, nuclear missiles, for and against, which one supposes was the KGB's intention. The voting's so close, the verdict can be read any way you like. The wheeling and dealing is still going on, but it looks as though we're going to get a wobbly coalition which can't claim a genuine majority in the country and which will try and ride both horses at the same time. That is, stripping out the double talk, their policy, if you can dignify it with that name, will be publicly against Cruise on German territory, but privately willing to do nothing much about it, provided they get more control. It's not quite the worst of all possible worlds, but it's in the running. The Right are already making noises about Reds in Bonn, and the security services are worried. The neo-Nazi wing are banging on about valour, and patriotic duty, and direct action, which means street violence, whichever way you read it. What's more, the bastards are getting weapons from somewhere. If I were sitting in Moscow, I'd make sure they got plenty. A violent, unstable West Germany, threatened with something very like civil war, must look like the jackpot from the Kremlin.'

He paused, possibly for effect.

Karen said impatiently, 'As a digest of current affairs, all that was predictable from the moment the Cruise deployment sites hit the headlines. If you just want an audience, I can tell you now, this half would rather go and eat somewhere.'

Goss glowered at her from under his bristling eyebrows.

'You're getting to be as impertinent as your partner in crime, young woman,' he said threateningly. 'I'm explaining the background to my decision, so just listen, as patiently as you can contrive. You may think

you have precious little to lose, but you have, and don'
you forget it.'

There should be a law of diminishing returns, Conroy
thought, when it came to threats, as with anything else
but there was not. Karen was staring at Goss, poised
and defiant, but in her eyes he saw an uncharacteristic
flicker of fear, which disappeared when momentarily
she forgot or pushed it to the back of her mind, but
which Goss could rekindle with one of his euphemisms
any time he chose. For a few seconds, Conroy allowed
himself the luxury of hating Goss, really hating the
brutish, ruthless, sardonic lout.

'NATO will survive,' Goss resumed more quietly. 'It
must survive, or none of us will. A crisis such as this
like the prospect of being hanged, sharpens the mind
wonderfully. Our political masters are bent on holding
together. They've realized that the leak on Cruise is
potentially more damaging and divisive than even the
mess in West Germany. If the source goes undetected,
if suspicions grow that it could be NATO headquarters
itself, or people in government in several different
countries, it could shatter the alliance. The Americans,
I need hardly say, take a piss-poor view of the whole
thing. If NATO begins to look like a really bad bet,
there's only one thing they can do, and that's pull out
completely, and rely on Fortress America. They never
have thought much of our security, from Fuchs to
Blake to Maclean. Garnett shook them badly again.
The Cruise thing has got them dusting off contingency
plans for bringing the rest of the boys back home.'

Over the years, America had progressively reduced
its forces stationed in a Europe which had a Gross
National Product higher than the USA and which
should, in American eyes, be able to look after its own
defence accordingly. The US element of NATO was
now little more than a thinly spread trip wire force. Put
another way, that could mean a force which need not

necessarily become involved in hostilities, and could be pulled out fast. The Nuclear Umbrella remained. Whether it would remain open should the storm break was the subject of agonized doubts by European commanders.

Goss glared at Karen. 'Am I still boring you?' he enquired savagely.

'I'm not bored,' Karen said. 'I'm restless. Yes, it's a big deal, I can work that out for myself, but we're not part of it. We're just two people under suspicion, but too small for you to bother to fry for the time being. How does it concern us? Where's the relevance?'

'This,' Goss said. 'I haven't gone into detail with the PM—PMs don't like details, least of all this one—but I rather coyly hinted that the department was looking into the possibility that what we're facing isn't so much high-level espionage on a grand scale, as a technical malfunction, allied with human error, which is being exploited by a single undiscovered traitor, or at worst a small group, but at a relatively low level. That appealed. It appealed a lot.' He waved at the scrambler telephones. 'I've been talking to Brussels, and it appeals there too. Generals and defence ministers are accustomed to being above suspicion. It spreads alarm and confusion when people start looking at them sideways. They don't like it. They don't know what to do. So, for the time being, I am basking in enthusiastic, universal approval. A way out has been revealed to our masters. Great careers which could have been in jeopardy may still flourish yet, if the buck of suspicion passes them safely by and settles at a convenient distance, somewhere in the lower reaches of some anonymous technician. With one accord, they like the idea. Unusually, even uniquely, I am suddenly a highly popular man. No, I shouldn't have put it quite that way,' Goss said modestly. 'I merely enjoy a small share of the reflected glory which is due to the department.'

'Very neat,' Conroy said sourly. 'You've turned us into the whitewash team.'

'Don't be grumpy,' Goss said genially. 'First of all you bore me rigid with your dotty ideas, and then you complain when I press them for you. You are a very hard man to please, sometimes. All the time, come to think of it,' he added.

On the face of it, the rebuke was justified, but Conroy knew that he was being used, and that was the source of his unease. How, and for what reason, he did not know. Only that he was.

'Since we're now working with the full approval of the great and mighty in the noble cause of getting them off the hook,' Conroy said, 'I assume you'll give us carte blanche. Is that right?'

'I wouldn't go that far,' Goss said cautiously. 'The next door opened, keep me in the picture, and then we'll see.'

'It still sounds like a cover-up to me,' Conroy said.

'Not if you manage to uncover something,' Goss said piously.

'It's like a Royal Commission,' Conroy said. 'Appoint it, feel that you've accomplished something, and forget about it, in the hope that by the time it's reported, the problem will have disappeared or been overtaken by events.'

'I trust you'll adopt a somewhat smarter working pace than a Royal bloody Commission,' Goss said. 'It's not intended to be a make-work programme for Conroy and Dewar. You two are still wriggling on your own hooks. That hasn't changed. I can't say that I want results or else, because, despite my honeyed words to the PM, I still think you're barking up the wrong tree in the wrong neck of the woods. But you might not be. Or you might fall over something by accident. Either way, I can't lose. But you two can.'

'You could too,' Conroy said. 'If the buck of suspicion comes to a stop in this office.'

'Follow that mirage, if it'll keep you going,' Goss said. 'Being pure of heart, soul, and mind, I'm content to take my chances.'

Goss was right, Conroy was thinking. He could not lose. If those fragile connections firmed up, if suspicion became something more and congealed into traces of proof that HOD himself could be guilty of treachery—then he and Karen would simply disappear.

Goss was studying Conroy intently. Possibly, he was a thought reader.

'At any rate,' he said softly, 'you'll just have to gamble that you're wrong about me. That's the chance *you* have to take.'

Conroy was not sure if he had lost heart, or was simply baffled. He clung desperately to the flaw which he imagined he had detected in the computer security system. That was paper-thin too, and perhaps it could be explained, but he was not going to take the word of a functionary like Mellish.

There were so many alternatives, in a period of dangerous international tension, when everything was in a state of flux, shifting almost from minute to minute.

Goss could merely be acting like any government servant, using them to divert the wrath of his political masters. Or, if Goss was personally implicated, he might be happy to let them go ahead, knowing that they were pursuing the wrong trail. Or it might be that it led in the right general direction, and Goss wanted to keep them under close observation, in case they came up with something dangerous to him.

There was another alternative which flitted briefly into Conroy's mind, and which he dismissed at once. That would entail Goss being a sensitive, perceptive, subtle man. An enigma, yes, that he was, but those things, no. That alternative could safely be consigned to the mental dustbin.

'I hate to interrupt when I'm sure is a delicious reverie,' Goss said, 'but your next door will now be opened. Who do you consider to be the organ grinder?'

'Someone way above Mellish,' Conroy said.

'Well, he's top man in his field in the department,' Goss said. 'The man with overall responsibility in the Ministry of Defence itself is the security superintendent, Bartlett. But he's a fairly recent appointment. Took over the existing system.'

'It might be better to talk to his predecessor, in that case,' Conroy said.

'Can't be done,' Goss said. 'Not unless you know a good medium. Ashby died eighteen months ago.'

'How?'

'Killed in a car crash,' Goss said.

'Was he?' Conroy said. 'In that case . . .'

'I'm ahead of you,' Goss said. He was making a note. 'Bartlett to be vetted yet again. Although I'm certain we'll find he's clean.'

'By we, you mean me and Karen,' Conroy said. 'We'll handle that.'

'If you wish,' Goss said. 'Up to you.'

'Richard,' Karen said impatiently, 'won't any expert simply play the same record as Mellish? From what I gather, security's programmed into the computer itself. If anyone wanted to break it, wouldn't they have to tamper with that? And is such a thing even possible?'

'We're going to be told no,' Conroy said. 'But it's a damn good point. It raises the question of who wrote the programme in the first place. The conveniently dead Ashby by any chance?'

'God, no,' Goss said. 'Ashby was a good man, and so is Bartlett, but neither rank as innovators. Remember, we're dealing with a branch of science. Just as, out of thousands of scientists, you only get one Einstein, so in the world of computer science, there are only a handful of geniuses. This was one of the most complex pieces of programming that's ever been designed. It had to be capable of recording every state secret there is, past and present, with infallible security built into it, and also be capable of handling certain functions which I happen to know something about, but which I shall have to take with me into the grave. The whole thing, even now, is such an amazing achievement, as to be on the very brink of known computer technology. Only a genius could have handled it.'

'All right,' Conroy said, 'who's Einstein in the world of computers?'

'In Great Britain,' Goss said, 'a man called George Spencer.'

'He doesn't happen to be dead too, does he?'

'No,' Goss said. 'Retired.'

'George Spencer,' Conroy said. 'Open that door.'

'I'll try,' Goss said. 'He tends to live in a world of his own.'

'Does that mean you'd prefer not to?'

'No,' Goss said. 'Just don't think you can bully him the way you do me, that's all. Anything else?'

'Yes,' Conroy said.

Karen was in London, vetting the oblivious Bartlett's security clearance. Conroy was in Cardiff. Goss had raised no objection to this temporary parting of the ways. The rein could be tightened again, any time he felt like it.

Conroy had driven into the Black Mountains with the police sergeant who had been called to the scene of the accident, and studied the point where Ashby's car had left the road, crashed into a deep gully, and burst into flames.

'Any other vehicles involved?' Conroy had asked.

'No,' the sergeant had replied. 'It was a filthy night, blowing a gale, pouring with rain. He must have clipped a stone marker and gone out of control.'

'Cars do not go up in flames nearly as often as American movies would have us believe,' Conroy had remarked.

'No, that's right, but there was a very full investigation, Mr Conroy. Well, there was bound to be, with Mr Ashby being an important man at the Ministry of Defence. Forensic couldn't find anything suspicious.'

'Who carried out the post mortem?'

'A Home Office pathologist in Cardiff,' the sergeant had said.

The pathologist, like the police sergeant, evidently imagined that Conroy possessed great authority and standing. Conroy did not disillusion him. It would be interesting to see when this backing was withdrawn. That would be when he would know that he was on to something.

The pathologist found the right file, and refreshed his memory.

'Ah, yes,' he said. 'The victim was travelling alone and was not using his seat belt. Cause of death, multiple injuries. The body was practically incinerated, of course. It's a lonely stretch of road, and by the time the fire brigade arrived . . .' He gestured.

'Could these injuries, or some of them, have been inflicted before the car crash, rather than have been caused by it?' Conroy asked.

'Are you suggesting that he might have been murdered?'

'I'm rather more interested in what might have happened to him before he died,' Conroy said.

'What precisely are you inferring?' the pathologist asked. He was a pedantic man. 'Beaten up or tortured, perhaps? With what object?' He took another look at the file. 'Oh, I see. The victim held high rank in the Ministry of Defence. To try and acquire information of some kind, is that it?'

'I'm simply asking if it's possible,' Conroy said.

'All things are possible,' the pathologist said. His lips pursed in a small, private smile. 'Although certain bizarre possibilities are less likely than others.'

Not exactly a waste of time, but no further forward. The possibility, in Conroy's world, was not as bizarre as the pathologist imagined. If there was such a thing as a key or a shortcut into the heart of a computer, Ashby might have known it. Someone might have extracted it from him, after which the car crash might have been staged, to account for the tormented body. No . . . too many 'mights' . . . such was Conroy's last thought but one before he fell asleep.

At the first ring of the telephone, Conroy came instantly awake. He had been trained, and had trained himself, to snap into full alertness no matter how deep and necessary his sleep. He glanced at his watch automatically as he lifted the bedside phone. It was 01:10.

'Hullo,' he said quietly.

'You meet George Spencer tomorrow,' Goss's voice said.

'Where?'

'I can't tell you that. It's a secret location. A vehicle will collect you at 07:00. For some reason, Karen Dewar doesn't seem to be answering her telephone.' Goss sniggered down the line. 'Should you happen to know where she might be, perhaps you'd tell her and save me the trouble of tracking her down.'

Conroy hung up and subsided on to his pillow. Beside him, Karen's eyes were wide open.

'I have a message for you,' Conroy said.

* * *

The vehicle which arrived at 07:00 was one of the ambulances with the blacked-out windows, used to ferry 'patients' to and from the Home; although Conroy guessed that the driver, who was alone, was from this secret location, wherever that might be, and not from the department.

Conroy and Karen sat opposite each other in the back. It was a long journey. Conroy was glad that his bladder was now behaving itself. Neither of them felt like talking. Conroy closed his eyes and listened to the steady grumble of the engine. Sometimes the driver changed down, but not often. Conroy opened his eyes, and smothered a yawn.

'If I'd known it would take this long, I'd have brought a book,' he said.

'Nearly three hours,' Karen said. She was keeping careful track of the time. 'Around a hundred and twenty miles. Probably more, if we've been travelling on motorways. It could be in Devon, Cornwall, Wales, the Peak District . . .'

'Or on the outskirts of London,' Conroy said. 'We could be going round in circles for all we know.'

Half an hour later, the ambulance came to a stop, although its engine did not. After just under a minute, it moved on. Passing through a perimeter gate, Conroy thought.

Moving slowly now, the ambulance drove on, pausing again for a few seconds, changed into bottom gear, and descended, moving in circles as far as Conroy could judge. Finally, it stopped, and the rear doors were unlocked and opened. Conroy and Karen clambered out.

It looked like the bottom section of an underground garage, except that the uniformed men were not car park attendants, but armed guards.

Conroy and Karen were asked to surrender any metallic objects before they passed through a scanning device. This one did not make any warning noises, but something must have shown up on their screen. Two guards closed on Conroy at once, frisked him from head to toe, and looked at each other, puzzled. Conroy wondered if they understood about myelograms.

'It's all right,' Goss said. He had emerged from a lift. 'There's nothing he can do about it. It's a reaction from stuff he carries around inside him.'

Goss formally identified them to the guards. Conroy expected to be issued with a pass, but instead he was handed a small object and told to put it inside his breast pocket. Karen clipped hers on to her dress.

'A modular automated system's used to open doors in the restricted area,' Goss explained. 'It's a small transmitter which emits coded signals. Serves to identify you as well, so don't lose it, or you get shot on the spot.'

He chuckled and led the way to the lift. Heavy steel doors closed, and the lift descended for what seemed a long way. They emerged into a corridor with fluorescent lighting. It reminded Conroy of the Home.

'Deep underground,' Goss told them. 'Proof against a direct hit by a nuclear missile. It has to be.'

They walked towards a steel door. As they approached, it opened silently. They passed through. Conroy glanced back and saw it close again.

'Remains open for thirty seconds only,' Goss said, 'so don't hang about chatting in the doorway, or you receive a nasty injury. Closes and locks automatically. If it's not closed after thirty seconds, an alarm rings on the central control panel, the area's sealed off, and there's a full alert in case somebody's up to a spot of no good.'

'What is this place anyway?' Karen asked. 'The Government Defence Centre, to be used after a nuclear attack?'

'More important than that,' Goss said. 'You'll see.'

Two more doors opened to allow them through and closed after them. Corridors branched off at right angles. They passed store rooms, offices, dormitories, and a dining room.

The final door opened and closed, and they were in a huge, open, vaulted area, like the top half of a sphere. Goss led them to an elevated observation gallery and seated them in comfortable chairs, where they could study the scene below.

It was the size of a cathedral, but only two men were on duty, checking panels, dials, and switchboards. The atmosphere was calm and quiet. There was a constant soft hum in the air.

It bore an eerie resemblance to some vast intensive care unit, except that there were no patients. It was, Conroy realized with a shock, a computer of staggering capacity.

From here, all the terminals, such as the ones he had seen in DI3's basement, were fed. This was the very heart of the system, the massive electronic brain, it's capacity far greater than Conroy had ever imagined. The scale of the thing was stunning. Beside it, he felt insignificant. The idea that this brooding monster could be tapped in some way, seemed not only puny, but inconceivable. Before the weight of man's achievement housed in this air-conditioned cavern, served by its duo of acolytes, Conroy's brain shrank into insignificance. He understood now the certainty of men like Mellish. It would resemble the sacrilegious not to worship at this awe-inspiring shrine.

'Manned twenty-four hours a day, of course,' Goss said, 'on a three-shift basis. Entirely self-supporting, power, food, air, water. Capable of operating, in a state of emergency, as a self-contained unit, for upwards of eighteen months.'

'I had no idea,' Karen said, evidently as impressed as Conroy.

'I thought I'd seen some big computers,' Conroy said. 'But this . . .' He shook his head. 'What on earth justifies a giant like this? How much material is stored here, for God's sake?'

'Those are things you shouldn't know,' Goss said. 'But I'm afraid you'll have to, if you're going to make any sense of what George Spencer will say.' He surveyed them both soberly. 'It's a ticklish problem, but you've created your own trap. To chase your wildcat notion, you must know. If it comes to nothing, and all the advice at my disposal says that it must, you're both in a worse spot than you are now. You become a profound embarrassment. Two people, still with question marks against them, who've been told far too much.'

'I'm sure you'll come up with some kind of solution to that little problem,' Conroy said.

'I hope I don't have to,' Goss said. 'OK. You're in the presence of MDC/2. MDC stands for Military Defence Computer. It has a number of functions. It's a kind of master storehouse of all information appertaining to defence, ranging from the trivial to the top secret. In some senses, that's the least important, although it's the aspect you're concerned with. It simply replaces miles and miles of files, solves storage problems, combines instant access with impregnable security built into the computer itself. That is, you'd be more fruitfully employed in trying to break into the Bank of England vaults with a bent hairpin, than trying to get information you shouldn't have from this fellow. You want to challenge that?' He gazed bleakly at Conroy. 'How do you fancy your chances now?'

'I'm just listening,' Conroy said.

'Right. So it's in effect a filing system of almost

infinite size. Also, just as you can use a computer to check and rectify some weakness in the design of a car, so this is used by the planners, to construct comparative probabilities. Deaths and property damage arising from a one-megaton explosion, either at ground level or an air burst, over Birmingham, for instance. The effect of twenty megatons on London. That sort of thing. Give it the logistics, the men, tanks, planes on both sides, and it'll fight battles for you and tell you the result, in the fraction of a second. How long it would take the Russians to reach the Channel coast if both sides used conventional weapons. What our casualties would be. What theirs would be. How long we could hold them up with the use of battlefield tactical nuclear weapons on the German plains. The Third World War has been fought over and over again, in every conceivable permutation of forces, tactics, and weapons, on this computer.'

'Whatever its complexity and sophistication,' Conroy said, fighting in defence of the few ounces of brain he carried around in his own head, 'it's still just a machine, dependent on the programme fed into it by human beings. Computers have been churning out wrong economic forecasts for decades. Not because they make any mistakes, but because they've been given the wrong models to work from. No computer can correct the model it receives. In that sense, it's still dumber than any village idiot.'

'This one's no idiot,' Goss said, 'but I'll leave that side of it to George Spencer. Otherwise, your analogy's false. There's one fundamental difference. Economic models, whether provided by politicians, Treasury officials, or economists, are constructed by people with an axe to grind. To one degree or another, they're all designed for eventual public consumption. To influence public opinion, or a sector of it, in one direction or another. When it comes to defence the results are definitely not for public exposure. The models are accurate, and any assumptions are on the pessimistic side. The results, therefore, are deadly accurate. Not reassuring. Far from it. Just accurate.'

'What does it make of a Europe in which West Germany is doubtful, and the Cruise missiles deployed may not be available?'

'What you'd expect,' Goss said. 'Not much. We're entering the most dangerous period the world's ever known.' He checked his watch, and brooded over the quiet, efficient scene below. 'We're dealing in margins,' he went on at last. 'Tiny tilts which upset the balance. Not all-out nuclear war. That would bring down the curtain for good. If both sides go mad and launch everything they've got, that's goodbye to the human race, and forget all the crap about civil defence, and fallout shelters, and survivors in remote areas outside target areas. They'd bloody soon wished they hadn't survived, and their wish would bloody soon be granted. The earth would become a dead planet, a radioactive monument to the insanity of homo sapiens. I can't prove I'm right, but I don't believe that will happen by intent. If it does, it'll be by escalation, after someone's decided that it's worth risking the limited use of nuclear weapons to achieve their aims.'

'I assume this computer is capable of assessing that risk,' Conroy said. 'Logistically, at least.'

'It'll bloody plot it for you,' Goss said gloomily. 'And the curve is rising. Europe is back in the position it occupied for centuries—the cockpit of the world. There it is, a continent, rich industrially and agriculturally, unwilling to defend itself adequately, riddled with self-inflicted internal strife and dissension. Talk about the internal contradictions of capitalism—if you dug up Karl Marx now, I'll bet his skull would be fixed in a permanent grin. And next door is Russia, historically always an imperialist power, and whatever its other weaknesses, militarily far more powerful. The politics of power has laws, just like physics. Water finds its own level. So do nation states. Recent history should have taught us that, but most people prefer to believe that water will run uphill. It won't.'

'What date does MDC/2 predict for the flow from East to West?' Conroy asked, fascinated by the grisly look into the future, despite himself.

'Anything from yesterday to the day after tomorrow,' Goss said. 'But there, even this beast is fallible. It can't forecast the result of human intervention. One man can sometimes change the course of history, at least for a while. It can't predict that. But I hope we're right, and the Russians haven't been able to develop computers which can perform like this one. If I were sitting in the Kremlin, reading the kind of printouts this fellow will give you, I'd be tempted to have a go.'

'You mentioned a final function the computer would perform,' Conroy prompted.

'That one I can't discuss,' Goss said. 'Nor will George Spencer.' He raised his hand briefly in greeting. 'Here he is.'

Conroy looked down from the observation gallery. A tall, lanky man with neatly greying hair, wearing a neat grey suit, had arrived. His back was to Conroy, and he was shaking hands with one of the supervisors. Conroy realized that Goss had, partially at least, been killing time, until Spencer turned up.

Something about the suppleness of the man's body as he moved struck Conroy.

'Why did he retire?' he asked. 'He can't be that old.'

'He's fifty-three,' Goss said. 'His wife died last year. Cancer. It was unexpected, and they were very close. It knocked the heart out of him. In fact, he didn't want to come today. I had to lean on him hard. So make allowances.'

Spencer turned towards the gallery and moved lightly up the stairs. Goss shook hands with him.

'Doctor Spencer,' he said. 'This is Miss Karen Dewar.'

'Miss Dewar,' Spencer said distantly.

'Richard Conroy,' Goss said.

'How do you do,' Conroy said.

Spencer sat down, and crossed his long legs. Conroy had never met Spencer before in his life, but he studied the man's face intently, comparing it with a mental snapshot which he had retrieved from somewhere in the recesses of his mind.

No, he was not mistaken. He had seen Doctor George Spencer before.

He had seen Spencer sitting four rows in front of Garnett, at Chelsea football ground.

EIGHT

Jenkins, cued perhaps by Spencer's arrival, appeared with a tray bearing a coffee pot and cups, set it on a low table, and went away again.

Karen poured coffee and silently handed it round. Spencer courteously asked her if she would mind if he smoked. She smiled her assent. Spencer nodded his thanks, but his eyes did not linger on her face for that fraction of a second which a smile from Karen triggered in nearly all men. He lit a cheroot and puffed at it absently.

After one cool glance, he did not look at Conroy again, who was able to study this computer 'genius' openly. Spencer's voice was soft and quiet. He chose his words with a careful, hesitant precision, as though he was unused to casual conversation, or had lived the life of a remote, introverted academic. His features were irregular, but the overall effect was sympathetic and pleasant. It was not a melancholy face but somehow, even as he smiled at some remark of Goss's who was treating him as though he were a piece of priceless Dresden china, there was sadness imprinted on what should have been the laugh lines around his eyes. And those deep blue eyes remained veiled, as though a gauze curtain had been lowered between him and the world outside.

'Well, I must thank you again for giving us your time in this way, Doctor Spencer,' Goss purred.

'You were extremely insistent,' Spencer said concisely. He gazed at the computer area below.

'Essentially, of course, sir,' Goss said, 'you're here to answer a few questions from Mr Conroy.' The lout was on his best behaviour.

'So I understand,' Spencer said. His aloof gaze turned to Conroy. 'Although I believe Mr Conroy has already received his answers from someone extremely well qualified to provide them. I fail to see what I can add.'

Conroy caught sight of the mocking twitch of Karen's lips. He gained a few seconds by leaning forward and sipping his coffee. The ground rules had suddenly changed in a way which he did not like.

By using the recall ability which was second nature to him, he had changed that mental snapshot of Spencer sitting in the stand at Stamford Bridge, two rows in front of Garnett, into a mental roll of movie film. He was positive that Spencer and Garnett had not exchanged words, or even signalled to each other by so much as a glance. He was certain that, when the game was over, Garnett had turned in the opposite direction and left by a different exit to Spencer.

But that meant nothing. The very fact of Spencer's presence could have been a pre-arranged signal, which would trigger a meeting later at some previously appointed time and place.

Did Goss know? Or was he oblivious? Was there a

conspiracy between men infinitely more important
than Burgess and Maclean and Philby, which would
place not only Great Britain, but the whole of Western
Europe in mortal danger?

Until those questions were answered, Conroy could
be signing his own immediate death warrant by pursuing the line of enquiry he had planned. Every instinct
of self-preservation shrieked at him not to risk exposing
his suspicions to Spencer, to play them down, to change
his tactics. But if he did, Goss would know at once.
And Goss would wonder why. He would be no better
off. And whether Spencer was another Fuchs or not,
there was only one man who could provide the answers
Conroy was seeking, and that was Spencer. Because
Doctor George Spencer had been responsible for designing the computer's incredibly complex programme
in the first place. There was no one else. There was no
alternative direction Conroy could take. Even if catastrophe lay before him, he could only go blindly ahead.

Goss was frowning. He shifted in his seat.

'I think Conroy felt that it would be best to speak to
you, sir, as the fountain-head, as it were,' he said
emolliently. There was nothing emollient about the
stare which he turned on Conroy.

'Where do you live, Doctor Spencer?' Conroy asked.

The slightest trace of surprise momentarily pierced
the veil over Spencer's eyes.

'The Cotswolds,' he said evenly. 'Quite near Stow-
on-the-Wold. Where I've lived for a very long time.'

'Would that be since you were married?'

Goss's bulky jaw jutted out in anger. The signal he
made to Conroy, out of Spencer's range of vision, was
easily interpreted: I told you to stay off that subject,
you fool.

'Yes, it would,' Spencer said. The veil was back in
place.

'Do you have any children?' Conroy asked.

'No. I do not.'

'Was that by choice?'

'No,' Spencer said. His expression remained unchanged, but there were small red patches on his cheeks.

'You both wanted them but your wife couldn't. Is that the way it was?'

'Look, Conroy, I fail to see what . . .'

'Did you consider adoption?'

'Mind your own bloody business!' Spencer snapped. The veil had gone. There was a glow of anger in those deep blue eyes.

'For Christ's sake,' Goss hissed.

Karen's expression of amusement had vanished.

Conroy kept going, rapid fire.

'Do you have a London address?'

'A pied-a-terre in Bayswater.'

'Have you had that, too, for a long time?'

'I have,' Spencer said dangerously. 'You could have looked all this up.'

'I'm asking you now,' Conroy said. 'You're very young to be "retired". What do you do with your time? Keep fit?'

'I play squash regularly, if that's what you mean,' Spencer said. Consciously or otherwise, his replies slowed the exchange down. 'I also play golf, I'm interested in gardening, I appear for my village cricket team . . .'

'How about soccer? Are you interested in that?'

'I used to be,' Spencer said.

'Goss tells me you're a genius.'

'Mr Goss exaggerates,' Spencer said drily.

'All right, you've got a brilliant track record, call it what you like. I find it hard to believe that suddenly, just because your wife dies, you're satisfied with village bun fights.'

'I didn't say I was,' Spencer said curtly.

'It's all you've told me.'

'I spend a great deal of time pursuing lines of theoretical research which interest me,' Spencer said. 'An attempt, if you like, to seek the solution to some fascinating problems I encountered during my working life.'

'For commercial application?'

'I'm not a commercial animal,' Spencer said. 'Pure research for my own satisfaction, which may or may not eventually lead to a paper on the subject in a scientific journal.'

'I very much doubt if, in your field, you can solve problems by sitting and brooding over them like the Ancient Greeks. You'd need a computer, and an advanced one at that.'

'That is a statement of the obvious,' Spencer said.

'So which one do you use?'

'This one,' Spencer said. 'MDC/2. I have clearance to use it for research purposes.'

'Any time you like?'

'Within reason,' Spencer said.

'Even though you've retired?'

'I was director of the whole project for a number of years,' Spencer said. 'And even during my retirement, I'm still subject to the Official Secrets Act, as you should well know.'

'Yes, I do know,' Conroy said cheerfully. He sat back in his chair. 'Right. Good. Anyway, I'm glad about one thing. It can't have been too much trouble for you to come along for this meeting. If you have access to the computer all the time, I expect you pop in and out pretty frequently.'

Spencer raised his eyebrows in Goss's direction.

'Am I to understand that my security clearance is being reconsidered?' he asked.

'No, of course not,' Goss growled.

'Then I really don't understand the purpose of Mr Conroy's questions.'

'Nor do I,' Goss said. 'I assure you that . . .' He broke off. A sequence of coloured lights was flashing on the wall. A look of worry replaced the mystified irritation on his face. 'I'm sorry. That's my code. There's a telephone call which I must take at once. Excuse me . . . I'll try not to be long.'

Goss got up and headed for the stairs. Spencer shot a glance at Conroy, followed Goss, detained him, and spoke to him, just out of earshot.

'Must be the prime minister's office to make Goss jump like that,' Conroy said.

'You are a cruel bastard,' Karen said quietly.

Yes, she was bright. She knew what he had been about. Or partially knew, at least. Conroy quickly modified that in his mind. She could well know all of it. Even if his sights were now ranged on bigger targets than Karen Dewar, he must never forget that she could be a part of it. Admittedly, even in her most unguarded moments, he had so far detected nothing to contradict her claim that she was, in effect, an innocent bystander, wrongly suspected. But Karen could just be extremely good at concealment.

'I don't want to waste my time with someone who's going to repeat all the received ideas when his mind's on something else,' Conroy said. 'Two-thirds of him wasn't even here when he first sat down. It was the only way to get through to him. I think he'll listen now, at least.'

'You're still a cruel bastard,' Karen murmured.

Conroy shrugged and watched Goss and Spencer. Goss seemed to be making reassuring noises. He patted Spencer's arm, and went down the stairs. Spencer came back and sat down.

'Is there any more coffee?' he asked politely. Karen

obliged. 'Thank you,' Spencer said. He sipped his coffee, and waited. But there was a tension in him now. Conroy knew that he would have his attention from here on.

'You know the purpose of this meeting, Doctor Spencer,' Conroy said in a friendly tone, as though nothing had happened. 'And why I need your assistance.'

'I'm not sure,' Spencer said neutrally. 'I thought I did.'

Spencer was bright too. He either knew or had deduced exactly what was in Conroy's mind. Still, that need not matter. That could be a positive advantage, provided someone else could . . . but who? Conroy could see Karen's slim legs, neatly crossed, on the periphery of his vision. If only he could trust Karen Dewar. Sooner or later, he thought despairingly, he would *have* to trust someone.

'But you would accept,' Conroy said, 'that the repeated loss of such highly secret information can only be accounted for, either by espionage on a previously unheard of political or military level or both, or by misuse of the computer by unauthorized persons to extract information.'

'I am obliged to rule out your second hypothesis,' Spencer said. 'You've already been told that it's impossible, I understand. I can confirm that absolutely, and I believe I am in a position to say that with some authority.'

'Your authority, I respect,' Conroy said. 'But are you claiming a kind of papal infallibility? Even his is open to some question, as far as I understand it.'

The slight crinkling around Spencer's eyes might have denoted some amusement. It gave him a very appealing look.

'I concede your point, Conroy,' he said. 'Let me rephrase my opinion more precisely. In the light of present knowledge and development, your hypothesis is so unlikely as to be virtually impossible. Will that satisfy you?'

'Fine,' Conroy said. 'The word "virtually" provides common ground where we can talk. You're operating on faith which is probably well justified, I recognize that. But there's a million-to-one chance that it may not be.'

'A billion to one would be more accurate,' Spencer said. 'In my opinion.'

'With those odds,' Conroy said, 'a few noughts don't make much difference.'

'Not to you, evidently,' Spencer sighed. 'Honestly, Conroy, all I can do is to repeat the explanation which Mellish has already given you.'

'I don't want you to do that,' Conroy said. 'Mellish has read the tablets of stone, but you're the bloke who wrote them. What I want you to do is change sides.'

'Not for the first time,' Spencer said, 'I fail to follow you.'

'I'm a layman with a mad theory,' Conroy said. 'You're the great authority telling me how mad it is.'

'I'm afraid it is,' Spencer interjected.

'OK, now stop telling me that,' Conroy said. 'Switch over from now on. Use all the weight of your learning and experience, every ounce of pure research you've ever done, to test that theory with the object of showing that it *is* possible. That, somehow, it *could* be done. Do you follow me now?'

'Indeed,' Spencer said. He stared at the coffee pot without seeing it, but his eyes were not blank or veiled. Instead, for the first time, there was a glimmer of interest. 'Viewed as a theoretical problem, that could present a fascinating challenge . . . highly intriguing, in fact . . . but the trouble is that I spent years covering the same ground. When I led the team which initially devised the microcode techniques for the computer, one of my principal objects was to ensure that it could *not* be done. What you're asking me to do is to double-check my own work.'

'Yes, exactly,' Conroy said, 'in case there . . .'

'But I not only double-checked at the time,' Spencer carried on, 'I tested all security aspects until they showed the slightest sign of failure, and if they did, I built in further checks. You're asking me to prove myself wrong, when I took every care to ensure that I was not. I'm afraid you need another mind to examine your theory.'

'Well, *I'm* afraid yours is the only one available,' Conroy said. Which was true. He wished it was not.

Spencer shook his head. 'No one could extract unauthorized material, and that is a fact,' he stated flatly.

'You could, Doctor Spencer,' Conroy said. 'Unless I'm very much mistaken.'

Spencer raised his head sharply. The face was aloof again, the eyes narrowed.

'Oh?' was all he said.

'When you devised the security programme in the first place,' Conroy said, 'you'd have left a "keyhole". Some way of overriding every single complex check you'd built into it. You must have done. It would have been necessary.'

'With how much authority do you speak, Conroy, in the field of computer technology?' Spencer enquired ironically. 'How much of an expert are you?'

'I'm not,' Conroy said. 'For reasons that don't matter now, I once did a crash course and a lot of reading. That only left me with a smattering, and I know it. Sufficient though to know that you couldn't have constructed such an incredibly complex programme without leaving yourself elbow room. That "keyhole" will still be there.'

'The "keyhole" as you term it,' Spencer said, 'is known only to me. That is proof, in my eyes, that MDC/2 could definitely not have been tapped, because I certainly know that I have never done so. The reverse kind of proof to you, however, I gather from your line of questioning. Proof that, since I *could* have done such a thing, your theory is not mad after all.'

'You have the means, Doctor Spencer,' Conroy said softly. 'You have the opportunity. You make frequent visits here. Your presence is taken for granted.'

'I see,' Spencer said. He shook his head as if he could not credit it. 'Somehow, I have become a suspect.'

'You're the only suspect,' Conroy said politely. 'Unless you can help me establish that it could have been done in some other way.' He gave Spencer a smile. 'It will provide a certain degree of motivation, sir,' he said. 'As well as being a fascinating conundrum.'

Karen's lips parted, as she carefully mouthed a couple of words. Skilled lip reading was not necessary. 'You shit' Conroy correctly interpreted.

'I quite agree with Miss Dewar,' Spencer said, straight-faced. Conroy thought that was interesting. Spencer's peripheral vision might be fantastic, but he was also paying rather more attention to Karen than was apparent.

Goss was on his way back. He came up the stairs with the tread of a tired man, and sat down.

'Has Conroy stopped playing the fool yet?' he asked Spencer.

'I think we could say that Mr Conroy is getting down to business,' Spencer said. 'He has succeeded in establishing that there *is* someone who could have milked the computer of the information which appears to have been passed to the other side. I am obliged to concede that he is right.'

Goss leaned forward eagerly.

189

'Really?' he asked. 'Who?'

'Me,' Spencer said laconically.

'Oh, Jesus,' Goss groaned. He rolled his eyes heavenwards, pained.

'What did the PM want? A progress report?' Conroy hazarded.

'On your brainstorm?' Goss shook his head. 'Forget it. To do with the pace of developments elsewhere, which is faster and worse than expected. I can't stay much longer, so if you've got anything sensible to say, get on with it.'

'It's up to Doctor Spencer to come up with something sensible now,' Conroy remarked placidly. 'Otherwise, he's left singing a familiar song. It could have been me, but it wasn't.'

'I hope I'm not expected to take this seriously,' Spencer said. 'Is it your practice to make accusations, merely on the basis of opportunity without a shred of evidence of any kind, let alone motive or proof?'

'I'm afraid that's the way this game is played, sir,' Goss said apologetically, if unexpectedly. 'It would be as well if you went along with him.'

'Perhaps Doctor Spencer is considering the problem,' Conroy said. 'Just to get the ball rolling, what about the physical removal of information from the centre here? Computer discs are duplicated, as I understand it. Could a disc have been taken away by someone?'

'By me, for example?' Spencer asked. He seemed amused for some reason.

Conroy said, 'I know that a disc in a carrying case is a bulky object, and I've seen something of the tight security net here. But is it cast-iron?'

'No disc could possibly be removed,' Spencer said.

'Come on,' Conroy said. 'No security system's infallible. There's always the chance of human error.'

'None of the Military Defence Computers use discs,' Spencer said. 'They use laser beams scanning a bank of molecular memory units.'

'I've read about that,' Conroy said, taken aback. 'I thought it was just a theoretical possibility. Something for the future.'

'The future is here,' Spencer said. He waved at the far wall with its rows of screens and dials, the altar in this technological cathedral.

'That means you've managed to construct something approaching the human brain,' Conroy said quietly.

'Approaching in the mechanical sense, perhaps,' Spencer said. 'We're working on the very fringes of our present knowledge. As yet, while it can deal in concepts, it cannot deal in ideas. Later on, that too may be possible. Although not in my lifetime, I fancy.'

'If you develop a computer which can deal in ideas,' Conroy said, 'you also have one which can accept them—or reject them. That is, the possibility of a disloyal computer.' For a wild fraction of a second, he wondered if the creature below had already reached that stage, alien and unsympathetic. He shook it off. The computer itself as a traitor? He could not cope with that conception.

'An interesting speculation,' Spencer said calmly. 'We shall just have to learn to brainwash them, as we do our own citizens, shan't we?'

Conroy was silent, going over what he had learned. He wondered if it had wrecked his already shaky theory or not. Something struck him.

'You used the plural,' he said. 'You said "computers".' He broke off, already half guessing the answer. He had assumed that MDC/2 meant Military Defence Computer Mark 2. It did not. It meant number two. There were several of them.

'Each NATO country has its own Military Defence

191

Computer,' Spencer said. 'They are all connected by an extensive multi-link network, so that even in the event of a considerable proportion of the landlines being broken—by sabotage or enemy action for example—the system as a whole will still function.'

'The logistics of a complex alliance like NATO make such a system imperative,' Goss said.

'But that means,' Conroy said slowly, 'that this computer could be "robbed" from another country! It could have been done from terminals all over Europe.'

'You're committing the classic error in logic,' Spencer said. 'You're taking a hypothesis as a conclusion, and reasoning from that. I have to say yet again, what you are suggesting *cannot* be done.'

'Prove to me that it hasn't already been done,' Conroy said sharply.

'I don't have to,' Spencer said, with the weariness of a teacher confronted by an exceptionally thick and obstinate pupil. 'How many more times do the security safeguards have to be explained to you?'

'They're wonderful,' Conroy said. 'Terrific. I can't imagine how they could be circumvented. They're a credit to your genius. But there's just one flaw.' His smile was a bit lopsided, half apologetic. 'At least, I think there's a flaw.'

'I see,' Spencer said. 'You've read a few books on the subject, half digested some technical magazines, and that equips you to walk in out of the blue, and spot something which eluded not only me, but every single member of the team working under my direction.'

'Put that way, it sounds pretty ludicrous,' Conroy admitted. 'But nothing Mellish said, and nothing you've said, has covered the point I have in mind.'

'I suppose it's this inspiration of yours which has made you so remarkably persistent,' Spencer said ironically.

'It's kept me going,' Conroy said.

'Reveal it to me,' Spencer said. 'I'm always willing to learn.'

'Suppose someone had managed to extract highly secret information, using any one of the terminals, it doesn't matter which,' Conroy said. 'Never mind how for the moment, either. Just suppose, for the sake of argument.'

'Well?' Spencer's half-closed eyelids did not hide the ironic amusement in his eyes.

'How would you know it had been done?' Conroy asked. 'How could you tell?'

'Any request for secure information is logged by the computer,' Spencer said. 'I understand that you have seen this demonstrated for yourself.'

'So you can check back and find out . . .'

'The computer would have informed us of any unauthorized request at once,' Spencer said. 'It automatically compares each retrieval with the duty officer's log, which is also fed in, of course. The aim of the entire design is to be self-checking. That is why the software is impeccable.'

'I'm afraid not, Doctor Spencer,' Conroy said. He took a crumpled sheet of paper from his pocket. 'Without the right passwords, I tried to get the computer to recall a particular meeting . . .'

'Mellish told me,' Spencer interrupted impatiently.

'Later, it said I had made eight attempts. I did not,' Conroy said quietly but emphatically. 'I made *nine*. I noted each one.' He held up the piece of paper.

Spencer shifted position. His body was tense. It seemed like a very small thing, but Conroy knew enough to know that it was not. Even if he had not been certain, the rigid set of Spencer's jaw muscles would have told him.

Goss leaned forward, interested. His big head turned from Conroy to Spencer and back again, as if he were watching a tennis match.

'With all respect,' Spencer said at last, 'the first explanation which comes to mind is human error. You probably made one less attempt than you imagine.'

'Conroy tried nine times,' Karen said. 'I was watching him. I counted.'

'The evidence mounts,' Conroy said, 'that your software is not quite impeccable after all.'

'Good God,' Spencer said, his voice rising, 'if you only knew . . .' He stopped and breathed in deeply. The man was rattled and on the defensive, Conroy thought. 'Years of work,' Spencer resumed, 'went into eliminating every conceivable bug. The problems were horrendous. Fifty or more terminals might be trying to access the same information at the same time. A power surge might create unpredictable conditions which could lead to secure information being thrown up when it shouldn't be. So we use an internal generator on a controlled voltage. As an extra safeguard the computer will identify a power surge, just in case. I spent sleepless nights eliminating one bug after another, being obliged to predict years ahead, with the object of minimizing every possibility . . .'

'So now it's "minimizing" not eliminating,' Conroy said.

'. . . and now you,' Spencer swept on angrily, 'you wave a bit of paper in my face, and on the strength of that you . . . can you tell me what you keyed in on each occasion?'

'No,' Conroy said. 'Some of them were at random. The fact remains, your computer missed one of them. Can you explain how that might have happened?'

'How the devil can I?' Spencer demanded. 'It's remotely possible that by pure chance you struck on a combination which would instruct the computer to recall your enquiries minus one. It's also possible that . . .'

'Let's stick to your first remote possibility,' Conroy said. 'If I can do that unwittingly, someone else could do it wittingly. That would effectively blow your security system.'

'Rubbish!' Spencer snapped. 'By accident, you may have created one minor malfunction, although you can't tell me how. We can't even be positive that it occurred at all. There's no proof. We only have your word.'

He was defending his baby like an animal guarding its precious cub, Conroy thought.

'Supported by Karen,' he reminded Spencer mildly.

'I don't wish to be rude, Miss Dewar,' Spencer said, 'but in support of a close colleague, people often see what they want to see.'

'Doctor Spencer,' Goss intervened heavily, 'there's no reason why you should know this, but for various reasons Miss Dewar would be unlikely to support Mr Conroy unless she was absolutely certain. She's a skilled observer. I'm afraid we must attach considerable weight to their combined evidence. At the very least, the fact that they agree enhances the possibility that they could be correct. Even a possibility raises very serious implications.'

'There only has to be one bug that you haven't ironed out,' Conroy said. 'If someone else could find that . . .'

'Suppose they could?' Spencer demanded. 'Remember the scale of this computer. It prints out literally miles of information every day, the vast majority of it purely routine and of no interest to anybody. Pay, equipment, requisitions, subcontractors' accounts, transfer payments to and from other government departments, that kind of thing. The dull but essential minutiae entailed in keeping our armed forces in the field. Ninety-nine per cent of it isn't even classified information, much less sensitive. If there were chance

access to data on one of the terminals due to some
undiscovered bug, the odds are heavily against it being
secure information.'

'I'm not talking about chance,' Conroy said. 'I'm
talking about deliberate manipulation.'

'Oh, my God,' Spencer groaned, as if in despair,
'you've witnessed for yourself how difficult it is to
obtain access to information, which you blandly choose
to ignore when it suits you . . .'

'Bland nothing,' Conroy snapped. 'You're the one
who's ignoring what doesn't suit you. Even though I
don't know how I did it, I bypassed your security
system. That means secure information *could* have
been extracted without anyone's knowledge. That's
quite sufficient for my purposes.' Goss was nodding his
head like a toy gnome out of control.

'It's not sufficient at all,' Spencer said tartly. He
looked at Goss. 'There's a fallback logging system to
guard against precisely this eventuality. Has that been
checked?'

'Checked and double-checked,' Goss said. 'Nothing
out of the way in the UK. Clean as a whistle.'

'All right,' Conroy said, 'but it now seems that it
could have been done from Germany or Italy or
Belgium or any NATO country. Have they been
checked as well?'

'Not yet,' Goss said.

'That would make it infinitely harder, not easier,'
Spencer said. 'Transmissions between the various Military Defence Computers are scrambled, and the scram-
bling code is changed every hour. Information itself is
stored in coded form. Not only would it have to be
decoded but descrambled as well. I'm sorry, Conroy,
you've made one valid point, but the fact remains that
the system is foolproof. There is quite simply no
reasonable way in which it could have been circumvented.'

Conroy was half inclined to regard all this as a smokescreen which Spencer was putting up to protect himself. On the other hand, perhaps not. If the system was as perfect as Spencer was arguing, he would be incriminating, not protecting, himself. On one level, Conroy rather liked Spencer, but that level was not one which ever entered into his professional calculations. Conroy had sent men he rather liked to their deaths before now.

'Doctor Spencer,' Goss said, 'in my experience, there is always a way, and if it is not a reasonable one, then it is unreasonable. Bend your mind in that direction, if you please. Tell us how a man could bring it about, no matter how way out it seems to you. A man working from the outside. A man with as much knowledge as yourself, if you like.'

'Call it a piece of pure research,' Conroy suggested guilelessly.

'By heaven, it would take a lot of that,' Spencer said. 'Years, I should think.'

'For a prize like this, they'd gladly spend years,' Conroy said.

'A large team would be required, working continuously under skilful and imaginative direction,' Spencer said. 'How do you think anyone could conceal work in progress on a scale like that?'

'Just assume that one's been solved,' Conroy said. But he knew what a serious objection it was. Computer time and expert teams were expensive and at a premium. He could not imagine how such a group could work 'for years' on the problem without someone wondering what they were up to. Except Spencer himself perhaps . . . he might be able to cover it up under the guise of his 'pure research'. But then why the hell should he go to all that trouble when he already possessed personal access by means of his own private 'keyhole'?

Spencer laughed.

'A large assumption,' he said. 'On a mundane level, one or more computer operators would have to be part of your espionage ring. Otherwise, the final extraction of information would be impossible.'

Conroy wondered how many computer operators were manning MDC terminals throughout NATO. Given the shift system, there must be hundreds. The idea of vetting that lot for one rotten apple was daunting.

'Why pick on computer operators?' he asked, trying to reduce the area of possibility. 'What's wrong with a bent duty officer slipping the right code-word to someone to use when an opportunity arises?'

'Not on,' Goss said firmly. 'No duty officer can ever predict the code-word. If you follow the chain back, the code-word's selected on a random basis by the computer itself.'

Conroy nodded, accepting the point. He also noted that, as time went by, it became clear that Goss knew very much more about the workings of the security system than he had chosen to reveal in the first instance.

Spencer said, 'The security procedures are not dependent on fallible or potentially treacherous human beings. They're built into the computer. In effect, it's automatically self-checking. That's the concept of the whole design. As to how anyone, starting from scratch, could crack open the computer as if it were some kind of safe, this is where we enter cloud cuckoo land with a vengeance.' He paused and scratched his cheek reflectively.

'You go first, and we'll follow,' Conroy encouraged him.

'I'm trying to think how to put it in reasonably simple terms,' Spencer said. 'Let's pursue my comparison of the computer with a safe. Both contain valuable information. Someone wants that information. The safe has a complex combination lock, but no matter now many permutations to that lock, in the end, they're limited. Compared with this computer, the safe is a mere child's money box. Because, with the computer, the number of possible combinations is infinite.'

'More or less still with you so far,' Conroy said wryly.

'Good,' Spencer said. 'Hang on to the concept of infinity. The various passwords and operators' codes and so on which you've already seen in use are merely, of course, representations in letters and numbers of the code to which the computer will respond. But that code, which the computer generates itself, is infinitely variable. Imagine the problem confronting someone who's trying to crack open a code like that.'

'Perhaps he should hire the traditional monkey banging away at a typewriter at random,' Conroy said. 'If he does it for enough millions of years, isn't he supposed to come up with the collected works of Shakespeare?'

'Well, our man would have to improve on chance since he wouldn't have a few million years at his disposal,' Spencer said drily. 'There would be some factors which would marginally limit his area of search. Since we use passwords for the sake of convenience, the prevalence of vowels, for example. Also, groups of numbers are unlikely to be too lengthy, or the possibility of human error would be enhanced. He would probably—rightly—assume that the computer would be designed so that no password would ever be repeated. In theory, any code can be solved, given sophisticated facilities and enough time, but in practice . . .'

'Stick to theory for the moment,' Conroy told him. 'Just tell us how. What would be needed.'

'Two things would be essential.' Spencer sighed. 'First, constant access to the target computer. That is, this one, in your scenario, Mr Conroy.'

'Because he'd need to keep asking it questions,' Conroy guessed. 'Trying to build up at least the skeleton of the code by a process of elimination.'

'More or less,' Spencer said.

'Don't see how that's possible,' Goss said. 'All the terminals, both here and in Europe, are in restricted areas, manned by selected personnel, and under constant supervision. Anyone trying that sort of game would come under suspicion in twenty minutes flat.'

'I have consistently said that, in practice, it is not possible,' Spencer pointed out.

'You said two things would be essential,' Conroy said stubbornly. 'What's the other?'

'Your hypothetical man and his team,' Spencer said, 'would also require constant access to another computer. They would use this second computer to test and evaluate, accept or reject, gradually constructing the code, fleshing out the skeleton you spoke of. Given those two things, it would be theoretically possible. Constant access to the MDC, plus the facility of a second sophisticated computer of great capacity.'

'Well, at least you've finally agreed that it could be done,' Conroy said. It sounded somewhat feeble.

'Doesn't sound very likely to me,' Goss grunted.

'I suppose that leaves me as your prime suspect,' Spencer remarked.

'Good lord, no, sir,' Goss said. 'Forget anything Conroy may have said. He indulges in hyperbole. You have my personal assurance that not a trace of suspicion is attached to you. It was always an outlandish idea, this business of robbing the computer. We're most obliged to you for giving us so much of your time.'

The ambulance was parked, waiting in a bay in the place that looked like an underground garage. They returned their small transmitters. Karen climbed into the ambulance. Goss laid his hand on Conroy's arm, and drew him aside.

'I'll let you have everything we've got on Spencer,' he said quietly. 'It runs to bloody volumes, but you can read it in bed, if you're not too busy doing something else. Or perhaps I should say, someone else.'

Conroy stared at him, trying to see beyond the unpleasant leer.

'I thought you trusted Spencer,' he said. 'I thought you'd written the whole thing off.'

'Any sensible man would,' Goss said. 'It's self-evidently pure cobblers, from start to finish. But it's the only game in town just now, so we may as well stick with it. "We" means you and your bedmate. I'm going to take a chance, and give you the carte blanche you asked for before,' he said generously.

'Such magnanimity,' Conroy said. 'Greeks bearing gifts make my skin prickle.'

'Try the one about the gift horse,' Goss advised him. 'As of now, you're restored to full freedom of action. Collect your operational equipment first thing in the morning.'

'Everything? Including weapons?'

'Standard issue,' Goss assured him. 'So if you've bought a shooter from a friendly villain in some scruffy pub, you've wasted your money.'

Conroy grinned.

'I've got an appointment with a mate of mine to-night,' he said.

'Cancel it,' Goss said. 'Anything you need, come to me. It'll be cheaper.'

'A bent computer operator somewhere'll be the first thing,' Conroy said. It would not be quite the first thing, but there was no need to tell Goss about that.

Goss nodded.

'I'll have all security clearances vetted double quick,'

he said. 'Any with anything remotely dodgy, from too much hire purchase to married lovers, you'll get their names.'

'Passport,' Conroy said. 'The offending party could be somewhere in Europe.'

'Got it here. Karen's too,' Goss said. He handed them over. 'And you may as well take this.'

Conroy took the small plastic case. Inside was a card bearing Goss's signature, Conroy's name, a series of numerals, and nothing else.

'What is it?' he asked.

'You'll find it'll open doors,' Goss said. 'In case I'm not around to do it for you.'

The ambulance rumbled along on its three-and-a-half-hour journey from wherever they were back to London. Conroy and Karen sat side by side and spoke in low voices. It was unlikely that such a noisy vehicle was bugged, but Conroy preferred not to chance it.

'If I know Goss,' Karen said, 'he's only turning us loose to see what we do next.'

'Leave Goss to me,' Conroy said. 'You take George Spencer. He's ready and ripe for someone like you.'

'I see,' Karen said. 'You've decided on him. You don't buy the other possibility, the team with their own computer and access to the MDC.'

'If I'm shopping for a tool to do a particular job,' Conroy said, 'and I'm offered two, one of which is complicated and the other is simple, I try the simple one first and see if it works. Spencer's the simple answer. Perhaps too simple. It's up to you to find that out.'

'I don't suppose I need ask how you expect me to do that,' Karen said.

Conroy said, 'Form a relationship with him.'

'Like Garnett, all over again.'

'Spencer's not queer,' Conroy said. 'It won't take so long.'

'Goss could be steering us into a dead end for his own purposes,' Karen said. 'Or are you happy about Goss now for some reason?'

'I'm never happy about Goss,' Conroy said. 'I intend to check his references.'

'Who with?'

'The one person in the world who should know,' Conroy said.

NINE

The air was warm, the sky blue, and reflections of the bright sunshine glinted in shifting patterns from the placid waters of the River Hamble.

The masts of moored yachts rose tall like forest trees. The river was busy with elegant boats, white sails tended by sweatered, sun-tanned crews, some heading downstream towards the Solent or more distant destinations, some returning to their berths. It was a peaceful, idyllic scene, a civilization quietly at leisure. The idea of war, of destruction, of mushroom clouds, of death or subjugation seemed so remote as to be inconceivable.

The tiny village strung along the curving river bank was still a shrine to the religion of yachting. The yacht brokers were still in business, the marinas were still crowded with craft of all kinds, the pubs were still full of yachting types, the yacht clubs still offered comfort and service in varying degrees of exclusivity, venues where like-minded men and women talked about their beloved recreation in a language of their own, mysteriously incomprehensible to outsiders.

Motor cruisers were slowly coming to be regarded as being as anti-social as cigarettes. Throttle levers were out; tall sails were in. The wind would still blow across the estuaries and bays and seas when all the oil had finally gone. There was still fuel to be had for power boats—at a price—but nowadays, only those who were both rich and insensitive thundered across the Channel on the plane, driven by twin engines at thirty knots. Even in a post-industrial expansionist society of living standards in creeping decline, there were still those rich enough to burn oil, no matter how high the price was pitched, on personal pleasure alone. Nevertheless, in the face of growing if erratic disapproval, an increasing number never took their gin palaces outside the marinas, or abandoned them in favour of the complexities of close hauling, tacking, and reefing.

Government policy, as had been the case since the first oil crisis set a complacent world back on its heels, was still, even now, a mixture of muddle, confusion, *ad hoc* improvisation, and blind hope that something would turn up.

Oil-fired power stations were being eliminated completely in favour of coal or nuclear power. None of the next generation of ships, which would probably still be sailing the oceans when the last reserves of oil were being painfully doled out, would be driven by oil, but rather by nuclear reactors, or coal-fired engines which burned their own smoke. No one knew what to do about aircraft. Travel in the modern world hinged upon the jet plane, and airlines continued to receive priority oil supplies, while fingers were hopefully crossed that someone would manage to work out—before it was too late—how to use hydrogen in place of oil to power jet engines, without creating enormous lethal flying bombs in the process.

Industry was being chivvied and encouraged to move from oil to electricity or back to coal, reserves of which were estimated in hundreds of years instead of the decade or two for oil. True, coal would run out eventually too, but future generations could be left to worry about that.

Intervention had long ceased to be a dirty word, and grants, ready-made plans, and assistance were thrust upon manufacturing firms in the drive to run down oil requirements.

Public transport had officially become the patriotic and cost-effective answer to personal mobility, its virtues only exceeded by those of walking. The usual fatuous advertising campaigns vastly irritated the man in the street, none more so than the poster extolling the health-giving merits of walking to work, the pub, and the football ground, displayed on boardings all over the country. It was discovered that the minister responsible not only used a ministerial chauffeur-driven limousine to travel from his home in Putney to Whitehall, but that the large garage alongside his detached house contained four cars, which were in constant use by various members of his family. His explanation that he studied official papers on his way to and from work, which he could hardly do while walking, and that his four cars had been up for sale for some time, was thought to be somewhat lame, if not dishonest. The prime minister was much annoyed, and the minister's political prospects were regarded as dim.

The once-despised railways became a 'good thing'. Line closures which had taken place on a large scale were seen as regrettable aberrations, and there was vague talk about reopening some of them. The rail unions pressed for parity with the miners, since they were such essential people all of a sudden. The miners curtly announced their own leap-frogging claim and balloted for strike action. The Pedestrians' Association morosely wondered what would happen if they struck against walking, and took to the buses and tubes, throwing the whole creaking system into chaos.

The private motorist, as ever loving his car next only to life itself, remained an obstinate pain in the neck. In theory, a combination of rationing and the price mechanism regulated the private use of petrol. In practice, prices could not be hoisted high enough to discourage use, as they had been with boat owners. Relatively few people owned power boats, whilst most families in the land owned a car. Boat owners could be written off as rich parasites needlessly burning fuel to no purpose; but every private motorist regarded every journey he undertook as essential and bitterly resented any restriction. The pragmatic solution was to allow motorists to queue for the diminishing official supplies, run out, or turn to the black market, which bloomed and flourished. A few priority groups, such as doctors, were created, issued with special cards, and assigned specific government filling stations.

Some of it was silly, some of it was useful. All of it came too late. The inevitable was round the corner, but since that corner had not been quite reached yet, the inevitable could be ignored. Science would find an answer. Or to put it another way, something would turn up. Meanwhile the oil left the ground, and some of it was used to build Rolls-Royces. The party might be on its last legs, but it was still in full swing.

Conroy was a few minutes early, and he strolled around for a while, enjoying the air and rather wishing that he had taken up yachting. It seemed like a nice way to pass the time. At three minutes to the hour, he turned back and walked to the yacht club.

Sir Lionel, wearing a white polo-necked sweater, was

sitting on the terrace, peacefully smoking a pipe. He saw Conroy coming and raised his arm in greeting. They shook hands warmly, and Conroy sat down beside him and listened as Sir Lionel chatted idly.

It was a long time since he had seen Sir Lionel, and he had forgotten that his former boss would have aged. The once flowing hair was now little more than a snow-white halo. There was a sagging paunch under that white sweater, and the face, as those of old men often do, had become round and placid, curiously innocent and babyish. Sir Lionel wiped his eyes frequently in the soft breeze; the skin on the back of his hands was loose, and the veins stood out blue.

The mental picture of Sir Lionel which he had retained from their last meeting was very different, and it was a shock. Sitting beside him was not the head of department he had known, but an old man. Conroy wondered if he had made a fruitless journey.

'Didn't think to ask you if you'd like to have lunch here,' Sir Lionel said. He pointed the stem of his pipe over his shoulder at the yacht club. 'They'll be serving now, so if you're hungry . . .'

'I'd rather not, sir, if you don't mind,' Conroy said.

'Suits me,' Sir Lionel said. 'Don't take lunch any more. One meal a day, now, that's me. Like a dog.' He laughed, clamped his pipe between his teeth, and sucked it back into life. He puffed out a cloud of smoke contentedly, and said, 'Well, young Richard, it's good to see you, but you've got something to talk to me about, I dare say.'

There were other people sitting on the terrace. A waiter came out bearing a tray of drinks.

'In private, sir, if you don't mind,' Conroy said.

'I'll show you my boat,' Sir Lionel said. He eased himself to his feet carefully. 'A bit of a dodgy hip,' he explained. 'A touch of arthritis, so I'm told. Damned nuisance, I can tell you.'

Karen studied the menu and told Spencer that she preferred red wine. He ordered a bottle of claret.

'It's quite a pleasant walk,' he had said. 'But we can take the car if you like, of course. They still keep sending me priority cards for some reason, so petrol's no problem.'

'Someone forgot to tell the computer that you've retired, I expect,' Karen had said. 'So it keeps printing out a new card for you every quarter. Computers never forget. That's why you receive a series of final demands, long after you've paid the bill.'

Spencer had laughed.

'Only obsolete models,' he had said. 'I suppose I ought to tell them, really. Feel a bit guilty about it sometimes, but my work is still important, at least to me, so I really do need my car . . .'

'Let's walk anyway,' Karen had said.

They had walked through Lower Slaughter, past the old water mill, and uphill across the fields to the hotel at Upper Slaughter where Spencer had booked a table.

The dining room was agreeably old-fashioned and comfortable, and Karen felt relaxed and at ease, as if this were a day off. It was not, of course. She had a target to achieve—a target who was sitting opposite her, tasting the wine, and indicating that it could be poured.

Like any good professional, Karen was well briefed. She had read Spencer's security file, which Goss had given to Conroy. She knew a lot about Spencer. She knew his date of birth, when he was married, what his wife's maiden name was. She knew that he had attended a Comprehensive school in Ealing, taken a first-class honours degree in electronic engineering at London

University, and then joined IBM, where he had worked in their research department at Hursley in Hampshire.

She knew the year in which he had taken his doctorate and the title of his thesis, 'The Use of Analogue Coding in Data Security.' She knew when he had been singled out and persuaded to join the Ministry of Defence, first on a consultancy, and later on a full-time basis.

She knew that he was a regular contributor to technical and scientific journals, and was the author of a standard work on computer systems.

She knew that, as his work inside the ministry became more secret, he had been positively vetted many times, and that there was not one single question mark against him. She also knew that that meant nothing. Garnett had been positively vetted many times too, with a similar clean bill of health on each occasion —until he was found out.

She knew a great deal about Doctor George Spencer, but there were some things which the bulky files had not told her. One was the way in which, when he was not on his guard, his eyes were those of a kindly man. He was much less wary now than he had been an hour before. Karen did not need telling that he liked her and was attracted to her. She could clinically assess the impact she made on any man and adjust the results to suit her own wishes—which usually meant the aims of the job in hand—as swiftly and efficiently as if she were turning a rheostat. Conroy was the exception which proved the rule. Conroy, unfortunately, was a match for her. She could lead him precisely as far as he wished to go in the first place, and no further.

On this occasion, she had dressed for the role and carefully chosen her make-up and hairstyle. Clothes, simple and elegant, with trim shoes which were still suitable for walking across fields. The latter was not the result of any clairvoyant powers. One of Spencer's listed hobbies was 'walking'. She wore no jewellery, except for a pair of plain gold earrings. She looked, she knew, the epitome of good taste, and extremely attractive in a quiet, ladylike kind of way. Her make-up was natural, and no one who did not know her well would ever imagine those delicately sculptured lips framing curt Anglo-Saxon words of the kind which Conroy had heard her use from time to time.

Spencer's dead wife had been educated at Roedean and Girton, had been born into an old county family, had a viscount for an uncle, money of her own, and before her marriage had worked in the kind of photo journalism for the kind of magazine which seemed to recruit a large percentage of its staff from the upper crust. Reading about her, and studying photographs of her, it seemed to Karen odds-on that she had been a 'lady' in the traditional sense.

Feeling that there might be something to be gained from carefully and delicately, taking care not to be too obvious, evoking certain pleasant nostalgic memories in Spencer's mind, Karen had composed herself accordingly. Judging by the way in which Spencer kept looking at her, unguardedly, even transparently, her combination of reason and instinct had been sound.

Karen smiled and nodded, kept the general conversation going, and thought that it would not take as long as she had anticipated. In her experience, a combination of passion and affection in bed usually hastened matters along wonderfully. With the exception of Conroy, where neither led anywhere. Karen smiled her ladylike smile at Spencer and revised her timetable.

Sir Lionel lovingly showed Conroy every inch of his boat, which was, Conroy learned, a forty-five-foot oceangoing ketch, teeming with sophisticated devices.

'I used to think I'd take her round the world single-handed,' Sir Lionel said, 'but this damned arthritis caught up with me. So, given fine weather, I just take her across the Channel now and then.'

Conroy made appropriate noises, and sneaked a look at his watch. The old boy had been rambling on about his boat for an hour. It seemed longer.

'Time for a Scotch,' Sir Lionel said decisively. They were in the saloon. 'Join me?'

'Thank you,' Conroy said. He watched as Sir Lionel took a bottle and two glasses from a locker. 'Perhaps I'd better put you in the picture.' It was high time he pinned the old man down.

'If it's about the department, don't want to know,' Sir Lionel said. 'Not my show any more.'

'You'll always be HOD as far as I'm concerned,' Conroy said.

'Kind of you,' Sir Lionel said, 'but I'm not.' He handed Conroy his glass. 'Good health.'

'And yours,' Conroy said. He toasted the old man sincerely. 'I only want to explain the background, sir,' he said gently. 'Officially, as former HOD you're still entitled to receive secret information, even though you are retired.'

'Only on request,' Sir Lionel said. 'I haven't requested it. Not going to. Retired means retired. What's the point in keeping up to date? Nothing I can do any more.'

'There is now,' Conroy said. 'I've got a rather difficult problem, and I need your help.'

'Take it to your present HOD,' Sir Lionel said. 'That's what he's there for.'

'It's about him,' Conroy said.

Sir Lionel eased himself on to a settee which converted into a berth, and grimaced.

'The quack keeps trying different pills, but none of them help,' he said. 'I suppose it'll be the hip operation in the end, but I'm not looking forward to that. Not at my age.'

'I need to know about Goss,' Conroy persisted. 'What your opinion of him is.'

'My opinion? As HOD? Done the job I expected him to do, I should hope. He got it on my say-so, after all.'

'Yours?' Conroy was surprised. 'I thought it was a personal appointment by the PM.'

'So it is,' Sir Lionel said. 'In theory. In practice, prime ministers always accept the recommendation of the outgoing HOD. Each head of department nominates his successor. In effect, appoints him. Always has. Always will, I expect. I thought Goss was the right man at the right time. Does that resolve your problem?'

'Hardly,' Conroy said wryly. 'My problem is, that I don't know if Goss can be trusted. If he's loyal to his country.'

'Oh, dear,' Sir Lionel said. He blinked unhappily. 'Pass my tobacco pouch, will you?' Conroy silently obliged. 'Give me a minute or two,' Sir Lionel said. Carefully, he filled his pipe and got it going. He seemed to be collecting himself, willing himself to concentrate, reluctantly calling upon reserves which he had gladly abandoned. 'I take it you have good reason?' he asked at last.

'If you won't listen to the background,' Conroy said, 'you'll have to take my word for that.'

'Your word's good enough for me, Richard,' Sir Lionel said. 'Yes. Well, in the circumstances, you're within your rights to call for my help, and I'm obliged to provide it as best I can. But should things go badly, turn nasty, keep me out of it if at all possible, will you? As a personal favour.'

'Of course, sir,' Conroy said. He felt guilty for disturbing the old chap's repose in this way.

'Not that I wish to avoid my responsibilities,' Sir Lionel said. 'If absolutely necessary, I'll accept them, of course, but . . .' He broke off, and puffed away absently. A full minute went by. 'Head of the department's a terrible job, you know,' Sir Lionel resumed quietly, at last. 'No one knows what it's like until they've done it. The knowledge that, to a considerable degree, you're ultimately responsible for the fate of your own country.' He turned his head and stared at Conroy. 'I've aged dreadfully since you last saw me, haven't I? Turned into an old man prematurely, long before I should have done.'

'Of course not, sir,' Conroy lied, his heart aching for the sad figure for whom he felt so much affection. 'You look fine.'

Sir Lionel shook his head.

'Kindly meant, I know, Richard,' he said. 'But I'm the one inside myself. I've watched myself crumble. What happens, you use up all your energy, all your stamina; never enough sleep, never enough rest; eating, drinking, doing the job night and day, year after year, and when it stops . . . nature presents the bill. You pay the price.' He gestured with his pipe. 'Mind you, I should be thankful. I'm the only head of department who's ever lived to retire, do you know that? The rest have died in harness; illness, accident . . . at least, it couldn't be proved that it wasn't an accident . . . one only lasted eighteen months . . . it's not a job any man should have to do . . . and yet someone has to do it . . . I've forgotten what I was saying,' he ended vaguely.

'I haven't,' Conroy said. 'You won't be troubled after today, I promise you. In fact, perhaps I should go now. I shouldn't impose on you like this . . .'

'No, no,' Sir Lionel said. 'My duty . . . an old-fashioned word these days, but it's in the bones, even old ones . . . I handed over to Goss gladly, but my duty . . . can't evade that . . . oh, damn and blast it!' he blazed suddenly. 'The thoughts are still there, as clear and precise as ever. Why won't the words come? Why do I start rambling?'

'You're making sense,' Conroy said. 'If you don't, I'll tell you.'

'Wish it sounded like sense to me,' Sir Lionel complained. 'Give me another drink, will you? And make it a stiff one. Didn't P.G. Wodehouse say that every Englishman was born two drinks below par? Perhaps I'm more than two, these days.'

Conroy refilled his old boss's glass, and topped up his own. Through a porthole he watched a graceful yacht heeling slightly in the gentle breeze as it sailed towards the Solent.

'How old are you?' Sir Lionel asked. His voice was stronger. A slight flush lessened the pallor of the parchment skin on his face. 'Thirty-eight?'

'Nearly thirty-nine.'

'Too young to understand.'

'I understand, sir,' Conroy said. After the Lubianka, he thought he did. He had never, even in the beginning, regarded what he was called upon to do by the department as a game. It was too ruthless, too dirty for that, and often shabby and shoddy too. He supposed that the fact that he was good at it, and never suffered from too much revulsion, said something, not necessarily much to his credit, about his make-up as a human being. But even so, the Lubianka bred understanding.

'Where do you want to start?'

'You recruited Goss. He was your man as much as I am. What did you think of him?'

'Never liked him,' Sir Lionel said. 'Couldn't stand the fellow, in fact. Disliked him intensely, from our first meeting until the moment when I thankfully said goodbye to him.'

'Yet you tell me you made him HOD,' Conroy said.

'Nothing to do with it,' Sir Lionel said. 'The man's a contradictory paradox. He's a lout and a bully. He's also immensely courageous. Both mentally and physically. The fiction that bullies always have a streak of cowardice somewhere is just that. A myth. The brave bully is a formidable animal, and that's Goss. Cares little for himself, and less for other people. He's foul-mouthed and well-read. He's a ruthless bastard, who'd have made a brilliant lawyer. But never a judge, except that Judge Jeffries might have been not unlike Goss. Although Goss has no secret illness that I know of. He's offensive, he's vulgar. He also has a subtle, complex, and delicately ingenious mind.'

'Goss? Now you do surprise me,' Conroy said. He recalled the half-formed possibility which he had rejected.

'Whatever your suspicions,' Sir Lionel said, 'don't underestimate your man. Should they be correct, that would be fatal indeed.'

'Could they possibly be correct? Could Goss be guilty of treason? Part of a conspiracy?'

'Yes,' Sir Lionel said flatly. 'He could.'

'In that case,' Conroy said carefully, 'weren't you taking something of a chance in nominating him as your successor? Or are you now using hindsight?'

'Only the self-satisfied or the bigoted never question themselves, or their beliefs, or their faiths,' Sir Lionel said. 'It may only be in their dark, private hours, but the man without doubt is a fool, without insight, or sensitivity or wit. Goss is no fool, he's sensitive in his own way, he has great insight, and although his wit is usually scatological, I suspect that's a mask he wears while he plays his part. We all play a part, we all wear masks. My country right or wrong is for dolts and sheep. There were occasions during my time as HOD when my country was so patently wrong, that I despaired.'

'But you never turned against your country,' Conroy said. 'You never worked for the other side.'

'The existence of doubt doesn't mean that you succumb,' Sir Lionel said. 'We know the names of some who have. There will always be more, about whom we don't know. Most don't succumb. Most subscribe to the doctrine of the lesser evil, or are subject to other constraints.'

'Is Goss subject to the kind of constraints you have in mind?'

'I don't know,' Sir Lionel said. 'Lord knows, background and education are no guide any more, we've learned that much. The feeling that England made me induces the final loyalty for many of us. Whether Goss is happy about what England made of him, I can't tell you. On the other hand, I don't believe he'd betray his country for personal gain, and I'm not sure that he's enough of an idealist to do so, which may sound like a play on words . . .'

'I know what you mean,' Conroy said.

'. . . but I could be wrong,' Sir Lionel finished.

'Did you ever gather what Goss's real opinion of me is?'

'In the personal sense, I'd say he doesn't like you at all,' Sir Lionel said. 'You're as tough and hard as he is, but there's a degree of compassion in your make-up which he would regard as a weakness. I wouldn't agree with that, I should add. I see it as a strength, but then Goss and I are very different animals. You have all his tenacity, plus something else, imagination or instinct, I'm not sure which, perhaps both, but in either event, a quality he's obliged to do without. The combination makes you a better man than he is in some ways, and Goss is acute enough to recognize that. He's also human enough to resent it, and I'm sure he wouldn't mind much if you took a tumble one of these days.'

'Suppose I were an obstacle?' Conroy asked.

'If you were an obstacle,' Sir Lionel said, 'he'd get rid of you with the greatest pleasure.'

'Or someone he could use?'

'Oh, yes, of course,' Sir Lionel said. 'But then Goss uses everybody. That's his talent. That plus his odious character combine to make him a good leader.'

'Hardly the conventional variety,' Conroy remarked.

'There's a lot of cant talked about leadership,' Sir Lionel said. 'The idea that the best leaders are those who inspire respect and affection, so the troops follow unswervingly out of love and loyalty and so on.'

'That was the way you led, sir,' Conroy said. 'That was how we all felt about you.'

'That was my style,' Sir Lionel said. 'Early training, the way I was brought up, and so forth. But do you imagine I didn't use it to manipulate you fellows and get exactly what I wanted?' He removed the pipe from his lips, and chuckled. 'Looking back, I'm ashamed of my own dishonesty. Even so, while it's one way, it's not the only way. Many of our greatest leaders have been sincerely hated as egotistic, vain, monomaniacs by those who were obliged to follow. Although hagiography and history usually combine to erase such uncomfortable and untidy defects in retrospect. But they were there at the time, and I speak from experience. I've served under some of those great men. I loathed the self-seeking bastards. But they got the job done, just the same.'

Conroy smiled wryly and said, 'I can't see Goss as a great man.'

'That may depend on whether he lives long enough,' Sir Lionel said. 'None of which helps you much with your suspicions, but then I don't suppose you expected a definitive answer.'

'No,' Conroy said. 'But you haven't told me that I must be wrong.'

'I haven't said that I think you're right either,' Sir Lionel said. His voice had grown fainter again.

Conroy stood up, realizing that the old man was exhausted.

'I'll get out of your way, sir,' he said.

'Good to see you,' Sir Lionel said. 'Come again one day.'

'I will,' Conroy promised.

'Remember one thing,' Sir Lionel said. 'Traitors are men who back the losing side. Benedict Arnold would have been a hero if America had lost the War of Independence. De Gaulle would have been a traitor if Germany had won the Second World War. Myself, I wonder . . . not if Goss is good at picking the side which is going to win . . . but if he cares much, in the end, about whether he's on the losing side or not. Whether the battle isn't everything, for that lout.'

Conroy nodded. When he left, Sir Lionel was leaning back, his eyes closed. Soon, he would be peacefully asleep on the settee.

After a long and leisurely lunch, Karen and Spencer strolled back across the fields. She had gently guided the conversation, apparently avoiding the real subject at issue, in fact sketching in details which brought Spencer into sharper focus.

She learned that, during his time with IBM, Spencer had travelled extensively, and taken part in many international conferences. He talked about those he admired and respected in his field, men and women of several nationalities, including Russians.

Karen had asked a question about one of them in Russian, and Spencer had haltingly replied also in Russian. She had expressed surprise. He had smiled modestly, almost bashfully.

'I have that kind of mind,' he had said. 'I can pick up the basics of a language very quickly. But where did you learn to speak Russian so fluently?'

After that, they talked about Karen Dewar, a subject which appeared to interest Spencer a good deal.

From Lower Slaughter, they took a footpath which

led them to the gentle valley where Spencer's house was tucked away. It was a one-time farmhouse, built of grey Cotswold stone, with mullioned windows, and a tiled roof.

Inside, there was an inglenook fireplace in the living room, which also had a beamed ceiling, but it was furnished without fuss or affection. It was a house in which any woman would feel at home, and it was easy to imagine Spencer and his wife in this slightly rambling place, with its unexpected nooks and crannies. Spencer offered tea, Karen accepted, and he went off to make it.

Karen looked into the adjoining room, which was evidently a library cum study in which Spencer worked. The desk was covered in papers, which in turn were covered with symbols which meant nothing to Karen.

She went back into the living room. There was only one photograph of Spencer's wife which she could see, and that was placed casually on a small eighteenth-century table, almost tucked away, not displayed prominently.

She heard Spencer coming but continued to look at the photograph as if she had not. She wanted to find out if he would say anything.

'That was taken the year before she died,' Spencer said. He put the tray of tea things down on a low table in front of a settee which faced the inglenook fireplace. 'We'll let it brew for a few minutes.'

'She was very beautiful,' Karen said.

'Yes, she was,' Spencer said. 'We didn't know when that was taken, it all happened very suddenly, but now I fancy one can see it, there in her face, the faintest warning.'

'Don't talk about it if you'd rather not,' Karen said.

'Usually, I prefer not to,' Spencer said. 'Even well-meaning people can be crass and intrusive, without wanting to be. But you're not like that.'

'Everybody loses somebody,' Karen said. 'Life and death, they're inextricable.'

'That doesn't stop one feeling sorry for oneself,' Spencer said.

'No, it doesn't,' Karen agreed.

'I took it for granted that I'd have her presence until the end of my days,' Spencer said. 'She was a lot younger than me. When I was told that she was going to die, I couldn't believe it. It was as though Fate had cheated, broken all the rules.'

'How much younger is a lot?'

'She was thirty-five when she died. A young woman. Well, that may not seem all that young to you, but . . . why are you smiling?'

'I think I'm rather older than you imagine,' Karen said. 'I'm nearly thirty-four.'

'Good lord! Are you really? I thought you were still in your twenties.' His surprise was genuine and transparent. 'In that case, why aren't you married?' He smiled, an oddly boyish, sheepish half grin which, Karen was learning, was a characteristic of his. 'I suppose that's a sexist question these days.'

'Definitely,' Karen said.

'Ah, well, my apologies,' Spencer said. 'It's none of my business anyway. Let's have our tea. Milk and sugar?'

'No sugar,' Karen said. She watched him as, concentrating on the task in hand, he poured two cups of tea. She said, 'There's a time for everything, the right occasion, including marriage. Mine came and went. Thank you.' She took her cup of tea.

Spencer said, 'Perhaps it wasn't the right time after all. That may be yet to come. And I doubt if there have been, or will be, any shortage of occasions.'

'You're endearingly gallant,' Karen said.

'I rather imagine you mean old-fashioned,' Spencer said, with his apologetic smile.

'Anyway, let's change the subject,' Karen suggested. 'Marriage doesn't figure much in my thoughts, I promise you. I can't remember the last time it even crossed my mind.'

'Presumably your work has something to do with that,' Spencer said, but casually, not probingly. Altogether too casually.

'I'm like most people,' Karen said lightly. 'My job and my private life are separate.' Which was about as untruthful a remark as she had ever made in a career of successful deception. 'I love this house,' she said more honestly. 'Do you come from this part of the world?' She knew perfectly well that he did not.

'No, but I've had a long-standing love affair with the Cotswolds,' Spencer said. 'My wife was born in the country. The first time we saw it, we both knew it was exactly what we wanted, and it never palled.' He paused, and his eyes grew distant. 'I never imagined that I'd ever live here without her, though.'

'And yet you choose to do so,' Karen said.

'People react differently,' Spencer said. 'Some need to get away, they fear reminders, and I can understand that. But I want to stay in the house where we spent all our married life. That way, I still feel close to her. That may sound morbid, or even maudlin . . .'

'It sounds as though you loved her very much, that's all,' Karen said.

'Why was Conroy interested in whether we'd thought about adoption or not?' Spencer asked abruptly.

'He wasn't,' Karen said. 'He was trying to goad you.'

'Why?' Spencer asked. 'Oh, I see. To gain my attention, I suppose.' He nodded gravely. 'My reaction may have seemed a little excessive . . .'

'Not to me,' Karen said.

'We both wanted a child,' Spencer said. 'Not immediately, we agreed that, but later. When the time came and nothing happened, we both had the usual tests, and anyway, they discovered it was her. They tried several things, but they didn't work. So then we had to face the fact that we couldn't. We decided to adopt. Went to an adoption society. Everything fine. There'd be no wait, of course, but still . . . she was so excited, so happy . . . then things began to move. Only the formalities left. One of the formalities was a full medical examination, for both of us. That was when they found that she had an inoperable cancer. She had a year. Or so. I took an early retirement, and we spent that year together. So that's why his question touched me on the raw. It may have been unintentional . . .'

'I doubt that very much indeed,' Karen said.

'If I may say so,' Spencer remarked, 'you don't sound very loyal to your colleague.'

'You may be confusing loyalty with liking,' Karen said.

Spencer nodded in acknowledgement. 'You must know Conroy pretty well,' he said.

'I first met him a long time ago,' Karen said. 'But I don't know him well. I don't think anyone knows Richard Conroy well. He doesn't reveal himself much.'

'Nor do I, as a rule,' Spencer said. 'Although I seem to be doing so to you, for some reason.'

'I regard that as a great compliment,' Karen said.

Spencer said, 'What does Conroy want?'

'He told you that,' Karen said.

'My head in particular? Or would any scapegoat do?'

'Conroy likes to create uncertainty,' Karen said. 'But Mr Goss is head of department, and he gave you his word that you weren't under suspicion.'

'I've had a few dealings with Mr Goss from time to time,' Spencer said. 'He treats me with a respect which I suspect is exaggerated.'

'It may not be,' Karen said. 'He believes you to be a

genius in your field. Even Goss respects genius. You should get him on the subject of Jane Austen one day.'

'Jane Austen? Really?' Spencer shook his head. 'Well, I find him an uncomfortable devil, and I think it would be a decidedly simple soul who took his word about anything. I may be a touch naïve, but I'm not that simple.'

'I don't think you're naïve either,' Karen said. 'You're wondering exactly what I'm doing here, aren't you?' She judged that now was the correct moment.

'I wonder why it's taken you so long to raise the subject,' Spencer said. 'Unless you wanted to get to know me a little first?'

'To some extent,' Karen said. 'But it was always going to take a day, including travelling. And it so happens that I find I've been enjoying myself as well.'

'Does the department allow such luxuries?' Spencer enquired quizzically.

'I decide how I enjoy myself,' Karen said.

'Just the same,' Spencer said, 'I've been conscious that the lady who is such pleasant company also works for the department, and must have a very different side to her. I've been waiting for that side to emerge.'

'For good or ill, you've seen the lady as she is,' Karen said, with the candour which had never failed to convince anyone, except Conroy, and did not fail now.

'Then I'm far from clear what your assignment is,' Spencer said. 'I assumed you were to question me, or make a report. Or even try and trap me in some way.'

Karen laughed gaily. 'What kind of trap did you have in mind?' she asked.

'I found Conroy much more believable than Goss,' Spencer said. But his tone was uncertain. Good. He wanted to be convinced.

'My brief,' Karen said, 'is simply to follow up the suggestion which both Conroy and Mr Goss put to you, and that's all. Nothing else. I say "that's all", but you must know how vitally important it is.'

'It's only important if Conroy is on the right track,' Spencer said. 'I don't believe he is, and I can't pretend otherwise, even if that does confirm his suspicions of me.'

'No one is suspicious of you,' Karen said. 'I know there's no reason why you should believe me, but it's the truth. I really don't know what more I can say.' Karen met and held his eyes. 'I give you my word,' she said quietly.

There was desire in those deep blue eyes of his. There was also relief.

'Very well,' Spencer said. 'Thank you.'

'But please,' Karen said, 'do as they ask. Imagine that you are on the other side, and that you want information from that computer . . . and how it might be done.'

Spencer nodded reluctantly.

'All right,' he said. 'I'll set my own work on one side. But you must give me some time.'

'Conroy may be mistaken, as you believe,' Karen said. 'But if he's right, there may be very little time left.'

'I'll do my best,' Spencer said.

'That's all we can ask for,' Karen said. 'And please regard me as your contact with the department. I'll give you my phone number, and do call me any time you like. I may as well warn you that if I don't hear from you, I shall call you. That's also my assignment. To keep in touch. Act as a kind of progress chaser. Worry and push . . . nag you continually, I suppose.'

Spencer smiled faintly.

'I shan't mind that too much,' he said.

'I've been admiring your stereophonic equipment,' Karen said.

'Do you like classical music?'

'I love it,' Karen said.

'How about the Resurrection Symphony?' Spencer got to his feet eagerly. 'Shall I put that on?'

'Please,' Karen said. 'It's my favourite.'

Spencer glanced at the photograph in the corner as he selected the records.

'It was hers too,' he said.

Karen returned his sad half-smile. She could not stand Mahler and thought his work altogether too sentimental and over-ornamented.

They listened to Mahler's Resurrection Symphony. Karen hinted that she would like to hear some Bach, and Spencer put on his First Brandenburg Concerto, which was a profound relief after Mahler.

For good measure, Spencer followed that with the Third Brandenburg Concerto. Time was passing nicely. Spencer seemed not to notice that, even when he absent-mindedly switched on a couple of table lamps.

They chatted at intervals, as if they had known each other for a long time, disagreeing about Tchaikovsky, but both approving of Shostakovitch. Eventually, having covertly tracked the hands of her watch past the point where it mattered, Karen sat up straight and reached for her handbag.

'I'd better make a move,' she said. 'Could you phone for a taxi to take me to Kingham, please?' She had chosen not to drive although, like Conroy, she had a priority card for petrol. With a car, short of a dense fog, there would be no excuse not to leave should the omens seem propitious, and even Karen could not conjure up a dense fog at will.

'I'll take you,' Spencer said at once. He looked at his own watch. 'But we'll never make it to Kingham in time for the last train.'

'Is it that late? I didn't notice . . .'

'I could drive you to Oxford,' Spencer offered. 'There'll be a train from there.'

'Oh, no, please. I don't want to put you to all that trouble. You must have a local taxi service . . .'

'It's no trouble,' Spencer said.

'No, really, it's my fault. I should have kept track of the time . . .'

'Look, I don't know if . . .' Spencer began. He broke off and started again. 'The thing is, I have to drive to London myself tomorrow morning. I can't go this evening, I'm expecting some documents first thing, special delivery. So unless there's some reason why you must be back in town tonight . . .'

'Well, no, not really . . .'

'Colleagues often stop over when they come to see me, so the guest room's always ready . . .'

'Well, it's very kind of you . . .' Karen said, inserting just the right trace of doubt, enough not to be too eager, but not sufficient to discourage him.

'I have a housekeeper who comes in every day,' Spencer said. 'She'll have left a cold meal . . . plenty for two . . . but not if you don't want to, of course.'

'If it's not putting you out too much,' Karen said. 'Thank you.'

'Splendid,' Spencer said. He smiled, struck a match, bent down, and lit the log fire which was laid in the inglenook fireplace.

They ate roast beef and salad in the kitchen, sitting at a sturdy pine table.

'I've tried to keep it much as it was,' Spencer said. 'I detest Ideal Home kitchens in old houses, and I refuse to replace good solid wood with plastic.'

'Someone I knew had much the same philosophy,' Karen said.

'Really? A person of good taste, I hope?'

'Only in preferring pine to Formica,' Karen said.

Afterwards, they sat in front of the log fire, sipped coffee and brandy, and talked until Karen delicately smothered a simulated yawn.

'It's getting late,' Spencer said promptly. 'I'll show you to your room.'

He led her up stairs which creaked comfortably, and along a passage.

'Mind the step,' Spencer said. He took her arm briefly. His fingers were surprisingly strong. He stopped and pointed. 'The bathroom's next door. You'll find a new toothbrush on the wash basin. As for night things, I didn't keep my wife's clothes . . . I didn't go that far . . . but if you'd like a pair of my pyjamas . . .'

Karen smiled up at the tall, lanky man.

'I think they might be rather on the large side for me,' she said. 'Don't worry. I'll be fine.'

'Well . . . good . . .' Spencer said. He opened the bedroom door and switched the light on. 'I think you'll be warm enough, and you'll find everything you need, but if not . . .' He pointed along the passage. '. . . mine's the room at the end.'

'I'm sure I shall have everything I want,' Karen said. She moved past him into the bedroom and put her handbag down on the dressing table. The room was furnished simply but very comfortably, and again it struck her how homely this house was, from top to bottom.

'Oh,' Spencer said. He crossed to the windows, drew the curtains, and turned to Karen. 'Well, I think that's it.'

'You've been very kind,' Karen said.

'It's a long time since I've had such a pleasant day,' Spencer said.

'I've enjoyed it too,' Karen said. 'Very much.'

'If I say you have a most uncommon beauty, that's a statement of the obvious rather than a compliment,'

Spencer said hesitantly. 'I'm sure you've not only been told often enough, but you're very well aware of it anyway. My wife was beautiful too . . . I could never really understand what she saw in me, although I was only too glad to accept it without question . . . but in a completely different way. You don't resemble her in the slightest. And yet there's something about you . . . I can't put my finger on it . . . something . . . a sort of repose . . . the way you hold yourself . . . your voice perhaps . . . I don't know . . . but something so familiar to me . . . you're quite different, and yet so like her . . . anyway, I'm not at ease with many people, but I've felt very much at ease in your company . . . I suppose I'm trying to explain why the last few hours . . . I've felt alive again . . . which is unexpected . . . and it's meant more to me than . . . God, what a long, rambling speech,' he ended sheepishly.

'It's a very nice speech,' Karen said. 'Thank you. I appreciate it. And I hope you know that it's been a good day for me too. But still . . .' She smiled at him. '. . . we're not saying goodbye, after all.'

After he had gone, she went into the bathroom and cleaned her teeth meticulously. Back in her bedroom, she undressed, sprayed a little perfume round her neck and shoulders, and slid into the large double bed between crisply laundered sheets.

She could hear Spencer moving about, and traced his progress to the bathroom. With her head on the soft pillows, she lay and waited.

Karen came awake the instant the door opened. She saw a plump woman wearing an apron.

'Doctor Spencer thought you might like breakfast in bed, Miss Dewar,' the housekeeper said.

'Thank you,' Karen said. She sat up and took the tray.

The housekeeper glanced at her breasts with something which might have been envy, or possibly surprised speculation, and drew the curtain.

Outside it was raining.

'Perhaps he's another bloody pouffter after all,' Conroy said. He looked at his watch. He was waiting for the telephone in his flat to ring, with the preliminary run-down on all computer operators at the various MDCs. 'Or else he's sharp, and he knew what you were up to.'

'He hadn't the faintest inkling,' Karen said decisively. 'And he's no more queer than you are. No. A great brain he may be . . .'

'With a more than even chance he's working for the other side,' Conroy said.

'That too,' Karen agreed. 'But otherwise, he's a living fossil, which you'd have thought was extinct long ago. You know what that is? A gentleman. And shy with it, as if that wasn't enough. That's what the poor mug is. At fifty-three years of age, he's a shy gent who sublimates his sex drive in his work. God, I never thought I'd live to see the day.'

Conroy thought about that. When it came to an assessment of men, there was absolutely no purpose whatever in questioning Karen's judgement. She was always one hundred per cent accurate.

'Well, what are you hanging about here for?' he demanded. 'Get back home.'

'I've been home,' Karen pointed out. 'He dropped me there.'

'For Christ's sake,' Conroy said irritably, 'from what you say, this is better than we could have hoped for. The idiot's either fallen for you already, really fallen for you, or he bloody soon will with a bit more encouragement. He's spending the day in London. Go home now. It's a hundred to one he'll call you.'

'He didn't say he would,' Karen said.

'He may be a slow burner,' Conroy said, 'but he'll get around to it before the day's out, and it's important that you're there, and available.'

'I sometimes wonder,' Karen said, 'why you're not sick every time you see yourself in the mirror.'

TEN

The telephone was ringing as she opened her front door. She ran inside and lifted the receiver.

'Hello,' she said.

'It's George Spencer,' Spencer's voice said. 'I've been trying to reach you for some time . . .'

'I've been out shopping,' said Karen.

They met at what Spencer had described as his pied-a-terre in Bayswater. It was no bed-sitter, suitable for the odd night in town. With two bedrooms, a good-sized living/dining room, and a balcony overlooking the garden square, it was the kind of flat which only people with money could afford in that area of London nowadays.

Spencer gave her a drink, repeated that he needed to see her urgently, and hoped that he had not disrupted any arrangements she might have made for the evening. He spoke jerkily, as though under some nervous tension.

'I didn't have any arrangements,' Karen said.

'Considering that I was a government servant most of my working life and retired on a reduced pension,' Spencer said, 'I suppose this place . . .' he waved at the well-proportioned room, with its high ceilings and period furniture, '. . . and a house much larger than I need in the Cotswolds, your people must be wondering . . . wondering where the money comes from, that is.'

'No,' Karen said evenly, feeling a trace of annoyance with the man. She had been almost certain that she had convinced him. Perhaps his apprehension had surfaced again after she had left him. Or perhaps . . . she wondered where Spencer had been that day. She knew that he was being kept under discreet surveillance. 'They know that this flat was your wife's, and that you inherited it from her.' She used the third person plural to distance herself from the sordid carryings-on of the anonymous 'they'. 'They also know that you bought your Cotswold home on a mortgage which your salary at that time would cover. You don't have to worry,' she said, smiling at him reassuringly. 'All the arithmetic adds up. In view of what's happened, you had to be checked out, but they're completely satisfied.'

Spencer said apologetically, 'I've never been the object of your people's attentions before. I'm probably getting paranoid about it. I began to imagine that I'd be watched all the time.'

'Oh, really,' Karen said amused. 'They wouldn't do that. It's simply not necessary. I gave you my word last night. I wouldn't have said that if it weren't true.'

Spencer said, with his engaging half-smile, 'Today, I found myself looking in my mirror as I was driving, taking roundabout routes, in case I was being followed.'

'All right,' Karen said. 'Were you being followed?'

'No,' Spencer admitted.

It was unlikely, given the highly expert nature of departmental surveillance, that anyone would detect their shadows. Even a high-class agent like Garnett had failed to do so. Karen wondered if Spencer's unease was that of an honest man bewildered by finding himself a temporary inhabitant of a world he had never seen at close quarters before. Or if Spencer was in an even higher class than Garnett.

'Is that why it was so urgent for you to see me?' Karen asked.

'No,' Spencer said. 'I had an idea today. In fact, while we were driving up to town this morning. I didn't mention it then. I wasn't sure if it could be done. Now I believe it can.'

'What is it?'

Spencer told her. Karen listened attentively. When he had finished, she said, 'I must speak to my duty officer at once. Have this logged straight away.'

'You can do it from here,' Spencer said. He indicated the telephone.

'Not on an open line,' Karen said. 'It's too important.'

'Yes, of course,' Spencer said. 'Although, I was rather hoping . . .'

'I'll be back,' Karen said.

She drove to DI3 headquarters in Victoria. She was surprised when she was intercepted and told to report to Goss forthwith and without delay. Her duty officer would have to wait. She went to Goss's office instead.

'A happy chance,' Goss said. 'Sit down. I've been after you but I was told you had Spencer breathing hotly down your neck. What brings you here? A sudden need for fatherly advice?'

'He's made a suggestion,' Karen said. 'One that my duty officer should know about.'

'Give it to me, and I'll pass it on,' Goss said. 'Especially if it's an immoral one.'

'It could be,' Karen said. 'I'm not sure. He believes he can set up something called a "trace" in the computer, which would monitor any future misuse.'

'I didn't think that was possible, with the molecular memory unit system,' Goss said. 'Otherwise, why wasn't it built in from the beginning?'

'The theory stems from research which Doctor Spencer has carried out since then,' Karen said. 'He's not certain it'll work in practice, it's never been tried, but he's discussed it with the engineer who worked on the original design, and they agree that it might be possible.'

Goss said, 'Will this "trace" tell us the source if there is any misuse?'

'If any unauthorized extraction of material takes place,' Karen said, 'Doctor Spencer is hoping that the "trace" will not only record that, but precisely identify where the leak is. But he's cautious about that, he can't guarantee it,' she added.

'Bloody good just the same,' Goss said. 'If he's on the level. That merchant could go on blinding us with science for as long as it suits him.'

'Possibly,' Karen said. 'I haven't had a chance to check today's reports yet.'

'They're here on my desk,' Goss said. 'After Spencer dropped you, he drove to the Ministry of Defence by a most peculiar route. There, he spent three hours with Wilfred Lewis, a senior computer engineer, who worked on the original construction and design. After that, he circled Hyde Park for some weird reason, and then went home.'

'I've had to tell him again that there is no question of his being under surveillance,' Karen said.

'He's still suspicious is he?' Goss said sombrely. 'I don't trust suspicious men.' He stared at Karen, his

eyes two flat pebbles behind his glasses. 'It's beginning
to look as if Spencer might be our man. Conroy
remembered seeing Spencer and Garnett in the same
section of the stand at Stamford Bridge. They didn't
appear to notice each other, but we've followed it up.
Spencer and Garnett knew each other. This didn't
come out during Garnett's interrogation, mainly because it wasn't something we were looking for. Also, of
course, Garnett may have concealed it, along with a
bloody sight more. Now, things could be beginning to
add up. Garnett was a scientific civil servant, remember. He had a first-class honours in physics. He was so
good, they offered him a research fellowship, but he
turned that down, plus some sweet offers from private
industry, and chose the civil service. Part of his responsibility was the scrutiny and funding of the kind of work
Spencer's team was doing. On the face of it, you
couldn't call it an association. They sat on the same
committee for a period, and at this distance in time, we
can't establish any more than that. If they met in
private, and if so where and how often, we've no idea.
But it looks as though Conroy's guess was dead on.
Except that Garnett was just the tool, passing on
information which Spencer could get any day he
pleased. If so, they've left Spencer behind to carry on
the good work. That would make him quite a lad, and
not easily fooled, even by you. You take my meaning, I
hope.'

'It hardly needs spelling out,' Karen said.

'You know what I want from you,' Goss said. 'Watch
yourself though, young woman. Be careful.'

Karen drove back to Bayswater. She had, or so it
seemed, been blandly exonerated, and in the fashion
she would have expected of Goss, in passing, without
comment, with no word of regret or apology for what
she had been forced to undergo at the Home. She had
sometimes thought about what she would like to do to

George, but George had merely been Goss's creature. Goss was the one. And, regrettably, she would never see Goss enduring the kind of suffering she would dearly like to witness.

'Sorry it took so long,' she said to Spencer, as she re-entered his flat. 'The duty officer thought it sounded important. He checked, and they'd like you to go ahead with the "trace" you suggested.'

"I'll phone Wilf Lewis now, and get things moving,' Spencer said. 'Oh . . . can I give you a drink first?'

'You make your phone call,' Karen said. 'I'll see to the drinks.'

She listened to Spencer's phone call while she filled the glasses. The evening lay before her and the night as well. There was no housekeeper here, and if she had not known before she talked to Goss, she knew now that she was not going anywhere else until morning.

While automatically memorizing what Spencer was saying, she also considered how to get him to talk about Garnett. She decided to tell him something of her involvement in the Garnett case. He might know all about that already, but his response could be illuminating, one way or another.

It was risky perhaps, but she could see no other course. And that was what Goss wanted.

It crossed her mind that Goss might also want to set her up.

Conroy had wandered along the Avenue Rogier, in Liege, Belgium, with the other Sunday strollers, and now joined the little group which was studying the National Monument to the Resistance.

Liege had, Conroy learned, been the centre for the Resistance movement against the Nazi Occupation in World War II, which was why the monument had been erected there on 8 May 1955.

There were two groups of statues, one of which

apparently symbolized the intellectual resistance, and the other the armed resistance. On the other side, carvings represented the underground press, and the Intelligence and sabotage services.

Conroy thought that nothing seemed to have changed very much, although he doubted if DI3 would ever be immortalized, symbolically or otherwise, by a group of graceful statues in Trafalgar Square.

He silently acknowledged the bravery of those men and women, who must have had little but faith to sustain them, and raised his camera, like some of the other visitors and tourists who were snapping the monument.

The telephoto lens which he first slipped on to his Pentax would hardly have provided a clear picture of the carvings at this range, but it was ideally suited to bring into sharp focus the woman who was glancing at her watch a few yards the other side of the monument.

Her name was Mademoiselle Colette Dubois. For nearly an hour, she had strolled about aimlessly like someone going nowhere in particular, except that she looked about her nervously from time to time. Now her gait was brisk and determined, and she did not look back. Conroy followed in the same direction, alert in case she decided to jump on a bus.

From behind, Mademoiselle Dubois possessed the slim, rounded figure of a young girl. In fact, she was forty-four, and her face, although pleasant, faithfully recorded her age.

She lived alone in a small apartment on the outskirts of Liege, from where a coach collected her every morning, and took her to her place of employment. Conroy supposed from this that the Belgian Military Defence Computer, MDC/1, which fed the hub of the entire NATO communications and command system in Brussels, was probably deep underground, somewhere in the lonelier stretches of the Ardennes. However, he was not concerned with the site of MDC/1. He was concerned with Mademoiselle Dubois.

She was a long-serving, senior computer operator, a faithful and reliable servant who, having enjoyed sterling' good health, had begun to suffer from minor illnesses from time to time, which necessitated a day or two off to recover. Also, she was rarely at home on her free Sundays, nor was it known where she went. It *was* known where she did not go. Her sole surviving relative was an aunt in Namur, who felt that she must have offended her niece in some way. Colette had been in the habit of taking her aunt out in her car for drives into the countryside. The pleasant trips which her aunt enjoyed so much had become much less frequent. Colette Dubois had explained that the shift system had changed, and that she was required to work more weekends than previously. It was true that her shifts had been reorganized, but not that her weekend working had been increased.

For such trifles could a woman in a sensitive job come under suspicion.

There had been question marks against three computer operators when Conroy had arrived, but the other two had been quickly cleared. The local people were inclined to dismiss the flimsy queries against Mademoiselle Dubois as well. She was a woman of a certain age . . . the aches and pains of which she complained to her doctor were typical . . . and as for the aunt, she was growing old and difficult . . . even a dutiful niece might well become weary of a trying old woman . . .

However, Colette Dubois was all that Conroy had left of his instinctive hunch, a leap of imagination which seemed to be petering out into nothing, and so he followed her to the station and boarded the same train for the sixty-five-minute trip to Brussels.

He took what heart he could from Colette Dubois's

use of the train. A well-maintained Renault was parked outside her apartment. It was an easy, fast drive to Brussels along the motorway. True, her confidential reports described her as the kind of earnest patriot who might well try and conserve fuel wherever possible. The Belgian system of fuel conservation was slightly different to that in Great Britain, but it amounted to much the same thing: graded rationing, exhortation, priority groups, and an unofficial black market.

Alternatively, Mademoiselle Dubois might feel that she would be more conspicuous, more easily checked up on, if she used her car for certain journeys which she did not wish anyone else to know about. It was little enough, but it sufficed to keep Conroy going, to ward off, at least for a few hours, the pessimism which was enveloping him.

Even so, even if Colette Dubois did prove to be a link in the chain, dealing with her would be rather like pushing his finger into a hole in the dyke, while achieving nothing to stem the rising flood waters.

For whether Conroy was right about the source or not, the flood was undoubtedly rising. The department briefings coming out of Germany told him that.

He wondered about the 'trace' which had been inserted into the British Military Defence Computer. If such a thing were technologically feasible, it should, at some point, establish beyond doubt, whether Conroy's theory could really account for the massive leakages of information which had taken place. But would the 'trace' be a real one, or would it be phoney? The trouble was that, since it was of Spencer's own devising, he could almost certainly manipulate it, should he so choose, to provide whatever result, or non-result, he liked.

There were good arguments for confining Spencer to the Home without more ado. There at least, he would do no further harm. But even if he *were* the spearhead of an amazingly successful KGB operation, he must have access to a large and highly sophisticated team as well. Of that team, which would be designed to operate if necessary without Spencer, not one single member had been identified. The former colleague of Spencer's whom he had consulted, Wilfred Lewis, had been rigorously vetted at once and reluctantly cleared.

Goss had decided to leave Spencer free, and see what happened. If, as seemed more and more likely, Spencer was the key figure, he would wonder what DI3 were up to, and worry about it. Worried men could make mistakes. There would naturally be some excellent excuse to deny him any further access to MDC/2, or any of its terminals, but whether by design, prudence, or chance, Spencer had made no attempt to use any of the terminals since Conroy had first met him. Meanwhile, he was, literally as well as figuratively, in the hands of Karen Dewar. He appeared to be spending much of his sleeping as well as his waking time with her. An agreeable perk for the man, Conroy thought, recalling his own experiences in that direction, even if likely to be a fairly short-lived one.

In the same coach were a couple of German businessmen, on their way to Brussels for a Monday morning meeting, and Conroy became interested in the gist of their conversation and joined in.

Anecdotal evidence, much of it inevitably second or third hand, had to be treated with reserve, but those staid, middle-aged Germans painted a gloomy picture. According to them, a near-total blackout had been imposed on the media. The ramshackle coalition, which had been stitched together between parties with little in common and very different aims, was proving even more shaky than had been feared. Riots were rending the social fabric apart. Civil order was breaking down. Both claimed that the police were no longer in control, that army units had been called in, and that the resultant heavy bloodshed had further fuelled the flames. One said that army depots as well as police stations were being attacked, and that something very like a full-scale urban guerilla war was going on; that the loyalty of the army itself was divided, and that at least one unit had mutinied.

It was true that most of this had been told him on good authority by someone who knew somebody else, but there was no mention of any violence against American or British bases, which, Conroy thought, could be significant.

The other German said, 'We used to be rather smug, I think. We took prosperity for granted. We took our stable social system for granted. The Germans, we thought, were an orderly people, and things like the Paris riots, and your war in Northern Ireland, happened to others, not us. We used to say that Great Britain was becoming ungovernable.'

'You don't think that some of the things you've heard might be exaggerated?' Conroy asked. They seemed to match only too well the information he had been receiving himself.

'I tell you frankly,' the German said quietly, leaning forward, 'Germany is very close to civil war. Not in the old sense, where there were two clearly defined sides. But these separate groups—if indeed they are separate —they all seem to be well armed. When you have bombings, street battles, people being killed, everyone afraid, no one knowing what to do, even if none of it makes sense, it is still civil war. And once that happens . . .' He broke off, clasped his hands, and stared at the countryside speeding by. 'Without order, a nation breaks down. The things we take for granted, transport, power, the distribution of food, water even, they stop working. Without order, it is hopeless. Something must be done.'

'No matter who it is who restores order for you?' Conroy asked.

The German leaned back in his seat and shook his head helplessly.

'Something must be done,' he repeated. 'Someone must restore order. Without that, we have lost everything.'

It was, Conroy thought, work which any private detective, even the portly-none-too-active-retired-copper variety, could have undertaken for a routine crust, without haste, while thinking about something else.

The far from opulent hotel off the Rue des Bouches, near the Grand Place, where Colette Dubois arrived first, and where she was soon joined by a tall, fair-haired, good-looking man, was par for the course for couples who wished to keep their meetings secret.

While they were inside, Conroy acquired, through the DI3 Brussels Controller, a self-drive car which he fancied he might need. Two hours later, Colette Dubois emerged from the hotel and walked away. Conroy let her go.

Ten minutes afterwards, the tall, fair man came out, walked to a car which was parked a hundred yards away, got in, and drove off.

At five-thirty PM, Conroy, somewhat bored by now, watched the tall, fair man arrive at a pleasant home in a Brussels suburb, where he lovingly embraced the two small boys who ran to greet him. After that, Conroy interrupted the Sunday rest of the local security people and made them do some overtime.

At eight o'clock that night, he telephoned Goss, who was still in his office, Sunday or no Sunday.

'Colette Dubois,' he said, 'is having it off with a dedicated EEC official in Brussels, who's so over-worked he goes to his office on Sunday, but needs a long lunch break in a discreet hotel. His name is Friedrich Hauser, a citizen of West Germany, married with two children. He's thirty-seven years old, highly paid, Nordic good looks, and with all respect to Mademoiselle Dubois, if he wanted a bit on the side, I'd have thought he could have done better.'

'Perhaps he fancies older women,' Goss said.

'Could be,' Conroy agreed. 'But he was born in East Germany. Crossed over to the West when he was twenty-two.'

'Here we go again,' Goss grumbled wearily. 'The number of times I've heard that refrain.'

'The old tunes still keep turning up in the charts,' Conroy said. 'Do you want me to lean on him, or just do some more digging?'

'Neither,' Goss said. 'You're needed. Pass him over to our Brussels people.'

'If you say so,' Conroy said, a little surprised. 'But he could be pretty important.'

'This way isn't going to work,' Goss said. 'It's like trying to lop tentacles off an octopus when you don't know which one is doing the damage.'

Conroy sighed. It was no use trying to keep track of what Goss was up to.

'Something very unpleasant's going on,' Goss continued. 'I have to be in Brussels tomorrow. I'm bringing Karen and Spencer with me. Make the arrangements and meet us at the airport.'

'Why bring Spencer?' Conroy asked.

'The man must have contacts,' Goss said, 'but I'm buggered if there's the slightest sign of them over here. Perhaps they'll show if we move him off his home ground. I think I'll have Karen chuck in a word out Mademoiselle as well. See if that bothers him.'

'Colette Dubois?' Spencer shook his head. 'I know some of the senior staff at MDC/1 of course, but . . .'

'Mr Goss thought you might remember her,' Karen said.

'If I saw her, perhaps,' Spencer said. 'But the name means nothing.'

As always, his honest, thoughtful eyes and face displayed complete integrity.

'She has a dubious contact,' Karen said. 'A man called Hauser of East German origin. She's trusted, has continual access to an MDC terminal. She could be the means they're using.'

'No, it's too simple,' Spencer said. 'One operator, using one terminal . . . she'd have her normal workload . . . she'd have to complete that, or she'd arouse suspicion at once . . . at best that would only leave her an hour or two a day, and even then she'd be working under supervision . . . it's not a feasible method.'

'I understood you to say that it was the only one possible,' Karen said.

'On reflection, I've changed my mind,' Spencer said. 'It simply does not stand up to closer examination. Even if by some means she'd been given the codes, and as you know, they're changed all the time, so God knows how that could be done, the information would comprise yards of printouts. Given the tight security and the random searches which personnel are subject to, how is she supposed to smuggle wads of paper out?'

'She could photograph the information as it comes up on the screen,' Karen said.

'That means taking a camera in,' Spencer said, 'and any one found with a camera is for the high jump. It means using that camera in an open area, in full view of many other people. Given the period over which information has been lost, it means getting away with all that for years on end. Karen, it's just not on. It may be a neat and easy answer, but it simply won't do.'

'All right,' Karen said. 'So what's the alternative?'

'I have to say that there isn't one,' Spencer said. 'I've done my best to act as devil's advocate, you know that. We've inserted a "trace" into MDC/2, with no result. I'm sorry, but the whole thing is a false trail leading into a blind alley. I've gone round and round in circles, and I always arrive back at the starting point. No one can steal information from these computers which they should not have. As I said at the very beginning, it's impossible.'

'Well, we'll be seeing Colette Dubois tomorrow,' Karen said. 'If you're there when she's questioned, perhaps something will come out of that.' She picked up her handbag. 'It'll mean an early start in the morning. I'd better go home and pack.'

'Oh,' Spencer said. 'Yes. All right.' Karen gave him a fond smile.

'I can't stay here all the time,' she said.

'I know,' Spencer said. 'It's just that when you're here, it seems . . . I don't know . . . natural, somehow. I get used to us.'

'See you in the morning,' Karen said. She kissed him lightly on the lips. 'Good night.'

She had been instructed to make certain that Spencer was left alone for a few hours, in case there were things which he wished to do.

Their flight had been called at Heathrow, when there was an announcement over the Tannoy. Would Doctor George Spencer kindly take an urgent telephone call.

'Well, well,' Goss said softly. He watched Spencer as he hurried away.

Karen fiddled with her boarding card, and suppressed a twinge of disappointment. After all these years in the department she should know better. Garnett had been, as a person, rather kind and pleasant, too. Jenkins was in his usual position, a few yards from Goss, constantly on the alert for any potential assassins, even in the unlikely venue of Terminal One.

'Should he, by some coincidence, have last-minute pressing business which detains him in the UK,' Goss murmured to Karen, 'you don't ask questions, and you come with me. Let's cut the apron strings. Give him his freedom. Under someone else's supervision of course. Someone he's never met.' A small, insignificant man was making enquiries at a desk not far from where Spencer was speaking into a telephone. 'I half thought this might happen,' Goss said.

Conroy was at Zaventem, the Brussels National Airport, to meet them.

'Breakfast,' Goss said. 'I need something to wake me up. Didn't get to bed last night.'

The lines which had always been there were cut deeper into his fleshy face, and his eyes were heavy. Conroy thought that Goss was beginning to look older than he really was. He was reminded of Sir Lionel.

They sat at a quiet corner table in the restaurant, drank black coffee, and ate croissants. Jenkins was at another table, with his back to the window and facing the doors.

'Where's Spencer?' Conroy asked.

'Last-minute phone call,' Goss said. 'Something to do with that "trace" of his. We were just boarding. He gabbled about how important it was, and he must verify it, but he'd catch a later plane. Anyone want that other croissant?' Conroy shook his head. Karen had eaten nothing anyway. She seemed withdrawn, and her face was set, as if she were trying to come to terms with bad news. Goss shoved the remaining croissant into his mouth and licked his fingers. 'We'll know the real reason by tonight,' he said.

'Spencer talked quite freely about Garnett,' Karen

said flatly, as though dictating a report. 'Said he found him a valuable member of the committee. Quiet, but a good grasp of details, capable of a surprising analysis of the subject. They dined together a few times, but apart from that, Spencer claims they never met, except on committee work. He found Garnett a very able man, and said he was astonished when he read about his trial in the newspapers.'

'How about Stamford Bridge?' Conroy asked. 'Did you manage to bring that up?'

Karen nodded.

'He seemed surprised to hear that Garnett used to go there regularly,' she said. 'Spencer said that he'd only been once in recent years, and that was to watch Chelsea play Southampton in a cup tie. Spencer said that he used to go and watch Southampton when he was with IBM at Hursley. He lived in Southampton at the time.'

'Yes, it was that game when I saw them both there,' Conroy said. But it meant nothing except that Spencer had a good memory, which hardly needed proving. All the pointers indicated Spencer now. It was not Goss. Nor Karen. He was rather glad that it was not Karen after all.

'It's of academic interest anyway, for the time being,' Goss said. 'Who, how, and why, they've all been left behind. Whether the assassination of Archduke Ferdinand was really one of the causes of the First World War may be of intense fascination to historians, but it didn't matter a sod to the poor bastards who got slaughtered on the Somme.'

'Is that where we're heading?' Conroy asked soberly. 'Towards World War Three? Is it that close?'

'We're balancing on the brink,' Goss said. He gulped the remains of his coffee. 'It's no scenario that anyone's ever fed into any computer. The politicians are running around in circles like headless chickens, and for once I don't blame them. It doesn't make sense. If the other side go through with it, it'll be an act of pure madness. But it's happening. That's why I'm due at the NATO Crisis Centre in Brussels this afternoon.'

A woman sat down at the adjoining table. Goss stood up.

'Let's go and talk to Colette,' he said.

Jenkins drove the Volvo towards the Brussels-Liege motorway. Karen sat beside him. Goss and Conroy were in the back.

'Two things,' Goss said. 'The first can't be confirmed. It's this. German Intelligence believe that one of the minority parties in their coalition so-called government intend to call for the assistance of their German brothers in restoring order. That is, forces of the German Democratic Republic.'

'They'd be crazy,' Conroy said disbelievingly. 'That'd be tantamount to inviting an invasion.'

'Germany's in chaos,' Goss said. 'What with violent marches by factions from all sides, people being killed right, left, and centre, strikes against the killings—as if strikes could achieve anything against men with guns—what amounts to pitched battles, the police and the army no longer at all sure where their loyalties lie, Germany's in the biggest mess any civilized country's ever been in, short of total war. There's panic buying, distribution's breaking down, queues at food shops, and the shutters going up because the shelves are bare. In some areas, people are going hungry. Breaking into warehouses. Being fired on by riot police who don't know if they're on their arses or their elbows any more. Everyone's blaming everyone else, and especially in Bonn. The government was always a rickety patchwork job, and they're not only squabbling, they're falling apart. It would be quite conceivable, if one minority party hung on while everyone else was resigning, for them to be theoretically the government of West Germany, if only for a few days. They'd only need twenty-four hours to formally, and at least with some tattered vestige of phoney legality, invite assistance from their neighbours, who happen also to be German, even if of a somewhat different political complexion up to now.'

'Yes, but just the same . . .' Conroy began impatiently.

'I know.' Goss waved his hand in the air. 'It's still crazy. Although they'd bloody soon have order restored with the East German army in control. And among various German characteristics, many of them splendid, is a profound love of order. On occasion, order at any price. The Weimar Republic was as democratic as you could wish. The Nazis were a small minority party in the Reichstag. But the Nazis gave them order, instead of the chaos caused by hyper-inflation and mass unemployment. So they bought the Nazis. That cost the world a five-and-a-half-year war and twenty or thirty million dead.'

'Are you seriously drawing a parallel between then and now?' Conroy asked. But even as he said it, he was uneasily aware that one existed.

'Human nature hasn't changed in a few decades,' Goss said. 'Teach a monkey a few tricks, it's still a bloody monkey. We're still the same animals we were thousands of years ago. We've learned some tricks, that's all. Just the same, I agree. The idea of West Germany "inviting" help, like the Hungarians, or the Czechs, or the Afghans, pure nonsense. Got to be. The ravings of a few demented demagogues at worst.'

'You also began by saying that it was unconfirmed,' Karen remarked.

As in other Western countries, reduced speed limits had been imposed to conserve fuel, and the Volvo seemed to be little more than coasting along the broad motorway. Traffic thinned considerably as they left the immediate vicinity of Brussels, but Jenkins vigilantly noted and assessed every vehicle ahead and behind. It was second nature.

'That brings us to the second thing,' Goss said, 'about which there's no doubt whatsoever. Our spy satellites show East German armoured divisions massing on the border. They've also surrounded Berlin. The road link's still open, but they could cut it any time they liked. Naturally, they've been asked in diplomatic language what the hell is going on. In equally diplomatic language, they've replied that troop movements inside their own country are their own business, and we can piss off. But the dispositions they're taking up mean that within hours they'll be poised to cross the frontier into West Germany in strength.'

'You say these are East German units,' Conroy said. 'What about the Russians?'

'That's the puzzling factor,' Goss said. 'The Russian armour's moving back.'

'You mean they're withdrawing? *Away* from the frontier?'

'That's right,' Goss said. 'Almost as if they're saying: "This is nothing to do with us. We're not responsible."'

'Bullshit,' Conroy said. 'They're Tweedledum and Tweedledee.'

'Of course,' Goss said. 'So it must suit their book to present it as a purely German affair, for the two halves, East and West, to settle between themselves.'

'But . . .' Conroy frowned, trying to make sense of the senseless and failing. 'Even if some rump in Bonn emerged, and asked the GDR to move in, no matter how they buttered it up with the Pan-German, we're-all-blood-brothers, time-for-reunification bit, they must know that NATO would react as soon as the first East German tank rolled across the frontier. Even if the

West German army *had* been neutralized from within, there are still forces from other NATO countries on the spot.'

'The Russian withdrawal may be intended as a signal to America that it isn't a matter for the superpowers,' Goss suggested, if dubiously. 'If the Americans could be persuaded to stay out of it in some way, that would leave us in a bloody dicky situation.'

'The Americans wouldn't fall for that,' Conroy said. 'At least, I hope they wouldn't. But with or without them, we could never allow a NATO country to be occupied by a Warsaw Pact power. Besides, we could beat the hell out of the East German army on its own.'

'Equally, the Russians would never allow that,' Goss said. 'And if it turned nuclear, their SS20s could wipe out Europe in half a day.'

'That cuts both ways,' Conroy said. 'Cruise may have been the cause of all the trouble, but we've still got a hell of a lot of them under our own control, even if the Americans did choose to stand aside. We've got nuclear missile submarines at sea . . . whichever way you look at it, for them to try and take over West Germany would be an act of lunacy. And I don't happen to believe they're lunatics.'

'I quite agree with you,' Goss said. 'They're not. If this is a try on, it doesn't stand a chance. Not on the face of it. That's what makes me think the bastards have got something else up their sleeves. Something we don't know about. At least, not yet we don't. But I've a feeling we bloody soon will. And I'd go banker we won't like it. This time, I think they're playing for keeps.'

Goss took off his glasses, rubbed his eyes tiredly, yawned noisily, and put them back on again. Conroy thought that his head of department looked rather like a fighter coming out for the thirteenth round of a fifteen-round contest, who did not know how he was going to last the next two rounds. Not for the first time, he wondered what went on in that large head, behind that fleshy ugly face. They were halfway to Liege, and had just passed exit number twenty-seven.

'If you could get out of your habit of talking in riddles,' Conroy said, 'we might know what the hell it is we're trying to find out.'

'Believe it or not,' Goss said, 'we have been trying. You, Karen, all of us.' His tombstone teeth showed, but it was more of a painful grimace than a grin. 'I've had this feeling for a long time. Ever since Garnett was convicted. Something didn't add up, but I didn't know what it was. It was there, I could almost grasp it, but no matter how hard I went after it, it always stayed just out of reach. Do you know what I mean?' Conroy nodded. 'Yes, of course you do,' Goss went on wryly. 'That's how you've been feeling ever since you were exchanged. Wondering if you were being told the real reason for your arse being kicked. Then you came up with that daft idea about the computer being robbed.'

'Blame Karen for that,' Conroy said. 'I'd never thought of it until she mentioned retrieving information, and something went click in my head.'

'Karen, you, I don't care who,' Goss said. 'It was still daft—and yet it wasn't. It was as though a fog had half lifted. I could see a bit further. Not far, but enough to change the perspective.'

'So you're now certain that's how they got the information about our nuclear subs, Cruise, and probably me and Harrington as well,' Conroy said.

'I'm never certain of anything until it's been proved,' Goss said. 'So far, it hasn't, although it's the best working hypothesis we've got. But how they knew all those things, that's water under the bridge. They do. Even if we close the stable door, the bloody horse has still bolted. OK, they've used that information to stir up trouble in Germany, and by God they've succeeded.

Now, it seems, they're on the brink of making another move. One that, on the face of it, could never succeed. That's what makes me wonder if there isn't something else they've managed to crack open.'

'What do you mean?' Conroy asked. 'Even more information?'

'I hardly know what I do mean,' Goss confessed. 'But there's another facet I've mentioned, to do with the fail-safe device against the accidental launching of nuclear missiles. Again, it's no more than a flickering glimmer, like a distant torch in a winding tunnel. It comes and goes, and you can't quite see just where it is, or what's there. I've chased this half-formed, half-baked idea with every expert we've got—except Doctor Spencer, of course. For obvious reasons. He may be our best brain in the field, but he's not the only one. I've said to them, suppose this, suppose that, suppose Spencer himself were a traitor, suppose he'd given the Russians this, that, and the other. They're unanimous. No way. Absolutely, flatly unequivocally, utterly impossible, no matter how much Spencer had passed on to the other side. To make matters worse, I can't even envisage the process I try to put to them. It's there, but I can't formulate it, I can't get hold of it. And I'm buggered before I start, because I was in the development all the way through, and I know we'd never have relied on it unless it was so perfect that in ten million functions, it could never fail to be subverted. I know all that as well as they do. On the other hand, that niggle, that worry, whatever it is, at the back of my head won't go away. Now, it seems, the Russians may be on the verge of taking a mad, crazy gamble. Well, they like a gamble, but only when the odds are heavily in their favour. And I keep thinking, if the incredible happened, if the Russians could manipulate *that* in some way . . . and even as I talk, I don't even know how or to what purpose . . . then perhaps it could make sense of this whole German thing. That would put the odds in their favour. And yet despite what we've seen, despite what Garnett achieved . . .'

Jenkins interrupted. Conroy had rarely heard him speak before, much less break in when Goss was talking.

'Sir,' Jenkins said. His voice was flat, even, emotionless. 'Some sort of pile-up behind. One vehicle coming up fast.'

Conroy twisted round and looked back. An articulated lorry blocked the motorway, just past the slip road. Two cars had already rammed it.

Between the lorry and the Volvo there was only a Mercedes pick-up truck, slab sides, nearly as good as an armoured car. Ignoring any speed limit, it was rapidly gaining on them. Conroy could see the tips of the gun muzzles pointing over the side.

Jenkins had floored the accelerator as soon as he spoke, but whatever the Volvo's other merits, its top gear acceleration was far from brilliant. It was no contest.

Flames flickered from those peeping gun muzzles as they opened fire. They were probably aiming at the petrol tank and body of the Volvo, but Jenkins had just begun to swerve, hoping to force the Mercedes to brake, and the bullets ripped into the engine and front tyres.

Conroy heard the grinding scream of the wheels' metal rims on concrete. Jenkins swung the steering wheel uselessly. The steering had gone.

The Volvo began to spin, and for a few seconds there was a crazy rotating kaleidoscope of sky, blurred road and grass, until it stopped with a bone-shaking shudder and the crunch of breaking metal, as the Volvo lurched over the hard shoulder and into a grass bank.

Conroy wrenched open the door, and crawled out of the crazily canting car. He was aware of the others, but he paid them no attention. He was firing at the Mercedes, which had stopped well past them, but was now backing up ominously. He heard the bullets from his automatic ricochet off the metal sides of the Mercedes. The bastards were professionals, coolly taking their time. The gunmen in the back were keeping their heads down, while the driver carefully positioned his vehicle so as to give them a clear field of fire when the moment came in a few seconds' time, while keeping the Mercedes angled, so as to shield himself.

Jenkins had kicked out the windscreen of the wrecked Volvo, and got out that way. Karen crawled through after him. Goss, like Conroy, was lying prone, gun in hand, using the edge of the hard shoulder as cover.

Jenkins was the only one with a sub-machine-gun, which he had wrenched from its clips inside the Volvo. He fired one quick burst before the gunmen opened up in earnest.

Jenkins fell, and his sub-machine-gun dropped to the ground. Conroy saw bullets stitch a swathe across Goss. Goss jerked up into a sitting position, and then fell and lay prone. He heard the sound of Karen's automatic, but compared with the machine guns their attackers were using, it was like a pop gun.

The Mercedes was manoeuvring again, backing slowly closer, like some deadly killing machine. Conroy cast a desperate look round. There was nowhere they could go. They would be cut down if they attempted to climb the grassy bank behind them. Karen was lying behind the rear of the Volvo, calmly aiming at the cab of the Mercedes. The window shattered, but the driver could not have been hit. After a moment's hesitation, the menacing vehicle resumed its inexorable backward progress. A few more feet and Conroy and Karen would be exposed and shot to pieces like clay pigeons.

'Get away from it!' Conroy yelled. 'Away!'

She grasped his intentions at once. While Conroy fired continuously, hoping to force the gunmen to keep their heads down, she ran, doubled up, towards him. Conroy put his last bullet into the petrol tank of the Volvo.

There was a sheet of flame and black smoke as the petrol tank exploded. The flame did not quite lick round the nearby Mercedes, as Conroy had hoped, but it threw them for a few seconds. They stopped firing, and there was a crash of gears as the driver hurriedly changed from reverse to first.

Conroy held his breath, leapt to his feet, and sprinted through the billowing smoke, past the Volvo, towards where he had last seen Jenkins.

He felt the blast of heat, covered his face with his arms, protecting himself as best he could from the flames, and then he was past the blazing car, and he could see again.

Jenkins was still alive, crawling unsteadily, trying to pick up the sub-machine-gun with his left hand. Conroy bundled him aside and grabbed the gun.

The Mercedes engine roared, and it began to accelerate away violently. Conroy had no time to wonder why. He loosed off a long burst as the change of angle exposed one of the gunmen, and saw his face turn into a blood-red pulp and his body collapse like a rag doll's.

Aiming high at the receding target, he tried to pick off the driver, but the range was too great. In a few moments, the Mercedes had gone.

Only then did Conroy identify the sound which had been buzzing in his ears for several seconds. It was the wailing siren of an approaching police car.

From first shot to last, slightly less than forty-five seconds had elapsed.

Jenkins, weaving like a drunken man, was stumbling

THE BRINK

towards where Karen was dragging Goss away from the
still-blazing car. Conroy ran to help her. Goss was dead
weight, his legs dragging limply on the ground.

His face had the pasty whiteness of old parchment.
Blood was trickling from his mouth like water from a
tap. Conroy helped Karen to prop him up against the
grass bank, and the flow of blood lessened.

Jenkins stood looking down at Goss's shattered
body. His face was contorted into a wild, manic expression.

'I let him down . . .' he moaned. '. . . to keep
him alive . . . that was my job . . . and I let him
down . . .'

The police car drew up, and its siren died. Karen ran
across and spoke to the driver.

There was a bubbling noise from Goss. His eyes were
open. He was staring at Conroy, as if making some
mute appeal. Conroy bent close to him. Goss's lips
moved. There were sibilants and consonants mixed up
with the awful, painful, gargling noise.

'. . . sss . . . satell . . . lite . . . you . . . you . . .
got . . . cah . . . cahd . . . go . . . mee . . . mee . . .
lting . . .'

'All right,' Conroy said. He nodded reassuringly.

There was a momentary expression of relief in Goss's
eyes, before his head fell back.

Karen was beside Conroy again.

'The ambulance won't be long,' she said. 'There was
one on its way to the accident. They're having it
diverted. It'll come straight here.' She looked down at
Goss. 'Is there any point? There are people hurt back
there.'

'He's still breathing, just about,' Conroy said. 'Christ
knows how. He's like a bloody colander.'

Karen nodded. Gently, she made Jenkins sit down.
She took off her head scarf, and began to improvise a
tourniquet for his arm.

258

'I'm all right,' Jenkins mumbled. 'See to him . . . Mr Goss . . .'

'Shut up and keep still, or you'll bleed to death,' Karen said.

Conroy could hear the ambulance coming. The Volvo was still blazing. Smoke drifted across the motorway. Jenkins' suit was drenched in his own blood. Goss was beyond first-aid. Absolution was probably all he needed now. Karen's dress was torn and dirt-stained. He himself, Conroy realized, was blackened by smoke, his hands burned and blistered. To the arriving ambulance crew, it would look like something out of Hieronymous Bosch.

'Well, now we know why Doctor George Spencer decided not to come along,' Conroy said.

ELEVEN

Goss had been rushed to the nearest military hospital, where Conroy gazed through a glass panel into the intensive care unit. Goss was in a coma and appeared to be wired up to everything in sight; less the remnants of a human being than a mere junction box, where machines met and performed their various functions. Without them, Goss himself would not function at all.

The doctor in charge said, 'His condition's critical and still deteriorating. If we can't stabilize it soon . . .'

'I need to talk to him,' Conroy interrupted. 'Can you bring him round for a few minutes?'

'It's a miracle he's still alive at all,' the doctor said. 'You can't expect any more.'

'I'm not concerned with whether he lives or dies,' Conroy said brutally. 'Only with what he might have to say, and if the effort kills him, that's too bad.'

The doctor stared at him with distaste. He turned away, as if Conroy was infectious.

'Listen,' Conroy said. He took the doctor's arm, detaining him, and winced involuntarily. Both of his hands were bandaged. The palms and backs were badly burned, and painful. 'You know who he is. He was due at a meeting at the NATO Crisis Centre this afternoon. He was trying to tell me something, and knowing Goss, it was no last-minute confession. I need to know what it was before that meeting takes place.'

'I know who he is, Mr Conroy,' the doctor said. 'But he's also my patient now. He cannot be brought round, as you put it, and that's final.'

'On ethical grounds?' Conroy enquired. 'Because if so, they don't apply, and he'd tell you the same if he could.'

The doctor said, 'Any attempt to restore consciousness at this stage, and he'd die at once, without being able to say a word. You'd hasten his death and achieve nothing. So as it happens, I don't face any conflict of conscience, thank God.'

'Your conscience is the last thing I'm interested in,' Conroy said. He released the doctor's arm, and walked away.

'And we haven't finished with you yet, Mr Conroy,' the doctor said, after him. 'Those burns are quite serious, and the dressings are only temporary.'

'They'll have to do,' Conroy said.

He joined Karen in the doctors' mess, where they drank coffee. Neither felt like food. Conroy had learned from the police that the driver of the articulated lorry, which was stolen, had been glimpsed running away, and a search was on for him. The Mercedes pick-up truck had been found abandoned. In the back were two dead men. Neither carried anything which could identify them.

261

'How's Jenkins?' Conroy asked.

'They're not making any promises,' Karen said, 'but they think they might be able to save his arm.'

Their luggage had gone up with the Volvo, but she had borrowed a sweater and a pair of slacks from someone and, apart from the strain on her face and in her eyes, looked more or less her usual self. She was the only one, Conroy reflected, who had emerged from the shooting unscathed.

Conroy could move his fingers, but holding the coffee cup was torment, and after a couple of sips he abandoned it with a grimace. Karen watched him as he put it down on the saucer with a clatter.

'I was lucky,' she said.

Conroy nodded, but he was no great believer in luck. Her own cool skill during that terrifying forty-five-second ambush had been at least a contributory factor, and possibly the major one.

They were sitting next to a large window. Outside was a pleasant vista of green lawns and, in the distance, quiet, peaceful countryside. Some nurses walked along a path, talking to each other and laughing.

'It's all coming apart, isn't it?' Karen said.

'Looks like it,' Conroy said. He glanced at his watch. He was surprised to find how little time had elapsed since he had met them at Zaventem.

'I don't know whether to be glad or sorry,' Karen said, 'now that we know about Spencer for certain. I'm beginning to think that anyone who does this job has to be the dregs. The absolute bottom layer. We're damn near certifiable, all of us. Wherever the stench is worst, we grub about in the dirt, and the only thing we can take pride in is how well we do it. Jesus!'

'Did you get involved with him?' Conroy asked. 'Is that it? Does it hurt that much?' He was surprised by her attitude.

'Oh, you're immune,' Karen said tightly. 'No guilts, no regrets, we all know that.'

'I do my best,' Conroy said. In his mind, he saw that tribunal again, sternly accusing him. He pushed them away.

'I couldn't do what I was supposed to do without becoming aware of George Spencer as a human being,' Karen said. 'Or at any rate, as he seemed to be. A sad, vulnerable man, in love with a dead woman. I had to get rid of her and make him think of me. So I set out to invoke reflections in the mirror of the past. And it was a good performance. In fact, it was brilliant, if I say so myself.'

Conroy said drily, 'We now know, after today, that he probably didn't fall for it.'

'Oh, yes he did,' Karen said. 'When a man's holding me, in the middle of the night, the things he whispers, I can tell whether he means them or not. I should be able to do by now.'

Conroy clenched his fingers unthinkingly and let out an exclamation.

'Sorry,' he said. 'Hands playing me up a bit.'

'They'll mend,' Karen said tartly. 'And if they don't, you can have plastic surgery. Your pain threshold seems to be getting lower though.'

'It is,' Conroy said.

'Mine too,' Karen said. 'Whatever decision Spencer had to take in the end, I know that I brought him to emotional life again. Not because he found me physically desirable, or he liked being with me, although he did, very much, both of those things. But because he came to believe that I cared about him. Really cared about him. I convinced him all right. And he was so grateful. So bloody grateful. The way his face softened when I walked into the room, and that private, shy half-smile . . . I can't tell you how corrupt and rotten it made me feel. Sometimes, after he'd gone to sleep with his arm round me, I'd lie awake, listening to him breathing. I could hear the steady slow beat of his heart. And I'd think, "I don't know which would be worse. Whether one day, if he's what he seems, to look at his face when he finds out that it's been all pretence, hypocrisy, what an evil cow I am . . . or whether this gentle, kind, loving man is really a . . ."' She broke off, turned her head, and stared out of the window. Her profile was as cold and lifeless as a death mask.

'Well, now you know,' Conroy said, 'and there's nothing for you to feel bad about. Christ almighty, the best you can say about him is that he might have felt a twinge of regret when, in effect, he signed your death warrant.'

'That's right,' Karen said, without looking at him. 'I'm just a whore who got screwed by a murdering, traitorous bastard. That's enough to make anyone feel good, isn't it? Really good.'

'Pimps are to blame, not whores,' Conroy said quietly. 'Let's face it, I did the pimping.'

Karen looked at him then.

She said, 'Yes, I've thought that from time to time, believe me.'

'I expect you have,' Conroy said. 'I should call London again. Make sure they've put Spencer where he won't do any more damage.'

'I'll wait here,' Karen said. Reaction had set in, and she felt numb and listless, lacking all feeling, even for a sense of time. A porter, wheeling a trolley for used crockery, took her cup away, and she hardly noticed.

Conroy came back, and sat down opposite her.

'Sorry I've been so long,' he said.

'Were you?' Karen lifted her head, willing herself back to the 'now', the man whose bandaged hands were resting on the table. There had been an odd note in his voice, she realized, and there was a strange expression on the masculine face which was usually so expert at betraying nothing.

'Did you arrange another car?' Conroy asked.

'While you were being treated,' Karen said. 'It's outside. Do you want me to drive?'

'Please,' Conroy said. 'I don't think I could manage it.' His voice was curiously remote. 'I spoke to the duty officer in London,' he said. 'Spencer was under surveillance all the time. He went back to London Airport, and his shadow called the duty officer. The duty officer used his discretion and told him to let Spencer go.'

'What?' Karen stared at him. 'Allowed him to catch a plane to Prague or Moscow? What made the fool do a thing like that?'

'The plane Spencer boarded was going to Brussels,' Conroy said.

'Brussels?' The rising pitch of her voice showed her astonishment. 'Are you positive?'

Conroy said, 'It was the same flight he said he'd catch.' He stood up. 'We can just about get there in time to meet him.'

Spencer came through the Arrivals gate with a flow of other passengers. He hesitated for a few seconds and then picked them out.

Conroy watched him as he approached. Spencer's face was set and worried, but it lightened for a few seconds as Karen gave him a smile of greeting. That smile, Conroy thought, would convince anybody.

'Hullo,' Spencer said.

'It's good to see you,' Karen said.

He put his arms round her and kissed her quickly, with a shyness which was strange in a man of his years. Karen hugged him in return and then released him.

'At one point, we thought you might not be coming,' Conroy said.

'I was afraid I might miss the flight myself, but

fortunately, it was a few minutes late taking off,' Spencer said. 'Where's Mr Goss? There's something he must know about at once.' He appeared to notice Conroy's appearance. 'What happened to your hands? And your suit—it's burned.'

'Goss has been shot,' Conroy said, ignoring lesser matters.

'Goss? . . . Oh, my God, no . . .' There was horror on that rather long, rather bony face.

Conroy briefly told him what happened, speaking in an undertone, while the crowds of passengers eddied round them.

Spencer grasped at the news that Goss was in hospital.

'Then he's not dead. Where is he? I must speak to him at once.'

'Join the club,' Conroy said. 'Technically, he may be alive, but only because life-support machines are doing his breathing for him, keeping his heart beating, the lot. He has multiple gunshot wounds, but he's too ill for them to operate. I wanted him brought out of the coma, even if it killed him, but it can't be done. He'll be lucky if those machines haven't been switched off by tonight.'

Spencer shook his head helplessly.

'Let's get away from this mob,' Conroy said.

They walked to the car, which was in a multi-storey car park. Conroy's eyes scanned the half-empty deck cautiously, but no one had followed them. They got into the car and closed the doors. Through the windscreen, over the parapet, planes could be seen taxiing, their engines a distant whine.

'Thank God you're all right at least,' Spencer said. Although his eyes only switched from Karen's face to Conroy's a second later.

'We thought it was down to you,' Conroy said. 'The ambush.'

'Me?' Spencer's eyes returned to Karen.

'Yes, I did too,' Karen said. There was no apology in her direct gaze. 'It seemed to follow.'

Spencer nodded. He clasped his hands and rubbed one thumb against the other.

'It probably was my doing,' he said at last. 'But not in the way you imagined.'

'In what way was it your doing, then?' Conroy asked sharply.

'I can't be certain,' Spencer said hesitantly. 'But I'm not sure they wanted Goss and you two. Not as primary targets, anyway. It's possible that they were after me.'

'You? Why?' Conroy demanded. 'Why should they want to kill you?'

'Well, you remember that I inserted a "trace" into the computer . . .'

'Of course,' Conroy said. 'What about it?'

'At Heathrow,' Spencer said, 'I received a disturbing phone call. That was why I couldn't travel with Karen and Mr Goss.'

'Yes, I've been told all about that,' Conroy said impatiently.

'I had to confirm it for myself,' Spencer said. 'I thought some kind of error must have been made. But there was no error. That "trace" had been negatived. Ceased to function.'

'Deliberately? It couldn't have happened by accident?'

'It was no accident,' Spencer said definitely. 'It was deliberate. Lewis was running frequent checks as a matter of routine. Simulating leaks to ensure that the "trace" was functioning, and identifying the source. Which it was. Perfectly. Until early this morning. Suddenly, it ceased to respond. Somewhere, some unknown third party was not only able to detect that the "trace" had been inserted into the system, but also to render it useless.'

There was a long, heavy silence. Conroy considered the implications. They were appalling. The fact that the 'trace' could be detected was bad enough. The only chance of tracking the source of the leakage of information had vanished. Even worse, the Russians obviously knew of DI3's efforts. The insertion of the 'trace' would have told them that, even if they had not been aware of it before. And their reaction had effectively blocked these efforts, with a casualness bordering on contempt. Conroy's neck prickled at the confidence *that* betrayed.

Spencer could be right. Perhaps he *had* been the target. With all the information now at 'their' disposal, they would know that Spencer was likely to be a key figure. His elimination was a logical step.

On the other hand, there was an even more simple explanation. Spencer could have negatived that 'trace' himself. But Lewis, who had carried out the practical work derived from Spencer's theoretical construction, was believed to be loyal. Could Spencer bluff such an able and experienced man? And even if he could, would he then catch the next plane to Brussels? He very well might, Conroy realized, if he had good reason to suppose that the only ones likely to suspect him were dead. And yet . . . Conroy saw again the expression on Spencer's face, when his eyes lighted on Karen at Zaventem. He would have staked his life that the look he gave her was genuine.

Spencer cleared his throat and spoke.

'I owe you an apology, Mr Conroy,' he said. 'If this could happen, then secret information could certainly have been obtained. You've been proved right. You were right all along.'

'Does the virtual cancellation of the "trace" help you to establish how it's been done?' Conroy asked.

'Not in any very helpful way,' Spencer said. 'It confirms that somehow a parallel computer system of great size, capacity, and flexibility, must be linked to our own, continually monitoring and decoding, twenty-four hours a day. How such a thing could possibly be achieved, I have no idea. But it's the only way.'

'So one bent computer operator on one terminal, like Colette Dubois . . . ?'

Spencer shook his head.

'She couldn't achieve what they're doing in a thousand years,' he stated. 'This requires the separate computer system I've mentioned, with teams of highly trained technicians and analysts, working on a three-shift system, seven days a week.'

'Good God, all that activity could never go undetected,' Conroy said, exasperated.

'Well, it has,' Spencer said. 'That's all I can tell you.'

'How? Short of subverting some organization like IBM wholesale?'

Spencer smiled faintly.

'In my experience of commercial computer companies, you can rule them out. Even if someone could disguise from the staff involved what they were doing, which sounds pretty incredible, or they'd been penetrated with sufficient agents with the necessary skills, which is even more incredible, the workload entailed would completely destroy their profit base, and that's why they're in business. No management team could possibly remain ignorant of what was going on.'

'We're all agreed now that it has been done,' Conroy said, disgruntled. 'But just the same, it's still impossible. And yet, there has to be a way . . .'

'Time to go, if you want to get to that meeting,' Karen said.

Conroy started the engine, and backed out. They left the airport and drove towards Brussels.

'One thing I need from you before we get there,' Conroy said. 'Goss was trying to tell me something, and I think it was to do with the meeting, but he was gargling on his own blood at the time, so all he managed were some weird noises. But I think one word might have been "satellite". Does that mean anything to you?'

Spencer said nothing. Conroy shot an irritable glance at the tall, lanky man sitting beside him.

'There are such things as spy satellites, of course,' Spencer said evasively.

'If I'd thought he meant that, I wouldn't have needed to ask a computer genius,' Conroy said. 'Spy satellites are in the field of espionage, and I do know a little bit about that. Come on.'

'This is extremely difficult,' Spencer began uncertainly.

'There's nothing bloody difficult about it,' Conroy said savagely. 'You open your mouth, and you talk.'

'You don't know what you're asking,' Spencer said unhappily. 'It's something so secret that only a handful of people have the full picture. I'd need authority first . . .'

'Who from? Goss?'

'Mr Goss is one of the handful,' Spencer admitted. 'Were he able to speak, yes, but . . .'

'Were he able to speak, I wouldn't have to ask,' Conroy said curtly. 'But he can't, because he's got bullets in his guts and across his spine. Goss might as well be dead already, and that leaves me. I'm taking his place at that meeting, and I need to know at least some of what was in the bastard's head.'

'Well,' Spencer said, 'I suppose if you could show me that Mr Goss authorized you take his place . . .'

'I'm going because I happen to be here, that's all,' Conroy said. 'It starts in fifteen minutes.'

'I could phone London from NATO HQ,' Spencer said. 'There might not be too much of a delay . . .'

'I haven't got time to fart about while bloody bureaucrats in Whitehall decide whether I've got the authority or not,' Conroy told him.

Karen, sitting in the back, leaned forward and placed her hand on Spencer's shoulder.

'George,' she said, 'the meeting's at the NATO Crisis Centre. Goss told us what it will be about. Richard's right. There isn't time. Please.'

Spencer had turned his head and was looking at her.

She said, 'I give you my word. You must. Trust me, please.'

Spencer nodded.

'All right,' he said.

A set of traffic lights ahead had turned red, and Conroy braked to a stop. A line of pedestrians filed across.

'The policy of Launch on Warning requires a perfect fail-safe device,' Spencer said. 'Mr Goss maybe was referring to that. It's called UDS. Ultimate Defence Satellite. A satellite which is in a geostationary orbit. That is, it remains stationary relative to the earth.'

The traffic lights turned to green. Conroy avoided a pedestrian who suddenly rushed out, risking the here-after rather than wait two minutes to cross the road, and drove on.

'Launch on Warning means exactly what it says,' Spencer said. 'There are no consultations between heads of government. On receipt of a warning, missiles are armed at once and fired. Now, our warning system has been much improved in the last decade, but it is still remotely possible to receive a spurious warning. It doesn't take long to detect, but while you could recall manned aircraft, in the days when we depended on them, you can't recall missiles. They're on their way.'

Conroy made a right turn towards NATO Headquarters.

'On firing,' Spencer said, 'a signal is automatically

relayed to the Ultimate Defence Satellite. There are then various time lapses, which I needn't go into. Longer for Cruise missiles, shorter for rockets. But before that time elapses, the UDS must have received a further coded signal from the nuclear commander, a new post instituted when the system went into operation. These are very senior officers, highly trained, whose duty is to ensure that no mistake has occurred, and that the strike should proceed.'

'So, in effect,' Conroy said, 'although it's Launch on Warning, there is later a positive order from Command Headquarters, or the strike is aborted.'

'Precisely,' Spencer said. 'Unless the coded confirmation is received by UDS, it will automatically explode all nuclear devices which had been launched. In the case of rockets, at a safe height. In the case of Cruise, that can't be done since they're hugging the ground most of their flight. So the course of Cruise missiles is altered until they're over a large stretch of water, or the polar ice-cap, anyway, somewhere safe, when the warhead is detonated.'

'And that's all programmed into the Ultimate Defence Satellite?' Conroy asked.

'Yes. It was probably the most difficult job I've ever had to tackle,' Spencer said. 'Even more complex than the MDCs.'

Conroy thought all that over. They were nearing NATO Headquarters.

'The Russians will know about it by now,' he pointed out. 'They'd know we must have something like it before we dared to deploy Cruise and go over to Launch on Warning. If they can identify the position of this extra satellite, what's to stop them destroying it?'

'Nothing,' Spencer said. 'But that would be against their own interests. Why should they interfere with a device designed to prevent accidental war? Because that's largely what it is. The final protection against

erroneous orders, spurious warnings, or local commanders gone mad.'

'What happens if something goes wrong with this
satellite, and it just falls out of the sky?' Conroy asked.
'Satellites have been known to do that.'

'A duplicate, standby satellite would be launched at
once to take its place,' Spencer said. 'In so far as any
man-made system can ever be foolproof, this one is.'

'You said much the same about the chances of
someone robbing the Military Defence Computer,'
Conroy reminded him.

Spencer sighed, and rode that one. They were there.
Their identity papers were examined, and they were
allowed to pass into the car park. Conroy located an
empty space, drifted into it, and applied the hand-
brake. For a few moments, he made no move to get
out. Finally, he shook his head.

'I don't understand what Goss was on about,' he
said. 'The one piece of equipment we've got which
works in the Russians' favour. The last thing they'd
want to do is to muck about with that.'

'If they've deduced what it is,' Spencer said, 'they'll
be anxiously keeping it under observation all the time,
to make sure it's still there.'

'Goss must have been delirious,' Conroy said decisively. 'Bloody raving.'

He opened the car door, climbed out, and led the
way towards the lift.

Karen followed. She felt Spencer tentatively take her
arm. She briefly squeezed his hand against her waist,
but she did not look up at him.

Some unpleasant questions had intruded on her mind
once more. Spencer had been genuinely unwilling to
talk about the Ultimate Defence Satellite. And yet,
once persuaded, what he told them must already be
known to the other side, if not in detail, then in outline.

It could no longer be so secret as to be known to only 'a handful of people'. Why then, his reluctance? Either what he had told them had a significance, which he had chosen not to explain . . . or he had deliberately held something back. If so, why? 'Trust me,' Karen had said. But was there some reason why he did not? Even more pertinent, could Doctor George Spencer be trusted? The euphoria which Karen had briefly felt when she saw him walking towards her at Zaventem had evaporated.

Conroy held open the door of the lift while they stepped in beside him. The door closed, and he pressed a button. For a fraction of a second his eyes were fully on hers. Then he looked up at the indicator lights. His expression had not altered one iota, but Karen knew. Words were unnecessary. All those disagreeable questions were back in Conroy's mind too.

They were shown into an ante-room, where they waited. Conroy grew increasingly impatient. Finally, a British Army brigadier arrived. He was thoroughly polite, but contrived to be also offhand and dismissive. He knew all about the ambush. Mr Goss's incapacity was especially deplorable. His presence on the Crisis Committee would be much missed. Mr Conroy's offer to take his place was appreciated, of course, but must be declined with thanks. Mr Conroy had no standing, certainly not until instructions to that effect had been received. While they were in constant touch with Downing Street, who were dismayed by what had happened to Mr Goss, no such instructions had arrived. The brigadier implied, with strained courtesy, that compared with the content of the other messages which were flowing to and fro between Downing Street and the Crisis Centre, the standing of Mr Conroy was a matter which took a decidedly low priority. Conroy argued vigorously, but it was no use. The brigadier said that they really must excuse him, and turned towards the door.

'I tell you that Goss wanted me to be here,' Conroy said wearily. '"Meeting", that was one of the words I'm sure he was trying to say. "Meeting".'

'If that were indeed Mr Goss's wish,' the brigadier said aloofly, 'it cannot, unfortunately, be confirmed.'

'Wait,' Conroy said. 'Just a minute.' He had seen again Goss's tormented face, heard once more those awful, bubbling, choking noises. 'Cahd . . .' That had been one of them. Conroy was almost sure it was. 'Cahd . . .' He fished in his pocket and found the card which Goss had given to him not long ago. It seemed like half a lifetime. 'Here. Show this to your Big White Chief.'

The brigadier took the card, on which Goss had scrawled some symbols, and his own signature. The plastic case had half melted and one corner of the card was singed and crumpled.

'I really don't see,' the brigadier began, 'what purpose will be . . .'

'Just ask him to look at it, for Christ's sake,' Conroy snarled. 'You don't need permission from the PM for that, do you?'

The brigadier allowed his feelings of offence to show mutely. The door closed behind him.

'And they tell us the Soviet Union is crippled by bureaucracy,' Conroy said. 'I only hope they're right, and the Red Army's infested with people like him.'

Spencer smiled faintly.

'I doubt it,' Karen said.

The transformation of the brigadier was swifter than that of Jekyll and Hyde. When he came back, he was respectful, apologetic, almost obsequious.

'I really am most terribly sorry, sir,' he said to Conroy. 'If you would be so kind as to come with me, Lieutenant General Price will see you at once.'

The brigadier held the door open for him. Goss had said, Conroy remembered, that the card might open a few doors, if necessary.

'Glad to meet you Mr Conroy,' General Price said, shaking hands. 'Please sit down. My apologies for the delay.'

'My fault,' Conroy said. 'It looked like a meaningless scrawl. I didn't realize it was Open Sesame.'

'A private code of Mr Goss's,' General Price said. 'It means that, temporarily, you are to be accorded all the authority which he himself would have commanded. You will know how wide-ranging that is.' The mouth under the neat moustache smiled pleasantly.

'I'd better make the most of my chances,' Conroy said lightly. 'I didn't miss the word "temporarily". It won't last long.' Just the same, he felt daunted. He devoutly hoped that Goss was in one piece and able to function.

Apart from the moustache, General Price had the quiet, thoughtful demeanour of some enquiring intellectual, rather than a military man. He seemed quite content to sit where he was. Conroy looked pointedly at his watch.

'The start of the meeting has been delayed, which gives me time to bring you up to date,' General Price said. 'Before I do so, you are of course entitled to have anyone else present whose advice you feel might be helpful. I have no idea what connection Doctor Spencer might have with DI3, but if you would like him to be here—or any members of my staff . . . ?'

'First tell me,' Conroy said, 'about the nuclear commander, NATO forces.'

General Price displayed no surprise at the question and answered at once.

'The duty of nuclear commander,' he said, 'is one

which rotates among the NATO allies, with the exception of the Americans. The USA have taken the view that since they could be confronted with a decision on the use of nuclear weapons anywhere in the world—in defence of their homeland, or in the Far East, for example—they must retain the right of their president to take direct action. Even as members of NATO, they cannot appear to be subordinate to the decision of an allied commander.'

'Or, to put it another way,' Conroy said, 'they prefer not to commit themselves to all-out war in defence of Europe, on a NATO say-so. Circumstances might arise in which they may want to opt out.'

'Their policy certainly leaves them with that option open to them,' General Price agreed. 'To be fair, Europe has taken the same attitude in reverse, as sovereign nations, unwilling to give blanket approval to American use of nuclear weapons. Going back a long way, in Korea, for example.'

'So the nuclear commander can be British, Dutch, Italian—or German. Which wouldn't seem to be a terribly good idea, at the moment.'

'We would all share your unease on that score,' General Price said. 'However, at the moment, *I* happen to be nuclear commander. A duty which will remain with me until the present crisis is resolved. Or otherwise.'

'I'm relieved to hear it,' Conroy said. He had quickly formed a good opinion of this quiet, self-possessed man. 'As nuclear commander, what do you know about the Ultimate Defence Satellite?'

'That it exists,' General Price said. 'And that its function is to abort any nuclear strike unless, in my capacity of nuclear commander, I transmit the war code of the day, confirming that the launch should proceed.'

'What more do you know about it?' Conroy asked.

'Nothing,' General Price said. 'If there is anything else to know about the UDS, it is not something which falls within my area of responsibility.'

'I see,' Conroy said. 'Thank you. We'll talk alone, in that case, and I'll use my discretion about how much anyone else should know later.' Spencer, he thought, should be kept at a distance until one way or another, he discovered what the man had been holding back, and why.

'Very well,' General Price said. He leaned forward, speaking quickly and concisely. 'In the last forty-eight hours, events have moved with bewildering speed. I take it you know that the German Democratic Republic claims to have received a request from West Germany for assistance in restoring order.'

'Does that claim have any conceivable basis?'

'In the view of the NATO allies—none whatsoever,' General Price said.

'You phrased that rather delicately, if I may say so,' Conroy said.

'There's a good deal of confusion,' General Price said. 'Confusion breeds muddle. Any advanced country is highly vulnerable to disruption. We've watched it happen to West Germany in an incredibly short time. Communications have virtually broken down. There's disorder everywhere, born of fear. Large areas are in effect under martial law. Normal newsgathering is impossible. Intelligence reports are contradictory. No one really knows who's in control in Bonn. Probably nobody. Effective government has ceased. They're drifting, like a ship, with no one on the bridge, and the engine room empty, while the crew argue and plot below decks, deciding nothing. In those circumstances, whoever controls the radio room may appear to be in command. As far as we can tell, that's roughly what seems to have happened. The foreign minister was injured in what was allegedly a road accident. His deputy, in the crazy coalition they put together, a man of the hard Left, took over, and issued an appeal for help to the GDR. The chancellor tried to dismiss him, but the Left now say they possess the balance of power, and deny his authority. It's a shambles, and any claim to legality is spurious. All one can say is that it's about as much as the Russians needed to move into Hungary, Czechoslovakia, or Afghanistan.'

'Or the Americans into Vietnam, come to that,' Conroy said. 'But this is different. They must know that we'd never allow Warsaw Pact forces into West Germany. Or any other NATO country.'

'Technically,' General Price murmured, 'the German Democratic Republic are offering assistance in the form of police contingents.'

'And these so-called policemen would be riding in the tanks they're moving towards the frontier,' Conroy said. 'They can't seriously expect us to allow those tanks to roll across Germany. Have they gone mad?'

'I can't think of any other explanation,' General Price said. 'But that is the position.'

Conroy looked at his watch again. The time seemed to be racing by.

'When's this Crisis Meeting going to start?' he enquired fretfully. 'Why the holdup?'

'Our American friends are waiting for an up-to-date briefing from Washington,' General Price said. 'From where, as one would expect, the hot line to Moscow is in constant use.'

'With what result?'

General Price said, 'Moscow state that neither they nor their armed forces are involved. They choose to regard the matter as an internal difficulty for Germany itself to resolve. Without, they emphasize heavily, any outside intervention from either side.'

'That's rich, even by their high standards of hypocrisy,' Conroy said. 'They can't really imagine they can persuade the USA to remain aloof from this.'

'They appear to be trying hard, just the same,' General Price said. 'Significantly, perhaps, they insist on referring to Germany as though it were one nation. They make no reference to the division between East and West.'

Conroy shook his head, puzzled and exasperated.

'The Kremlin must have turned into a nuthouse,' he said. 'Even if they did some deal with the Americans, Britain and the rest would fight on their own. We can't allow the reunification of Germany on communist terms, which is what they seem to be aiming for.' The trouble was that, in Conroy's opinion, the Kremlin was not populated by nutcases, but by hard, calculating men, who carefully assessed the odds and knew exactly when to gamble and when to pass. 'What the hell are they really up to?' he enquired rhetorically.

'The virtual Finlandization of Germany, perhaps,' General Price said tentatively.

'Something they know they can't get, at the certain cost of a shooting war? It doesn't make any sense.'

'Well that seems to be their aim, judging from the offer they've made,' General Price said. 'Quite unacceptable, of course, and already rejected in private diplomatic exchanges.'

'Goss might have known what that offer was,' Conroy said. 'I don't.'

'It's surprisingly detailed,' General Price said. 'One gets the impression they've spent months drafting it, if not years. The main headings go like this. First, what they call the joint restoration of order in West Germany. This is to be followed by a loose confederation between the two halves of Germany, with the aim of reaching further political agreement. During this period, both Germanys will—as they put it—enjoy equal access to the trading privileges open to the other. It's designed, I suppose, to sound moderate and reasonable, but it still amounts to Warsaw Pact forces on the banks of the Rhine, from where they could command the whole of the rest of Europe any time they liked.'

'True,' Conroy said slowly, 'but there may be something else behind it.'

'You know what they're really after?' General Price asked.

'I think so,' Conroy said.

Equal access to trading privileges. That must refer to Comecon and the European Economic Community. Comecon had nothing to offer. The EEC had. Priority access, painfully negotiated three years before, to British North Sea Oil.

Russia, like other industrialized nations, was desperately short of oil. Her Siberian oil fields had proved to be a chimera. In the North Sea, as marginal fields were exploited while oil world-wide was drying up, reserves were predicted to last, given the most careful husbanding, close to two decades, and perhaps more.

Through her satrap, East Germany, Russia would siphon off North Sea oil, as she had taken Rumanian oil long before, as she took Polish coal, as she took Czechoslovakia's advanced engineering products.

It would give her a breathing space until—and if—practical energy alternatives could be perfected, heavily weight her advantage against the rest of the world. Oil, as vital to a country as the blood in a human body. Russia was after a transfusion which would maintain its strength through the next few crucial years. A transfusion which would also fatally weaken the donor, render it, at one stroke, dependent on the USSR and effectively bring the whole of Europe into the Russian sphere of influence, and eventual direct domination.

'What I don't know,' Conroy said, 'is what makes them think we'd ever fall for it. It's the one thing NATO'll defend, even more than German territory.'

One of the telephones on General Price's desk rang. He lifted the receiver, listened, spoke briefly, and hung up.

'Half an hour ago,' he said levelly, 'the East Germans closed the autobahn to Berlin. Their tank formations have completely surrounded the city. A couple of travellers who were turned back report seeing more tanks moving towards the frontier.'

'They daren't go through with it,' Conroy said. 'It's a bluff. It's got to be.'

General Price stood up.

'Tell the Crisis Meeting that,' he said. 'They're ready to begin.'

Conroy, Karen, and Spencer had been assigned rooms in the underground command centre, normally used by duty personnel. It was three hours later when Conroy tiredly found his way to Karen's door, knocked, and went in. Briefly, he summarized what had happened.

The meeting, attended by field commanders and political advisers, had been gruelling, and had examined all known facts in exhaustive detail. Finally, there were no dissentients. With the reservation that the Crisis Centre would be kept on full alert in case any new factors came to light, the NATO powers were of one mind.

'Unless there's something we don't know about yet,' Conroy said to Karen, 'it looks like Cuba all over again. In that case, the Russians have got it wrong. They're bluffing, and they'll back down.'

'Suppose they don't think they have got it wrong?' Karen asked.

"They've had a straight message,' Conroy said. 'No

diplomatic bullshit. The first plane to invade West German air space, the first tank to cross the frontier, the first armed man—and it'll be regarded as an invasion. An act of war.'

'So the shooting could start any time now,' Karen said soberly.

Conroy shook his head.

'Not that way,' he said. 'It's never worth it, and the Russians know that.'

'Not that way?' Karen queried. 'What do you mean by that? Is there another way?'

'I don't know,' Conroy said wearily. 'I'd have staked my life that the USSR wouldn't blunder into a position like this, where they only stand to lose face. I was certain they'd learned that lesson from Cuba.' He sighed. 'Too much has happened in one day,' he said. 'I don't know what to think any more.'

TWELVE

The unthinkable, the horrifying impossible, the incredible, took place at midnight precisely the following day. There had been no reply to the blunt NATO rejection. The answer came, but not in words.

The commander of a British nuclear submarine, lying on its sea bed station out in the Atlantic, sent a frantic radio signal. As the second hand registered the expiry of that day, one of the submarine's thermonuclear missiles had armed itself and fired itself. All 'on board' controls had been locked on 'safe', and remained so. Such a thing could not possibly happen. But it did. The missile was targeted on Moscow. Its warhead was capable of completely destroying that city and every human being within it.

Simultaneously, a tactical nuclear missile left its launch site near a village forty miles south of Hamburg. Its target, changed only hours before as the crisis developed, East German tank formations.

A Cruise missile deployed in East Anglia took off—destination Leningrad.

Within less than a minute, General Price had been roused from the cot which he would occupy during his period as duty nuclear commander, and was in the suite of war rooms which comprised the Crisis Centre. Conroy joined him there seconds later.

The scene was in stark contrast to the calm, if grim, atmosphere which had prevailed when Conroy had been there before.

This time, it was one of despair, incredulity, and disbelief, tipping over into panic and downright terror. Harassed radio operators received and passed contradictory messages. Keyboards connected to distant capitals chattered out, like machines gone mad, urgent requests for information. Telephones rang constantly, and high-ranking officers of several nations, some only half dressed, spoke in their own languages to prime ministers or defence ministers—themselves tired, frightened men, who demanded to know what had happened and why and what was to be done.

No one knew. There were contingency plans for everything but this. With no prepared ideas, with nothing to go on, senior officers and their aides moved aimlessly about, snatching up and reading pieces of paper, grabbing telephones, as if movement of some kind were imperative, as if even meaningless actions might bring order out of random chaos.

It was like some bizarre, military Tower of Babel.

The panic which had surfaced, briefly reducing men accustomed to discipline and the responsibility of decision-making to a state of shock, the instinct to run away reminiscent of any terrified stream of refugees, only lasted a couple of minutes at most. But Conroy thought that, in that short time, he had witnessed how a powerful alliance could come asunder as though the bonds which held it together were no stronger than tissue paper.

What all had grasped at once, both here in the Crisis Centre and in the respective capitals, was that, through some awful and inexplicable malfunction, NATO missiles had been launched against Russia itself. Already the Russians would be tracking the rocket aimed at Moscow on their radar screens. Cruise was designed to pass underneath Russian radar, but it was believed that they had been working on other methods of tracking those missiles by means of satellite observations.

Inevitably, the Soviet Union would retaliate against what must appear to be an unprovoked attack. It was the beginning of World War Three.

That much was immediately apparent as soon as the reports of the launchings which could not have taken place, but had, were incredulously confirmed. It was in the next sixty seconds, in the first frantic exchanges, that the alliance fell apart, as instinctive national self-interest took precedence.

The commander of the American forces in Europe, much depleted anyway in recent years and now little more than a token force, was speaking urgently to his president. The American attitude and intended course of action was immediately and understandably clear. The details of 'how' and 'why' were of no interest at this stage. This was a massive European bungle, and nothing to do with the USA. No American-controlled missiles had been fired. Moscow must be informed of this at once. Made to understand that America had played no part, and was not involved in any way.

Other leaders wanted messages sent disclaiming responsibility for this terrible accident, and begging the Russians not to respond in kind.

All this took place in the first chaotic couple of minutes before General Price regained control and imposed some semblance of order on the various national factions. His quiet, decisive authority eventually brought this about. There was nothing he could do about the Americans. They would no doubt be using their Washington-Moscow hot line even now. He flatly refused to send the kind of message for which others were clamouring, but relayed his own instead.

It was brief and to the point. Moscow was informed that there had been a technical malfunction, which would be urgently investigated. There was, however, no danger to Russia. The Allied fail-safe device would ensure that the missiles concerned never reached the Soviet Union.

Conroy watched as senior officers looked shamefaced and visibly pulled themselves together. The activity remained hectic, but ceased to be frenetic. Under the immediate stress of what had seemed to be the imminent obliteration of Europe by means of Russian retaliation, nearly everyone had forgotten, in those first crucial moments, about the Ultimate Defence Satellite, and its function.

Without the war code of the day, which of course General Price as nuclear commander had not transmitted, the various strikes should automatically be aborted.

Or at least, so they must hope. This was the test. The Russians might wait in the light of Price's message, watching the track of that thermonuclear missile as it rose on its parabolic course, but they would not wait long. As soon as the rocket reached its maximum height and began its downward descent for Moscow, the SS20s which constantly threatened Europe, and which would have been armed as soon as that rocket was detected—and that would have been before the receipt of General Price's message—that awesome array of rockets with their multitargeted warheads, would be fired.

The time left could be measured in seconds, rather

than minutes. The whole of Europe was that close to complete and utter destruction.

For one fear overtook another and gripped them all like a flesh-crushing vice.

If an inexplicable and unknown malfunction could cause the firing of deadly missiles, in some mysterious way bypassing and overriding the battery of careful, highly developed, technical precautions, believed until this minute to be as infallible as human ingenuity could devise, then might not the fail-safe device also be affected and fail to function? If so, every living thing in Europe was as good as dead already.

There had been no answer from Moscow to General Price's message, which was being repeated at thirty-second intervals. On separate radio links, anxious operators begged for an acknowledgement at least, confirmation that the message had been received. But none came.

The second hand of the clock on which Conroy's eyes were fixed began to tick away another minute. The radar screens remained blank. No cluster of electronic dots appeared which would signal the imminent end of Europe. Nothing. The second hand wound its agonizing way round the clock face, and entered into another minute. The radar screens remained dark and empty.

Conroy began to hope. He glanced at General Price. Price had taken an empty pipe from his pocket, and was absentmindedly sucking it, but otherwise he might have been waiting for a cricket match to begin.

Still there was no acknowledgement from Moscow. Yet still the radar screens showed nothing. The Russians too would be watching their own radar screens. Surely, by now, they would have retaliated. Unless the accidental strike had been successfully aborted.

'The fail-safe device *must* have worked,' Conroy said. He watched the clock as another minute receded into the past. 'If it hadn't, two Russian cities would be in ashes. They'd have hit back with everything they've got before now.'

'Let's hope you're right,' General Price said.

Karen was there, awoken from her light sleep by the sounds of activity.

'Where's Spencer?' Conroy asked.

'Sleeping through it,' Karen said. 'Do you want him called?'

'Not yet,' Conroy said.

It took forty-five minutes for all the information finally to filter through.

The tactical missile forty miles south of Hamburg had exploded almost immediately after launch, rupturing all telephone communications over a wide area. Miraculously, the explosion had taken place over open farmland, and there appeared to be no casualties. The report came by radio from an army unit, which was moving in and assuming control.

'I thought this Ultimate Defence Satellite was supposed to explode warheads in a safe place,' Conroy said edgily. 'Not far from Hamburg doesn't strike me as very bloody safe.'

General Price sighed and shook his head.

'It shouldn't have happened,' he said. 'But then, none of it should have happened.'

The Cruise missile from East Anglia had exploded over the North Sea. A gas rig caught in the shock wave was sinking. The gas wellhead was on fire. Numbed survivors spoke shakily of a gas explosion so powerful as to resemble an atomic blast. None of them were aware that it *had* been an atomic blast.

The thermonuclear missile from the British submarine had exploded in the stratosphere. To those awake and about in Lapland, Norway, and the Shetlands, it had given a new meaning to the term Northern Lights.

When the last report came in, when it became clear that all the strikes had been successfully aborted, the few moments of sheer relief in the Crisis Centre were almost palpable. There was even something resembling a hesitant cheer.

With little justification, as Conroy well knew. The worst had not actually happened, and that was all that could be said. What *had* happened was bad enough in all conscience.

Nuclear devices, supposedly incapable of being fired without the most stringent, well-drilled, frequently rehearsed procedures, had armed themselves and launched themselves, without the knowledge or intervention of those responsible. It was something which could not possibly happen. And yet, it had happened. For a few minutes, Europe had been on the brink of all-out nuclear war.

A devastating Russian response would have followed, had it not been for the final fail-safe device incorporated in the Ultimate Defence Satellite. But although the UDS had prevented those nuclear missiles from reaching their targets, its operation seemed to be haphazard, to put it mildly. Conroy thought that there were a number of urgent questions to be answered. He moved from one desk to another, collecting the information he wanted.

Nearby, a grim-faced, angry American five-star general was telling General Price precisely what he thought about NATO, its so-called precautions, its so-called procedures, its so-called Ultimate Defence Satellite, and offering strongly worded suggestions about what General Price and his European colleagues should do with the whole God-damned lot.

'If you people think this fucking so-called alliance is going to pitchfork us into war because of your fucking incompetence, you must be fucking . . .'

The bitter night-long inquest was well under way.

And still there had been no response from Moscow. Not so much as one word.

Spencer's fitful sleep ended abruptly. Conroy snapped the light on, ripped his bedclothes off, dragged him forcibly out of bed, and threw him across the room. Spencer ricocheted off a chest of drawers, hit the wardrobe, and fell to the floor with a cry of pain. His pyjamas torn, he shakily raised himself to his hands and knees and, dazed and bewildered, stared at Conroy's face, which was set in taut anger, not one fraction of which was simulated.

'Conroy . . . have you gone insane?'

'Let me tell you what's happened while you've been in the land of Nod,' Conroy snarled. He spoke fast. Spencer remained where he was, incongruously crouching in his torn pyjamas, subconsciously rubbing his bruised elbow, until Conroy had finished.

Then Spencer stood up, stumbled to the wash basin, and sluiced his face with cold water. He raised his eyes and gazed at Conroy. Water dripped on to his pyjama jacket.

'Those missiles couldn't possibly have armed and launched themselves,' he said.

'Well, they bloody did,' Conroy snapped. 'How?'

Spencer shook his head, groped for and found a towel, and dried his face.

'Try another one,' Conroy said. 'This one you should know. A thermonuclear warhead exploded in the stratosphere over the North Pole . . .'

'As programmed,' Spencer said. 'A giant firework display but perfectly safe.'

Conroy said, 'I haven't finished. Two to go. One ignited a gas field in the North Sea and sank a rig. The other is providing practice for fall-out precautions in Germany. Do you regard that as perfectly safe too?'

Complete disbelief was written all over Spencer's face.

'That can't be so,' he said. 'You must have it wrong.'

'For God's sake, man,' Conroy shouted. 'Take these.

Maps. Grid references. Exactly where both missiles went off. On-the-spot reports which have come in so far. Look for yourself, damn you.'

Spencer studied the documents in silence, frowning, his long face pale.

'Hurry up,' Conroy said savagely.

'I can't explain it,' Spencer said. He shook his head. 'There simply is no explanation.'

'Those missiles weren't under the control of your bloody satellite. Is that it?'

'Partly . . . the fact that they exploded . . . but the course they took, no . . . nor the points of explosion . . .'

'They could have wiped out London and Hamburg. Our own bloody missiles!'

Spencer's hands were shaking. Like a man sleepwalking, he slowly crossed to the bed, sat down, and bowed his head, gazing sightlessly at the papers in his trembling fingers.

'Look at me,' Conroy said. His voice was quiet, deadly, menacing.

Spencer lifted his head obediently. His blue eyes were dull and unblinking.

'There's one explanation,' Conroy said softly. 'You devised the programme. You either got it so wrong it's not true—or you fixed it to happen the way it did.'

'I swear to God . . .' Spencer began.

'Shut up,' Conroy told him brusquely. 'I need to know one thing before I finally make up my mind about you. You made a great song and dance about telling us anything about the Ultimate Defence Satellite. Bullshit about how secret it was. Yet what you did tell us must be known to the Russians already, in principle at least. That means you were holding something back, and that's what you're going to tell me. Now.'

'There's nothing I can . . .'

Spencer stopped speaking, and fell sideways. Conroy had hit him backhanded across the face.

'No more evasions,' Conroy said. 'No more holding anything back. All of it. There isn't the time to ask you nicely.'

Spencer pulled himself erect. One cheek was flaming red. He was afraid, that was obvious. Vicious, controlled violence was outside his experience. But there was a kind of defiant dignity about him, even though he spoke with difficulty.

'Some things are so secret . . . it's impossible . . . you of all people should know that . . .'

'Goss knew though, didn't he?' Conroy paused, but there was no denial. 'Well, now I'm standing in his shoes. I'm Goss, God help me.'

Conroy pulled up a chair and sat down close to the pale figure in the crumpled, torn pyjamas. His tone changed, became quiet, conciliatory, reasonable. In so far as such a feeling achieved tangible form, he mildly regretted the necessity to strike Spencer. For all his height and long limbs the man was as defenceless as a baby. Conroy could crush him as casually as stepping on a cockroach, or reduce him to a mere outward husk of a man screaming in agony. The psychological shock of the blow was necessary, in Conroy's judgement, but ultimately Spencer had to be persuaded. If he could not be persuaded, that would be proof enough. He would have ordered his own elimination.

'Missiles must be armed and keyed before they can be fired,' Conroy said. 'Yet tonight, three of ours took off, warheads activated, though no man had armed them. When your fail-safe device operated, two of them exploded where they shouldn't have done, but it could have been much worse. It could have been the end. Curtains. No one knows how these things could have happened, but by God we've got to know and soon. If our own nuclear missiles are no longer under our own control . . .' He broke off, staring. Something was happening to Spencer's face. Sweat was standing out on his forehead. His teeth clamped his lower lip as if in pain. 'We must find out,' Conroy went on. 'Tonight, we took a look over the brink into the abyss of death. It didn't quite happen. Not quite. Not this time. But if there's a next time, it very well could. It's too late to worry about secrets. You know something which none of us know. Perhaps it won't help. But it's no longer up to you to judge that.'

Spencer said in a strange voice, 'There is something.' He drew his forearm across his forehead, wiping away the sweat. Glistening droplets appeared again at once. His lips were dry. He licked them, and swallowed. 'The UDS has one additional function. An ultimate function. Hence its name, I suppose. When the system was constructed, every possible scenario had to be considered and incorporated, especially one which the policy of Launch on Warning would not cover.'

'And what scenario might that be?' Conroy demanded. But he had half-guessed already. The monstrous vision induced a feeling of nausea.

'That in which, despite a warning, our missiles could not be launched,' Spencer said, his voice shaky. 'For example, if the personnel manning those weapons had been incapacitated by means of a massive initial strike using nerve gas or neutron bombs, stocks of which the Soviets have been building up. That wouldn't take out our nuclear missile submarines, of course, but the Garnett affair made it clear that they had been manoeuvring to be in a position to do just that.'

At least that particular fence had been mended, Conroy thought. A sudden chasm of appalling doubt yawned open in his mind. Suppose the arrest of Garnett had not put an end to the flow of information eastwards? What if they still knew those submarines' sea bed positions, but had simply withdrawn their own hunter killer subs out of range of detection, but in a position to move swiftly in again and strike?

'Go on,' he said grimly.

'In such a contingency,' Spencer said, his voice hardly more than a whisper, 'if no one in the field were left alive to arm and key and fire the missiles . . . there is a final emergency system . . . only to be used if all else fails . . . but the code is known only to heads of state . . .' Spencer's half whisper had taken on a note of anguish.

'They can press the button from some underground government bunker,' Conroy said bleakly. 'How?'

'By means of the Military Defence Computer, linked to the Ultimate Defence Satellite,' Spencer said. 'That emergency code, or codes I should say—there's a master code or lesser variants of it—would override everything. All missiles, or a group selected at will, would be automatically armed, keyed, and launched. No human intervention would be necessary. It was built in,' he said, as if appealing for understanding, 'as the ultimate deterrent, in the event of the worst possible scenario . . . to prove to them . . . in the hope of achieving a ceasefire, even at the last minute . . .' He stopped, and waved his arms in a futile gesture. His hands and wrists were those of a rag doll.

The technical means, Conroy had not known, but the philosophy behind it did not surprise him. It was that of doomsday minus one.

Then it came to him. Shocked, he opened his mouth to speak, but the tormented expression on Spencer's face told him that the man had arrived there already.

'It's not credible,' Spencer said. 'It's not practical . . .'

'Someone who knew the code supposedly known

only to heads of state,' Conroy said stonily, 'could fire those missiles. The fail-safe satellite would explode them. If they've managed to subvert the entire system, they could be exploded wherever they chose . . .'

'There are too many codes to be broken!' Spencer cried. 'It could never be done. It's utterly impossible.'

'You said that before,' Conroy said. 'But someone detected and negatived your "trace". That couldn't be done either.'

Spencer slid off the bed. In silence, he pulled on his shirt and trousers, not bothering to remove his pyjamas first.

'I shall need authority for exclusive use of all the facilities in this place,' he said. He picked up a bulging briefcase.

'I think there's a strong chance,' Conroy said, 'that what happened tonight was a demonstration. If that were to happen again . . .'

'We can't close down the linked MDC system, if that's what you're thinking,' Spencer said decisively. He was beginning to recover from the inner blow he had suffered. 'Any credible defence is dependent nowadays on the operation of the MDC and the UDS. Without them, we'd be as helpless in the face of attack as a medieval rabble. And if the Russians have managed to tap our computer communications in some incomprehensible way . . .'

'There's no "if" about it,' Conroy said. 'Not any more.'

'Then they'd know as soon as we shut it down,' Spencer said. 'If ever there was a green light, that would be it.'

'They're aiming for checkmate,' Conroy said. 'At midnight tonight, they made their penultimate move. We'll soon know what their final one is. I don't think you have many hours at your disposal, Doctor Spencer.'

The onward tread of time that night dragged by in leaden clogs. Until nearly dawn, Conroy and Karen sat in the computer area. Operators and analysts from the NATO staff had been assembled to form a makeshift team. Spencer, apparently unhurried, moved from one terminal to another, giving quiet instructions, watching, discussing, turning to his analysts, poring over printouts.

Conroy hoped to God that he knew what he was doing. General Price had been put in the picture, and had nodded abstractedly, without speaking. Still, there had been no word from Moscow.

Stiff, bleary-eyed, fighting off their weariness, Conroy and Karen eventually left the computer area in search of coffee and something to eat. There seemed no point in staying anyway. Neither had the remotest conception of what Spencer was hoping to glean from the growing yards of printouts, except that he did not seem to be getting anywhere.

Munching sandwiches and holding plastic cups of coffee, they met General Price in the communications room. Price had one piece of news, which he told them in a conversational tone, as though he were remarking on the weather. The remaining American units in West Germany were being moved to assembly points near military airfields. Giant transport aircraft were on their way across the Atlantic.

'In their colloquial way,' General Price reported, 'our American friends remark that if we will light the flame, and can't stop the pot boiling over, they see no very good reason why they should stew along with us.'

At 07:45 the message from Moscow arrived.

It was couched in bleak, uncompromising terms. Using highly advanced—though unspecified—techniques, it said, a team of Soviet scientists had established beyond doubt that the control system of the NATO nuclear armoury had developed a dangerous instability. The truth of this had already been forcibly demonstrated. Now, it was predicted that a missile deployed near Dungeness would behave in a similar fashion before 08:00.

In issuing this warning, Moscow was extending the hand of friendship to the peace-loving peoples of Europe, as the German Democratic Republic had done in offering assistance to restore order and tranquility to West Germany, now in a state of utter turmoil.

It could further be predicted that, within hours, all nuclear missiles under NATO control would simultaneously become completely unstable. It was feared that when this took place, the warheads would explode over major centres of population very close to the point of launch, destroying European cities, like London, Amsterdam, Brussels, Rome, Bonn, and a number of others.

Moscow was as anxious as NATO would be to avert this catastrophe. Accordingly, at ten o'clock that morning, GDR units would cross the frontier to come to the aid of their German brethren. They would be accompanied by teams of technicians, who would assist their Western friends in disarming and making safe the nuclear weapons which now threatened the destruction of Europe from within.

Aeroflot aircraft would take off at the same time, transporting more technicians to the other countries in the alliance on whose territory nuclear weapons were based. Formal NATO agreement to this course of action was expected before l0:00.

There was no time for discussions. There was no time for anything, after hurriedly scanning the text, but to

issue frantic orders for the immediate evacuation of the area around Dungeness.

At 07:59 the missile took off. It exploded almost immediately. The Dungeness nuclear power station was badly damaged, and a severe radioactive leak was recorded, although fallout caused by the missile itself was not heavy.

'Their final demonstration,' Conroy said. 'The only thing left now is their ultimatum.'

General Price nodded, took the unlit pipe from his teeth, and lifted a red telephone.

'Give me a few minutes,' he said to Conroy, quietly.

With such self-possession, Conroy thought, with the calmness of those already dead, must the men of Haig's armies have waited on the Somme for the barrage to lift, for the moment when they would leave their trenches, and walk through the mud into the lethal field of fire of the stammering machine guns which would kill them.

Conroy and Karen left the chaotic activity of the war room, with its atmosphere of frenzied, fractured uncertainty. They were not exactly in the way. You could not be in the way of men who did not know what to do next.

They sat in silence in General Price's office. They did not speak. There was nothing to say.

General Price was more than a few minutes. It was nearly half an hour before the door opened, and he walked in and sat at his desk.

'What's been decided?' Conroy asked.

'Nothing,' General Price said. 'No alliance can stand a strain like this. We could find ourselves facing a *fait accompli*. The German government has virtually disintegrated. The smaller nations can see no alternative but to accede to the Russian . . . er . . . request, and who can blame them. Our PM's talking to the US President. The only chance any of us can see is for the Americans to threaten a strike against Russia itself, if the events predicted by the Soviet Union take place.'

'Will they do that?' Conroy asked doubtfully. 'They've got to mean it, or it would be no more than a futile, useless gesture.'

'Making threats, that's easy,' General Price agreed. 'Carrying them out, that's different. We're asking America not only to go to war, but to enter into an all-out exchange of thermonuclear weapons, when the Russians themselves won't have fired so much as a single rifle shot. If the worst happens, we're asking them to accept the annihilation of half North America, when Europe itself would already have been destroyed. And destroyed moreover, by its own missiles, not by those of the enemy. If we don't do something, the Russians can take us out without lifting a finger. Subsequent American retaliation would be precious little consolation to us. Every living being in Europe would be dead or dying. In my judgement, the USA will regard all that as a very bad bargain indeed. I don't think they'll buy it. As they see it, this bizarre mess is of our making, not theirs. Outside Europe, they can still defend themselves. Their ICBMs and so on aren't affected. I think they'll settle for that, leave us to make our own decision, and live with the consequences, rather than prematurely die for them. We're required to decide whether to commit suicide, in one form or another, or not in . . .' he glanced at his watch, '. . . rather less than an hour and a half, but they're not. The time scale is too short honestly to expect them to volunteer for obliteration.'

'Deliberately short,' Conroy said. 'This is what the whole thing has been leading up to. Ten o'clock this morning.'

'There appear to be only two practical alternatives apart from surrender,' General Price said, as though he were lecturing at the Sandhurst Military College. 'The first is to shut down the entire control system. The MDCs, the UDS, everything. That would avoid a nuclear catastrophe. But without the MDCs we couldn't even fight an effective conventional war. Apart from the fact that it's doubtful if we could rely on the West German Army or indeed many of the other contingents as I've already indicated, every damned thing, communications, logistics, the command structure, everything is geared to those computers. So closing the system down inevitably means . . .'

'Defeat,' Conroy said. 'Germany in the Soviet bloc. The rest of us, with Russian "technicians" at our elbows, existing by Russian sufferance, drained of oil, raw materials, manufactured goods, food—colonial outposts in their empire.'

'The second alternative,' General Price said, 'is to decline the Russian terms and hope that they're bluffing.'

'They're not bluffing,' Conroy said. 'They're playing for the biggest prize of all time. The conquest of the whole of Europe, without the loss of a single Russian life.'

'Quite,' General Price said. 'So no realistic second alternative exists. We're defenceless. The only chance, a remote one I know, is somehow to break the stranglehold they've managed to achieve in controlling our own nuclear missiles. As to that, the PM is waiting for your report and advice, which will clearly influence the eventual decision.'

Conroy nodded.

'Yes,' he said.

He suddenly felt more alone, more completely isolated than ever before in his life, even in the Lubianka. He would have given anything to be a mere spectator, for Goss to be sitting there, the subject of General Price's direct, serious gaze, hunching his shoulders in that characteristic gesture as he accepted, swearing obscenely, the awesome weight of final responsibility. But nothing could grant that particular wish. Goss might be still technically alive, according to an EEG, but in his condition he would neither know nor care whether he died from multiple gunshot wounds, or in the dreadful heat of a nuclear blast.

'Failing any suggestion you may be able to make, Mr Conroy,' General Price said, 'it looks like surrender, I'm afraid.'

George Spencer bore all the marks of an exhausted man. There was nothing in his appearance to suggest that he was not a defeated one, too.

'We need more time,' he said. He scrubbed the bristles on his unshaven face with the palm of his hand.

Printouts were still being spewed out of all the terminals, the machine clatter as busy as ever, but otherwise it was apparent that Spencer's team was as weary as he was. The operators' skilled fingertips were moving more slowly, they were making mistakes, cancelling requests, keying in fresh ones. The concentration of the analysts was fading. Everything was slowing down.

'There isn't any more time,' Conroy said, and told him why. 'Have you been able to come up with anything at all?'

'All we have is a possible hypothesis,' Spencer said. 'Evidence for it is empirical and slender. It could take several hours more before we really know whether it will stand up.'

'Several hours aren't available,' Conroy said. 'Only one hour, twenty-one minutes, to be exact. The hypothesis will have to do. And keep it simple, for Christ's sake.'

'Very well,' Spencer said. His eyes were red-rimmed, and bloodshot. 'We had to begin with some assumptions, or there was no hope of getting anywhere. I chose a negative one, followed by a positive. First, the security code could *never* have been broken in the way we've been investigating up to now. That was a blind alley, from beginning to end.'

'But they've done it!' Conroy said. 'First, information, then the "trace", now . . .'

'That was my positive assumption,' Spencer said, interrupting. 'But it had to be by some other means. So my hypothesis is that they've managed to locate and tap one of our landlines. That is, they've been "listening in", as it were, to the flow of information from our computers which is constantly passing through the system.'

'But if they were just trawling,' Conroy said, 'like electronic bloody fishermen . . .'

'That's the idea, more or less,' Spencer said.

'They wouldn't know what they were going to get,' Conroy objected. 'You told me yourself, ninety-nine per cent of all transmissions are garbage. How could they know they were going to get Cruise missile deployment sites, or submarine sea bed positions?'

'You're quite right,' Spencer said. 'They couldn't. But . . .'

'They'd want to be able to select information, the top-secret stuff they really wanted,' Conroy said. A deep well of disappointment overflowed inside him. 'No, Spencer, it won't do. It's not good enough.'

'If you'd try and listen, damn you, instead of interrupting . . . !' Spencer flared, with the sudden flash of anger of an overtired man. He took a deep shaky breath. 'Bear with me for a while. Will you do that, please?'

Conroy shrugged, barely able to control his angry impatience. He thought of General Price stalling the prime minister, trying to keep some shred of hope alive. He thought of the Warsaw Pact tank commanders, waiting for their radioed orders to roll across the frontier. He thought of the choice, submission or oblivion. Spencer had been their last hope. Whether the nations of Europe lived in virtual slavery or died in a nuclear holocaust, all had come to depend on this grey-haired man, whose face was now grey as well.

'You may wonder why I didn't mention this remote possibility to you before,' Spencer said. 'The truth is, I didn't really believe in your theory until my "trace" was negatived, and that was only twenty-four hours ago. Until then, despite everything Karen said, I didn't think you really believed there was any fault in the system. I thought, and I fancy I was right, that you assumed I was a traitor, the source of the leakage of information myself.'

'It's of precious little consequence now,' Conroy said. 'But if it makes you feel any better, you're right.'

'My feelings are unimportant, but I should have considered this hypothesis before,' Spencer said. 'That is why I did not. I wish I had. I might have been able to be more definite. As for your objections, let us suppose for the moment that the Russians *have* been able to tap one of the landlines. They would be able to record the transmissions for weeks, months, years for all we know, and examine them at their leisure, probably back in Russia itself. There, they would have the use of sophisticated computers, one element of our original . . . er . . . discussion, which would still be a necessity. With time at their disposal, they could break the codes. The more codes they solved, the more they would be able to solve. The process would become progressively easier. The knowledge of our MDC system which they could build up would become greater and greater.'

Conroy was listening with close attention now. Reluctantly, he was coming round to the possibility that what Spencer was offering made sense—reluctantly, because, as far as he could see, it could only lead into a further quagmire of doubt. He thought of the multi-link network which Spencer had previously described. A complicated cat's cradle of landlines extending over many hundreds of miles.

'Can you identify the point where a line might have been tapped?' he asked, without much hope.

'No,' Spencer said. 'We've been trying a process of elimination and deduction—which is, I fear, only a polite term for guesswork. Tracing the flow of those four pieces of information to which we can reasonably assume they have gained access. There are only two possible centres. London and Brussels. None of the others ever had access to all four.'

'Yes, I reported my Berlin meeting to Brussels,' Conroy remembered. 'That would then have been forwarded to London . . .'

'The NATO Commander in Chief would have constant updated access to sea bed positions and Cruise deployment sites,' Spencer said.

'Yes, but what about Harrington? That was a private British ploy run by Goss. Nothing to do with NATO.'

'We have established that Harrington was stationed in Brussels when he received his orders,' Spencer said. 'But equally, of course, those orders were transmitted from London.'

London or Brussels? Which? It could be either. You could hardly toss a coin, Conroy thought grimly, when the cost of losing could be reckoned in hundreds of millions of lives. He caught sight of the time. The hands of the clock seemed to have mysteriously changed pace since those long, endless hours before dawn. Now, the minutes were racing by.

He tried to shrug away the sudden, despairing temptation to give in and accept the inevitable. And yet this was too much to require of one man. And even if he guessed right, how much further forward would that take them? It was hopeless, useless . . . the other side had won . . . they had NATO in a trap from which there was no escape . . . why not admit it here and now and be done with it?

'In their position,' he said, keeping his voice even with an effort, 'if I were starting from scratch, and supposing I could choose, I'd opt for Brussels.'

'As the site of NATO Headquarters,' Spencer said, 'there'd be the maximum inward flow of secure information. It is also the place where all landlines converge, providing the densest concentration, the best opportunity. Yes. That would be the logical choice.'

'It's not really logic, Doctor Spencer, it's blind hope,' Conroy told him. 'There isn't enough bloody time left to get to London.'

'You do your instincts an injustice,' Spencer said mildly. 'Brussels is also the one centre we could not isolate and bypass, should we become suspicious, without rendering the entire system inoperative.'

'I take it your magic box of tricks can provide us with the location of all the landlines in the Brussels area,' Conroy said.

'It can,' Spencer said.

He moved to a vacant terminal, sat down, and tapped the keys deftly. Conroy assumed that he was using his own personal 'keyhole', which he would have left when designing the original system. He watched as a network of lines swiftly appeared on the screen while simultaneously being printed out.

'One big question,' Conroy said, 'is how the hell they could have found out where the landlines were in the first place.'

'Garnett, possibly,' Spencer suggested. 'As a member of the steering committee he might have been able to obtain access to that information.' He picked up the printout. 'As I told Karen, I found him an astonishingly able man. Even so, looking back now with the benefit of hindsight, I suppose he was, in fact, concealing the extent of his theoretical insight. At the time, I thought him brilliant, although rather wasted, but of course as things turned out . . .'

'He was sitting in the middle of exactly the right spider's web,' Conroy said grimly. 'I should have killed the bastard when I had the chance.'

In General Price's office, with less than an hour left, they pored over the routes the underground landlines took, superimposed on a street map of Brussels. None of them were remotely near any of the Eastern Bloc embassies, which had been the first thought in Conroy's mind.

'It was in ours, too,' Spencer said drily.

Trying not to be hasty despite the time slipping by, fearful of missing something, Conroy traced those fragile lines on the map again, comparing them with his mental picture of the city above ground.

'I'm far from clear,' General Price said fretfully. 'You say a team of experts would have to work continuously, descrambling and decoding . . .'

'If we're right, it needn't necessarily be done on the spot,' Spencer explained. 'Our transmissions would be recorded on tape. There's a man in Moscow, I met him once in Stockholm, Professor Stashinsky, a brilliant theoretician. Given the facilities and enough time, it could well be within his capability. The tapes could be flown to Russia as diplomatic baggage, or even sent over a landline of their own.'

'One thing occurs to me,' Karen said hesitantly. 'Forgive me if I haven't understood, but if they're capable of tapping and decoding everything, won't they have been able to do that to the information you were accessing all night? And if so . . .'

'You're quite right,' Spencer said. 'They could. Whether they did or not, there's no way of knowing.'

'But in that case . . .'

'If we're on the right lines, they could well be aware of it,' Spencer said. 'It's an inevitable risk. We had no alternative. But their suspicions could have been aroused, yes.'

'They probably don't give a damn anyway,' General Price said. 'Not with less than fifty minutes to go.'

Conroy raised his head, and looked at Spencer. His eyes ached from tiredness and his intense study of the map, and his head ached from his effort to recall the facades of shops, offices, hotels, all the buildings which lined the streets of Brussels anywhere near those lines, zigzagging to avoid underground obstructions.

'We've got to have some limiting factor or it's hopeless,' he said. 'Tell me again, the things they must have. And put yourself in their shoes. What you'd look for, ideally, over and above the essential.'

'Access to the ducts,' Spencer said calmly. 'That is, distance measured in yards, unless there was something which might conceal what was being done, such as building activities. Premises which would offer good, ideally a perfect, cover. On-site computer facilities of a high order would be necessary. If I could find it, I'd prefer a building where computer operations went unnoticed, and technicians of all levels could come and go without question . . .'

'And a landline of your own,' Conroy said, his voice rising with excitement. 'You said something about transmitting information back to Russia over a land-line.'

'Well, yes,' Spencer said dubiously, 'although I should have said that was only in theory . . .'

'But if you could have the perfect circumstances. Exactly what you wanted?'

'As a counsel of perfection, certainly,' Spencer agreed. 'In fact, of course,' he went on, his brow wrinkling into a frown, 'it doesn't have to be a landline as far as Moscow. Provided it went to, let us say, East Berlin . . .'

'Jesus,' Conroy said. In his head, he saw the rubble of the vast building site when he had passed through Brussels four years before. He saw the office which backed on to that building site. He saw the sign above it. Quickly, he told them.

For the first time since they had met, General Price exhibited symptoms of unease.

'This is no more than speculation,' he said worriedly. 'At best a wild possibility . . .'

'Both,' Conroy said. 'But I know it, General. I know it in my guts.'

'I mean no disrespect when I say that I wish Mr Goss were here,' General Price said. 'Acting as HOD in his place, you have the authority, Conroy, if you insist, but you also carry complete responsibility.'

'If you haven't heard from me by ten,' Conroy said, 'it'll have failed. You're back in the saddle. You'll have to make whatever decision you think fit.'

'Your own life, you're entitled to gamble with,' General Price said. 'But you're staking every man, woman and child alive today in the whole of Europe.'

'I've told you what I want done,' Conroy said. 'Unless Doctor Spencer says that it's not feasible . . .'

'It's certainly feasible,' Spencer said. There was no guarantee in that phrase.

'But even if by some extraordinary intuitive insight you've got it right,' General Price protested, 'you'll never get into the place.'

'I'll get in all right,' Conroy said. He smiled mirthlessly. 'I have my own Open Sesame.'

The car stopped after its brief, hair-raising ride. Conroy stepped out. He glanced up at the multi-storey building in the background, towering above the shops and offices, the building which had not been there four years before, and crossed the road. ‾

It was 09:38 when he walked into the Aeroflot office in the Rue Raunestein.

In the windows were alluring advertisements for Arts Festivals in Moscow and graceful models of Ilyushin aircraft, new generation planes now in operation. Aeroflot, he noted, was always at his service. A poster proclaimed, 'Our motto is speed, comfort and hospitality'.

In his travels around the globe Conroy had noticed before that, despite its proud boast of being the largest airline in the world, Aeroflot offices were rarely hives of activity. So it was here. Booking clerks sat behind a high desk, each with her computer terminal, doing nothing very much. Working for Aeroflot seemed to be something of a sinecure. Low, comfortable couches flanked glass-topped tables on which attractive brochures were invitingly laid out. Discreet pop Muzak floated in the well-heated air. It was a warm, agreeable, well-lighted haven in which no one sat browsing through the brochures, and no customers stood at the long counter, which Conroy approached unhurriedly, carrying a large attaché case.

On the way in, there had been double doors, separated by a small vestibule, no doubt to protect the inmates from draughts, which entailed a necessary pause after passing through the first door while pushing open the second. Conroy had not wished to risk lifting his eyes and searching for a scanner while making his entry. He simply prayed that he was right.

He was approaching one of the booking clerks now, his footsteps noiseless on the soft carpet. Before he reached her, two well turned out, courteous men materialized, wearing polite smiles.

310

'I am most terribly sorry, sir,' the larger of the two said, indicating the attaché case in Conroy's hand. 'But we must check your case. A formality only. You understand.'

'Of course,' Conroy said.

'This way, sir, if you please.' He indicated that Conroy should walk in front.

They passed through a door in the panelling, almost indistinguishable, and also sound-proofed. There the courtesy evaporated, along with the sound of the Muzak. Conroy was slammed against a wall, and searched for weapons with no ceremony or consideration for modesty. He made such noises as an innocent bystander might utter and was told to shut up. In any case, for a few moments, his mind was not entirely on this preliminary charade.

As the door in the panelling had closed, he had seen that someone had entered and was sitting on one of the comfortable couches, engrossed in a pamphlet. She had glanced up momentarily, and for a fraction of a second, Karen's eyes had met Conroy's.

Her presence was not part of this despairing last throw. He had assumed she would wait at the Crisis Centre. Why was she here?

He had little time to worry about it. His briefcase was passed through a scanner and gingerly opened, but it contained only blank sheets of paper.

Satisfied, the two men grabbed him and hustled him down a long flight of stairs. Conroy made only a token show of resistance. He was bundled along a long corridor, through a door, and into a control room, in which were two men.

The older of the two took the attaché case and nodded. The goons left.

'Good morning, General,' Conroy said.

'You recognize me then.' He was about sixty years

old, heavily built, with a strong face, and grey eyes. He wore his neat suit uneasily, like a man who was not accustomed to civilian clothes.

One wall of the office was of glass. The other side was a fully equipped and busy computer area.

'You were Andrei, I believe,' Conroy said. 'That was when you were being friendly.'

'I am sure there is no reason why we should not be friends now,' the KGB general said.

'You choose your friends badly, General,' Conroy said.

He looked at the second man, the one with the beard, who was sitting behind a desk. The smell of peppermint hung in the air.

Garnett's white teeth showed under his beard as his lips parted in a small, prim smile.

THIRTEEN

Neither the general nor Garnett appeared to be particularly perturbed by Conroy's presence. Garnett was staring at Conroy with detached interest. The general was studying a bank of monitor screens against the far wall. On them were relayed, from several angles, street level scenes at the front and rear of the Aeroflot offices. Neither the busy traffic at the front, nor the service road at the back, indicated any unusual activity.

Conroy noted with relief that the General was not paying any attention to the screen on the far left; the one which was a view of the booking hall and showed Karen picking up a fresh brochure and glancing at her watch.

'It seems unlikely that you would have come alone,' the general said calmly. 'I assume your men are stationed out of sight.'

'Just me,' Conroy said. 'No one else.' He hoped that the frequency with which Karen was looking at her watch would pass as the impatience of a woman waiting for a friend who was late.

The general gave him a disbelieving smile.

'Underneath the panelling you passed through is reinforced steel,' he said mildly. 'This area has now been sealed off. It is encased in a kind of cage. It would take some while to break in. Long after ten o'clock anyway. In any case, it would be a useless exercise. Control, if necessary, can be exercised from elsewhere.'

'That's what we assumed,' Conroy said. 'That's why I'm alone.'

The general had opened the attaché case.

'With a few sheets of blank paper,' he said.

'They'll come in handy later,' Conroy said.

'Later?' The general raised his eyebrows and regarded the clock. It said 09:42.

Conroy ignored Garnett. There was no doing business with a man like him. The general, however, might be another matter. The general was a fellow professional.

'We knew of your efforts almost at once, of course,' the general said, conversationally. 'Your people spent a busy night.'

Conroy indicated the computer area outside the control room.

'You're now able to decode on the spot, are you? With a radio transmitter beamed on the UDS as well?'

The general nodded.

'But there was nothing to lead you here,' he said. 'One assumed you would rule it out, as being too far from the nearest landline.'

'It seemed to fit your requirements,' Conroy said. 'And you had the opportunity to lay your cable four years ago, when the site at the back was being redeveloped. Not all that hard to infiltrate a few men into an electrical contractor's workforce.'

'And you guessed it from that?' the general said admiringly. 'A good piece of work.'

'Thank you,' Conroy said.

'General,' Garnett said, searching the desk top for a fresh peppermint, 'it occurs to me that Conroy seems quite content to stand around and be congratulated. I think he's waiting for something, don't you?'

'Like all of us,' the general said. 'Today, we witness great events.'

'Would I be right that it was Garnett who thought up the original idea?' Conroy asked interestedly. 'The suggestion came from him?'

'In broad outline,' the general said. 'It was an exciting concept. He was in a perfect position to play a major role. Until, that is . . .' He raised his hand in a stop signal, delicately avoiding mention of Garnett's arrest and imprisonment.

'For the purest of motives, I'm sure,' Conroy said. 'Like the future well-being of mankind.'

'As you say,' the general agreed. 'Also, Mr Garnett feels, probably rightly, that his experience of government could be more usefully exercised at a somewhat higher level than that of a senior civil servant.'

'Running a satellite Great Britain?' Conroy laughed. 'He can forget that particular ambition. He's been wasting his time. And yours.'

'As you are, also, Mr Conroy,' the general said gently. 'Mr Garnett was right about that.' His eyes flickered to the monitor screens again. 'And yet nothing seems to be happening. Not here, anyway. I think you should explain your presence.'

There was only the slightest change in the general's quiet tone, as hard to detect as a single instrument marginally off-key in a symphony orchestra. But for a fraction of a second every muscle in Conroy's body contracted in the fearful anticipation of pain which was unbearable, but must be borne. He had heard that note in the general's voice before, in the Lubianka. His mind might try and banish the recollection, but his flesh remembered, and knew that the goons would be waiting on the other side of the door.

It was 09:45. By now it should have been done, but it had not. The computer area, which he had been covertly watching, was staffed by men who were still calm, carrying out their functions with relaxed composure. If Doctor George Spencer had failed in his crucial tasks . . .

'I shall not ask again,' the general said. 'Objectively, I was rather impressed by your . . . er . . . resilience during our former conversations but in retrospect, compliance with the British insistence that you should be included in the exchange arrangements was a mistake. There is much to be done in the next few minutes, and your presence, indeed your existence, is a nuisance.' He turned towards the door.

'That would be another mistake, General,' Conroy said hurriedly. 'I'm here in place of . . . someone else.'

The general paused.

'"Nikita"? Now identified as Nicholas Goss? Deceased, I am given to understand.'

'I've brought an offer,' Conroy said. 'And it's the only one you'll get.'

'We are not interested in offers,' the general said impatiently.

'It's this,' Conroy said. 'Safe conduct for yourself and your technicians on the first Aeroflot flight out of the country.' He waved at the computer area, which was as quietly busy as ever. What the hell was taking Spencer so long? 'In return, withdrawal of your ultimatum.'

'No ultimatum has been presented,' the general said. 'Merely a suggestion for mutual, friendly co-operation. However, we shall not quibble about semantics.'

Garnett said, 'It can't be stopped now. They cannot

possibly interfere with our control of the system at this stage.'

'Something seems to have gone wrong already,' Conroy said, with quiet relief. In the computer area, work had come to a stop. Puzzled men were staring at blank display screens. Printouts remained stationary, half finished.

'What does this mean?' The general was addressing Garnett, not Conroy.

'They've closed their system down,' Garnett said. 'They've surrendered. It's all over.'

'Far from it,' Conroy said. 'Our Defence Control System remains fully operative. The landline which you tapped has been cut, that's all.'

'Impossible,' Garnett said, amused. 'The tap was deliberately placed near a junction, so that it could be any one of three. You can't have identified which. You'd have had to cut all three.'

'Yes, quite right,' Conroy agreed. 'But as you well know, it's a multi-link network.'

'Cutting those three would isolate the Brussels Centre,' Garnett said, with weary tolerance. 'Even if you're telling the truth, you've lost control.'

'You were out of action for a long time,' Conroy said. 'During your enforced absence, the system was further developed, additional links were created. Apparently, you failed to check on that after your, what shall we say, return to duty.'

'He's lying,' Garnett said to the general contemptuously. 'It's part of his stock in trade. He's good at it.'

'Somewhere out there in those yards of printouts,' Conroy said, 'is an up-to-date track of the landlines, which we accessed this morning. Evidently, somebody failed to appreciate its significance. You'll find it shows the extra links.'

The general's expression as he regarded Garnett was far from friendly.

'If what I have been led to believe is correct,' he said ominously, 'even if Mr Conroy is speaking the truth, it makes no difference.'

'Perfectly correct,' Garnett said. He stared at Conroy. 'A coded radio signal to the Ultimate Defence Satellite arms, fires, and directs your nuclear missiles. That radio signal can be sent from anywhere. A standby transmitter is beamed on to the UDS.'

'From inside Russia, I suppose,' Conroy said. He dare not postpone the final moment any longer. He could not know if Spencer had been successful or not. There was a big difference between what was 'feasible' and what would work in practice. Well, he would soon find out, more than likely in the few remaining moments before he died.

'I think your diversionary tactics have lasted long enough, Conroy,' the General said brusquely.

'Before you bring in your goons, General,' Conroy said, 'I should tell you that the self-destruct mechanism on our UDS has been activated. A standby satellite has been launched to take its place, and will now be in orbit.' Please God, let it be in orbit. 'The programme in that satellite has been changed, and you no longer have the facilities to decode it.' He pointed at the blank display screens outside. 'You no longer control anything, General.'

'Is this possible?' There was ice in the general's voice, as well as in his eyes.

'It's pure invention,' Garnett said tightly. He could be right, Conroy thought. 'Don't believe him. They know they can't stop us. It's a transparent attempt to make us hesitate, to gain time . . .'

'General,' Conroy cut in, 'if you don't do something, in less than nine minutes' time, your tanks will cross the frontier into West Germany. I am authorized to tell you that such an action will be regarded as an act of war. They will be destroyed at once by our battlefield tactical nuclear weapons, which, I repeat, are once more entirely under our own control.'

'He's lying,' Garnett stated flatly. But his eyes had widened fractionally in doubt. His face was that of a man who could not bring himself to believe that his beloved brainchild could possibly be less than perfect. 'They're helpless. It's just a stupid, last-minute bluff.'

'It will take very little time to find out,' the general said. 'Excuse me, Mr Conroy,' he said civilly.

He went out. The door closed behind him. A few seconds later, he reappeared the other side of the glass wall and lifted a telephone. After a brief interval, his lips moved, as he spoke into it.

Conroy stood watching. He could tell nothing from the general's impassive face, as he listened, nodded, and spoke again. So much could have gone wrong . . . a malfunction in the launch rocket . . . the satellite might have failed to achieve a geostationary orbit . . . There was the faint rasp of a drawer being opened. Conroy glanced round. Garnett had an automatic in his hand.

'I wouldn't do that just yet if I were you,' Conroy said steadily. 'Your superior officer might not be too pleased. On the other hand, he might applaud—or prefer to do it himself. Better wait half a minute to find out.'

Garnett smiled, and laid the gun on the blotter. His hand went into the drawer again, and came out with a new packet of peppermints. He held it up, showing it to Conroy ironically, took one of the mints out, and delicately popped it between his lips.

In the computer area, the general finished speaking, put the phone down, and walked out of sight. The door of the control room opened and he came back in. His eyes registered the automatic on Garnett's desk. The general signalled the goons to remain outside, and closed the door.

'It appears, Mr Conroy,' he said courteously, 'that, according to our scientists, your nuclear weapons system is no longer unstable, and there should be no further malfunctions. I was also happy to learn that the civil authorities in West Germany have succeeded in restoring order, and the assistance of their brethren and fellow countrymen will, therefore, no longer be required. You will share my personal pleasure in this good news, I am sure.'

The general's pleasure was, apparently, not infectious. Garnett's face had assumed the pallor of a man suddenly taken ill. He had ceased chewing.

'I need to make a phone call,' Conroy said. The general waved his agreement. Conroy dialled the number which would put him straight through to General Price. It was six minutes to ten.

'Give George Spencer my heartfelt thanks in case I don't see him for a while,' Conroy said. 'Hold on.' He handed the receiver to the general, who repeated what he had told Conroy, and hung up. His eyes rested on one of the monitor screens.

'I see that our transport has arrived,' he said. A coach had entered the service road at the rear of the building. The general picked up his briefcase.

'Safe conduct does not include Garnett,' Conroy said. He placed one of the blank sheets of paper on the desk. 'After he's signed a brief statement, he comes with me.' Conroy took out a fountain pen, removed the cap, and held it out towards Garnett.

Garnett stared up at him. Suddenly, he laughed, and his fingers touched the automatic as his hand grabbed for it. At that moment, there was a 'phut', and a hole appeared in his forehead. Garnett fell forward on to the desk, his lips frozen in a grimace. Blood ran down his face and formed a dark pattern on the blotter.

Conroy put his fountain pen away. The single bullet which it fired had done its work.

The general said mildly, 'My men were very lax. They will be rebuked in due course.' He glanced at Garnett's lifeless figure. 'I believe Mr Garnett died some time ago, however.'

'Of a heart attack,' Conroy said. 'Cremated in Parkhurst Prison.'

'I suggest we leave the civil police to clear up this mystery,' the general said. 'No man can die twice, after all.'

Conroy saw the general and his staff into the service road, and then made his way to the booking hall. Karen's worried face cleared as she saw him.

'You cut it fine,' she said.

Conroy took her arm as he led her out, and unobtrusively squeezed her handbag. Inside was a hard metal object.

'What the hell did you think you were going to do?' he enquired.

'Come and find you,' Karen said.

'You stupid bitch,' Conroy said affectionately. 'You wouldn't have had a chance.'

FOURTEEN

It did not much resemble peace, but it was not quite war, either.

The countries of NATO did their best to unscramble the mess and glue the alliance back together again. One thing all governments agreed on was that it would be much better for the public if they never knew precisely what had taken place. The media were only permitted to print or transmit the official version. Curious journalists might—and did—put something very like the truth together, but what was common gossip in Fleet Street pubs never reached the ordinary man in the street. Government information officers revelled in their new-found importance and authority. Censorship had returned in practice, if not in name.

East and West, each for their own reasons, solemnly played out their roles in what amounted to a mutual if unspoken conspiracy of deception.

What was described as a massive blow-out in a North

Sea gas field attracted least attention. By comparison with the explosions at nuclear power plants, which had, the official statements admitted, taken place in Great Britain and West Germany, it was small beer.

Urgent enquiries, the public were assured, were being launched, to discover the fault which must be common to those separate installations. This meant giving the anti-nuclear lobby a strong hand which was seized and played for all it was worth, but that was considered a necessary price to pay in the circumstances. Better that the public should demand 'no more nuclear power stations', which would merely set back the cause of nuclear power for a few years, than 'no more nuclear weapons', which would, those in authority decreed, endanger the freedom of the West. Through the good work of the censors, free citizens were guided away from such a fearful risk.

Russia was accused of breaking the Test Ban Treaty by exploding a thermonuclear warhead over the Arctic Circle. The Soviet Union indignantly labelled this as a lie and charged the West with doing likewise.

On a lesser level, NATO protested vigorously about the cutting of the Berlin autobahn by armoured columns. The German Democratic Republic replied stiffly that the autobahn had been briefly closed for essential repairs, and that any nearby tanks had merely been on internal manoeuvres.

Private talks were initiated between East and West. Both now wished to disengage from a Launch on Warning policy. Neither could agree on who should do what first. The talks bogged down. If SALT was anything to go by, they would drag on for years.

In the meantime, the fragility of the Western control system had been exposed. Doctor George Spencer was urgently invited to return to government service, and agreed. His brief was clear. In the light of Russian obduracy, the allied Launch on Warning system must

be improved, made more effective and—this time—
genuinely foolproof.

As badly shaken governmental nerves recovered, the
terrifying brink was rationalized into a brief period of
danger, analogous to Cuba, now mercifully moving
into the past. If any lessons had been learned, it was not
noticeable. The world's oil continued to run out.

Conroy paid a second visit to 10 Downing Street.
When he emerged, Jenkins opened the door of the car.

'That arm's still a bit stiff, isn't it?' Conroy asked.

'No, sir,' Jenkins said, straight-faced. Conroy let it
go. He knew that Jenkins had practically worn out his
young, enthusiastic physiotherapists in his drive to be
returned to duty, fully fit. Jenkins sat behind the wheel
and glanced in the mirror.

'Back to the department, sir?'

'No,' Conroy said. 'I want to make a couple of calls.'

Karen handed him a drink.

'I suppose congratulations are in order,' she said.

She sat down opposite him and crossed her legs. She
looked different again, another aspect of the chameleon. Perhaps she had changed her hairstyle.

'I want to talk to you about your future in general,'
Conroy said. 'They'll know a good deal about you now,
from Garnett. I think you should be withdrawn from
work in the field. I do have one firm suggestion, which
concerns me as well. My future too, if you like. After
all, there was a time when . . .'

'Before you go any further,' Karen interrupted, 'I'd
better tell you that I shall be applying to be placed on
the reserve list. I'd like to get away from the department and everyone in it.'

'You've only just had two months' leave,' Conroy
objected, put-out.

'Ideally, I'd prefer to resign altogether,' Karen said. 'I know Goss wouldn't allow any resignations, but now he's gone . . .'

'Where did you spend your leave anyway?' Conroy asked.

'The Cotswolds, mostly,' Karen said.

'Ah,' Conroy said. 'I see.'

'We talked about getting married,' Karen said. 'The idea appeals.'

'It appealed once before, I seem to remember,' Conroy said tartly.

'This time, I'd have a home and a husband,' Karen said. 'Not an empty flat and a man who was always somewhere else. I want children before I'm too old.'

'I hope he knows you got rid of the last one,' Conroy snapped.

'He knows everything,' Karen said steadily.

Conroy drained his glass, and stood up.

'Well, thanks for the drink,' he said. 'Put it in writing, will you?'

'I already have,' Karen said. 'I wanted to tell you first, and get the worst part over with. I rather thought it might turn out like this.'

'You know me altogether too well,' Conroy said wryly.

'Yes. Exactly,' Karen said.

'I got one or two things wrong,' Conroy said. 'Getting together again . . . even if it was in a somewhat peculiar way . . . you at the Aeroflot office, prepared to take on half the KGB if I didn't appear . . . I added it all up and got my sums wrong.'

'Not all that wrong,' Karen said quietly. 'But while George Spencer may have the brain of a genius, otherwise, he's just a very ordinary man. Whereas, while you're no genius, you're not ordinary at all. Now, it would be even worse. Perhaps I could cope with it, but even if I could, I can't face it—if that doesn't sound too contradictory.'

Conroy put his arms around her and kissed her briefly on the cheek.

'You're doing the right thing,' he said. 'Anything else, it wouldn't work.'

The car drew up outside the long, low building. Conroy was out before Jenkins could open the door for him. Jenkins' pained expression tactfully rebuked him.

Conroy walked into the rehabilitation centre, spoke to the porter on the desk, and received directions. He walked along the vinyl-floored corridor, followed the signs, and pushed open the door marked PHYSIOTHERAPY. It was a large, open area, with mats on the floor, wall bars, and curious arrangements of weights and pulleys.

Goss was between parallel bars, supporting himself on his arms. He was wearing a track suit, attempting to swing his hips, and force one dangling leg forward after the other.

Goss saw Conroy and, distracted, inadvertently placed his weight on one limp leg and fell sprawling on the floor.

'Oh shit,' he said viciously.

The pretty young physiotherapist sat him up.

'Are you all right?' she asked.

'Bloody marvellous,' Goss said. 'What do you think?'

'That's enough for one session,' the physiotherapist said. A wheelchair was standing nearby.

'Let me give you a hand,' Conroy said, moving forward.

'Fuck off, you,' Goss snarled.

'Mr Goss,' the physiotherapist said, 'you are easily the worst patient I have ever had.'

'You've led a bloody sheltered life, my darling,' Goss remarked, 'that's all I can say.'

It was astonishing how such a slim, small girl could move Goss's bulk from the floor and into the wheelchair with no apparent effort, but she did. Two elbow crutches were hooked over the back of the frame.

'I can stand up with those things,' Goss told Conroy. 'Like when I want a pee. The only trouble is, you then need three hands, and so far they haven't issued me with an extra one. I've tried to get her to hold it for me, but she won't.'

'How about a pair of tongs?' Conroy suggested. He gripped the rubber-covered handles and started pushing.

'Very funny,' Goss said. 'And take your hands off. I can drive this thing on my own, thank you very much.'

He spun the wheels, and the wheelchair banged open the swing doors and trundled along the corridor. Conroy followed behind.

Goss came to a stop in an annex, where there were rows of battered armchairs.

'Visitors' area,' Goss said. 'Park your bum. I'll stay where I am, if it's all the same to you.'

Conroy sat down.

'I saw the PM today . . .' he began.

'No need to thank me,' Goss said.

'I wasn't going to,' Conroy said. 'What do the quacks say? Any chance of getting back on your feet?'

'What the hell do you care?' Goss enquired aggressively.

'I don't,' Conroy said. 'I'm asking, that's all.'

'There's fuck all they can do for a severed spinal cord,' Goss said. His language was more basic than ever, understandably so, probably. 'All they aim to do in this dump is teach you to adjust and how not to get pressure sores. It's the wheelchair bit for me from now on, my lad. So if you were thinking I might get back on my pins, and you could slide out of it, discard that notion. You're lumbered.'

'Jenkins wondered if he could come in and have a word,' Conroy said.

'No, he couldn't,' Goss said savagely. 'This is between me and the half of me that doesn't work any more. It's private. You're my first and last visitor. Got it?'

Conroy nodded. He had been about to ask if there was anything he could do, but he swallowed the empty words. What could anyone do? He sympathized with Goss's attitude. If it ever happened to him that, he thought, was how he would feel.

'I suppose you'll be shacking up with Karen Dewar for good now,' Goss said.

'No,' Conroy said. 'She's going to marry George Spencer.'

'Women are practical animals,' Goss reflected. '"Till death" might be altogether too short a period, in your case. As a husband, you're a bad buy. I doubt if your reign as HOD will be one of the longer on record. The opposition know who you are. They owe you one anyway. As soon as they find out you're running the department you'll be their number-one target. You won't just need Jenkins, you'll need a bloody battalion. You'll be lucky to see forty-five, let alone fifty.'

'I've already worked out that you haven't exactly done me a favour,' Conroy said.

'Lionel couldn't stand the sight of me,' Goss said. 'My ways weren't his ways, he never did understand what made me tick, and I'll bet it was with a bloody heavy heart that he put my name forward, but he had enough sense to know I'd be the right man, even if he didn't know why. Now the wheel's turned, and I've had to do exactly the same thing. Part of life's rich tapestry, as they say, I suppose. When it mattered, you pulled it off. Maybe I would have done too. But maybe not. So now you'll reap your just reward.' He laughed. It sounded like a cracked gramophone record. 'And may the Lord have mercy on your soul.'

'I expect I've strained his patience a bit already,' Conroy said.

'I suppose Garnett's on your conscience,' Goss said solemnly.

Conroy laughed.

'Only at the bottom of a fairly long waiting list,' he said.

'That trial at the Old Bailey was a farce,' Goss said. 'We now know that Garnett was innocent of the charges brought against him. The evidence was pure bullshit. He never had personally handed over the nuclear subs patrol routes, as alleged. By rights, he should have been found not guilty.'

'A gross miscarriage of justice,' Conroy agreed. 'Some bastard must have framed him.'

'What's the betting a bright-eyed do-gooder'll dig it all up one day and want the case reopened?' Goss wondered. 'You killed a man who'd been wrongly convicted.'

'I'll have to try and live with that,' Conroy said.

'Time to go,' Goss said, 'or I'll be late for occupational therapy. You know what the half-wits are making me do? Build a doll's house. Me. Goss. The terror of the Secret Intelligence Service. A fucking doll's house. Jesus.'

He wheeled himself away along the corridor. Conroy watched him go, the spade-like hands attacking the wheels as if it were a matter of life and death to go as fast as possible, the bulky figure leaning forward, swaying to and fro with effort. Goss's voice floated back.

'Good luck to you, my son,' he called. 'And by God, you'll need it.'

Jenkins had the car door open, waiting. Conroy climbed in.

'Mr Goss isn't feeling up to another visitor,' he said. 'He asked me to thank you for everything you did for him.'

'Thank you, sir,' Jenkins said, his face impassive as ever. 'He must have changed. Gone soft, has he?'

Conroy grinned. So Jenkins had a sense of humour. Another revelation.

'Not noticeably,' he said. 'No.'

Jenkins drove out of the car park, paused at the main road, and turned towards London. The radio crackled.

'Sir,' Jenkins said.

Conroy lifted the radiotelephone receiver in the back.

'Conroy,' he said.

He had long ago faced up to the possibility of disfigurement or disability or death. But life played with a concealed hand, and there was one unpleasant fate he had never envisaged in his worst nightmares. To be obliged to do Goss's job.